Nemesis
in the
Mearns

OTHER BOOKS FROM SCOTTISH CULTURAL PRESS

Roots in a Northern Landscape: Celebrations of Childhood in the North East of Scotland, edited by W Gordon Lawrence; 1 898218 79 X

North-East Song and Story: an anthology of narrative verse and song from NE Scotland, edited by William Morrice Wilson; 1 898218 81 1

A Doric Dictionary: Doric~English, English~Doric, compiled and edited by Douglas Kynoch; 1 898218 80 3 (pb), 1 898218 86 2 (hb)

North East Passage, Tom Bryan; 1 898218 57 9
(part of the Scottish Contemporary Poets Series)

Nemesis
in the
Mearns

Love, Laughter and Heartache
in the Land of Grassic Gibbon

Clarke Geddes

SCOTTISH CULTURAL PRESS
EDINBURGH

First published 1996
Scottish Cultural Press
Unit 14, Leith Walk Business Centre,
130 Leith Walk
Edinburgh EH6 5DT
Tel: 0131 555 5950 • Fax: 0131 555 5018

British Library Cataloguing in Publication Data
A catalogue record for this book is available from the British Library

ISBN: 1 898218 78 1

The publisher acknowledges subsidy from the Scottish Arts Council towards the
publication of this volume

Printed and bound by
Cromwell Press, Melksham, Wiltshire

For Lesley

**With grateful thanks to James Leslie Mitchell
(Lewis Grassic Gibbon, 1901–1935)**

And the Mowats looked at the Segget burn, washing west to the Bervie flow, and were ill-content that it should go waste. But it didn't for long, the jute trade boomed, the railway came, the two jute mills came, standing out from the station a bit, south of the toun, with the burn for power. The Segget folk wouldn't look at the things, the Mowats had to go to Bervie for spinners, and a tink-like lot of the creatures came and crowded the place, and danced and fought, raised hell's delight, and Segget looked on as a man would look on a swarm of lice; and folk of the olden breed moved out, and builded them houses up and down the East Wynd, and called it New Toun and spoke of the dirt that swarmed in Old Toun, round about the West Wynd.

Cloud Howe, Lewis Grassic Gibbon

Clarke Geddes spent his boyhood in Grassic Gibbon country in the twenties and thirties at the time when *Sunset Song* and *Cloud Howe* hit the Scottish literary scene.

After five years in the wartime RAF and eight years in the Civil Service, his career took a turn for the better. In 1955 he resigned from the Civil Service, matriculated as a mature student at Aberdeen University and married Lesley, a teacher of French from Fraserburgh – all in the one year.

Clarke's enthusiasm for Scottish literature earned him a first class degree and a post as a teacher of English at Robert Gordon's College. Other appointments followed and, in the twenty years before his retirement, he enjoyed the privilege of directing the Department of Extra-Mural Studies at the University of St Andrews. There he set up the University's Open Association and a wide range of courses including the university's Scottish Studies Summer Schools and a programme of study tours which he and Lesley took to France and Switzerland.

Clarke retains his affection for the Mearns and the north east. In his retirement he continues his lecture programme on Grassic Gibbon, Sir Patrick Geddes and other east coast personalities. His researches into Scotland's past have resulted in the present tale, but the flavour of it, he says, owes as much to his earliest memories of scout campfires in the grounds of Arbuthnott House and the winter he spent after his release from the RAF when he took the job of part-time postman at the Bervie Post Office. From there Clarke trundled his postman's bicycle all the way past Hallgreen Mains, Peattie Farm and across the Bervie stream at Mill of Allardice into Leslie Mitchell's 'Kinraddie'. There could have been no better introduction to Mitchell's thinking, he argues, than a winter spent delivering the Royal Mail, whatever the weather, to places like the Mains of Allardice and Millplough, and on past the Gallow Hill to Craighead and Auchendreich.

'It was coarse land and lonely up there on the brae... red clay and rough.'

When the mists closed in and the foghorn moaned over Kinneff way, he felt he really was pushing into an uncanny land that was weird and spooky, 'up and out of the world' into Leslie Mitchell's legendary 'Blawearie!'

ACKNOWLEDGEMENTS

I am most grateful to Mrs Rhea Martin for granting me permission to quote freely from her father's books. Some of the incidents and thoughts in Leslie Mitchell's early works are accepted as being of a semi-biographical nature, and any attempt at a fair reconstruction of his early days must take these into account.

I am also much indebted to Jane Ann Webster, John and Kathleen Webster, Madge Laing, Molly Middleton, Sandy Couper, Isles Burness, Gerald Bannerman, Roy Souter, Alexander Whyte Low, Alastair and Moira Reid, Norman and Dorothy Geddes, Alick and Bette Clarke and Russell and Rita Clarke for their help in reconstructing the events of those early 'Segget Years'. I have also had considerable help from Professor Ian Campbell, University of Edinburgh and, in St Andrews, from Dr Ronald Cant, Robert N Smart, Ken C Fraser, Marjorie M Moncrieff, Hugh Richardson, Gordon Christie, Alistair Armit, Madge Geddes and Imogen Scott. My researches into the Battle of Cambrai were much helped by George McLennan of the Gordon Highlanders Museum in Aberdeen and Joe Hughes of the Anstruther-Bapaume Twinning Association.

I am also grateful to the following institutions for their help: the Scottish Records Office; the Bervie Parish Church Heritage Society; the *Mearns Leader* Office; the County Buildings, Stonehaven; University of St Andrews Library and the University Computing Laboratory; Dundee City Library; Aberdeen City Library; Woodside Library, Aberdeen; The Gordon Highlanders Museum; La Mairie at Bapaume; Musée des Arbis, Albert; and Historial de la Grande Guerre, Peronne.

I owe a very special thanks to my wife Lesley for her help and linguistic expertise during our Cambrai battlefield tour and for her constant support and forbearance while the work was taking shape.

The complete draft of this book was produced by my younger daughter Frances with commendable speed and accuracy on her word processor. I am most grateful to all of you and to the scores of others with Bervie and Arbuthnott connections who have helped to put this tale together. It was a tale that just had to be told.

ONE

He'd stayed over long in the Royal Toun. John had warned him about the coarse place. 'They're a clannish lot, those mill tinks,' John had scowled. 'When their dander's up, they'll clout you or have the breeks off you if they spot you're a teuchter. The mill quines are worse. If a crowd of those mill hoors get you down by the Back Well they'll do you an injury.'

There was a quiver of excitement about the place. That wild year of 1911 was ending in storms and gales. But it was Saturday; Christmas and all the Hogmanay capers were still to come and the crowds were making for the King Street and the Square, trigged out for a weekend of boozing, flirting and dancing. Most were wandering up the brae from David Street where Webster, the mill laird, housed his workers. The mill lassies had started their jostling and flirting with any lad daft enough to be on the pavement by himself.

'Get home before it's dark, Leslie,' John had urged. John was only fourteen himself, but he'd grown up fast. Handling the beasts and listening to the speak of those uncouth bothy billies had given him a wisdom beyond his years. Those billies were well versed in the most unlikely copulations they all swore they understood.

Leslie mulled over John's words. A bit of an alarmist, John, at times. Strange how George and John were so different. And nothing like himself. He often wondered at that. George was nineteen now and shaping a life of his own. Father spoke of little else but crops and fertilisers, and mother, with all her fanciful notions, had little time for tales now that father was breaking into new land high up there among the whins.

He'd be eleven himself in the New Year, and he'd be expected to give more of a hand on those 70 acres of clay that father sweated his guts over. Even now on those coarse December morns, the darkness still on the land, he'd hear father rise at five. Father would scowl at him, the day's work well begun, when he set off down that long road to school, the clock striking eight. Well they could say what they liked. They'd never turn him into a country teuchter. His brothers never tried to hide their country ways.

1

They'd swank about them. Their country speak picked them out for the farming billies they were and they took a pride in that, forever jabbering on about horses and cattle shows. They might wear a serge suit and an odd tie at times down in the Royal Toun, but as often as not they'd clump in across the Bervie Brig in their heavy worsted coats, old cord breeks and tackety boots. They'd tales enough of the times they'd faced up to the spinners, a bunch of pasty-faced little runts, and they'd aye held their ground.

'Those Bervie tinks treat the Gourdon fishers much the same,' John had added, 'but the fishers go round in packs and are well able to take care of themselves.'

The rain had stayed off, though, and he was determined to explore. He'd had a good look at the new charabanc at the garage, watched the sparks fly in the smiddy and listened to some weird tales at the barber's shop, where Barber John the Spanish Don snipped away, paying little heed that most were only in there for the heat and the entertainment. He'd watched a shunting engine at the station, and ended up on the beach, spellbound by the waves crashing ever closer to the road.

'The seventh wave's aye the biggest,' a young nipper had shouted, dashing back with a cork float in his hand. Leslie stood fascinated a while as the waves thrust up the beach, then sucked the pebbles back for another charge at the shore. He turned back up the brae, the salt spray in his hair. It was a good six miles back up to the Reisk, but he'd hitch a lift, as like as not, from some farming billy getting home late. The Royal Toun had a stir the countryside lacked.

Mother had slipped some coppers into his hand, so he headed for the Kirkburn, the road they called The Great Divide. It separated the mill tinks, who swarmed in the David Street, from the gentry and those more genteel bodies who lived along the Terrace. He returned to the Square and made for the back of Shand's bakehouse where the worthies were said to gather. It was fine and warm at the back of the bakehouse and the smell of those steak pies in the oven fair gave you an appetite. George Shand had fixed up some benches and it was a grand place to be as the day wore on. You could buy a hot pie, drink tea and put the Toun's affairs to rights. You'd get all sorts in there on a Saturday. They'd flock in from the pubs in need of a bite, but they'd leave their pub tales behind when they came in about. Old George Shand was fell religious in his way and would suffer no coarse language in the place. Teuchter speak or spinner speak, it made little odds to Big George as long as it was clean and wholesome. A kindly, genial man, George, but he was big framed and strong, so most held their tongue. Besides, he turned out some of the tastiest meat bridies and pies in the whole of the Mearns.

Leslie eyed Big George with some interest, watching him hand a hot bridie to a poor, frail woman he'd guided in from the shop. George, he'd heard, had a special religion of his own, not Auld Kirk and not of the Wee Frees, not Episcopalian even, but more like those Brethren chields, or as near as damn it. So that bothy billy had said, but then bothy billies were never that clear of their facts when you tried to pin them down. You'd find teetotallers there, the billy had laughed, and Good Templars up from Gourdon. Good Templars avoided pubs like the plague, he'd said, but they had to find some place away from their wives on a Saturday night.

Getting at the facts was Leslie's big problem, and the scattered crofts on Arbuthnott's braes were never the easiest places for that. Good Templars, he learned, were crazed teetotallers who'd go marching with their bands and banners, getting fair excited by the thing.

Leslie sat down on the bench and munched away at his hot bridie, a real steak bridie, he was assured, piping hot with onions and savoury gravy. He was glad he'd stayed on. He was mesmerised by the speak though. What an odd bunch of characters they were and they'd a speak of their own, all about toun politics and women. Now and then, one would recite a bit of verse or come out with some strange Bervie tale most seemed to understand. Most often they were about charters and kings, and the grand Bervie times there had been in those days that had long gone.

It was some time now since he had made up his mind: he'd drop the coarse teuchter tongue and speak always in good plain English. That was how you escaped and got clear of the dreadful life on those sodden clay parks. He'd little wish, either, to take a job in those terrible mills. Lads of his age were doing part-time work among the stour of the breaker, untangling the flax down in the Bervie Haughs. He knew plenty of good English words now, and facts as well, from those books he'd borrowed from the manse. H Rider Haggard, Conan Doyle and H G Wells were among the best. But he had to work at it real hard, listening all the time to their teuchter talk and putting up with their daft teuchter ways.

The worthies in the bakehouse eyed him with droll-looking smirks. He'd a touch of the yokel about him, this lad, with his boots and his breeks, but he didn't quite fit in. He wore a collar and tie and had light brown eyes that pierced right through you. Nosey young devil. His brown hair was soft and cannily combed, but he'd shuffled in with a stoop. Something to hide maybe? He'd spoken up clearly enough though and tendered his pence. 'Thank you,' he'd said, for God's sake, when the lass handed him his steaming bridie. But he was just a lad, after all, putting on airs. There were plenty like him from the other end of the Toun. But what an odd way to be rigged out; half teuchter and half posh he was.

An argument started up between one of the older worthies, Toddler Ben they called him, and a fisherman from Gourdon, a Good Templar, no doubt. The crowd went quiet while Toddler had his say; a man to be listened to, a man who knew his facts.

'Na, na,' he was saying, nodding the while. 'Gourdon's part of Bervie Parish. You're right enough there. But Gourdon folk have no claim to fish for trout in the Bervie waters. That's reserved for us folk in the Royal Toun alone, the only Royal Toun in the whole of the Mearns. King Davie insisted on that when he handed us our Charter, and we've to thank Old Guthrie for that.'

Big George stood beaming at the two of them. 'You good folk of Gourdon have little need to come up and fish for finnocks in Bervie's wee stream,' he grinned. 'With that fleet of boats you've got, you've aye got more fish than we will ever have. You'll never be short of a good fry at night.' It seemed he was a bit of a peacemaker, George, with that strange religion of his. 'We're off down to David Square to sing a few hymns to the Lord,' he added. 'You're all very welcome to come, and there'll be a bite to eat in the chapel when we're done.'

Only two of the older men and the frail woman got up and followed the smiling man outside. Leslie had finished eating his second meat bridie, so he stood up and trailed on after them. Daft curiosity, he told himself, but he might as well see as much as he could of this strange Royal Toun as long as he was here.

Out into the Market Square, the chill wind bit hard and he wrapped his thick woollen gravat round his neck. In the warm, comforting atmosphere of the bakehouse he'd forgotten just how sharp and bitter the weather had become. He'd a mind to turn left and cross The Square and head for home, but a crowd of mill workers were capering with some women by the Market Cross and rather than push his way past, he took the easy way out, turned right and headed on down the High Street. The big new Craigview Works they all spoke about was standing there on his left, its boilers steaming away quietly in the gathering darkness, its gates tight shut. What a carry on they'd had a few years back, he'd heard, when old Jock Webster had opened the place. It was the newest and the most modern of the Toun's seven mills. Some were less sure about it now because of all the incomers the mill had drawn in, but most were fine pleased because of the extra silver folk had. That's what he'd heard.

It was now four in the afternoon and the winter's gloom was settling in. It would be another hour at least before the toun scaffy started lighting the gas lamps. John had been right enough about the bairns. They were all over the place. 'Swarming like lice at the fit o' the Toun,' he'd said. Leslie turned into David Street and there things were even worse. The houses were jumbled against each other and he had to cross the narrow street to avoid a rumpus outside the Modelly, the name they gave to Laing's Model Lodging House. He could just see Big George and his band of supporters out there in front. There was a crashing of glass and a drunken chield came staggering out of the Modelly. Some of the bystanders cheered.

'Away back to Stonehive,' yelled a wiry little tyke, giving the chield a whack with a stick. Something soft and sticky hit Leslie's face and he hurried on. Two young lads, not over six years of age, disappeared into the mouth of a close, laughing. He had to get out of this as fast as he could. He came to an open space on the right where George Shand and his small group were assembled. Four or five paraffin lamps threw some light on the scene, and a bright-eyed, cheery-looking woman was playing some rousing music on a harmonium.

Leslie edged round the back of the group trying not to be noticed. George Shand said something to the crowd he couldn't quite make out and the singing started. It was a rousing hymn, all about being washed in the Blood of the Lamb. Gruesome and gory, Leslie thought, trying to move away from some young lassies giggling near to him in a darkened doorway. One of them, much bolder than the rest, slipped up beside him. She was big bosomed, but not more than fifteen he guessed. She rubbed herself against him and put her cheek to his face. Her hand clasped him tight and he felt her fingers fumbling.

'Let go you daft quine,' he shouted, pushing her off. His words were drowned by the harmonium, but the lassies heard.

'He's a teuchter,' one of them howled. Leslie took to his heels.

He stopped to gulp down some air when he reached the Bervie Brig. Stupid, he'd been, to use a word like quine. They never spoke of quines down in the Royal Toun. They were all lassies down there. Quine was a teuchter word, if ever there was one.

He was at Arbuthnott Crossroads before a chield with a pony and trap caught up with him. 'Jump up, young Mitchell,' shouted the chield. 'This is no place to be wandering about at this time of night.'

'Thanks, Mr Middleton,' Leslie gasped. 'The traffic's all going in the direction of Bervie tonight.'

'Just call me Rob,' the chield laughed, chirking his sheltie to move on. 'We don't stand on ceremony up here on the Reisk.'

'They're a frisky lot, those quines in the Royal Toun,' Rob laughed when Leslie had told his tale. 'Steer clear of them lad or they'll have you for breakfast.'

'What has Guthrie to do with the Royal Toun?' Leslie asked, explaining Toddler Ben's tale in the bakehouse. If anybody on the Reisk knew the truth about the thing, it would be Rob Middleton, their neighbour, from Hareden.

'Oh, they were on about Guthrie's tale were they? They never let up on that if you give them half a chance.' Rob cackled and gave the sheltie a slap. They were passing the farm biggings at the Gobbs and had a bit to go to Leslie's place at Bloomfield. 'That's how they got their famous Charter, or so they say. King Davie and his quine were shipwrecked on the cliffs at Kinneff and a Bervie chield took them in and helped them dry out. They say the wife took out the pan and said she'd gut twa herring for the royal pair, but at that her man was firm. "Na, na," he said, "you'll gut three." Well the young King Davie had still enough smeddum in him to chip in, "From this day on, my mannie, your name shall be Gut Three," he said. And then he gave the Toun their Charter, and Guthrie, as they named him, got his lands down there in the Bervie Haughs. So they say, but damn the thing about it can the scholars find in their books. You can still fish for finnocks in Guthrie's Dam though, so there's maybe something in it.'

After he'd dropped off Leslie, Rob stabled his sheltie up at Hareden and his oldest quine ran out to give him a hand.

'That young lad of yours got a rare fleg in the Royal Toun this day.' Rob said, glinting at her as he lit up his pipe.

'I've told you before,' Becky scowled, annoyed at her dad. 'Leslie Mitchell's not my lad. He never says a word if I meet him on the road, just glowers·and stares at those old stanes on the braes. George and John have aye a cheery for you. Leslie looks on the rest of us as if we were dirt.'

6

TWO

'David Webster's planning his own Christmas dance at Hazelgrove this year.'

Madge looked at Teen's excited face. Her eyes were shining and her cheeks were flushed. Teen Strachan always reminded Madge of those glamorous photographs and postcards of Gladys Cooper she pasted into her album upstairs, away from the prying eyes of Father and the boys. Since she'd gone to that College at Atholl Crescent in Edinburgh, Teen had inhabited a fabulous world of actresses and romance, daring conversations and suffragettes. Then there was the handsome David, Jock Webster's son, with his obsession for the flying machines that kept landing on the sands at St Andrews. David had been at boarding school there but now he was back in the Royal Toun.

Madge looked forward to those meetings with the vivacious Teen; they brought a sparkle and some fun to her own sober existence. They brought a twinge of guilt too when she lent her ear to some of Teen's more outragious suggestions. Teen spoke about things no-one ever dared mention, especially in a house full of boys.

'You should know about these things, Madge,' Teen had said, and Madge knew she was right and wanted to hear more. If Father had overheard, she would have died.

Madge glanced at the shop door, but Teen had timed her visit well. The shop of R Clarke, Painter & Decorator, was handily placed halfway along the King Street and a few doors down from the new garage of the Bervie Motor Company. With Bervie's seven mills and the mills in Gourdon and Johnner working flat out it was a boom time in the place and most folk in the Royal Toun were at work. Father had taken on a big contract at Brotherton Castle and he would be down there with Bert and Harris painting and decorating before the Christmas capers got started. Albert would be stitching away cross-legged on his tailor's board, and young Laurie, the brightest of the bunch and two years Madge's junior, would be at his lessons 'Under the Dome' at Montrose Academy. Madge often wished she'd accepted Father's offer and stayed on there herself, but her duty lay here in the family business looking after Father and the boys. Duty was a fine thing and it brought you a tingle of pride at times, but Teen's world was a deal more exciting.

Madge sighed. 'David's dad will never agree to that,' she said. 'Those fiddle entertainments he's forever laying on at Hazelgrove are for older folk. Bert was up there with his fiddle last week and he enjoyed himself fine, but there was nobody there under 30, and Young Alice looked a bit bored with the whole thing, he said.'

'Oh, Young Alice is going to have a go at Old Jock,' Teen laughed. 'David says his mam agrees it's time they'd some young folk into the place now he's come back from his school at Clifton Bank. David was fifteen last week and he thought they would have had a party for him then.'

'I can't see Old Jock putting up with modern dancing at Christmas time,' Madge said doubtfully. 'Bert says he's invited Scott Skinner back. There's a lot more chance of him turning up with his Hazelgrove Jig and his Bervie Quadrilles for Jock and his old cronies.'

Teen put her arm round Madge and gave her a squeeze. 'You're a pessimist, Madge. That father of yours works you too hard. Tell the Bailie from me he should let you out a lot more. We're all fifteen now. It's the twentieth century and girls are doing all sorts of jobs these days and becoming more independent. There's a picture in the paper of Kitty Kent – you know that actress, the Girl from Utah – taking off in an aeroplane with her friend from the airfield at Hendon. Tell your father we'll all be getting the vote soon, along with the men.'

'Shush Teen.' Madge looked at the door again. 'Father was going on again last night about the wicked Suffragettes.'

'I'll pin a poster up on his shop door if he's not careful,' Teen laughed. 'But I'll have to rush. David's promised to let me know how his mam's got on with Old Jock about the dance. It's high time we had some real fun in the Royal Toun. Those millworkers have made the Burgh Hall dances on a Saturday night far too rough, even for me.'

Madge trundled away at the handle, trimming the wallpaper on the new cutting machine Father had bought for the shop. There were no more visitors to the shop that morning, but there was plenty of wallpaper to trim, and it gave Madge time to daydream. Maybe she should have stayed on at the Academy. They'd all travelled by train along the coast line to Montrose each day. David had been great fun then, before they sent him to that boarding school in St Andrews. She missed those train runs along the 'Smugglers' Coast' to Montrose. The little stations with their coal fires and the warm railway compartments with their plush upholstery and photographs of far-off places like Largs and Strathpeffer, were a comfort on cold east-coast mornings. The rail journey took less than an hour, but they were happy times. They took her through the fishing villages of Gourdon and Johnshaven where the train would reverse to pick up the fish waggons. It paused at Lauriston, the only station with two platforms, where they would peer into the coaches of the train travelling north to see who was venturing there at that time of the day. They then went on to St Cyrus and the cliff-top run high above the sandy beaches, the most beautiful run in Scotland, some said. Then came the fast run down the Warburton Brae to the North Water Viaduct and across the North Esk river to Montrose.

There were no corridors on the Bervie train and the boys had usually kept to their own compartments. One day David and another boy shared the compartment with Teen and herself. It had been great fun and they'd crowded the window at Gourdon station to keep folk out. When the train crossed the high bridge at the Den of Finella, they had peered down into the deep gorge where water poured over a precipice some 70 feet deep. She felt light headed as she gazed down at the water, disappearing among the luxuriant growth of heart's tongue fern. Teen's sweet voice held them spellbound as she told how Lady Finella, the assassin of Kenneth the Third, had been overtaken by her pursuers. Rather than fall into their hands, the bonny Finella had thrown herself from the edge of the rock. David, she remembered, was quite carried away when Teen recited in her clearest English voice:

> She leapt from the rocks to a wild boiling pool,
> Where her body was torn and tossed.

Teen had stopped suddenly then. When Madge turned round, she saw that Teen had turned a bright scarlet. Yes Teen, who'd never blushed in her life! At Johnshaven Station a surly porter had put the boys out of the compartment 'to stop any nonsense'.

'Just a few words with the Bailie, Madge, before we meet the rest of the Council.'

It was later that evening, and the Provost, a douce and canny man, nodded quietly as Madge showed him up the darkened staircase. The glimmer from the gas light in the hall cast a shadow before him as he rounded the stair corner past the grandfather clock. He had a soft spot for Madge, the Provost. Last summer he'd had a quiet word with the Bailie when Madge left the Academy at Montrose after her third year. 'Madge would make a grand school teacher,' he'd urged. 'Things are changing, Bob. Young lassies with talent are getting university degrees these days. They're more independent now than when the Old Queen was alive.' The Bailie had given Madge the chance, but he'd not pressed it on her, and Madge knew fine she was needed to look after Father's business, as well as Father himself and the four boys.

The Provost's words came soft and friendly, but Madge had seen a tightening of his lips when he'd passed her in the hallway. She could guess fine what the trouble was. This was not the best of nights for the Provost to have a quick word with Father. Father had been in one of his coarser moods that night and the boys had got the rough edge of his tongue. The job at Brotherton had gone badly. Harris had left the long ladder behind and Bert's attempt to quieten things had only stoked his fury.

'There are high ceilings in that place,' he had shouted. 'I just can't afford to lose another day on the job. The estimate was low enough in all conscience, and we'll be hard pressed to finish that work at Hazelgrove by Christmas.'

Father always took on too much. When Mother died, Father had flung himself into a frenzy of work to blot out his torment. Bert, the oldest, had explained this to Madge one night when he'd found her sobbing her heart out at the back door. They had to see what Father had come through, he said.

'You know yourself, Madge, Father never fails to make his peace with all of us at the day's end,' Bert reminded her. Bert had been only thirteen when Mother died and he'd taken on the job of watching over Madge and the other boys when Father's rages were at their worst. Bert had explained how, after nearly killing himself with too much work, Father had turned to religion, filling his bookcases upstairs with Hebrew bibles and Greek dictionaries. Father's folk in Montrose had strong Free Kirk beliefs. Madge was only five when one of the Montrose aunts held her up to kiss the cold, stiff face of Mother as she lay, decked out and coffined in the crowded parlour upstairs. Since that terrible time, Madge's chief preoccupation had been the likelihood of eternal damnation for all of them. This she'd picked up from Father's biblical pronouncements and the helpful reading plied on to her by the Montrose aunts. It was confirmed each Sunday when Father shepherded all of them down to his Free Kirk in the Kirkburn where the Reverend Whyte had strong views on hellfire and damnation. Damnation was even a greater certainty at night time when Madge tried to get some sleep in her lonely wee room upstairs. Her fears were little helped by the view that she had when she looked out over Newbigging's fields and remembered the tales she'd read about the boiling of that sherriff on the Garvock hills beyond.

After religion had failed to help Father, he'd turned back to his work and got himself on to the Council. His energies were now directed to cleaning up the morals of the Toun, and now that he was Senior Bailie, he was fair set to speak his mind in those cosy chambers up the Glebe Close.

Madge could hear the two of them at it. Provost Boath was certainly trying his hardest to persuade his Senior Bailie that this was a time to practice a little diplomacy.

Madge had little interest in what went on in those hallowed Council Chambers, but there would be much to discuss that windy winter's night up there in the Glebe Close. Madge strained to catch a word. Father, she knew, was set to fall out with the mill laird, Old Jock Webster. Jock was the Council's Treasurer, and if that were to happen, Madge convinced herself, there was little chance of Old Jock giving in to David's plan. There was even less chance, Madge was sure, that she, the daughter of the fiery Bailie, would be invited up to the Big Hoose to go dancing along with the rest of them.

Madge had been to Christmas treats at Hazelgrove in her younger days when she and David and Teen had romped round the huge Christmas tree and played their party games. David was the only son of Jock and Young Alice. They called her that because she was twenty years younger than Jock. She was a bright and flirty sort of lass, full of fun and aye keen on parties, but Jock had soon put a damper on any capers of that sort.

The argument upstairs came to a sudden stop and Madge heard their footsteps on the stairs. The front door banged, a fairly loud bang she thought, and Father came into the kitchen. He looked flushed and out of sorts. 'Folk aye want to think the worst of you Madge.' He shook his head.

11

Now that she did the books for Father, Madge had a deal more confidence in coming straight to the point. 'Because Uncle John in Dollar has recommended this man, they shouldn't hold that against him,' she said. Father was chairman of the Parish Committee and he had strong ideas about the kind of man they should appoint as their new Inspector.

'There's nothing like a hint of nepotism in a Council appointment to raise their hackles,' Father retorted. 'I quite agree with them there, but I've explained to the Provost, as clearly as I can, this man's no relation of mine. He does come highly recommended. He's had a good Dollar education and he's well used to handling the books. The ratepayers need have no fear on that score. But we need more than an adding machine for this job, Madge. We need a man of the Kirk that can handle the young folk in this place and bring back some respect to the Toun. We've had over 30 applicants for the Inspector's job and they can all add and subtract and produce a balance sheet for Webster at the Council. I've read all their references, every last one of them, but this is the only one with the kind of experience I've been looking for. Of course I've still to meet the man,' he went on, 'and so have my committee. At the end of the day, that will decide it, not all the slanderous gossip made up by folk with little else to do.'

'Then I shouldn't worry yourself Father, said Madge, bored with all the nonsense of it. Why was there any need for Father to go upsetting the Toun Treasurer at this time of year? If only he could keep in with him they'd all be in the best of spirits for Christmas. Teen had hinted David would be bringing a few of his school chums up from his St Andrews school at Clifton Bank. She'd be sixteen next year and she'd never even met a boy that looked like the ones she'd read about in the *Weekly Welcome* Teen passed on to her. St Andrews boys had a bit of class to them, Teen had said. They were nothing like those coarse characters Harris or Bert brought into the house at times!

'Aye,' said Father, 'we need a young man that can organise the young folk in this place, get them out into the open air at weekends, get them into clubs and healthy, wholesome sports. With all those incomers finding jobs in the new mills, Bervie's becoming the Speak of the Mearns. What goes on at weekends in this toun is a crying disgrace. Bervie's getting itself a reputation worse than Sodom and Gomorrah.'

Madge was well enough versed in her bible and knew something of Sodom and Gomorrah. Teen had whispered some of the thrilling details of what went on between the mill lads and their lasses down on the back braes on a Saturday night. She'd found most of it hard to believe though Teen's words had stirred up some tinglings in herself she still blushed to think on. Why could Father not leave Jock Webster and the other mill lairds on the Council to get on with their plans? What sort of Christmas would it be if David's dance at Hazelgrove was put off for another long year?

THREE

Hebrew Bibles and Hazelgrove parties were never a bother in Arbuthnott. Surviving the winter was trouble enough. Leslie had mocked their teuchter ways, but teuchter skills were all they had. He knew that well enough, but Father made him mad having mother chauve on the way she did.

He lay listening to the sleet drive up from Bervie's Haughs, a sunken, flax-smell of a place with its clutter of mills, steaming quietly now, their boilers banked high for the night. Closer by, at Hareden and Greenden and all the other crofts on those braes, chields like Father would be lying, comatose, by their wives, knackered by days of howking and ditching to keep the flood waters from the door.

The better parks were lower down. Places like Milltown and Pitcarles, Townhead and Hercules Haugh lay stretched out from the railway track at Fordoun to the Royal Toun itself, all thirled to the Big House. The Home Farm and the Big House itself were mortgaged to the hilt, crumbling away and overrun by rats. The laird was poorly, they said, and he never gave a damn. Those ploughmen would be back now, from their Saturday night binges in Laurencekirk and the Royal Toun, sick and wretched in their dreary, sodden bothies. What a hard, grey, miserable life all of them had. The injustice of the thing he could never understand. What right had any man to lord it over the rest of them? Some marauding king in the distant past had decided the thing, and so it went on, forever and ever it seemed.

8>

Milltown of Arbuthnott, where the Queens lived, was close by the Bervie road and just a short dander to the shop and the school; a much handier place for the bairns than the three mile plod that other bairns like Leslie Mitchell or Becky Middleton – who lived far up there on the Reisk – had to thole, day after day. This was just as well for there was no shortage of bairns in Arbuthnott's Milltown. They were a cheery bunch, the Queens. Bobby was near thirteen, Chris ten, Mary eight, Jane four and wee Alec just two. They had all been bedded down at last, so John and Jane Ann Queen had time for a crack. They'd manage again this Christmas, they'd none of them starve, but she'd be hard at it again in the morn, making do with what they had. There would be no Christmas frills at Milltown. Thank God the Reverend Dunn was planning his Christmas concert and his social forby. The word was they would be handing out hot Bervie bridies and cakes, and Peter Bannerman at the shop was giving them a ham to slice up.

'I keep thinking of those Bervie spaewives and the fortune they held out for young Jane,' Jane Ann laughed. 'It helps to cheer me up when things are hard.'

John had spent his whole day ditching among the coarse clay round the door. The waters from the parks had been a worry for a time, but he'd saved their bit place and steered the stream further over and down across the Bervie road. The laird could handle it all from there, he'd grinned.

'I doubt if the Bervie spaewives ever get things right, with those readings from their tea leaves.' John looked across at Jane Ann. The logs were blazing now and the kitchen was snug and warm. This was the best time of the day. She was a real bonny quine his Jane Ann, and they'd a bonny bunch of bairns. The storm could rage on now, their place was safe and secure. They'd get through the New Year fine if they just took a care.

'It's a fine thing to dream John. Gives you something to try for. It was an odd thing though, what the Provost Doctor said that night. I felt an odd notion when I heard of it. You looked real pleased yourself, when you told me the tale.'

John Queen settled back in his chair and lit up his pipe. Jane Ann was aye most content when talking of the bairns. He'd made a good move when he'd given up the white fishing and left that cliff-top place at the Crawton. Life as a ploughman was coarse enough, but that fish toun at the Crawton had fallen on hard times. Besides, tossing about on that wee boat by the cliffs near Stonehive had been a damned risky business. They'd had grand times, though, down there on the cliffs in those Sabbath days of June before they were wed, chucking pebbles into the Crawton burn. They'd watch them tumble over the Trollachy cliff to the sea below, the two of them lying there on the seagrass, with the kittywakes crying in the summer heat. There were kittywakes by the thousand along the cliff face of the Fowlsheugh all the way to Stonehive. Bobby, Chris and Mary had all been born at the Crawton before they'd moved on. Then had come little Jane at New Mains of Ury. She'd been born in the summer of 1907, and that was what put the Provost Doctor on to his tale when little Alec was born. Jane Ann had had a hard time of it then, but she'd fair brightened up when he'd passed her the news.

Down in the Royal Toun they called Dr Aymer the Provost Doctor. They called him that long after he'd stopped being a provost and Provost Boath had taken on the job. Dr Aymer had a solemnity about him, but he was never over proud to roll up his sleeves and deliver a bairn, or give a hand at bandaging and cleaning up the soss of the filthiest wretch whatever the cause. He'd get on his horse and trot out the road to Garvock or Arbuthnott if some half demented chield hammered at his door and shouted, 'for God's sake doctor, you have to come.' Whatever the weather, the Provost Doctor would keep a calm souch and tease out the facts in that quiet, soft-spoken way that he had. His sharp blue eyes soon summed up the state of the gasping tyke before him while his lad was readying his horse.

That November night in 1909 when wee Alec Queen was born, Jane Ann was just sixteen months old as she stood there, wide-eyed, listening to the first gusty howls of wee Alec. The Provost Doctor had given her dad a wry look as much as to say, 'at it again, John,' a thing the well mannered Dr Aymer would never have put into words. But he did say, patting the lass kindly like, 'and how old are you, little miss?' Wee Jane Ann grabbed her dad's hand and hid her head in the warmth of his worsted breeks.

'That's Jane Ann, doctor,' said John Queen, proud and unabashed. 'She was born at New Mains of Ury on the 24th of July, 1907, at one o'clock in the morning.' He was a proud dad was John Alexander Queen. He'd a great respect for the Bervie Provost Doctor, but he'd take no rebukes from him.

The Bervie doctor smiled quietly at that and looked thoughtful then. The year 1907 had been a big year in the Bervie calendar, and he'd heard what the Bervie spaewives had said of all the bairns lucky to be born in the year of Bervie's *Annus Mirabilis*. Little Ella McLeod had been born at no. nine the King Street in 1907 and her father, Andra McLeod, the horse hirer, had regaled the Provost Doctor with the tales the spaewives had been putting about. Great things would come to pass, they said, for bairns born in Bervie in that great year, for that was the year Jock Webster's big new mill, the Craigview Works, opened its doors for the very first time.

The Provost Doctor minded all this and his face broke into a quiet smile. 'Great things will come to you little Jane Ann,' he said to her, stroking her bonny locks. 'You were born the year Bervie's Craigview Mill started to spin its flax. That was Bervie's *Annus Mirabilis*. They do say down in Bervie, to be born in that year was a very lucky omen.'

John Alexander Queen was fine pleased at that bit of news. Any good news about his bairns was aye pleasing and he thanked the Provost Doctor as he showed him out the door. It was the blackest of nights and Milltown of Arbuthnott had not been the easiest of places for the Provost Doctor to get to, but the doctor was as courteous as ever as he took the reins of his docile bay hunter from Bobby who'd got a hold of him. The night was quiet, the stars were bright, and the track down to the Bervie road shone clearly in the light of the oil lamps John Queen had rigged up earlier.

'Come along, Dobbin,' said the doctor. He raised his hand. 'Take good care of your lady now, Mr Queen,' he said firmly. 'She's a wonderful woman, but she'll need a good long rest now.'

'Have no fear doctor,' cried John. 'She'll be kept in her bed for the rest of the week. We've plenty of busy hands here ready to help.'

'Fancy calling a grand horse like that Dobbin,' said Bobby as they got back inside and shut out the cold November night.

'Och, that's just the way of the gentry,' said his dad, giving Bobby a friendly slap, 'but the Provost Doctor's a fine man. Did you hear what he said about little Jane Ann?'

They had a good laugh at that when they gathered round mother's bed and had their first keek at wee Alec. 'Bervie spaewives say such daft things,' said Jane Ann. 'Lucky omens are chancy things though.' But she was real pleased and smiled at little Jane Ann when she said that. 'Born in the year of Bervie's... what were the words he used?'

'*Annus Mirabilis,*' said Chris, who'd a good memory for such things, 'the year the Craigview Mill started up.'

'Ah well, we'll wait and see,' said mother, giving Jane Ann's hair another ruffle, 'but I'm over tired John lad,' she said, giving his hand a squeeze. 'I think I'll just lie quiet and rest for a bit.'

John shoo'd the bairns out of the room at that and set about bedding them down in the kitchen. Jane Ann dozed off just then, for the Provost Doctor had given her a draught from a wee bottle he carried. So little Jane Ann had been born under a lucky star, had she? These were her last thoughts as she slipped into a deep, deep sleep. A lucky Bervie star, but maybe none the worse for that, was the notion she took to her dreams.

John's eyes began to droop. He'd had another hard day of it, working out there with Bobby in that ice-cold wind. They'd settled in fine up here in Arbuthnott. The life was hard but no harder than it had ever been. The speak of the place was odd and coarse sounding in your lugs, but there was a couthieness to folk. They'd come rushing to help if you ever needed a hand. The Reverend Dunn, especially, was a dab hand at getting the best out of folk, and the ploys he got up to made the world of a difference. Thank God the minister was a body you could speak to. There was precious little help from the Big Hoose over the road. Jane Ann had never ventured into that tree choked land behind the high dyke. It would be five or six feet high, she thought, and you could see damn all but trees and weeds if you keeked through the lodge gates. Folk said the Arbuthnott lairds had run through all their silver and that the place was falling about their lugs and swarming with vermin. You could well believe it. Most had never seen the laird and there was a tale of their being more than one laird, and that you were hard put to tell which was the real laird. There had been a daft laird once, she'd heard, but there had been a grand one too, back in the Old Queen's time. He'd left four sons in the place and they'd all lived on there. One had been poorly and died out of turn, but the rest had all had a shot at the lairding.

From what Jane Ann had heard, they did damn all but potter about the place and shoot the rabbits that swarmed both sides of the Bervie burn as far afield as Fordoun and Garvock. Except for Bill Allison the game-keeper, the only person she'd ever seen come out from the trees was an odd character called Preddy. She'd met up with Preddy at the shop one day when she was in for a fill of paraffin. He'd toddled off with his messages and there had been a bit of a laugh. Peter Bannerman, the grocer, had soon put a stop to that. Preddy, they said, was the real laird who ran the Big Hoose. He handled all the business, if business it was. He was housekeeper, manager, handyman, and God knows what else, if you believed all the claik. They said that he'd been taken on to look after the brother that was poorly, and that when the brother had died, Preddy had kept his room just as he'd left it, as a sort of shrine, they said.

But tales like that just added to the riddle of the place, and Bobby would try to frighten his sisters with yarns about the goings on at the Big Hoose and the old kirk down by the Bervie Water. They had been there since antique times, Bobby had said, and were haunted by knights and gryphons and other wild winged beasts of long ago.

Jane Ann smiled as she thought of that. Young Chris and Mary were over smart to be taken in by such tales and would give Bobby back stories they'd made up and were a lot better still. Young Jane though, who'd be old enough for school next August, would look wide-eyed and wondering as she listened to it all. Maybe there was something in what those Bervie spaewives had said. Strange things did go on in that haunted valley of the Bervie. She'd heard a tale that when the Bervie burst its banks, something ill was aye sure to follow. Well maybe there were good luck signs as well, like Bervie's *Annus Mirabilis.* Maybe young Jane would end up as mistress herself of one of Bervie's big hooses. Which big hoose would that be, Jane Ann wondered. There were only two big hooses run by the Mill Lairds down in the Royal Toun. One was Bridge End, where Pappa Jim Gibb, as they called him, kept a close eye on his big mills in the Haughs. The other was at the opposite end of the Toun at Hazelgrove. Jock Webster had built that for his young bride Alice. Jock owned two other mills in the place, besides the new Craigview he'd started the year young Jane was born.

Jane Ann gave herself a shake. It was fine to dream when the day's darg was done, but the fire was burning low and you'd to get back to what you had. At least the bairns had the Reverend Dunn's Christmas social to come, with its bridies and hot pies, so thank God for that!

'Time we were in bed John lad,' she laughed. 'Those spaewives have got me dreaming the daftest of tales. I've been trying to work out if wee Jane will end up in Pappa Gibb's hoose at Brig End, or maybe Webster's new place at Hazelgrove!'

FOUR

Jim Geddes stepped off the train at Fordoun Station into bright December sunshine. The day had caught folk by surprise. Even dour old Grant who'd got on at Laurencekirk gave Jim's 'grand day' a grudging 'aye, for all its glaur and spleiter there are worse places on God's earth than the Howe o' the Mearns.'

What sort of doric was this, Jim wondered. His genteel Dollar accent had encountered some coarse expressions along the Hillfoots, but this earthy tongue was of a different order. The breezy Banff words of his younger days had been nothing like this. Yet the farmer man, for all his scowls, had an eager glint in his eye. The mysterious ways of the Mearns they'd warned him about were maybe far worse than he'd imagined.

Country wives, humping their bundles and their parcels, shot him sharp, suspicious looks. He looked a fine enough figure of a man, all of 22 summers maybe, a bit quiet and solemn like and clean shaven, but a braw lad for all that. But who did he think he was, him with his leather case and his brand new overcoat. His polished shoes and his collar and tie marked him out as a government man of some sort, a city gent from Doon Sooth maybe, Dundee or Glasgow even.

However, you'd other things to think about today than government inspectors. That sea-piner had gone at last. Days on end it had sore tried you, ripping at the steadings and tearing off the roof tiles. It was over a week past since the howling north-easter had flung itself against the sea rocks at Kinneff and chased the wee boats bouncing back to their shelters at Gourdon and Stonehive. Within hours, so the *Mearns Leader* said, the concrete slabs on Stonehive's fancy promenade had been flung and smashed beyond repair. A bit of a laugh that for the locals. Only the toffs and the hotel folk had worried about that bit stishie. A trouble maybe for the tourists from Doon Sooth, daft enough to waste their holidays up here in Stonehive.

The real hurt as ever had been to the folk down by the shore, struggling to wrest a living from it all. The 'Mayflower' from Gourdon had

19

foundered and lost four of her crew. That was earlier in the month. Now news had come of the trawler 'Robin' from Granton, smashed on the Gourdon rocks at the foot of those hills beyond Garvock way.

The word was their prayers had been answered. Prayers were fickle things, and maybe the Granton crew owed their lives more to the rocket line and the breeches buoy than to the mission hall prayers. John Cargill and his lifeboat crew had crawled over the rocks with lights and heaving lines to grab at the survivors. They'd got five shillings each for that bit of foolhardiness. Now the Granton men were being coddled and fed by the fisher wives in the quiet dark of their fish-smelling bens. Here in the Howe they said coarse things about the fisher tinks who'd clout you as soon as look at you at the Saturday dancing, but fine you knew if you nearly drowned on their precious rocks, they'd feed you and bed you till you were up and ready for another bit clouting. So they said, but folk would say anything for a laugh.

That week of the sea-piner and the Granton wreck, the high gales had veered to the sooth. They'd stopped a while, just long enough for the Fordoun Winter Show, the best show ever, and then started up on another rampage. This time the storm had howled up through the Howe, an Atlantic, wetter gale, splattering the higher lands with snow and sleet.

Up the storm had swung, past Forfar and Brechin, tearing slates and chimney cans the whole length of the Howe to Fordoun and Stonehive. A mighty swirl had swung round at Fordoun, and on down the glen of the Bervie flow, uprooting the trees in Arbuthnott's parks and in the haughs beyond, to the sea at Bervie. As the auld sang had it, the winds that week had been frae a' the airts.

Jim felt a bit put out and flummoxed at the sour looks folk gave him. He could hardly have guessed that the glint in old Grant's eye had something to do with the weekend of drinking that was before him, and that maybe there was a thought too of the Christmas and Hogmanay capers still to come. Jim's worries had little to do with drinking orgies.

If he'd declared himself as the Good Templar that he was – one of that odd crowd, Grant knew, swarmed down in those fisher touns like Gourdon – they might have had a breezier palaver.

Jim made for the footbridge which connected with the station buildings and the down platform. A Glasgow-bound express thundered through, shrouding the place with steam and smoke. Up on the bridge he took stock. So this was the heart of the Mearns. He'd read plenty about the place that last week. Best to know what you were letting yourself in for. They'd covered their tracks well those early Mearns men, not just the Romans and the Picts, but the later lairds and earls. They'd confessed things enough with the different yarns they'd left behind. They'd swept the Howe clean, helped no doubt by the Grampian storms. St Andrews and the Borders still clung to their ruins, but here in the Mearns, not an antique stone was left to confound their tales.

Fordoun, he'd read, was where St Palladius had built the earliest kirk of all. That had been behind the hill there, up Drumtochty way, where they still held their Paldy, or Paddy Fair as they had it. Over there had been Kincardine Castle, that antique home of kings, capital of the Mearns and much else besides. The Third Kenneth had died there. At the hands of his own men? The more romantic tale of the Fair Finella appealed the most. Wife of the Mearns Chief, she'd lured poor Kenneth on, they said. They said much else, but maybe that's the way history was. The past was the way you liked it to be.

Never mind the railway trains, the porter lads and all the stir in the station yard, this Howe that was hemmed in there had a feel about it still. Jim felt he was in among them, those hard-nosed men of the Mearns. Behind him were the Grampians, and to his right the Howe widened out to the richer soil and bigger farms by Laurencekirk and beyond. On his left the hills closed in on a narrower strip of farmland. That would be the way, Jim guessed, to the place they called Stonehive.

The Mearns that December Friday noon was having a grand day of it. The higher Grampian lands behind him were still mottled in sleet, and ahead lay the road he must take. A winding road it was, along the flat at first, then edging slowly up through the gap in the braes. The high ground on each side looked bare and rough with great patches of fir trees, splashing their different greens on the braes. There was a redness on the slopes where the plough had been. Higher up it was moor country, bare but for the weather-torn broom.

Nearby came the rush of water, heard but not seen, tearing away at the red clay, carting it into the Bervie flow now swollen and breaking its banks. The word had got back to Fordoun Station that the lower lands at Arbuthnott and Allardice were well under water. It had spilled across the wider stretch of the Bervie Haughs and was swirling near the sandbagged mills of the Royal Toun. To the joy of the young and the exasperation of the mill lairds, the Bervie flow, a douce bit trickle for most of the year,

21

was now on one of its wilder bents. From Fordoun to the sea the cry had gone up, 'The Bervie's in spate!'

Jim could only guess at some of the jokes and laughs flying about the station yard. For all that he'd heard of Mearns folk being a dour-like crowd, there was a restlessness about the place. Maybe it was the shock of seeing the sun out for a change, or maybe it was just the way folk were, lifting parcels onto their traps, their long-suffering ponies docile and quiet as the bundles piled higher still on the creaking boards.

Some of the banter he picked up, was on the Fordoun Show. A grand time that had been; fair stirred you up at the black time of the year. The best show and the best prices they'd ever seen had fair put the Stonehive folk in their place. Reid at Alpity had got the premium prize for his heifers and Milne at Leys of Barras, second prize for his shorthorn bull. It was Alexander of the Bents who had made the biggest stir with his red tickets for four black heifers. Fine fleshy beasts they'd been and herded off for a grand price by George Diack, one of the butchers down at Bervie. There was no shortage of silver in Bervie these days. The greedy lairds would be eating their way through all that meat before the weekend was over.

The new charabanc of the Bervie Motor Company sat fair and square at the front of the station yard. It had a flat roof and was open-sided, the only bit of glass a windscreen for the driver. There were four banks of seats, a separate open door leading on to each. To get to them you'd to hoist yourself up on to a long plank of a step, a fair bit from the ground, then on to another, a bit higher at the back. The seats were arranged in a handy way so folk at the back had a good view of the road out in front. A solid looking machine it was, with sturdy iron wheels rimmed with hard bits of rubber to give them a grip. Judging by the laughs of farmers nearby, the Bervie charabanc had a reputation for having wheels that stuck on the braes and sulked in the mud.

'Would you like a loan of my sheltie, Frank?' laughed a young orraman, loading some boxes on to a farm cart. 'You did a fine job sliding down the Townhead Brae, but I'll warrant the mud will do for you on the way back up. You'd be safer with a couple of Ellison's Clydesdales,' he added. 'It would be a shame to lumber a wee sheltie with that fancy load of wood and iron.'

The charabanc driver, a clean cut young lad in a peaked cap and a chauffeur's uniform complete with leggings, took it all in good part.

'You'll all be driving motor trucks in another year,' he laughed. 'Your ponies will be fit only for race tracks and circuses.'

Jim climbed on board and settled himself on the bench behind the young driver. A young couple with two rowdy bairns piled into the back seat, off to grannie in Bervie for Christmas and Hogmanay, to judge by their chatter. The only other passengers were an elderly couple who sat themselves in the middle, on the far side, away from any disturbance, and a young foreign-looking man who seated himself next to Jim, apparently with the intention of enjoying some conversation on the journey to the coast. All of them were bound for Bervie, for the few farmers and other country folk heading in the same direction were already starting off in their traps and carts. The driver took a good look at Jim. 'Arbuthnott billies have little faith in modern kinds of transport,' he grinned.

Jim had had an early start that morning, the advice of John Alexander, the Bailie's brother in law, still ringing in his ears.

'Speak up for yourself, Jim,' he'd urged. 'These Bervie mill-men and traders are a hard-headed lot. I've done all I can, but it's up to you now. They'll judge you as they find you.' But there had been a worrying note to that last conversation. 'Some of the Council think the Bailie's trying to foist one his relations on to them,' John Alexander had whispered. 'The Bailie's wife was a Geddes,' he'd added by way of explanation.

The cheerful charabanc driver settled down at the wheel and turned round with a grin. 'I'm Frank Riddell,' he said. 'Just ignore those farmer billies. It's a bit muddy on the roads today, but we'll take it nice and steady up the Townhead Brae. We should be all right from there on.'

Frank Riddell heaved the heavy gear lever forward and the charabanc lumbered out of the station yard on the first stage of its Bervie run to the cheers of the small crowd of bairns who had gathered round the forecourt to see for themselves how this contraption worked.

'I'm Pasquale Canale,' the friendly foreigner introduced himself. 'I bring the delicious Italian ice cream to Bonny Scotland. One shop in Bervie and one in Gourdon, just one mile away by train.'

Jim was quite cheered by the friendly approach. Italians were much more forthcoming than the locals in these parts, but he eyed the jovial Italian before he answered. 'Jim Geddes, from Dollar,' he said and added quietly, 'paying just a short visit to Bervie.'

'Ah! You will be the Bailie's man to be the new inspector.' Canale's eyes lit up and Frank stole a nosey.look. 'I wish you every success in your interview. The Bailie is quite right. We need a good man to organise the young people in the place. I am having a billiard table for my shop. That will give them something better to do than drinking in the public houses each night.'

There were no secrets in the Mearns then. News of his coming, and no doubt his credentials, had gone before him. The charabanc lumbered on, cresting the summit and circling round the trees and dykes of Arbuthnott estate.

They rumbled past the village shop, showering excited bairns with mud and water. 'Bannerman's Economic Stores' proclaimed the sign above the door. Jim noticed a neat display of whisky bottles in the window. There was a butcher's shop on the left, and on the other side stood the open doorway of a small garage.

'Howe o' the Mearns Whisky,' announced Frank. 'The best there is outside the Spey. Old Peter Bannerman blends the stuff himself.'

'High up behind there the land gets bleak and coarse,' he continued. 'Bare, grudging soil, you'd have to be bleak and coarse yourself to survive on those dreich heights. An Aberdeenshire man took over a place they call Bloomfield some two years back. Little chance of much blooming there, folk said, but he's been working away at it fine, breaking in some hill land. A hardy lot those Aberdeen teuchters. But look there's Bervie on the skyline.'

'Many tower'd Camelot'. The words of Jim's Dollar Academy teacher struck him then. Not so many towers though. The Bervie silhouette, etched crisply on the clear December skyline, brought a thrill of pleasure. Jutting high above all the rest stood a tall, square church tower with four slender and sharpened minarets pointing skywards. Two long, narrow chimney stacks stood out sharply in the clear midday light, one on either side.

'That's the auld Parish Kirk,' said Frank. 'The stack on the right is the Laurel Mill, built by the Burnesses, but the Gibbs soon took that over. A lot of good it did them. The winds had the stack down twice and did a fair bit of damage to the machinery below. But there it is, smoking away as fine as ever. Must be plenty of silver in the flax trade, if they can take knocks like that.'

'That stack on the left is Webster's main mill,' said Canale, showing off his own knowledge of the Toun. 'It's called the Springworks. They call the newer part of it the Klondike because the spinners earn an extra penny or two working the new spindles. It stands right behind my ice cream shop in the middle of the Toun.' Canale's Italian accent was spattered with a

Scots-Bervie twang Jim found fascinating.

A sailing of geese swung in from the sea, crossing the Haughs to some well-kent loch, deep in the heart of the Howe. A chilly breeze had started up from the sea, waving the leather straps on the rolled-up canvas above the open sides of the charabanc. Jim breathed in deeply the salty tang of the sea air. This would suit him fine, he thought, then he remembered what John Alexander in Dollar had said. Half the Toun was already lined up against him!

By the time Frank had steered his heavy bus on to the high standing Bervie Brig, Jim's two guides had pointed out and explained all seven of Bervie's smoking chimney stacks. Down to the right, the brown flood water had spread itself into a lake covering most of the valley, splashing at the mill walls in a tumbling rage. On the other side, looking towards the sea, Frank pointed to a low-lying, one-storeyed building. It was an older-looking mill with a short, thick smoke stack and it had a water wheel splashing away wildly in the mill race.

'That's the Linty Mill I was telling you about,' Frank said. 'The one Old Jock Webster got from his mam, another of the Gibbs.'

The bus made a sharp left turn at the end of the brig and Frank moved down a gear to climb up the Cowgate Brae into the Royal Toun.

'Bridge End House.' Frank waved his hand to a solid looking villa on the left. 'That's where the early mill lairds all lived. Provost Alf Gibb built those two big mills in the Haughs. The Auld Mill and the New Mill, they call them. No fancy names for the Gibbs. It's his brother, Captain Pappa Jim, that runs the place now. He ran off to sea when he was a lad and ended up as captain of a west coast puffer. They call him Pappa Jim because of all the bairns he has. Bridge End is crawling with Pappa Jim's bairns.'

The Bailie stared long and hard at the young man in front of him. The lad had stood up well to his questions, and he had a steady, honest look about him, staring you straight in the eye. He had a fair understanding too, of an inspector's problems. Living with Inspector Fraser's family that time in Dollar had given him a good training. You could never beat that sort of experience when you got it at first hand. The Bailie sighed. The lad knew his catechism. His Dollar education had done a good job there, and he was sound on doctrine. Pity he was an Auld Kirk man, but the Auld Kirk and the Free Kirk were little different now. He preached in the David Street gospel hall himself, when he got half a chance.

No, the young lad looked just what his sister Jean's man had said he was. But had he smeddum? He was a bit soft spoken, gentle in his ways. Would the wilder lads be too much for this man? You could never trust appearances, though. Folk thought that he, the Bailie, was a hard man, and that suited him fine, but look how he'd cracked when his Louie had died. God forgive him for that! He was no better than most men that he knew. Five bairns his Louie had borne for him in those ten short years. It had all been over much for the lass. He blamed himself for that, lusting after her the way he'd done. And the sins of the flesh were with him still. Those burning cravings he suffered would never let him rest. Women had been put on earth to tempt a man, to test him out and he'd been a miserable failure. Marriage never gave a man the right to treat his woman that way. He'd rot in Hell one day for his sins if the Good Lord willed it. The Bailie sighed. Maybe this lad in front of him was different. Maybe he'd an inner strength, was tougher than he looked.

Jim wondered at the silence. The Bailie's eyes had glazed over. Jim cast his eyes round the wee parlour. There was a Victorian clutter about the place, framed family photographs everywhere. An upright piano stood angled across one corner of the room. On top lay a wooden stereoscope beside a bunch of cards, the top one showing two identical pictures of the Forth Bridge for three dimensional viewing. He noticed a small harmonium, a cornet, two fiddle cases and a crowded bookcase. Jammed between an armchair and a sofa, stood a swivel bookcase of dark oak with a complete set of the *Encyclopaedia Britannica*.

The Bailie spoke. 'Folk are saying I'm making too much of this appointment. They say all we need is a good book-keeper we can trust who can keep a tight grip on the ratepayers' silver.' Jim made no reply. 'We've seven mills in the place now, five of them built in the last twenty years, as well as two new mills in Johnshaven and Gourdon. There have been hundreds of incomers, many of them are decent and hard working folk, but there are plenty of the other sort. Bervie is the only industrial place of any size in the Mearns. If you've been keeping an eye on what's been going on down in Dundee, you'll see the kind of trouble we might run into here.'

'Industrial trouble?' Jim had often debated on industrial problems at his kirk guild in Dollar. He'd have to watch himself here. 'There's been a lot of talk about strike action by the Dundee dockers these last few days.'

'Aye, and among the carters as well,' said the Bailie, getting quite animated. 'They'll be having strikes in the Dundee jute mills next. Dundee handles jute and Bervie flax, but we get our flax from the ships that dock in Dundee.'

Jim nodded. 'Are you likely to see a mill strike in Bervie?'

'Not just yet,' said the Bailie. 'They're all looking forward to their Hogmanay holiday, but if trouble breaks out in Dundee, you never can tell. We have a direct railway line to Dundee. What we need is somebody that can encourage the young folk in the Toun to take a pride in the place, get involved in things. The kind of things you've been organising in Dollar, like discussion groups, cycling clubs and athletics, would be far healthier for them than the kind of capers most are getting up to these days. If we could get a few of the more talented men involved, they'd soon keep a grip on the wilder lads. There's more to life than drinking and brawling, aye, and fornication too, if it comes to that.' The Bailie glowered at Jim to see how he took that.

Jim nodded again. How would a parish inspector keep the peace among a crowd of ruffians like that?

'You don't involve yourself in politics do you?'

Jim thought a moment. A bit of an empire man himself, he'd strong feelings about what had been going on in India that week. The papers had been full of the Royal Durbar and India's new King Emperor, George the Fifth, touring around in his grand train. Painted all over in white, the royal train had caused a fair stir. There had been no stinting on comfort or expense, the papers had claimed, every coach had been magnificently upholstered. But what about those pictures of all the beggars and scraggy bairns they'd shown, rushing along the track crying out for baksheesh? Now those dockers and carters were asking an extra shilling for the choking, dangerous work they did among the jute boats in Dundee.

'No,' Jim said at last. He didn't involve himself in politics and he certainly wasn't a socialist.

'Aye,' said the Bailie. 'That's fine.' But he'd noticed Jim's hesitation when he'd spoken about politics. Surely the man's allegiance should lie with the bosses. Where would they all be if there were no bosses to provide the work and the silver in the first place? 'Well, Mr Geddes, there are three of you to be interviewed. My committee will see all three of you in the Council Chambers in the morning. It will be up to you to persuade them that you are the man for the job.'

He'd botched things at the end. He was sure of that. Ah well, he'd have another chance in the morning. He'd still one chance in three of becoming the new inspector. With half the Toun against him though, and this grim Bailie having his doubts, what sort of chance was that?

A sweet young lass with bright, shining eyes showed him to the door. She wished him a pleasant enough 'good day', but even she gave him a suspicious sort of look. She was clearly upset at his coming!

The interviews next day were long and wearisome. They were as grim a body of men as Jim had ever met. They might have been appointing the Prime Minister! But then they'd the safety of the Royal Toun's silver in their care! One applicant had been sent on his way, ungraciously, Jim thought.

The Committee were evenly divided, the vote split between Mr T D Phillips of Lochgelly and Mr Jim Geddes of Dollar. They were having another try at it. The door opened suddenly. They'd spoken themselves to a standstill.

'Gentlemen,' said the young clerk, embarrassed at what he had to say. 'I have to tell you that the voting of the Committee remains divided, so the decision has been left to the chairman. Bailie Clarke has given his casting vote to Mr Jim Geddes.'

Jim was not prone to great shows of emotion, but he felt a burst of relief and then some real excitement at the news. He turned to the unhappy man at his side and shook his hand, offering what condolences he could. At last he'd done it. He'd landed a job he could do something with. It was later on, though, that the notion struck him. He was fully beholden now to that dour-looking, cantankerous Bailie. Did that mean that he'd hitched himself up to that strange looking man and all his odd notions for the rest of his life?

FIVE

The Bailie's fears of a workers' revolution proved real enough. In the days following Jim's appointment, three hundred sodgers of Dundee's own regiment, the Black Watch, were rushed by train to the city. They marched through the streets with rifles and fixed bayonets, to the jeers and boos of the crowds. A strike of carters and dockers had broken out and the city of Dundee was virtually paralysed.

'You've come to quell twa or three carters,' jeered the crowds, and the lads of the Black Watch, red in the face, returned to the hard floor of the drill hall with one army blanket each to hap them up for the night. They soon perked up though, with big helpings of bully beef, bread and butter, and scalding tea.

Next day, the dockers threw a lorry into the docks, and in the days that followed, the bobbies conducted a running battle with thousands of the toonies who'd taken to the streets. The crowds hit back at the mounted bobbies with stones and bottles and were rewarded for their pains with baton charges and with being trampled underfoot if they got in the way. The police force up in Aberdeen were asked to help, but that canny lot kept their heads down and said, 'Na, na. We've no bobbies to spare.' So it raged on with a kind of anarchy and undeclared martial law, disrupting the city. By 23 December, all the mills and factories in Dundee, though still not on strike, had closed down completely.

Back in the Royal Toun, folk looked on fair amazed, but here and there a deil among them would be takin' notes and biding his time. The turn of the mill workers was yet to come, they vowed, but not yet. By Christmas Day, concessions had been made. The strike collapsed and the men of the Black Watch prepared to leave, glad to get out of the place and plan their own bit skirmishing for Hogmanay.

It was noted though, that as a result of that bit stishie, the carters now had an extra shilling a week and the dockers another penny for every hour they put in. An odd spinner here and there on the north side of the Kirkburn wondered if they'd have some kind of Bervie stramash in the New Year.

There was little the Bailie could do to stop the boozing revelries of Hogmanay except turn the lights out early and see his family safely indoors. But next day, the New Year's Day holiday, the Bailie had his chance. As chairman of the Highland Games Committee, his plans were well in hand to raise money and provide a night of entertainment more in keeping with a royal toun.

Cold and wet as it was that New Year's night, the Burgh Hall was packed with folk from both sides of the Burn. The mill lairds and their wives sat there on the one and sixpenny seats in front, close behind the wee orchestra with Bert Clarke and Cockie Davidson tuning up their fiddles and Jim Douglas testing out his cornet.

You looked down from the back row in your sixpenny gallery seat, over the heads of some shopkeepers in front. If you stood up you'd a grand view of the crowd packed down below, most of them on the sixpenny forms. Nearer to the front were a few forms with backs to them and there, on the ninepenny's and in the shilling rows, sat some teachers, shop folk and maybe a mill foreman or two.

You'd queued up in the cold and got in early. The place had soon warmed up. The gas lamps hissed and, along by the front of the stage, a row of shielded gas mantles threw a glare up on to the stage curtain. The curtain was rolled right down and it got a jolt at times from the stage hands and the folk in the opening chorus shoving around at the back.

You kept looking back at the huge curtain. It had been dropped from near the roof and it stretched right across the hall. Painted on the curtain was a huge picture of the Bervie Bridge. It brightened up the place and towered high above the whole assembly. The great arch of the thing in its brown sandstone and sets of white, spiked iron railings, fair got every man, woman and bairn staring at it. The bright blue of the sky and the Bervie water below, the green of the high banks on each side, and the sharp white of the old toll house high up on the right made a grand sight.

Aye, the Bailie and his men could fair paint a bonny picture when they liked! It reminded you of the long, hot summer days of long ago when you guddled for burnies in the Linty Shots. It gave you a fine feeling inside, a comfortable feeling, for this was hame, the folk around you, your folk. Making a dreadful noise they were, but a cheery, laughing noise, slapping and hand shaking, wishing each other 'good health' here and 'a Happy New Year' there. Determined they were to enjoy themselves.

The tunes and the singers, they'd most have heard before, but that was what they'd come for, the old songs and the old tunes and maybe some of the new music hall tunes too, from the banker and the dominie, from the dressmaker and the quines that served in the shops or worked in the mill office. Old Annie's voice might be getting a bit thin like, but my she could fair sing in her time, and that took you back a bit! You'd clap at the Indian Club Display by the young lads from Gourdon. You'd clap loud and long after every chorus, every duet and every solo. You'd cheer the young lassies up doing the highland fling for the very first time. The comic would crack the jokes you'd heard him crack before, but dammit, it was New Year's Day, so you'd all howl and laugh and stamp your feet. You never boo'd at a New Year's Day concert, it just never occurred to you. By the time the show was well begun, the condensation was streaming down the walls and the place was like a hot house.

It would never be a Bervie concert without some well remembered Bervie songs and verses. Bervie should be named the Poets' Toun, some said, and my certie, you knew most of the words by heart, and you'd sing along with the rest of them when Andra gave voice to all five verses of The Bervie Lasses, with a rousing chorus between ilka verse:

> O, hae ye seen the mill maids,
> The mill maids, the mill maids,
> O ye seen the mill maids,
> The bonny maids o' Bervie?

Then you'd lie back, fine and proud like when the Major recited 'The Bervie Volunteers'.

Lassies were collecting pennies for their penny programmes, mostly from folk at the front. Cockie Davidson and his lads were still tuning up with Miss Moir at the piano. Old Will was going round with his long pole and hook, lowering the flares of the gas lamps. As seven o'clock struck, the Bailie rose to his feet and stood at the side of the stage. The band stopped their tuning and the shuffling feet and back slapping stumbled to a stop. A hush of excitement fell on the place. A bairn spoke a few words at the back. The hiss of the stage lights added to the thrill. Before saying a word, the Bailie fixed the crowd with his dour like glower. The new year of 1912 was about to be properly started!

SIX

Nineteen twelve was a good year but there were disasters for some. A parish inspector sees some of the worst, and young Jim, in his new job, did what he could. Jim's parish office was a small two-roomed building at number three the Cowgate, at the north end of King Street and just a few doors up from where Pappa Gibb kept a sharp eye on all that was going on at the haugh mills down below. It could be said that Pappa Gibb eyed the workers to see they were busy, and Jim Geddes eyed the rest that were down on their luck. The site of Jim's office was a handy one, for Pappa Gibb could keep an eye on that as well. The ratepayers' silver was never there to be flung away on every wastrel that had moved into the Toun.

That road down the Cowgate had other attractions for some. Mary Williamson's Whisky Shoppie lay between Jim's office and Pappa Gibb at Bridge End. It served the Toun well, but times being what they were, you'd to pick your time with care. None thought it odd if Pappa Gibb or the other mill lairds dropped by. They'd be entertaining, and would need to keep up their supplies. But those douce folk that lived down Castle Terrace or in other genteel parts had to be circumspect. They'd saunter down from the Terrace and up the waterside. On a dark night, you could dander up from the brig, slip into Mary's Shoppie, and never see a soul.

If you'd a bad thirst in the daytime, you covered up as best you could, but Isobel made a real hash of things that day she'd a drouth. Her man kept racing pigeons, so she chanced her luck at the Shoppie with the doos' basket in her hand. That rash caper cost Isa dear. Mistress Jamieson spied Isa cutting across the Square.

'Out shopping, Isa?' Mistress Jamieson asked, with a smirk.

'We're just fleein' the doo,' Isa snapped back, as red as a beetroot.

After that bit sally, there was little you could chance in the Toun. If you'd a box or a bag in your hand, folk would give a bit laugh. 'So you're fleein' the doo again?' they'd smirk, before you'd time to explain.

In April word came through about the Titanic, and you could hardly get a worse disaster than that. For us lads in Pappa Gibb's mills the whole thing was a disaster, and a month before the Titanic hit the news, we made a bit of news in the place ourselves. It was big Dod started the thing, early on in March. Big Dod told how the Dundee dockers had forced an extra penny an hour from the bosses for the filthy work they had to suffer. If anybody suffered more for less silver than the lads in the preparing sheds he'd never heard of them. Big Dod was right, of course. Mixing rough Russian flax and shoving it into the breaker was the roughest job in the mill.

The clouds of stour the breaker threw out were hard to bear. You choked and gasped, and some lads were laid low and weakened with the stuff. For all that chauving you got little more than tuppence ha'penny an hour. Over at the Pitcarry Mill, Dave Burness paid the lads a penny extra. For cleaning out the ash from the flues and chipping away the lumps from inside the boilers, Dave would pay five shillings a day, but you didn't get a chance of that very often.

So the rest of us joined Big Dod and made our demands to the foreman. Pappa Gibb would have none of it. We could clear out of the place for all he cared, so clear out we did. We'd a grand day of it, marching up and down the King Street whistling and singing. The looks we got from the shopkeepers, you'd have thought the revolution had come. One lad started the singing with words he'd picked up at the dancing, but when we got into the square and near to Shand the bakers, Big Dod started shouting, a bit tuneless like, the words of 'Scots Wha Ha'e.' That fair took a trick and we all bellowed out:

> Now's the day, and now's the hour;
> See the front of battle lower;
> See approach proud Pappa's power;
> Chains and slavery.

Millar, the chemist, lowped back into his shop as though the Germans had landed. That fair tickled us up. But we soon tired of the singing, and fixed up a football game down in the park. We felt a lot better for that day in the fresh air, but we'd to get to work next morning again, with not a penny on our wages and a day's pay lost.

So that was the tale of the Bervie strike. Two weeks later Jim pinned up a notice in his office window telling of the free pamphlets he had, if you wanted to emigrate to Canada. A hundred and sixty acres of good Canadian land could be yours for the asking. Two or three farming billies from Arbuthnott and Garvock said they'd take a chance on it, but the lads in Pappa Gibb's mills knew damn-all about working the land. You got precious little silver for working in the bloody mills and the hours were long and coarse, but there was aye the weekends and a chance for some fun with those teuchters that came inby to the pubs!

SEVEN

Soon it was summer, and the Bailie had Jim organising most things in the Royal Toun. The June days lengthened, and Jim had his programmes and his posters for the Bervie Games well in hand. The Games were to be better than ever this year, with bus excursions from all over the Howe. A special train was laid on to cover the fisher touns along the smugglers' coast. There was excitement in the air.

Even those teuchters in their bothies were touched by the bustle, for there were prizes to be won down there in the Haughs. At Milltown, the Queens were as excited as the rest. It had been a long hard winter, but now that was past, and thirteen year old Bobby was already earning some silver to take home to mam. Ten year old Chris and Mary who was eight, could scarce wait for the holidays to start. Jane Ann would be five soon and would be joining them all at the wee school in August, but for now, all they could think of were the holidays that were near, and those long summer days that never seemed to end.

There was much on the go. The Reverend Dunn's picnic and Arbuthnott's own sports were always the best. Then they'd be down to Bervie to join the crowds at those wonderful Games. Scarce a soul would be left through the whole of the Howe on a day such as that.

The loons and the quines were kept well apart by the high dyke in the playground, but they'd all rush out together when the day's work was done, along the road to the shop to see what was new. The bairns from the Reisk joined in with rest. There was little need to struggle away back up that hill now the long bright nights were here. Young Jim Allison, the game-watcher's lad, said he'd more futrats to show them down in the woods, and he and Bert Lemon were off at the gallop. Leslie Mitchell took his time, making his way to the manse.

'Getting books for the holidays?' Chris called out to him and they ran away laughing.

Chris and Mary, with Becky Middleton close behind, made off for the shop with some of the rest. Would old Peter Bannerman be trundling out that strange looking motor car of his that he steered with a stick? Some said it was French, an odd sort of thing.

It was 17 June and life for the Queens was as hard, but as good as ever it had been. The sports and the Games and the holidays were all they could talk about, when suddenly it happened. Jane Ann heard the shouting from out by the shed and a coldness came over her then. She dropped the baking tray on the table and ran to the door.

Her John was doubled up on the ground. He'd been bothered with an ulcer, but this was different. John was gasping for air.

'I've wraxed myself, Jane lass,' he burst out and clamped his mouth shut. A trickle of blood seeped over his chin.

'Dad was shifting the sacks Mam,' Chris cried. 'He should have waited. They were too heavy for him to lift by himself.'

'Lift him gently, Chris.' Jane Ann took John's shoulders and they eased him slowly indoors and through to the bed. Jane Ann's face was white. She felt John grip himself with the pain of it.

The Bervie doctor was a while in coming, but they'd done all that they could with kettles of boiling water and basins and cloths galore. The Provost Doctor looked grim, working there in his shirt sleeves. John had ruptured himself and was coughing blood. It was a night they'd none of them forget, Jane Ann keeping up the supply of hot water and Bobby carting off the blood filled basin to the yard. It was a battle they'd never win, and by half past nine the next day, Tuesday, 18 June, it was all over. The Bervie Provost Doctor, Charles Aymer, MB, CM, certified that John Alexander Queen, ploughman of Hilltown, Arbuthnott, was dead.

Only the doctor knew the full torment of Jane Ann that bright June day, for Jane Ann was four months pregnant. There were arrangements to make and bairns to feed. Was it only yestreen the place had been ringing with their laughs about the holidays and the Games? It seemed an age ago. The summer solstice was upon them, but the brightness of it all and the summer fun were smothered in the gloom. A shocked numbness fell over the place.

The Provost Doctor showed his mettle. He took things quietly and steadily, as was his way. The quiet, commanding voice of the man that had cooled many a council row in the Royal Toun, brought a drug-like calm to all of them. The bairns were gathered together in the wee kitchen, Bobby and Chris, Mary and little Jane Ann, their tired white faces, smeared and scared, looked on in disbelief. A world without their Dad was something they had yet to meet up with. The bairn, wee Alec, sat huddled and quiet on Mam's knee. The Provost Doctor spoke quietly and gently, and there was, you felt, a kind of holy silence on it all. What the doctor said, you'd none of you remember. The way he said it, you'd mind all your days.

Jane Ann never cried then. That came later. First, there were things to be done, and it was then that you saw she really had smeddum. With the Provost Doctor's help, a woman was brought in to give a hand. Soon they all gave a hand. When a disaster like that hits a young family, nobody stands by. The Inspector was there, the Reverend Charles Dunn was there, and neighbours Jane Ann had never heard of turned up to do what they could.

There had been drearier burials in Arbuthnott's kirk yard, in the driving rain and in the sleet of a winter's gloom, but there had been none more wretched than the burial that day. It was under a high summer's sun they buried Jane Ann's John, pulled away from them all in his thirty-eighth year. With five bairns at her side and one yet to be told of and yet to be born, Jane Ann was never more alone.

A tied house is a tied house, and they all had to move. A place was found for Jane Ann and her bairns at Mains of Kair over Fordoun way and the last of her bairns was born there on their bleakest November yet. They named him John after the dad he would never see. Times had been rough at Milltown but they'd been nothing like this.

If Leslie Mitchell and Becky Middleton could trudge down to Arbuthnott's school from the Reisk, the older Queens could make it from the Mains of Kair. Chris and Mary cut through the parks, and Bobby trudged on, tending the beasts and grabbing any job he could find for what silver that was there.

The Provost Doctor's lucky omen was holding back then for little Jane Ann. She'd been real keen to join Chris and Mary at Arbuthnott's school, but that coarse trek across the parks was over much for the five year old. She went instead to Fordoun's wee school at Redmyre and stayed through the week with her Aunt Mary who lived almost next door.

Other bairns had been born in Bervie's lucky year, but little Molly Cushnie, down on the Bervie banks at Mill of Arbuthnott, was not of their number. By some odd chance, Molly had been born a year earlier, Doon Sooth, in London of all places, so when Molly came back up north, it was she who turned up at Arbuthnott's fine school. So there was Molly from Mill of Arbuthnott at her classes instead of Jane Ann from Milltown! All a bit confusing, and over much, you would have thought, for those gods and spaewives alike, hatching out their plans for the quines on those braes.

Some said that was why wee Molly ended up playing a part of her own in the tale that was now taking shape!

EIGHT

New Year's Day 1914 saw the Bervie mill lairds in fine fettle. The flax trade was booming and there were plans on the go for still more and better mills. Jock Webster planned yet another mill in the Royal Toun itself, and Jim Gibb's brother Ed, who'd built the mill down in Johnner, planned the new Invercarron mill up in Stonehive. That would fair put the poverty toffs' noses out of joint – spinning frames with all their noise and stour in Stonehive's genteel streets!

The mill men were having a grand time of it. The silver kept pouring in and, if you'd been in an English way of speaking, you could say it was a golden time for the Royal Toun.

Just four years back, the Bailie had paid his first instalment on his Gold Keyless Hunter English Lever Watch (no. 3288 at £15) and his nine carat gold Albert Chain (no. 115566 at £6-6/.) to J W Benson Ltd of 62/64 Ludgate Hill, London EC, and if you'd kept a look out for that sort of thing, you'd have seen the weskits of the master joiners, plumbers, chemists, bakers and butchers all vying with their gold chains and gold, keyless watches. By 1914 no self-respecting mill manager, stationmaster or insurance man in the Royal Toun would have ventured out on public occasions without his gold chain, fixed through a button hole, high up on his weskit, and looped on either side to his weskit pockets. In one pouch would be the gold watch he'd flip open for consultation, in the other his second best, maybe a silver-looking ingersol. But gold was the standard, and a golden sovereign would be the token a Burness or a Gibb, a Webster or a Peter would present to a new bairn at christening time.

Among the spinners, the reelers and the rest that chauved hardest to bring in all this wealth, there was deil the sign of gold. The year past had seen trouble in the mills, when an increase in pay to the spinners had upset all the reelers. The wildest times were in Johnshaven, or Johnner as most had it, where Ed Gibb paid a lot less than brother Jim. The Johnner mill quines were a hard-necked bunch and a shade nearer to the socialist billies in Dundee. They pelted Ed and his cronies with stones and brought out their flags and a chield with a drum. Then they got themselves a pot of coal tar and splashed it all over Ed's noticeboard. Ed was ceremonially drummed back to his house after that. A coarse and foul-mouthed lot, those Johnner quines, when their dander was up.

What next did they do but descend on Bervie to stir up support among the mill folk there, but damn the help they got from the Bervie quines. They could come and work for more silver in Bervie, they were told. There were idle spindles crying out for good, nippy-fingered spinners. A concert and dance was held in Bervie to raise money for the Johnner strikers. Scarce a soul turned up at the concert, but the dance went well enough. The Bervie lads cared little for socialist billies, but the notion of dancing with a wild quine from Johnner fair kittled them up.

Folk gave little thought that January of 1914, that they were living in historic times. All times are historic. Plans were laid the length and breadth of the Howe for the annual booze-ups they called Burns Suppers, the Mearns being the true fatherland of Burns. The most memorable event of 1914, folk were agreed on that, would be the unveiling of a new statue high up on the Knock Hill to let Rabbie look on to places like Clochnahill, Bogjurgan and Brawliemuir where his folk had farmed for generations.

They'd a grand time of it with their suppering and their boozing in Stonehive and Auchenblae, Laurencekirk and Johnner, Gourdon and Fetteresso. In the Royal Toun, the Bailie sang 'Robin Tamson's Smiddy' and 'Whistle o'er the lave o't', the party pieces he knew by heart. Young Harris, the Bailie's lad, sang 'The Deil's Awa' Wi' The Exciseman'. A bit of a comic, Harris, when he got started. John Burness, the owner of Pitcarry Mill, recited 'To a Moose'. Ogg, the mill manager, sang 'Deoch and Doris', and young Jim Geddes, the new Inspector, was roped in to give 'The Immortal Memory of Rabbie Burns'.

Leslie Mitchell thought all the excitement about Rabbie Burns was daft. It was too close to that teuchter stuff he found hard to thole. Women were kept well away from Burns Nights of course, except up there in Arbuthnott, where the whole parish could join in if it had a mind to. They would all be there, bothy chields, grey-haired matrons, troublesome bairns or flirty quines, it made little odds.

Leslie's experience in the Royal Toun had made him a lot more suspicious of flirty quines. Sex was a filthy business, much the same as those other bodily functions you never spoke about at home. He'd asked a simple question of mother once. 'You filthy little beast,' she'd shouted. 'Where did you pick up all those dirty words?'

It was the same at school, the loons drawing dirty pictures on the lavatory walls and the quines giggling away among themselves in the corner. No wonder they'd built a high wall in the playground to keep the loons and the quines apart. He knew the practical mechanics of sex, of course, from those books he'd read, but they'd nothing to do with him. The Reverend Peter Dunn had shaken his head once when he'd borrowed a book on the physiology of sex without batting an eyelid. 'My, you're growing up very fast, Leslie,' he'd said.

However, Alexander Gray, the new Dominie, refused to leave it at that. 'Quines or no quines,' he'd laughed, 'Burns Night will give you a chance to show what you can do.'

The new Dominie was a young man, still in his twenties, and he'd a grand stock of books he let you borrow. He was a man you could speak to. He took an interest in those flints you'd collected on the braes and he'd laughed at what you'd written about those Bervie folk and their famous bridge. So to please the Dominie, you'd mugged up 'The Cottar's Saturday Night', and that had pleased them. The Laurencekirk 'Squeaker' thought you'd been the star performer, but then the 'Squeaker' would say the daftest things.

The Dominie had some great books. How could those silly quines read such muck when there were books like those to be had? Leslie looked away with a start when Chris Queen caught his eye on her. Chris saw the thick, dreary books sticking out from his bag. Her bag was stuffed with bright and colourful magazines. She pulled them out and showed him some pictures of actresses and the like. The bonny Chris intrigued him. She'd a sweet face and nice legs. Her thin dress moved above her knees when she wriggled at her desk. Why that should bother him, he couldn't understand. She was a damned nuisance like all the other quines in the place. 'What makes you want to read rubbish like that?' he said, fed up with her capers.

Chris laughed. 'They're a lot better than that dreary stuff you get from the dominie and the minister,' she sparked back, fine pleased to make him mad.

Alex Gray grinned. The Mitchell lad had a good turn of phrase, but he was over shy. Alex had come up from Kirkcaldy High School and taken over from Dominie Mason the year before. Some said he'd been daft to leave Kirkcaldy for those god forsaken hills, but this wee school was his own and the bairns were keen. The bonny Chris Queen liked books of a different sort: romances and novels and brighter like tales. A true romantic, Chris, but a thinker too, in her own cheery way. She could write a good essay when she made the effort.

An essay competition in the *Journal* was just the thing to settle them down before the holidays. The bairns aye got a bit restless in the summer term, and this would give them something to think about.

'Here's your chance,' he said to the class. 'They want you to write an essay on Robert the Bruce. There are lots of prizes, and if you really tried, you could make the rest of the Mearns sit up and take notice.'

He held up the *Journal* for them all to see. Leslie gave a bit laugh at the banner headlines. 'Boys and Girls of Scotland,' they said, 'Rally Round the Standard. Join the *People's Journal* in Celebrating the Great Victory that Won our National Freedom. £100 in Prizes for Scholars and Teachers. Open to Boys and Girls between 14 and 17. "Robert Bruce – His Place in Scottish History".'

'I've not read a great deal about Robert Bruce,' Leslie said, a bit puzzled, 'and I've only just turned 13.'

Chris Queen, put up her hand. 'Robert the Bruce watched a spider before the Battle of Bannockburn,' she whispered. What a daft thing to say.

'That's right, Chris,' the Dominie laughed. 'But we'll need to read a bit more about him. We've got time enough before the closing date on the ninth of May. I see there's a competition, as well, for twelve to fourteen year olds on "The Fight for the Brooch of Lorn", and there's a medal for the best essay in the Mearns. You've all got as good a chance as anybody. I'm sure you could write better essays than those clever folk up in Stonehive.'

'And better than those tinks doon in the Royal Toun,' mumbled a wee nipper in the front row, who thought that was a deal more important.

'Right,' said the Dominie, 'we'll start tomorrow, and we'll learn all about the Brooch of Lorn and the Battle of Bannockburn. It was fought on the 24th of June in 1314 – that's 600 years ago this June. I wonder how many Scottish folk have had to be reminded about that famous anniversary?'

Leslie sighed. He was half way through *The Origin of Species*. He'd little time and little patience for those daft Scottish battles. But the Dominie was persuasive, and he and the rest were soon writing essays like mad. Even Chris Queen stopped reading her magazines and was caught up in the dreary books she'd just been laughing at. They spoke about little else in the weeks that followed. 'It will give you a rest from Darwin,' the Dominie grinned.

Leslie's dad took a different view. 'You should be out there in the parks,' he growled. Old James Mitchell had little time for dirt of that sort. The lighter nights were coming in, and they'd to make the most of them.

His mam shook her head, but her approval was needed, and she signed the next coupon from the *Journal*, when the Dominie sent it along. Jane Ann got hold of the *Journal* from the folk at the Mains, and signed her name to please her bonny Chris.

The competition fairly had folk thinking about Scotland for a change, though most were a bit bamboozled, their heads filled with them being North Britons in that empire upon which the sun never set. The *Journal* soon put that to right by running a serial story on the Great Bruce, entitled 'Scots Wha' Hae', which they were strongly advised to read. That changed their thinking for a time.

The essays were finished at last. They'd all had a go and now they'd to hang on and wait. The waiting was the worst part. The weeks dragged on and old James Mitchell lost all patience with his youngest son. They seemed to take a deal of a time those clever billies in Dundee to work out where to send their tenners and their medals.

The winners were announced, at last, on 6 June. It was a quine, Margaret Low from Blairgowrie, who had won the top prize. The editor was amazed. 'Girls,' he declared, 'you have beaten the boys hollow in the competition.'

But in the Mearns it was a lad that proved best. The medal winner's name was there for the whole world and, more important, the whole of the Howe to see. The 'Squeaker' of 12 June summed it up best. 'SUCCESS OF ARBUTHNOTT PUPILS IN ESSAY COMPETITION' it shouted. James Leslie Mitchell of Bloomfield, Arbuthnott, had beaten all comers and won the Robert Bruce medal for the best essay from the Mearns and Chris Queen of Arbuthnott had won a consolation prize. Two prizewinners from Arbuthnott's wee school. That caused a stir through the Howe and put a good few noses out of joint. Maisie Deans of the Kirkburn, down in the

Royal Toun, along with a wheen of others, had got herself a consolation prize. But it was Arbuthnott that made the headlines. Jane Ann was thrilled. Leslie's mam was fair dumfoonered. Even old Mitchell scratched his pow and gave a bit nod. Down at the shop the claik never let up. 'A medal, by God!'

By Sunday though, young Mitchell was put in his place. 'He should be out there working like the rest, not wasting his time with high falutin dirt like that,' was the verdict at the kirk door down there in the Den. 'You can't eat medals,' said one jealous wife, tossing her head with a smirk.

When Dominie Gray spoke of sending Leslie to the academy at Stonehive, old Mitchell tightened his lips and growled, 'Na, na, we canna spare him. He'll hae to take his brother's place now he's of age.'

Leslie learned something else that hot summer of 1914. When some of the prize winners asked if they could see their stories in print, the editor's answer was short and to the point. 'I regret I am unable to oblige,' he said. 'Space is extra valuable in the *People's Journal* at present.' It was going to take Leslie the best part of twenty years before a publisher gave him a second look.

But the bonny Chris Queen was never to be worried by thoughts of that sort. The thing now was for Jane Ann to get the lot of them settled in Bervie where workers were in great demand. For all her love of books, Chris would have to leave school and find a job. What chance had she or any of them got of earning silver on that wind-swept hill?

So the Queens of Arbuthnott became the Queens of Bervie. They got a fine terraced house at the corner of Montrose Road and Townhead, at the south end of King Street. It was a neat little place with a garden in front, just over the way from the Terrace where the toffs all lived. They took over that corner; Queens' Corner, folk called it. When the lads and lasses of the place paraded the pavement on a Saturday night, by the glimmers from the gas lamps and the shops, they'd set off in their twos and threes. 'Off for a dander,' they'd say, 'from the Square up as far as Queens' Corner.'

There was nothing could stop any of them now, Jane Ann thought, having got them all settled in this famous Royal Toun. Even Jane Ann Queen, though, in those high days of the Bervie mills, could scarce have guessed where it was all going to end. No spaewife in her senses would have put up a tale where Molly and Becky, Chris and little Jane would be caught up, one day, with those Big Hooses at Hazelgrove and Bridge End.

They'd all be caught up too, in some sort of fashion, with the true tales and fictions of Leslie Mitchell's Segget.

NINE

David Webster looked down on the lawns and close-pruned bushes the gardener kept neat and trim. It was one of those bright, clear mornings Bervie wakens up to with some surprise in early Spring. A farm milk cart clopped briskly along the Montrose turnpike beyond the railings at the far end. Sharp shafts of sunlight stabbed through the high trees that edged Hallgreen's castle park in the field beyond. The sky above Craig David was the deepest blue. David flung open the window and breathed in the clean sea air. Dad had done the right thing to bring him back to Hazelgrove. Bervie in the spring was a grand place to be.

He missed the good times he'd had in St Andrews though. They'd have started their tennis down there by now. Mam had said the tennis courts in Bervie were never ready till well after Easter. The one on their own front lawn would be of little use till they got some real heat in the air. The tennis court below, for all its neat appearance, was soft and sodden. It would take more than a day of spring sunshine to dry that out.

Dad would expect him to put in an appearance at the Linty Mill today. Dad had wanted him to start full time, but Mam had said he should have another year before he was lumbered full time with that kind of work. It was a canty wee mill the Linty, with its big splashing water wheel. Of the three mills they owned, it was the one he felt most at home in. It was the family mill after all, the one his grandmother, Madge Gibb, had brought to his grandfather many years back. That had ended in a tragic way, Dad had explained to him once. The Bervie had been in full spate when Grandma Madge had fallen in. Some said Madge Webster's ghost still haunted the old Linty Mill.

David grinned at that. You were no sooner back in the Royal Toun, but you were listening to the spaewives and their tales. There was a feel about the wee Linty though. If he did have to follow Dad as a Bervie millman, it was the mill that would suit him best. That was nonsense of course. You couldn't let romantic notions of the family past get in the way of business. The big Springy and Craigview mills were where the future lay, along with the new mill Dad had planned over the bridge in Kinghornie's fields. The wee Linty paid its way, but it could scarcely last for ever.

In truth, he'd no wish to take over any of the mills. Surely there was a better way of earning a living? Life had been a lot more exciting in St Andrews, with those planes coming down on the West Sands. There were more planes landing there than ever now. One had landed in the playing fields once and they'd raced the lads from St Salvator's School to get to it first. He'd enjoyed that. The St Salvator's boys in their chocolate blazers and their blue St Andrews badges thought themselves a cut above the Clifton Bank boys. They were a more academic lot, the swots that they were, but when it came to practical things like helping the pilots refuel their planes, the lads from Clifton Bank aye beat them to it.

David glanced at his red and yellow blazer on the chair. He'd have no need for that any more. He'd enjoyed those days at Clifton Bank with his collections of birds' eggs and butterflies, but it was those aeroplanes that brought the real excitement. Where else would you see aeroplanes landing out there in front of your window as he had in St Andrews from his room on the Scores? They'd swoop down over the houses in front and skid to a halt on the wide stretches of the West Sands. They'd been on their hedge hopping runs from Farnborough to the air station at Montrose, and had dropped down for some oil and petrol. That's when he and the other lads had bounded down the road to give them a hand. David picked up his scrap book and thumbed through the pages. That's where the future lay, up in the air, not stuck in the noise and the stour of the Bervie mills.

How did those men land exciting jobs like that? He turned the pages where he'd pasted in their pictures. There was the 1911 Avro with C Howard Pixton on the Sopwith Tabloid taking off from Brooklands, and Mr Noel at Hendon on the Maurice Farman with Miss Kitty Kent, the 'Girl from Utah'. He studied a Bristol Scout single seater and a photograph of O T M Sopwith, the winner of the first Aerial Derby on 8 June, 1912. There was a picture too, of Gustav Hamel, winner of the second Aerial Derby in September of last year and another of Howard Pixton with his Sopwith seaplane taking off from the sea at Monaco.

Life at Clifton Bank had been all right. Watty Mair, the headmaster, had been easy on them and his wife had seen to it they were all well fed. She could dish up some fantastic meals. Maybe they didn't get the classical education the swots got further along the Scores at St Salvator's, but he was none the worse for that. Mr Le Maitre, the headmaster there, drove his lads real hard for the full certificates of the Oxford and Cambridge Joint Board, but they'd a much easier time of it at Clifton Bank. It was because things had been slipping of late that Dad had brought him home. Dad was always on at him to take up shooting. It was more of a man's sport, dad said, than collecting birds' eggs and butterflies. But where was the pleasure in shooting defenceless rabbits? He'd had a go at fencing though, and that did no harm to anyone. That was a man's sport, and surely flying was a man's game? That had been a great experience when he'd paid for a flight over St Andrews. Why couldn't he become an aeroplane pilot instead of spending his life in those dreich Bervie mills?

David stretched himself. There were some compensations for living in Bervie. He got on better with the lassies here. They spoke the same language, though Teen insisted he'd picked up an English twang since he'd gone to Clifton Bank. In St Andrews, the St Leonards' girls were kept under tight control, but when they did slip away, for some reason, they made for the St Salvator's lads. Maybe it was the plummy way that crowd spoke, or their classical education. It could have been their chocolate coloured blazers! Did they think yellow and red stripes were a bit common?

David made for the door. He could hear Mam moving on the stairs. Tonight should be a bit of a laugh. That Carnival Ball Jim Geddes had organised should be a cut above the usual Bervie type of entertainment. Teen would be there, and Madge and Alice and all the rest of the crowd. There was no silly nonsense with that lot.

It was to be a fancy dress affair. He'd wear those goggles and that pilot's outfit he'd borrowed. Better get there early, he'd one or two ploys to fix that would stir things up for Teen and Madge. It would be a bit of a laugh!

TEN

Things were dropping into place that long hot Summer of 1914. Leslie looked on at it, fair amazed. What else could you do at thirteen but watch and wait? The future lay out there, all fixed up it seemed, biding its time.

He said that to John one day, and John laughed, 'You think over much, Leslie. Last week it was flints and all those dead lairds in the Den. You'll be joining up with the Bervie spaewives next. They can tell when the next spate's due on the Bervie.'

'That's maybe it,' Leslie wondered. 'It's all waiting to happen.'

John would be seventeen in November and looking for a fee somewhere, as George had done before him. What made them so different? They were all brothers, when you thought about it, and he thought about it a lot.

Father had lost all patience with him after he'd won his medal, lazing about with those damned books, as he had it. But Dominie Gray had pushed him real hard, and he'd made up his mind.

'I've won a bursary,' he said, surprising them one day. He'd get £25, he told them, if he stayed on at school and sat the entrance exam for Stonehive.

Father scowled at the thought and dug in his heels. So the Dominie came up.

'He's a born scholar, your lad,' Alex Gray pressed. 'He'd make a fine schoolmaster if you gave him a chance. A year or so in the feeder class and he'll have no problem winning a bursary for Stonehive.'

The Reverend Dunn had a go with notions of his own, but the words were the same. 'Your lad's a natural scholar, Mr Mitchell,' he said, 'I can see young Leslie in a Kirk pulpit yet. He just gobbles up those books on the Picts and all their capers, and he's a real expert on the stars and the planets.'

Leslie wondered at that. Did the Reverend Dunn think Heaven was out there on Mars or Jupiter? But the strangest thing happened. Father gave in. No, you could never guess the future, but sure as death, it was waiting for you, hanging back till you got there. Father had got lost in all their speak.

He'd run rings round them on fertilisers and crops, but when they started on about books and bursaries, it threw him in a fankle. He'd looked over at Mother.

'We'll not keep the lad back,' she'd said, with a tightening of her lips, and so it was fixed. He'd be doing Shakespeare and French in the Dominie's feeder class next year. But he'd no great wish to be a preacher or a headmaster either, if they'd bothered to ask. There would be something waiting for him though, when he'd read all those books they'd have to get for him now.

It was Saturday 4 July at last, and the whole of the Mearns had just one place in mind. The Royal Toun was decked out with flags and streamers. Maybe other things were dropping into place, far off in foreign parts, but folk neither knew nor cared. A day or two back some had read a paragraph in the *Advertiser* about an Archduke and his Duchess being murdered in Sarajevo, somewhere in Bosnia, wherever that was. You paid little heed to daft tales like that.

The Bervie Games would be on a grander scale this year. The new Inspector had taken charge and had spread his posters wide. He'd organised a special late train to take folk back home along the coast line to Gourdon and Johnner, and on to Montrose with connections further Sooth. The prize money had drawn in champion runners from places like Motherwell and Dundee. The Montrose Band paraded the King Street and the men were swanking about in their shirt sleeves, the lasses in summer frocks. You were hard put to pick out the mill spinners from the lairds and their quines.

A lot more of the new buses were rumbling down from Garvock and Benholm, Arbuthnott and Kinneff, and there were more traps and gigs than ever this year clattering over the bridge. Country folk were still shy of trusting themselves to those new motor contraptions. The whole of the Mearns was there, into the shops, buying up the cakes and biscuits. At Canales they were queuing up for a taste of Scotland's best ice cream. But Canale had planned it well. His ice-cream tricycle was early on the road, down the long stourie slope to the Haughs. Saturday was a half day, but the mills had shut down early and the spinners had all fled.

When John and Leslie burst out of the Square and through the School Wynd to the top of the Gassy Brae, what a sight met their gaze. The quick way was down by the gasworks and along by the old mill lade which would keep you clear of the traffic on the long Haugh Road. But they stopped a bit and stared at the sight of it. The yellow broom had flowered early in the heat that year, and it spread itself on both sides of the Howe. On the left it stopped short at the lush trees of the wood. To the right it spread round and beyond Pitcarry Den, past Burness's Mill and on up Arbuthnott's parks. Green and fresh those parks, up and out of the world, as the Bervie folk had it, past Auchendreich way.

Beyond that again, were those coarser fields of Bloomfield and Hareden. Father would be bringing Mother down when he'd hitched their pony to the trap, later on, he'd said.

Away in front, beyond the Upper Mill and Guthrie's famous dam, stood the castle at Allardice, white and clean and sharp in the July glare. Behind that, and much further on beyond Arbuthnott House and Fordoun, clear as ever they'd seen them, rose the Grampians, firm and secure. Leslie had a notion, just then, that those years that were waiting, would bring this all back to him, sharper, more poignant than now.

But he snapped out of that. Down there, past the dozing mills, the full fun and colour of the Games jumped up at him. He stared at the stretched coloured canvas of the huge marquees and the rows of wee tents and stalls. There were two dancing boards, one for the experts for their highland flings and sword dances, and the other – a huge specially-built affair that was the speak of the Mearns – was where the quines and their lads would be dancing their hearts out till darkness fell. The park was filling up fast. Kilted bandsmen and lone pipers were strolling about and, pouring in through the gate, were the folk themselves, turning the park to a scatter of colour with their summer sarks and their cotton frocks. John gave him a nudge. 'Come on, we'll take the short road down. I promised Jean I'd see her at the tea tent.'

They plunged down the Gassy Brae, with the swarming, stumbling crowd. The Gassy Brae was nearly vertical. Most poured down the long road, the cars and the carts shoving them aside. The gentry were as keen as the rest to get down there at the start.

'We've got a damn good team this year,' John gasped when they reached the level by the mill lade. 'Jock and his lads have been practising behind the smiddy for weeks. There's thirty bob for the winners and a pound for the runners-up. Those tounie's will be no match for the Arbuthnott lads. There'll be no shortage of drink in the Star Hotel this night.'

'That's big money for pulling a rope in the tug o' war.' Leslie turned that notion over. A whole miserable week ploughing those awful parks would bring just a fraction of that. There would be some bloodied noses this day, if we teuchters as they called us, ran off with that kind of silver. But why did John want to waste his time seeing this quine he'd spoken of? What was so special about quines, for God's sake!

Madge crossed the mill lade and paid for her ticket. She smiled to the new Inspector. The ticket table was cannily stuck on the narrow brow of the lade bridge, the only way into the Games, unless you splashed through the Bervie or swam the lade and struggled under the sacking. That happened when a spinner or an orraman thought the coast was clear.

The local bobby, whose father was the blacksmith, kept a sharp lookout for capers of that sort. Jim Geddes, the Inspector, was standing behind the ticket sellers, checking a list with one of the judges. That would keep him busy for the rest of the day, Madge thought.

She reddened when she remembered that caper at the Carnival Dance. David Webster had paired the two of them off when he'd slipped her the Duchess of Plaza Toro's pink tag. The Duke's blue tag had found its way on to the lapel of the new Inspector. He'd hugged her real close in the last dance, she thought. They'd met often enough when he called to discuss Council business with Father. But this Jim Geddes had aye a worried look on his face. Did he think of nothing but work and those jobs Father kept flinging at him? Maybe he was afraid of Father. He looked so lonely at times. And he'd nice smiling eyes. Surely he didn't think she'd had anything to do with fixing that dance? She could strangle David Webster!

Madge and Alice and Maggie Elliot, the stationy's lass, enjoyed the racing and jumping, the caber tossing and the dancing. They watched the Open Events and cheered on the locals, cheered the bairns and admired the horses. Then came the Tilting at the Bucket. Motor bikes would tear along the grass, slow down under the bucket to let the passenger, sometimes a lass, push a pole through the slot. As often as not the pole would miss, the bucket would tilt, and a gallon or two of good Bervie water would drench the pair of them.

Off then to the tea tent and that pungent smell of new cut grass, hot canvas and steaming tea urns. Madge marvelled, as ever, at the burnished brass tea kettles Bervie women brought out at times like this, family heirlooms from kitchen dressers, decked out in the Games ribbons of blue and white. Young farming billies were devouring huge steak-filled bridies. What appetites! Building up their strength for the tug o' war and their work with those horses later on.

'Hi Madge! We saw your Jim at the ticket table.'

Madge flushed, annoyed with herself. What had young Laurie been saying about her? It was Cousin Alec from Montrose, grinning and sun-burned as ever. Alec was one of the Montrose cousins who'd come home from South Africa because of the troubles out there. He was good looking and eternally sunburned. The Bervie lassies could hardly keep their eyes off him, and Madge got a thrill being seen with him. But now she was mad. Alice and Maggie were laughing beside her.

'He's not my Jim,' she burst out. 'Laurie's been talking rubbish as usual.'

Laurie was pretending to be fascinated by a brand new motor bike parked by the side of the tea tent.

'Sorry Madge, no offence,' Alec apologised. 'Laurie says you'll come down to Montrose with him next week to watch our challenge match. A walk on Montrose Links will do you good.'

'Yes, Father says I can go. He's giving me the day off.' Madge made a quick recovery. You couldn't stay mad with Cousin Alec. He'd taken Laurie under his wing and the two of them were never off the golf course now, blethering on about niblicks and birdies. Alec was quite a celebrity at Montrose that week. He was the new golf champion at the academy and had lifted all the prizes, the Milne Medal as well as the Paton Championship Trophy. Why weren't there any boys in Bervie with the looks of Cousin Alec? Pity the new Inspector couldn't play golf. Too busy with his committees for frivolous games like that, he'd have said.

Cousin Alec and Laurie hurried off. 'Come and see the tug o' war Madge,' Laurie shouted. 'It's going to be a bigger laugh than ever this year.'

The Montrose band was thundering away with Colonel Bogey and that stirred them up. 'I suppose we'd better give the Bervie lads a cheer,' Madge said to the girls beside her. Alice and Maggie nodded, not too sure about it though. J H Johnstone, the Gourdon Dominie, would need all his height and authority this year if the rumours about the Dundee dockers and bobbies were true. J H, as they called him, was the committee man who took over when things threatened to get out of hand. He was the only man Madge knew, who'd a specially made bicycle. It had two cross bars, one above the other, to give it extra height and strength.

J H fingered his waxed moustache and fixed his steely eyes on the Arbuthnott team till they came to rest on the mark. A bunch of Bervie mill workers were nudging some of the farming billies, and a group of orramen were wandering over from the harness judging, eyeing the situation with sappy grins on their faces. Madge and Alice drew back a bit. The Gourdon Dominie could usually handle those coarse chields, but you never could tell.

Alice pointed to a lonely looking lad standing quite near. 'That's the lad who won the Bruce Medal I was telling you about,' she said. Alice picked up most of her news from her dad, Ake Goodfellow, the joiner, who got as many folk into his workshop as Barber John or Criggie the Tailor did when the wind was in the east. There was no shortage of places in the Royal Toun where you could get in out of the rain and pass on the latest gossip. Madge looked at the shy lad with some interest. She'd long had a notion to write a novel or two herself.

The shy lad brightened up as the mill men and the country lads edged closer. But the Dominie, all seven foot of him, was for none of it. He powered in between them and wedged the spinners and the billies apart. The Arbuthnott Billies took the strain, and that ended the carfuffle. There were those pints in the Star to think about.

'That'll stop them bragging about their charters and their brig,' Leslie Mitchell laughed, when the Bervie team were dragged across the line. But the locals were having a tougher time of it this year. Two hefty teams had turned up from Dundee and caused a bit of a stir when the word got round they were the Dundee police and the harbour porters. Folk could mind fine when the Dundee bobbies had cracked the skulls of the porters and the porters had showered them with bricks, flinging a truck into the docks for good measure. So a fair crowd was gathering in the hope of a stramash. It would be a much better rammy than you'd get from the mill men and the teuchters.

Folk cheered on the locals, but none were a match for the Dundee bruisers. The Arbuthnott billies were still in the game though, and the odd thing was, once they took on the Dundee men, you cheered them on. Arbuthnott lads were Mearns lads, you thought, you had to back them against those foreigners from Doon Sooth! And so it turned out: nobody could match the Dundee porters. Shifting those bales of flax and jute had given them arms like tree trunks, but a great cheer went up when the

Arbuthnott billies pulled the bobbies over the mark and pushed them into third place.

'You'd never get a mill man to cheer a bobby,' a Bervie lad muttered, fair affronted that he'd cheered on the teuchters.

The teuchters spent the rest of that night knocking back the drams, fair chuffed with themselves. It all ended fine and satisfactory like, with another rammy in the square. By that time, the Bervie bobby had gone home, well pleased he'd done as much as folk could expect of him.

But before the tug o' war had ended, the fiddlers and the cornet player were stirring folk up at the dancing board, a famous board by now, 60 feet by 24, built for the Bailie by Alice's Dad, the joiner, just two years before. Ake Goodfellow's dancing board fair pulled in the crowds and had more than paid for itself at all those games, sports and picnics that kept the Mearns entertained through the long summer nights. Madge saw David and Teen heading towards it. Maggie went off with her lad, and a young lad from the Montrose band asked Alice for a dance. She felt a touch of sadness just then. It had been great fun until now.

'May I have the pleasure?' It was Jim, the Inspector, at her elbow, smiling and looking more relaxed than ever she'd seen him. Madge smiled. Why not?

So that was the start of Madge's golden time. Jim smiled and his grey eyes lit up. The day had gone so well. They'd taken a record amount of cash. Well over two thousand had paid their entry money and that was in addition to the hundreds of free tickets they'd given away. It was all due to the weather, he beamed, but Madge could see he was pleased with himself. The organisation had gone as he'd planned and now his men were getting on with the clearing up. His part of the work was over, so he said.

Madge let him chatter on. She looked up at him. He was a lonely man at heart, but now he looked happy. They were both lonely. She had an urge to hug him, but caught herself in time. The spell was broken. He called her Madge. She wondered if he noticed. That had been the first time. She'd call him Jim when she had a chance.

She would remember that night in the months and years ahead. They didn't dance for long. The mill men, they knew, and the farming billies, had come to the Games for a night of fun and were all itching to get on to the board. They held back when they saw the Inspector and the mill laird's lad with their quines. The fiddlers and the cornet player saw what was up and kept the tempo slow and romantic. Alice and her lad were there, and

David and Teen, and soon they were joined by a couple of schoolteachers and their lads. The high summer sun had still some way to go before it dropped out of sight over Auchendreich way. Then the young mill quines would stop their reels and strathspeys and quieten down in the arms of their lads as the soft July light drifted away.

But now it was their turn and, self-conscious maybe, but keeping step fine, Jim had caught on to the old fashioned waltz at last. It could have been the warmth of the night air, or the far-off sounds of hammering through the music as the stands were broken up, or the clopping of the horses and gigs as they made off up the brae, but the crowds round the board were hushed as they waited. Madge felt Jim's hand holding hers. She caught Teen and David looking at her and she laughed. Daft, she'd been, to worry like that in her wee back room. Worrying about the future and what it might bring, and now this was that future. But nothing stood still, she thought. An odd notion came over her then. If only you could, she thought, hold things still for a time, dancing close like this with Jim. They all seemed so content, down here in these Haughs. The fiddles and the cornet rang clear in the still air. Would there be bitter sweet memories for some, in those years out ahead? For now though, it was the present that mattered. It was good to be alive and to be young, this warm summer of 1914.

The six of them, Teen and Alice, and now Madge too, started off with their lads, up that long road to the Toun, content with their day. Behind them came the shouts and the laughs as the mill men and the country lads let themselves go and clowned with their quines. Leslie stared on, entranced. The word had gone round that the minister and the Inspector and all the mill lairds had gone. He watched the ploughmen and the spinners make a grab for their quines and give them a bit squeeze. Things looked a bit rough, but they lined up at last for an odd sort of dance. 'Drops of Brandy' the cornet player shouted above the din. The pace was slow enough at the start as they linked arms and gave a bit twirl. Then the thing hotted up and the real whirling began with all the hooching and the skirling. The men had their jackets off and an elderly billy ripped off his collar which had been a bother from the start. A red-faced ploughman, well whiskied by the look of him, let out a yell when his galluses snapped.

John had gone off with his Jean, so Leslie took the chance of a lift back on Rob Middleton's box-cart. They spoke little at first, each with his thoughts. Rob had had a grand time with the horses, a great man for horses, at times he'd speak of little else. It seemed he'd talked himself dry. Back up in Hareden his new wife had brought forth another bairn a couple of weeks back. A man of astonishing energy, this Rob.

The sheltie was taking its time on the brae by Pitcarry Mill. The sounds down below had quietened and even the wildest lads were exhausted, shuffling close against their quines in the darkening gloom.

'Old Hilly was up on that board making an utter fool of himself,' said Leslie, at last. He'd been turning the thing over and over in his mind. 'That young quine he was near strangling was less than half his age. I just can't understand it.'

Rob glinted down at the thirteen year old by his side and gave a bit laugh. 'Give it a couple of years Leslie,' Rob grinned, 'and you'll understand it fine. Losh, Leslie man, you'll be thinking of little else.'

ELEVEN

The summer belonged to Madge and Jim. The days were longer, the sea more blue and the hills more inviting. On an evening they'd see Father seated with his easel and his palette, quite engrossed as he studied the stepping stones that crossed the July trickle of the Bervie; the cruives they called them. But they left him to his work and to his thoughts.

They stepped and slithered over the cruives themselves. Crossing the cruives had an excitement to it no footbridge could ever bring. You'd clutch your lass by the hand when she stepped on to the big shiny boulder. Then you'd grab to save her from a soaking, and it would end up with both of you in the burn. The cruives had a lot to do with a lad taking his lass o'er the Bervie Water.

Madge discovered herself on those summer rambles. There was much, too, for Jim to learn about the Royal Toun and its secrets. There was the Pental Stone, Robb's Cove and the King's Leap itself, along the cliffs by that well trodden path. There was the little crevice where you might place a lucky pin, or find a penny if some superstitious worthy had been there before you. Then up and up you'd scramble, past the Chapel Well and Kinghornie farm to the brow of Craig David. Hardly a name in the place but had some royal or kirk connection. If they'd miscalled a place in the past the Council had soon put that to rights. Madge pointed this out, the two of them high up on the rock, looking down on the Toun, fair and square at their feet between the rock and the Knox Hill beyond.

'There's David Street,' she pointed. 'It was once the main street of the place. They called it The Fisher Gate, but just before Father came, the Council had boards painted and named it David Street. Much more fitting,' she laughed, 'for a place with royal connections.'

Away to the south stretched the coastline of Angus to the hills of Fife. To the west lay the ridge of the Grampians, blue now, in the summer haze. 'Some day, David will own those three mills.' Madge pointed to the tall stacks of the Springy and Craigview and the smaller, stumpy chimney of the wee Linty.

'And much else besides,' said Jim. 'The houses in the east end, as well as Kinghornie farm, will all be his.'

'This rock we're sitting on will be his,' Madge laughed. 'But he'll make a good employer. I can't see David letting his workers put up with things the way the older crowd do.'

'I'm sure you're right,' said Jim, 'but he'll have to watch not to be too much of a reformer. A good boss has to have good business sense as well. I suppose it's a question of balance again.'

'Oh, you and your balance,' Madge teased. 'You'll be telling me we should put more ugly words into our Bervie poems again.' They'd had a long discussion on Bervie's Kailyard Versifiers on that first time they'd met. Jim's notions had been over much at odds with Madge's sentimental view of the world.

Jim smiled. He enjoyed those sparring matches with this sweet young romantic. She had lovely red lips.

'Bervie folk are not all romantics,' he countered. 'The place is full of eccentric, colourful characters. You couldn't call them romantics.'

'Oh, they give such weird names to each other,' Madge smiled. 'Have you heard of Toddler Ben and Echty Tips? However did they get names like that, I wonder?'

'There's one called Geordie Gip, and there's Nosey Legg.'

'What about Moshy Tite and Mossy White,' said Madge, 'I bet you don't know half of them.'

'The one I like best,' said Jim, 'is Barber John the Spanish Don. He's a grand barber, but I go there to learn more about Bervie and all its folklore.'

'He's put a striped pole on the railings at the top of the Kirkburn. They say he once shaved a farmer's pig before they took it to the Fordoun Show,' Madge laughed.

'I noticed that young lad who won the Bruce Medal. I think he goes into Barber John's just to listen to the yarns.'

'Well it all sounds a bit romantic to me, Jim,' said Madge. 'I don't think Barber John would be regaling his customers with spiteful stories like those you spoke about in that house with the green shutters.'

'No, but some of the yarns their customers tell would make you gasp.'

Jim put his arm round Madge and held her close. High up there on David's Rock, the sun warming the Haughs and the Toun below, it was the most natural thing in the world to be sitting cheek to cheek. They turned together and had their first kiss. This is more like it, Madge thought. It's taken him a long time.

Other nights, they wandered on the braes and looked out over the Haughs to Pitcarry and the wee mill there, and up to Allardice, steeped in its past with its hauntings of William the Lyon. The summer nights were warm and dry. They'd pass folk with an 'aye, aye' or a 'grand night'. Some, more concerned about the crops, would say, 'could do with some rain now', and on they'd go.

But the rains never came. The fields were parched and, up the waterside, by Guthrie's Dam, the fleas and the glegs, and the golochs too, began to fuss and bite. There were swarms of midges everywhere. The boys were out with their rods. It was a time for the fly, they said. Over by the little dam young Laurie was standing quietly in his waders. Six or more other lads, some mill men among them, were spaced along the banks on either side, flicking gossamer lines, trying first one fly, then another, to tempt the lazy trout.

They stopped, watching quietly as the flies kissed the surface, but nothing stirred, a sheen on the water maybe. The fish were not to be tempted. None of the lads seemed bothered. They were fine pleased just to be there, together, not speaking, quietly knowing the others felt as they did, a communion of a sort, but they never thought of it like that. Other times you'd catch fish. Other times when the Bervie was in spate and the brown torrent threatened the banks, then you and the whole toun would be there, with your hooks and your worms, hoisting out the trout by the basket load. But that wasn't fishing. Any fool could do that. Tonight, you were with the anglers, the men who knew how to cast a fly. Only tonight they weren't rising, tomorrow maybe. However, it was reward enough to be there, at peace with it all. Over yonder was Burness, the mill laird. Further back was Archie, the roadman. You seldom spoke. When you did, it was to the point, about the fly. Madge's young brother, Laurie, saw them and came softly across.

'Laurie makes his own flies,' Madge whispered. 'They all do.'

Laurie opened his fly box. More flies were hooked into his bonnet. 'They're not rising tonight,' he grinned. 'Thought I'd try the Blue Dun. They were going well for it yesterday.'

'They've got attractive names,' said Jim.

Laurie reeled a few off with pride. 'That's the Olive Quill. There's a Greenwell Glory, a Light Partridge and Yellow, a March Brown. There are a few more in my bonnet, a Hare Lug and a Woodcock. The water's quite low but there are some burnies lurking there in the dam.'

The three dams sluiced their waters into the three lades for the different mills, relics from the past when water power was the driving force. Now only the Linty Mill and the Auld Mill still used their water wheels as a back up for their engines. Down by Crookerty they stopped again. 'This is another example where Bervie boasts it has the best,' said Madge. 'They say this spring has the purest and cleanest water in Scotland.'

'You'd better keep that tale from the Stonehive Provost,' laughed Jim, who was catching on to the local patter. 'He says Bervie folk are always going on about having the oldest and the biggest, like their mills and their brig.'

'I've a mind to recite some of Bervie's romantic verse to you,' Madge kept on. 'You'd be amazed at the number of poems there are about Crookerty's clear spring water and those Haughs out there. They're all about daisies and buttercups, and rubbish like that, as you would have it Jim.'

'Why don't you write a short poem for me? I'd like that.' Madge took his hand; the summer had a long way to run.

'They're trawling tonight' – the word had gone round.

'You must see the trawl, Jim,' Madge told him. 'Half the Toun will be there.'

Long before eight, with a bit of a breeze from the south, warm and balmy like, folk were moving cannily down to the bar of shingle which held back the Bervie flow, now reduced to a trickle in the summer heat. The trawl was at eight, but how folk knew this was a wonder. Some sort of communal consciousness thought Jim, reminded of what he'd read about bees in the hive. They were dandering down from all directions. Most came by the Kirkburn, in wee groups of threes and fours, others by the waterside down from the brig.

At the end of the bar of shingle was a narrow lapping of water where the incoming tide pushed in to hold back the flow. Young lads could just jump across without wetting their feet, but the gap was wide enough for salmon to smell the fresh water of the Howe. Out there they'd be moving about in a stishie before taking the plunge up-stream to the spawning grounds. But the odds were against them this year, so dry was the stream.

The crowd assembled on the beach as the coble was readied for its loop round the mouth of the Bervie burn. The evening calm lulled folk into a satisfied expectancy. Half of Bervie was a gross exaggeration, Jim thought, but a fair crowd was on the move. Mill hands, by the look of them, were stumbling on the dry grass by the back brae, past the Back Well from David Street. There was no rush, no hurry and scarce a word was said. The Bervie trawl had a soporific effect, a quiet stroll at the day's end; a mid-week stroll at the back end of July and then off to bed. In the darker months folk would be bedded down by now, cuddling under the blankets, then dropping off to build up their strength for the next early start.

A summer trawl made a fine change to things. Weekends you promenaded, drank in the pubs, got wild at the dancing, or had a clout or two at the teuchters if the fancy took you. But mid week, in the summer calm, a Bervie trawl was a chance to dander and laze. You just left your door, no need to shut it, you were just off to the trawl. You'd take your wife with you, or your lass. Or you'd wander down and catch up with the folk in front – no need to waste words on a night like this, just, 'aye, aye', or 'fine night for a trawl', and on you'd dander.

Over the time-buffed pebbles, Jim took Madge's hand, stumbling as they went. Mostly grey and white, the stones slid beneath their feet, but here and there they'd come on a burnished red granite, a mottled black and green or the glint of a sparkling quartz. The wide grey curve of the Bervie beach marked the end of the steep Kinneff cliffs. From Fowlsheugh in the north to Craig David here by the Royal Toun, the cliffs stood their ground.

They kept off intruders and salmon alike. Half way, at Todhead, stood the lighthouse with that horn the farm lads cursed if it sounded in the night.

It was at Stonehive, or here at the Bervie gap, that the salmon had their real chance to reach high up the waters of the Mearns and spawn their lives away. But the salmonies, the coarse tinks, would be trying to grab them in their nets. So the true anglers said, but tonight they held their peace. For tonight folk were there for the show and most would have snared a finnock or whipped out a trout with a worm in a spate, given half a chance.

More than a hundred folk had gathered now, from the very young to old Toddler Ben himself. You were never that old for a Bervie trawl. Still they came, spinners and shopkeepers, a schoolteacher or two. Some labourers, Jim recognised, who'd landed themselves jobs on the roads, Elliot, the stationy, and yes, there was Burness, the millman, having a quiet word with Jock Webster at the back of the crowd.

A Bervie trawl attracted all sorts. There wasn't a penny in it or a fish for any of you. It was a ritual you enjoyed before turning in for the night, a kind of a nightcap, as they would say at Hazelgrove. The salmonies, sturdy lads and a fair age, most of them, faces like leather, had stacked their nets at the back of the coble. A lad was left on the beach with the line in his hand and they paddled off in silence with barely a splash. Old Will paid out the net from the stern, the rest heaving on their oars, firm and steady and slow. Out they went, a row of bobbing corks behind them, in a huge sweeping bend, then back to the beach again, hard up against the water mouth. Little chance of a frisky fish getting past that line of net.

The peace and the slow calm of it all lulled you into a quiet sort of dwam. You'd as soon have shouted out in the Kirk as spoken out at a time like that. The salmonies leapt ashore and split into two lots, grabbing the rope at each end. The trawl started in earnest, real steady like. The salmonies on both ends moved closer on the wet pebbles at the water's edge. The coble swung back to sea again, one man on the oars, splashing away outside the ring of the net to chase the fish back in.

Madge and Jim caught up with Teen and David. A bit close they were, Madge thought, with folk all round them. But folk had other thoughts then, the nets piling up on the beach in two neat bundles, side by side. The loop of corks had shrunk in size, and not a fish was in sight. The boat closed in behind, then the last few yards saw them, in twos and threes at first, stuck squirming high on the net, silvery clean. They came then in a rush. The salmonies leapt into the sea, waist high in their waterproof breeks for the end of the net was heavy and full, bulging hard now with wriggling silver salmon. They were as large and as strong as you'd wish. Folk thrilled at the sight, as the net, bag-like, was lifted bodily onto the shore. The salmonies behind grabbed the stragglers and threw them high on to the pebbles. Then came the count.

You waited for the final tally as basket after basket brimmed over. 'Sixty-two tonight. Not a bad haul that. I mind the night...' Then off you strolled, as quietly as you'd come. Off to bed. Up the Kirkburn, past the bowling green, the last foursome lifting their bowls to the club house. The tennis courts, had shut long since for the night. David and Jim walked up, chatting away, the lassies in front, voices lowered.

Two nights later, up Townhead they wandered, Madge and Jim, high above the Toun with the sea behind. Clouds were gathering now, the summer sun low but dropping still beyond the Reisk far off to the right. Madge clutched Jim's arm as they passed Newbigging Farm and she shivered, though still it was warm. That farm, quiet and at peace now in the late July dusk, she'd looked out on in her sad times, from her wee window at the field's end. They crested the brae and strolled by the trees. The trees and the hills of the Mearns were theirs. 'A change from the night of the trawl,' Jim mused. 'It's another world up here.'

Who's the romantic now, Madge thought, but held Jim close. This was a different Jim. She picked up his mood. 'These hills have seen awful sights in days gone by,' she said. 'That place beyond Garvock, they still call Sheriff's Pot, where they boiled the sheriff. Some call it Brownie's Kettle. It's beside Brownie's Leys farm. I wonder how true it all is? Folk don't do things like that nowadays. This is the twentieth century.'

'I hope you're right, Madge,' said Jim. 'We are lucky though. The country's never been so prosperous and things can only get better.' He kissed her bonny red lips. She kissed him back and put a stop to all his blethers.

Up on the Reisk, Leslie Mitchell had little time for daft nonsense of that sort. He made up his mind, sitting there, his back against the Big Stane by Leys of Barras and Greenden. Those words of Rob Middleton came back to him then. Quines were a damned nuisance when he'd so much to do. He'd think of little else, Rob had said. Time then to put them in their place. He'd be in the Dominie's feeder class in August and there would be a quine or two beside him there. He'd ever only seen quines in the feeder class. They sat apart from the rest, the quines' class they called it. He'd have to stop using that teuchter word, though. Look how it had branded him down in the Royal Toun. How they'd all howled!

He took out his notebook and started to write. He'd done his best to rid himself of those teuchter ways, but now he'd plan the thing in earnest. When he got down to the Mackie Academy at Stonehive, there would be none who would dare call him a teuchter. But there was more to it than the odd word like quine which he still let slip. He'd watch that from now on. He'd speak in plain English, but with no fancy accent like the lairds and those uppity folk they called the gentry had.

He divided the page in two. On one side he listed all the teuchter words he could remember. On the other, he started to list the best alternatives. Times though, there were no alternatives, and he puzzled over that. There were other things he had to watch. Those giggling girls – yes, girls – down at the shop had been his biggest problem. He'd had a go at that before coming up the brae. He'd looked at that girl straight in the eye and been really firm, polite but firm. She'd been away to start her giggling again, but he'd stood his ground and she'd been embarrassed in the end. There were other things that could single you out. He listed them down. There was the way that you dressed, how you walked, how you ate. Country folk rolled when they walked, a ploughman's gait, he'd heard a tounie laugh. And they ate with their mouths open and sloshed their food about on their lips. That book from the Dominie had been a great help. He'd soon sort himself out. And washing – teuchters seldom washed, certainly not all over. Nakedness was indecent, they said. What nonsense! He'd wash himself all over, every day. He'd strip down naked. There would be problems with that bath in the kitchen. He'd wait till Father was up on the hill. He'd have to explain it to Mother. She would be scandalised, of course, but he was thirteen now and it was time he explained there was nothing indecent about the human body.

Next day, a paragraph in the *Advertiser* spoke about skirmishes by the Serbs and how the Russians were ranting on about things. Neither Leslie nor the Dominie, Madge or Jim or any of the rest, paid it much heed. There were better things to think about than daft paragraphs in the *Advertiser*.

Folk called it a heatwave. Up in the Howe, away from the coast, those last days of July grew hotter still. The sun's heat sizzled in Strathmore and the Borders. Doon Sooth folk sunbathed and splashed on the sandy beaches, and played daft games like cricket. Some thanked God for the sunshine; things were as good as they'd ever been.

Early in August Jim made a sentimental journey to his native Banff. He'd left it some fourteen years back, before moving down to Dollar. Those early Banff years had left their mark, though. Father, he knew, had been married before. When his first wife died, Father had married Mam in his declining years. But that was ancient history. Father had died, Mam said, before he'd seen his young Jim's second birthday.

'The poor old brute had been fair sucked dry,' he'd once heard an auld wife smirk. Mam had shut her up, but they were words he never forgot. Father had lumbered his ailing Mam with a kirn of trustees, Auld Kirk elders and the like, to keep a grip on young Jim's Christian education. He'd been named after Father who'd run a prosperous painter's business in Banff High Street for as long as most could remember. Like most of his breed, that older, mysterious Jim Geddes had been a dab hand at the preaching. That much he'd been able to ferret out. Father had been a staunch presbyterian of the old school, who'd worked out his own way of things, how God's bairns had been set on the road to salvation at the start of time, before all those ungodly capers had come in about. Father Fraser had confided that to him when he'd been a bit older. The sour Auld Kirkers had kept faith with the auld brute, Father Fraser had reminded him, grinning, when he'd spoken of what he knew. Jim had accepted that. Folk in the north had a coarse way of telling things.

His younger Banff days had been a succession of Sunday schools, bands of hope, prayer meetings and the like. It had all been over much for his bed-ridden Mam, he could see that now, and the Auld Kirkers were no doubt right when they used Father's silver to get him a good Dollar education. He'd been about ten when they'd kitted him out and escorted him down to Banff Bridge Station with his one-way ticket to Dollar. That's when he'd been taken in hand by Robert Fraser, Dollar's much respected parish inspector, an Auld Kirk man of more settled opinions. The canny Banff trustees felt they'd discharged their obligation when they presenting him at the station with a substantial tome on South Africa's explorers and missionaries. They'd inscribed it: 'To James Geddes with best wishes, Banff, the First Day of the Twentieth Century'.

Jim had now returned to lay the ghosts of his past. His Mam, he discovered, was now being tended to in the Broch, and it was as he passed through Macduff, that he got the news. War had been declared. The naval reserves had been called up earlier and postcards were on sale showing the crowds of navymen and their families assembled at Macduff harbour. 'The Naval Reserve leaves Macduff', the postcard said. He bought one straight away, for it seemed an appropriate postcard to send on to his Madge.

'Spending the afternoon here,' he wrote, 'expect to be at Fraserburgh tomorrow, Jim'. The postmark was stamped, 'Macduff, 5.45 p.m., 5th August, 1914'.

Leslie read the news in the paper he got down at the shop. He cycled back up the Reisk, fair excited by it all. It was time that Prussian Kaiser was taught a lesson. There was no place in the twentieth century for brutality of that sort. Rob Middleton was less impressed. 'Silly buggers,' was all he said, and he chirked to his horse, and went on his way.

In the Royal Toun, there was a deal of excitement. What could those Germans be thinking about, risking a war with the British Empire? The French were there too, with a huge army and an empire of sorts. Had the Germans never heard about our navy?

Jim smiled when he got back. 'It's a pity it should come to this Madge, when everything's going so well. I can't see it lasting that long though. Most folk say it will be all over by Christmas.'

TWELVE

But it was not all over by Christmas.

There was a fair stir in the place when the Gourdon men were called up. Near every boat in Gourdon had men in the naval reserve. It made a fine bit caper with a trip Doon Sooth and some silver to spend.

Folk were pouring down from Benholm and Garvock to join in the stir. It was the start of the Gourdon holidays and the mill quines were there in their summer frocks. Willie Peter's new mill, the Selbie Works by the shore, would be shut for the rest of the week. Already crowds had set off on a cheap train excursion. It would take more than a foreign war to upset the Gourdon holidays.

Not since the coronation four years back, had Gourdon seen so many Bervie folk and country chields swarming the harbour edge. On coronation day, the rain had come on and spoiled the dancing, but today the skies were clear and the sun was out. Even the older men carried their jackets and had their sleeves rolled up. You soon picked out the navy men, with their dark blue suits and their collars and ties, all trigged out as if they were off to a wedding. They sweated away in the summer sun, their women folk and bairns trailing on behind.

Most were crowded down by the station, some were on the wooden bridge that crossed the railway line. Over the bridge, in Queen Street, the latecomers were queueing up with their cases and gear. God, Gourdon could turn out a fair sized navy by itself! You wondered how the Kaiser could be as daft as take on the British navy. Our battleships could sink his fleet in an afternoon, and here were reserves that could handle the rest.

When the train moved off, you all joined in. What a waving and a cheering! They'd have heard it far up in the Howe. A coarse-like lot, those seamen from Gourdon and you'd swapped a few clouts with them at times, but man, it was fine they were on your side when you'd to deal with foreign tinks like the Germans. The Germans were raping the women and bayoneting bairns in their prams. We British would never stand for that!

The war was all handled Doon Sooth. The territorials were heading in the same direction, and ten planes from Montrose were off to Farnborough. You started to read the papers. Those editor billies could fair stir you up. The Jerries were having a hard time of it, they said. But we lost a destroyer and a minelayer just off the coast, and a cruiser was blown up. You could expect that sort of thing, they told you. The Jerries were getting a hammering and our army had landed in France without a man being lost. That would put a stop to all their nonsense.

Even in Stonehive, where folk were a cut above the rest, the 33 territorials under Captain Riddoch, the rector at the Academy, and Lieutenant Falconer, the lawyer, had all volunteered for service at the front. The territorials had joined up for home service, so you granted that it was real patriotic of them. You'd to let bygones be bygones at a time like this.

In the Royal Toun four hundred mill quines were knitting socks in their spare time, and they'd precious little of that after a long day in the mills. The more genteel women met in Hallgreen Castle where they cut and stitched up shirts for the sodgers. The gentry provided them with the cloth

64

and they'd a cup of coffee in the drawing room when things got hard. The papers kept up their tales of the pounding Jerry was getting and there were cartoons of the Kaiser ordering his chauffeur to turn back. 'Home, James!' he said, and folk had a good laugh at that.

The Bailie and Jim were determined the New Year concert would be on a grander scale than ever. Jim booked Willie Goodfellow's Band and the best of the local talent. For the first time ever, he booked a professional, Percy Ford, an entertainer from Aberdeen. The fee was two guinees plus expenses, but Jim thought it well worth it. They'd to go in for things in a big way now. They'd need more prizes next summer, for the Games would be crowded out with all the victory celebrations that would be going on.

They were a coarse lot, those Germans though, and couldn't see when they were beat. They kept battling on. But Leslie had battles of his own to fight that winter. There were guffaws and starings when folk watched his capers. 'Pretending to be a gentleman', was the speak at the shop. 'Thinks he's gentry. Did you see him raise his hat to the minister?'

'He's been proud and conceited ever since he won that medal from the *Journal*,' snorted Reid up at Alpity, but his wife had a worse tale than that, straight from the grocer lad that very day. He'd taken the bread in from the cart and dumped it on the kitchen table, and there, as naked as the day he was born, young Mitchell was standing there, as bold as brass, scrubbing himself by the fireside.

'And he never batted an eye,' the grocer lad grinned. He could scarce wait to get back to the Royal Toun with that bit tale.

'The dirty limmer.' Mistress Mutch was thrilled at the news which she got at the shop. 'Shaming his folk like that.' Her man came from respectable God-fearing stock that went to bed with their drawers on, which was only right and proper. When they washed, their lower regions was a mystery you never dared speak about.

'You're a lazy brute,' Father Mitchell howled at him, digging his graip into the reeking cattle dung he was spreading on the park. Leslie was dandering down the next drill, a graip in one hand and one of the Dominie's books in the other. 'I'll show all of you yet,' he muttered. He could be real thrawn, when he had a mind to it.

There were three of them in the Dominie's feeder class, and they sat at a bench by the wall out in front of the rest. He paid little heed to the two quines sitting next him, though one was Rob Middleton's lass, Becky, from Hareden, next door near, up beside them on the Reisk. She was hard to avoid, at times, on that wearisome road they'd to trudge, going and coming to the wee school.

Girls were bothersome enough, but his real enemy was Nick Taggart, a ploughman's son, who swaggered about the place and bullied all the younger bairns. When he saw Leslie sitting apart in the feeder class he smirked and winked and made kissing noises with his thick fleshy lips.

'You should be in the quines' playground, now you're in the quines' class,' he shouted to him one day and the rest of them laughed. They were all a bit nervous of Nick Taggart and it was best to laugh. Nick would grab their schoolbags and throw them into the hedge when the mood was on him. One of his favourite ploys was to hold a younger lad under the tap and give his head a droukin.

Leslie seethed away under Nick's taunts for about a week. If he ignored Nick maybe he'd give up. But Nick thrived on the thing, and the lassies in the class began to catch on and nudge each other when Leslie appeared. The thing bothered him a lot, and he lay there at night wondering what to do. But what could you do? He'd little wish to start up a slanging match with the stupid teuchter. Besides, you could only slang Nick with daft teuchter words. If he slanged him in the English he was now determined to speak, the whole school would laugh. Bullies were a curse on the earth. Those Romans he'd been reading about were bullies, clever and well organised, but bullies just the same. That slave, Spartacus, had stood up to them, though, and given them a threshing. Maybe that was the answer.

He took a book of the Dominie's home one night, *The Art of Self-Defence,* and he read it in one go. Footwork and watchfulness, were all you needed, it seemed. Nick was a slob. He'd cut him down to size. 'I'll see you in the playground when the Dominie's gone,' he told him, and Nick smirked and nodded, uneasy like.

Well that was the speak of the place for a week or more, but it ended Nick's career as the laird of the playground. It was all over in minutes. The word had spread and the whole school was there. That fair roused Leslie to the job in hand. It was like one of those gladiatorial battles he'd been reading about. But he kept cool and thought of what he'd read. Watch him like a hawk, jump around on your feet, and hit him hard on the nose. So they rolled up their sleeves and Nick lumbered at him with a soft grin on his face. It was a shame really, Leslie thought later. He kept an eye on that fist, danced to one side, and thumped him hard on the nose. It was the shock of Nick's life. There was blood everywhere, and the whole school yelled and clapped.

If the Dominie ever heard, he never let on. Leslie could do little wrong after that. He could speak all the English he liked. Even Nick picked up the odd English word when he thought it sounded grand. A more douce and canny lad was Nick as the winter closed in. He and Leslie got on fine after that, scouring the braes for flints and odd relics the Picts had left behind.

Winter tightened its grip and early in December, blizzards swept the Highlands. The Howe of the Mearns and most of the coast lay buried in snow. The week before Christmas, the snow had vanished and the winds were light. The Royal Toun was asleep.

It was after three in the morning the cry went up: 'The Mill's on Fire!'

Madge looked out of the window. Not a glimmer had she seen when she'd turned out the light. Now a great orange glare filled the sky, away over to the right. Bert's words galvanised them all. Father was down the stairs like a shot, half dressed and pulling on his jacket as he went. Where did he get all that energy? Harris was soon after him.

Madge, taking time to make herself respectable, arrived down last. Father and Harris had gone by the time she reached the door but Bert was there. 'It's been going for some time by the look of it,' he said. 'I heard them running and shouting in the street.'

'You'd better stay with me,' Bert said, 'there's a bit of moon about, but you'll need to watch your step.' The gas lamps had been snuffed out by the scaffy hours earlier, but lights were going on all down the King Street as folk were roused by the din. A car with its headlamps blazing came hooting down the street and passed them at the top of the Kirkburn.

'That's Webster's car,' said Madge.

'But it must be Pappa Gibb's mill that's on fire,' said Bert. 'I hope they can save it. It will be a real disaster if that's gone.'

The two of them stopped at the top of the Gassy Brae. A large crowd had gathered. Some were talking quietly but most were struck dumb at the sight below. Was this the same spot you'd stopped at last summer on that glorious day of the Games? In the summer sun, the colours of the tents, the crowds and the bands had thrilled and excited you. Now, you were standing, in the cold December gloom, the last Thursday before Christmas, watching the redness and the glare from the buildings below.

The fire was in the buildings to the left where the roofs had already fallen in. Nothing could quench an inferno like that. You could just pick out folk running about beside the Gas Works building. Nearer to the fire, on the other side of the lade, you could see men silhouetted by the flames. Someone had started up a pump. A hose snaked over in the direction of the lade.

'It's the Old Mill that's gone up,' said Bert. 'They're trying to save the New Mill. There's a gap between the two of them.'

They stood for a time, the heat from the fire reaching up in the raw December breeze. Deep roarings and crashings from the blaze mingled with the cries of the fire fighters down below. A noise like thunder signalled another mill roof gone.

The crowd were subdued. This was a major disaster for the Toun. There would have been no-one down there when the fire had started, around midnight, somebody said, and they'd only discovered it after three and by then it had got a good hold. Folk whispered when they spoke.

The flames grew less. Once the timbers and the roofs had gone, they'd nothing else to feed on. It looked, too, as if the spread of it had been halted. The New Mill to the right stood intact and in darkness. A faint glimmer from the moon was a help, and some were moving off. Most still had jobs to go to.

The five thirty mill horns were sounding, first the Springy's deep throated boom, then came Craigview's high pitched scream. These were the warning horns, and there was little time left before the starting horns at six.

Harris joined the two of them. He'd been down at the fire for over an hour and he was breathless when he reached the top. The Gassy Brae was fine for sledging when snow was on the ground, but it was a hard, vertical climb if you tried it on the way up. The older mill workers aye took things more cannily and came up the long way round.

'They've saved some of the frames,' Harris said when he got his breath back, 'but the Auld Mill's gone. The whole of the reeling department's gone and so has the engine house. They say the fire started in the engine house. At least the New Mill's still there.'

Father joined them then. He'd been standing along on the Braes, discussing the disaster with two councillors. There was little more to be said, and the four of them, Father and Bert in front, made their way back up the King Street.

Bervie's Golden Year had started off so well. Another mill was to be built, and still better times were in store. Now near to Christmas, and things were ending like this. The news from the war was getting worse by the day. And here in the Royal Toun the Auld Mill had gone. The Auld Mill had changed a lot down the years, but for a century and more, Bervie folk had looked down on her with pride and a kind of affection. She was a well kent sight, Scotland's first spinning mill. All the engineering and spinning skills Bervie possessed had started down there, at the Auld Mill in the Haughs.

The chorus of the starting horns blared out as the four of them passed the Auld Kirk at the top of the Kirkburn. That, you might have thought, was a sound of hope for the future. But the Auld Mill had been Bervie's talisman. Was it a sign, you wondered? What was out there, in those days that were waiting to come?

THIRTEEN

The Auld Mill was smouldering still when the tongues started to wag. Strange how the mill had been blazing for three hours or more and not a cry gone up. The McDonalds and the Bruces heard the roof crash about three. They were some 200 yards away from the place, but Dave Stewart at the gassy was just over the lade, hard up against the mill dyke.

Was the man deaf and blind you wondered. He'd a contraption that roused him sharp if the gas tank fell low. Then he would loup for his shovel and go like the clappers. But Dave was over long in the tooth for that ever to happen. He'd timed his wee gas tank fine. Precious little gas was used at nights once the scaffie had dowsed all the lamps.

Surely Pappa Gibb had a lad in the place to keep an eye on things? No, no; once the fireman had banked the fires for the night, the doors were slammed shut. Old Gibby would not pay good silver for a lad to do damn all at night time. The sly chields in the pubs soon had it that Pappa Gibb would be fine pleased with the Auld Mill gone, but that kind of speak was soon shouted down. A man would as soon set fire to his own bit place as fire the Auld Mill of Bervie.

Oh, aye they'd glint, the strikes and the grumbles of the mill quines had fair plagued Jim Gibb those months past. Pappa had been thumping his desk and swearing he'd see them damned before he paid the Auld Mill spinners the same rate as the quines in the New Mill. It was simple economics, he said. The output in the New Mill was higher so the workers there got a shilling more. What folk deserved had damn all to do with it. But, they'd argue, to settle the thing, the big engine they'd put in some time back was over heavy and expensive to run. It was handy it was the Auld Mill was in ruins.

Pappa Gibb soon put a stop to lies and rumours of that sort. The fire had started in the engine house, and they'd saved 22 of the 40 frames in the place. They would be shoving them into the New Mill. The machines were nothing like as antiquated as folk made out and they were as up to date as any you'd find in the North East. The insurance lads would be well-pleased at that bit tale, you said, but then a tale went round that Pappa Gibb had paid not a penny for insurance. So you took what you could from that speak on the mill blaze at Bervie.

The mill blaze caused a lesser stir up on the Reisk. A commotion outside brought Leslie to the window and he stared a while at the big red glow in the sky. But he'd his book to read and he picked it up and carried on where he'd left off. It had fallen from his hands just an hour before.

They'd left him well alone after that fight in the playground. Father too had held his peace and taken on a hired man who slept under the eaves up there in the garret. The £25 for his bursary had quietened father for a time so he was left to his books.

The three of them would have to sit the Stonehive entrance exam in a year's time, but that gave him little bother. The trouble was laying his hands on more books. The Dominie was hard pressed keeping up with his needs. Dickens and Wells, Shaw and Huxley, Darwin and Scott, it made little odds. He read the lot. Anthropology and science, the Picts, the Romans, exploration and time travel. It was fascinating stuff.

He could never forget that problem he'd had over language when he'd thought of slating Nick Taggart. The teuchter tongue was much better for that. But there must be as many words and more in good plain English. If the day was fine he climbed the brae and settled behind the Big Stane with a dictionary and a thesaurus and when a new word took his fancy he wrote it down in his book.

The dreadful lives of his parents were past belief. From five thirty each morning till nine thirty at night they each had their jobs. They'd little time or patience for the finer things in life. Love and affection had no place in their existence and at the end of each day father would collapse into bed still wearing his heavy woollen drawers. Leslie could scarcely imagine his mother looking on father with anything more than a long suffering acquiescence.

What a hellish existence the two of them had. How could you describe such a life in words of plain polite English. Teuchter words or coarse English words were the only ones of use. He'd thought of that when he'd watched mother planting herself on the three-legged stool. She stuck her head into the ribs of that big docile cow, then grabbed the teats in her red, roughened hands. The cow stood there cud chewing and farting as mother pulled away at an amazing rate. He lay back against the Big Stane and searched his thesaurus for an alternative to farting. The best he could find was borborygmus, a daft like word and not quite right, but he wrote it down. A rumbling of the stomach! He'd use it one day, but he still preferred farting!

Words were the keys to escape. Words and knowledge. He often thought about mother. She was medium sized like himself, five feet and a half or so. Like himself, she'd a vivid imagination and a sharp tongue when she was roused. Father was slower, a man of few words and fewer ideas. He must have got his ideas from mother. But mother's hair was red and his was a soft brown. Father's hair was black. Heredity was a fascinating subject. His own features could be described as dolichocephalic. He'd looked that word up and written it down. His head was longer than it was broad. Father, with his square, weather-beaten face, could scarcely be described as dolichocephalic, nor could George or John. Strange. John had passed an odd remark one day, which had troubled him ever since. He must ask him about that.

The war dragged on, disaster upon disaster. He'd changed his mind about it being a grand crusade against that awful Kaiser. Folk were slow to realise it, but the war was still going to be raging away next Christmas. It was 20 May before the Bailie and his committee realised the Games that summer would have little to celebrate. Jim reported that the Montrose Games had been cancelled and that Forfar were calling off theirs. So they cancelled the Games and pressed on with their plans to raise silver for the summer after next.

Long before Christmas, however, J H Johnstone, the Gourdon Dominie, had taken over the Games secretary's job – 'pro tem', as he put it. Jim, the Inspector, had volunteered and was off to the war.

Madge could scarce believe it had happened. They'd all gone, every single one of them. All of a sudden, it was a different war, with awful telegrams and casualty lists in the papers. Madge's worries of long ago came flooding back, but this was no time to lie and gloom out over Newbigging's fields. The talk was all of duty and sacrifice and being patriotic. The house was empty, uncanny and empty. Just Father and herself now, all on their own.

Madge shut her eyes. Those summer months of 1915 had been sweet. Not intoxicating as the summer of 1914, but sweet just the same, with Jim and the boys. She and Jim had climbed Craig David again and laughed and cuddled and remembered the year before.

There was that great day when David had run the four of them to Gourdon in the new car and they'd set sail in the 'Alice Webster'. She even remembered its number: ME 242. Motor boats were rare and they caused such a stir when David took the helm and steered them out past the breakwater to the open sea, Teen and David, Jim and herself. A perfect summer day. So impossible to believe there was a war going on, away over there.

'Watch out for the submarines,' a youngster had shouted as they left the Gourdon pier, and they all laughed. There had been incidents with fishing boats, but what could happen on a day such as this? The sea was blue and smooth, like those postcards she'd seen. Bervie looked different from far out in the bay. She could see it still, the grey-white curve of the bay, framed by the green of the Knox Hill and Craig David, and there, straight ahead, the square, safe church tower with the grey, dry Kirkburn road climbing to meet it. The mill lums looked so sharp and true in that cobalt blue sky.

They had cruised round the bay in the summer heat and watched a train leave and puff its slow way along the shore line to Gourdon. David was working in the mills now, full time. His dad had insisted he spend a week or two in each department to learn how things were done. He'd been in the mills often during the holidays, but David was a bit of a dreamer.

'Enjoying your taste of mill life, David?' Jim asked him, with a laugh.

'I'll enjoy it a lot better next week,' David smiled that lazy, happy smile of his. 'Dad gave me the rough end for a start. Nothing could be worse than working in the stour of the breaker. I think my lungs are bunged up for good.'

'Breath in that good salty air.' Teen flung her head back and breathed in the good seaweed smell of the North Sea. They all had a go then, and they laughed and filled their lungs with it all the way back to Gourdon.

'Your mam and Douglas are waiting for us,' said Teen, waving.

'Your mam looks so young and cheerful,' said Madge and they clambered to the pier. Alice, David's mam, greeted them with a wide cheery smile. Douglas Ogg, David's chum, had driven her down. David and Douglas were of the same age. How strange, Madge thought, David's mother seemed not much older than the two of them. How full of life and what fun she was. She and Douglas then sailed out to sea in the motor boat that bore her name. What must it be like to have a mam of your own, Madge had wondered.

She shook her head. Life had been good those last two years. It had all happened in a rush. She wanted to blame Father but that was hardly fair. He'd not encouraged them. But he'd not stopped them either. It was all the talk about duty and patriotism, and single men and shirkers. Yesterday a shop girl had handed a young boy a white feather. What a stupid thing to do! They were just boys. Jim and Bert and Albert and Harris. Now young Laurie and Cousin Alec from Montrose had volunteered by cheating on their ages. It was as though a terrible sickness had come over them all. Seventeen year olds, little more than schoolboys. There was little sense in any of it. The world had gone mad.

FOURTEEN

Nineteen sixteen was a terrible year. It began in wind and rain. Crowds gathered at Montrose, Bervie and Stonehive to hear the bells ring out the old year and ring in the new. They got drenched for their pains. December had been a foul month. On Christmas Eve heavy seas had sunk a steamer off the Tay. Easterly gales had lashed the coasts of Aberdeen and the Mearns. The 'Bohemian' was lost with all hands off the harbour bar at Aberdeen, eight men grasping the rigging to the very last.

It eased on Christmas Day, but stayed wet and dismal. That was a ploy to fool them all, for straight from the north came a screaming storm with a terrible force, smashing scores of wee boats coaxed out for a catch by Hogmanay.

The war news was worse. The newspaper billies did their best. The *Advertiser* boasted we'd hoodwinked the Turks. We'd got all our horses and mules off, it said, with their vehicles, ammunition and stores. But a whole army was lost out there in the Dardanelles.

There was to be no let up in the New Year. A hurricane screamed over the Royal Toun, and the houses Jock Webster was building for his workers on Kinghornie land were smashed and levelled. The bricks were flung wide and far on the new mill road he'd built above the brig. That cost the contractors a fortune and set back the work on the mill he was planning. On the fourteenth, the skies opened up for a last wild fling. Stonehive got the worst of it that time, and there was a trail of wreckage right across the Howe.

So that set the shape for 1916. Madge had to run the house and the business for Father. Soon the letters came pouring in, from Jim and the four boys, and from cousin Alec and John Elliot, the Stationy's lad. They came in, as well, from Bervie lads she barely knew, all looking for news and tales from home. On and on they came, long rambling letters, about all the dirt and the nonsense they'd to put up with Doon Sooth.

Madge was doing a job the newspaper billies could never do. She filled a book with addresses that changed with every post. If she'd done little else but write letters she'd have been hard put to keep up. Madge could write a good tale and was soon scribbling like mad, as were all the rest of the quines throughout the Howe and beyond.

Harris, cousin Alec and John Elliot found themselves in the Royal Field Artillery. Laurie, at seventeen, landed in London in the Royal Garrison Artillery, soon with tapes on his arms and rising fast in the ranks because his young, sharp wits got the hang of the new signals and telegraph machines, whatever they were. Albert and Frank Riddell, the bus driver, got into the Royal Army Service Corps, and dear Bert found himself in a strange sounding regiment called the Fife and Forfar Yeomanry.

Jim, for reasons no-one could make out, landed in a crowd called The 64th Divisional (Highland) Cyclists Company. That seemed an odd sort of ploy. Maybe he let out, in the factual way he had, that he'd done some biking along the Hillfoots in his day, but bikes sounded as daft for fighting the Germans as horses, the Bailie said. But the generals knew best. It seemed they were fell keen on bikes now as well as on horses. It turned out that Jim's bikers were for home defence round the Norfolk Broads, though a boat would have been better for that you would have thought. Madge thought bikes round the Broads were fine, much better than being away out there in France. There was a picture, in the *Advertiser,* of the bikers on manoeuvres, making an assault with their bikes strapped to their backs. How you fought the Germans with a wheel round your neck was never explained.

It was Harris who came back from the real war first. Madge first knew he'd been at the front when a photo arrived with Harris on a garden seat. 'On the plage at Dieppe', he'd written on the back. He'd already got a wound stripe on the arm of his tunic. But the cheery Harris grin had gone. He looked thinner and saddened but fit and ready for another shot with his Number One seige company he gave as his address.

Harris turned up at the back door in a filthy mess. He'd a day's growth of beard on his face. Alice had seen him come up the Kirkburn from the station and had passed him by. Old John Elliot, the stationy, had already stared hard before he'd spoken.

'You're in an awful hurry, Alice,' Harris joked. Alice, trying to give this dirty looking sodger a wide berth, stopped in her tracks. It was not just the sight and the dirt of the brute made her keep her distance, but the vile smell as he came near. 'It's all right, lass,' said Harris. 'Madge will soon have me into a tub and I'll be put out to dry.'

'It's Harris!' Alice gasped.

Harris had been the most pernickety of the lot, a bit of a dandy when he'd gone courting with Bella, his Stonehive lass, the maid at Hazelgrove. He'd never sported as much as a whisker in his life, when whiskers were all the rage. But if you looked closer, beneath all the hair and grime, there was Harris, a bit of a twinkle in his eye still, but tired-looking. The same Harris, but not the clean shaven, neatly trigged out Harris Alice knew, off to visit his cheery wee lass from Stonehive. Harris humped his pack, gave a bit of a wave, and trudged up the Burn, past the Free Kirk and a group of young lads that were staring, quietened at the sight.

Madge ran to the back door. No-one came in at the back door unless it was Father or the boys come back from their work. Now there were no boys coming back and Father was down at the Square seeing about a shop sign he was painting for Shand the baker. Painting signs was a work of art, and now that he was on his own, sign painting was a more practical way of keeping the business going than driving himself on with all those rough decorating jobs. But he did that as well. He'd still a living to earn.

'It's me, Harris, Madge. I'm in a terrible mess. I'm stinking. If you could put the boiler on, I'll sit out in the store shed till it's ready. I'm crawling with lice,' he added, to drive the message home.

That was the day that went into the family folklore: the day Harris came back from the trenches covered in lice. It was the day that knocked all the daft notions, if Madge and the Bailie had any left, of the war being some glorious, heroic crusade against the Germans.

'It was a shambles,' Harris said later. 'I'd have waited for hours and wasted half my leave. A crowd of us just kept on north once we'd got our passes. The troop train from London took ages and we've been sleeping most of the time. The lice have been having a banquet.'

Madge worked like mad to get Harris respectable before Father came home. The boiler had been lit for the weekly wash and the water was on the boil. She dashed back and fore between the kitchen and the store shed. The louse-ridden uniform and underclothes, she held at arm's length in a bucket, and dumped them in the boiler. A basin was rushed out with a shaving bag and some disinfectant. Harris was scouring his hair with something Madge took to be paint remover.

'You'll skin yourself if you use that stuff, Harrissy,' she shouted.

'Never fear, lass,' Harris laughed. 'I've thinned it down. It's one of the tricks I learned in the trenches.'

Father soon heard the tale of Harris and his filthy state, for little happened in Bervie you wouldn't hear in Shand's shop within the hour. Father was none too pleased at that bit speak. He bided his time and got back for his dinner not a minute early. Harris might be back from the trenches, but you'd to be professional at your work or you'd soon end up in a soss.

'What's all this I've been hearing?' said Father at last, and Harris explained how it had been. But it was later that night, up in the parlour, that Harris told of the madness and the killing on the Somme. First he spoke of the filth and men who lived like animals, only animals never lived that way. Madge felt Harris spared them the worst. He was quiet at first in his answers to Father's questions, but then out it came. Life in the trenches was not as you'd thought, with our gallant boys, as the papers had it.

The Bailie was shocked. 'But your guns had been blasting the barbed wire for days,' he said. 'You must have cut some roads through the wire.'

'That's just it, Father,' said Harris. 'Any sodger at the Front knows fine if you shell wire for a month it will still be there. The shells just lift the wire up and it falls down again in bigger tangles than ever. The generals know more about their horses than they do about barbit wire. Our men walked into the stuff and the machine guns cut them down in their thousands. It reminded me for all the world like a trawl on Bervie beach. Instead of salmon stranded high up on the nets, there were our men, dangling on the wire.'

Harris stopped. From that day on he was loath to mention the Somme again. After he'd slept and wandered round the old Toun for a while, a strange look in his eyes, back he went to his seige guns. There was no turning away from the thing and all the madness that went with it.

It was just a year since Madge and the rest had laughed at the thought of German submarines coming in to Bervie bay. But all that summer U-boats had been sinking fishing boats off places like Scarborough and Whitby. It was three months before they heard what happened to the wee Gourdon boat 'The Bella', a family affair with dads and sons on board. Then a telegram arrived to say they were all safe and sound in a German prison camp. They'd been captured in broad daylight, within sight of Tod Head.

Nineteen sixteen was a terrible year too, at Bervie's Big Hoose, Hazelgrove. Old Jock Webster died there on 18 August, a passing that would change Bervie's fortunes in ways none could foresee.

Jock was not that old, you'd be told by the worthies. He was still in his 66th year and a grand shot he'd been in his day. The crack shot, they'd go on, not just of the Bervie Volunteers, but the best shot in the land. You looked with a smirk at that kind of speak and then they'd stand up for the man. They'd been Volunteers themselves, they'd say, and if the crack shots of the Bervie Volunteers had been there now, neither the Jerries nor the Turks would be getting away with things the way they were.

It was the speak in the pubs for a month or more and fair knocked out the war as an excuse for a dram. The Volunteers, and there seemed more of them than ever as the days went by, stood up for old Jock Webster. He'd won the Caledonian Shield in Edinburgh for his shooting and most could well mind the day, back in '79 when he'd beaten the best shots in Scotland with his Bervie gun. He carted off the Lord Advocate's Cup, presented by Colonel MacDonald, the Solicitor-General of Scotland, no less. He did better still in '86, old Tam would chip in, down there at Wimbledon, would you believe, where he carried off the Kirkman Cup itself.

The tongues were wagging again when the will was read, and that was no secret. Scarce a soul in the place but knew every line and paragraph of the thing. He'd left three mills, Kinghornie Farm, half the houses in Bervie, and God knows what else with his shares and all, in the charge of his trustees. He'd left a bit of cash to Abner Wheatley, his manager, the lucky devil, and some guineas to his trustees, but the whole damned lot would go to young David in time. David was over young yet, he'd judged, to handle the workings of a business like that, him with his talk about aeroplanes, his butterflies, birds' eggs and the like. David would have control when he turned twenty if the trustees thought fit. The trustees were to pay Alice a monthly wage and the life rent of Hazelgrove. But here was the catch, and it was down there in black and white. If Alice was ever to wed again, she'd lose the lot. Now what put that thought into old Jock's head?

Nineteen sixteen had been Leslie's worst year yet. Things started well enough; he and Becky and the rest got through their entrance exam with little bother. Dominie Gray had made sure of that. There were some sniggers though, from the trimly clad Stonehive scholars, lawyers' bairns and the like, when Leslie and the other scholars from the Howe walked in.

'Country bumpkins, that's what they called us,' he complained to mother next day, certain he'd failed his exam. However he tried, there was no concealing his country origins, with his tackity boots and heavy worsted breeks. When the results came out, though, he and Becky headed the list. They'd got their bursaries and could go to Stonehive.

The battles raged in France and the sun blazed on the Reisk. Father kept ranting on about the crops, so Leslie volunteered to burn the whins high up on the moor. He cleared out each morning with a box of matches and his bag of books and propped himself against the Big Stane, fine pleased to be shot of all the dirt. Grand to soak up the sun, to read on and dream on about the Romans and the Greeks and all those early folk who'd delved on those braes, before the Picts came and hoisted their stones and carved out their squiggles.

Leslie started well enough at Stonehive. His essays took a trick with the teachers at the Mackie and some were read out as a model for the rest. He kept his distance though, suspicious from the start of those tounies and teuchters alike. He and Becky tramped in the opposite direction now, down the road past Mondynes to the station at Drumskite. They caught the eight o'clock train in the morning and got back at five thirty each night. They spoke little though, and, once the train arrived, Leslie searched out a compartment to be on his own and get on with his book.

Becky wondered at that. On the road home he was always out there in front, scrambling up that rough track past Mondynes. He'd have a book in his hand and she'd watch, certain he would trip on the roots or the boulders that cluttered the road. He must have mapped it out in his head, she thought, watching him swerve at every ditch and slope, his eyes glued on his book. As the nights darkened, they'd exchange the odd word, groping their way over the rotten bridge at Mondynes and the paths changed by the floods. They'd speak of their day and the teachers they shared. 'A bunch of promoted Orkney fisher-louts and Kincardineshire ploughmen,' he burst out one day, and that made her laugh.

Did he realise, Becky wondered, even the country lads who had joined the train at Fordoun had a nickname for him. They called him Caliban, which seemed a bit odd. But that was the way those teuchter lads were. They came from as far as Tipperty, near the source of the Bervie stream, on bikes and on foot, to catch the horse bus at Auchenblae. You could hardly get further into teuchterland than that. The tounies were wary of him and the country lads laughed. He'd give them polite answers if they spoke, but she could see he was a loner. There was no-one really close to him, she felt. Maybe Caliban was right, Becky mused, but she doubted if he cared.

It was close to Christmas when she noticed the change. He tightened up even more and spoke scarcely a word. She knew his moods, walking with him so long. Something had upset him and he was working it out like that last time she'd watched him, the week before his fight with Nick Taggart. Whatever it was, it must have hit him really hard. Even that English teacher who'd praised him at times, lost patience. Becky could see he'd been hurt.

&

John had shied away from the thing at first, but Leslie had pressed him for an answer and John told what he knew.

'You mean, we've all of us got different fathers. All three of us?' He couldn't take that in. Not all at one go.

'Father married mother in 1898, on Hogmanay, the last day of the year. I would have been a year old at the time and I can remember nothing about it. George was about nine at the time, and he once explained some of it to me. You were born about two years after that.'

'But what about your father? He must have left you and mother right at the start!'

'It wasn't quite like that.' John was uncomfortable at the way the conversation was going, but this young brother of his worried away at things once he got going. 'I doubt if my father saw mother on more than the one occasion.'

Leslie shut up at that and scowled; his world was now on its head. Mother was not like that. She was such a stern sort of figure, always slaving away for them all. He'd always thought she was overworked. Exploited, that was the word, honest, reliable, God-fearing and exploited. It was mother who saw them down to the kirk in the den every Sunday.

John was now saying she was immoral. They'd teuchter words for that kind of behaviour. But no, not mother.

'My father was a farm servant, Alex Hall, from over Banchory way. George said she tried to sue him, but she got precious little out of that.'

'And George? What about his father?'

'God knows,' said John, and walked away after that. He shouldn't have opened up to young Leslie that way, but he was such an inquisitive young devil. He'd have found out for himself anyway, sooner or later.

Leslie went back up to the Big Stane and he sat there until dark. Nothing was ever what it seemed. He held his head in his hands. Things were far, far worse than he'd imagined. His parents had angered him at times, the deferential way they accepted their lot. Then he'd felt for them and been angered at himself. He'd looked on them, always, as a dependable, steady pair, doing what they could for this family of theirs. What a terrible life they led, and getting precious little for all their drudgery and pain. The 70 acres that was father's was feud to Arbuthnott Estate, and that itself was in a muddle of debt. So they said. The laird's man, when he was sober, would visit father at times, as he did the other farmers on those braes. All that ever came out of those visitations were lost tempers and flaming arguments. Father would stump about for days afterwards. The laird's man must have spent his drinking hours dreaming of quarrels he could pick. They said he drank more than half of that Howe o' the Mearns Whisky Peter Bannerman sold down there at the shop. It was maddening to think of all those hard pressed farmers, still stuck in a feudal treadmill centuries after those laws had been passed, laws settled by the sword. They'd no more right for them than that, Charlie Smith, the roadman, had once explained!

Now this! Not only the lairds were to blame. The workers themselves used each other. The rewards went to the coarsest and the strongest. He could hardly blame mother. She'd been one of a family of twelve and put out to service when she was still just a bairn. She'd told him that once when he'd asked, but she'd said little more. What chance had a young lass got where men took what they could?

There were men everywhere grabbing what they could, not just the lairds, though they were at it too. Those bothy billies he'd listened to were no better than those lairds and kings he'd read about with their sordid lives and their bastard bairns. This was the other side to those braggings he'd listened to in that bothy down the brae. They were all of them at it. Even this family he was in had been forged out of one drunken orgy after another. It made some sense now, he could see, why the three of them were all different.

He was father's only son. So why did father pick on him? Was it because he was his only son and he'd let him down with his daft notions of getting clear of the land? Why had father married mother in the first place? Had it been because she was just available? After all, she'd two sons already. Had he planned it that way, so they'd be there to work their guts out for him one day?

He'd been right in thinking that love and affection had little place in that family of theirs. Mother, at times, had shown her feelings for them all, but life was too hard for nonsense of that sort. That's what he'd felt. And father was so caught up with his crops and those few beasts that he kept.

Was his parent's marriage just a piece of paper to cope with father's lusts, whatever they might be? That's what Peter Dunn, the minister, spoke about on Sundays. Father had wed mother to use her and make her his fulltime, unpaid servant, there was nothing more to it than that. He hated the lot of them. Those sloppy poems and songs by folk like their precious Rabbie Burns they all droned on about on Burns' Nights were full of lies and drivel. Men were filthy and coarse by nature. His own mother had been used and enslaved from the day she was born.

'Go to hell, the lot of you,' he shouted over the gloom of the parks. He picked up a small boulder and threw it into the night. He wiped the tears from his eyes and slunk off down the brae.

FIFTEEN

'Dad's got a bed for Jean and me in Stonehive.'

It was Friday night, and the track past Mondynes was ankle deep in mud. Last night's snows had melted, but on either side of them the drifts were piled high on the dykes. The sky had cleared at last and there was an uncanny silence as the two of them picked their way home in the eerie light of the stars. Leslie had been jolted out of his moodiness the night before by the severity of the blizzard, and they'd had to battle that same road with the sting of the hail and wind in their faces. But he was his old moody self again tonight. Becky could see he was embarrassed.

Last night he'd had to grab her hand over the rickety bridge. She'd been glad of his help floundering about in the dark, knee-high in snow. He'd held on to her and they'd had to laugh, lost and blotted out from the world. She'd held on to him close, frightened and pleased. She remembered him giving her frozen fingers a squeeze. He'd put her hand in his pocket for warmth. They'd laughed again and to cover her confusion she'd started to sing. He'd joined in and they'd struggled and huddled against each other all the way up to Hareden. She'd never known him so happy. Pity there was no snow blowing tonight, she thought, and her cheeks reddened in the dark. She remembered how their cheeks had touched, the strange tingling she'd felt, his cheek against hers, sliding warm and wet with the melted snow. They'd stopped at her gate, cheeks touching, and he'd kissed her gently on the lips. She'd kissed him back then, for an age!

He was embarrassed now, crossing the bridge in this weird stillness. What an awful thing they'd done! She'd never been kissed by a lad, not like that. Those kissing games at Christmas were different, daft pecks that were nothing. And she'd kissed him back. He'd never kissed either. She could tell. He'd been strangely roused and she'd had trouble sleeping last night.

'Dad said we'd end up with pleurisy, getting soaked like that.' She just had to keep on talking. Jean was the other lass from the Dominie's class they'd left at the road end. 'If we share the same bed, Dad says he can manage it, now he's got the bursary money. Besides, there's precious little room for all of us in Hareden those days.'

'You'll have a chance to get on with your lessons then.' He'd an urge to apologise for that kiss last night but that would have been daft. Rebecca had enjoyed it every bit as much as he had. He was relieved she'd spoken the way she had, for he'd felt silly trudging on and not speaking. She was behaving very sensibly. Lassies must mature more quickly than lads. He felt so naive and inadequate about the whole business. He'd been shocked by the way that experience had stirred him, taken him over almost.

'It's a wonder there's room for you all,' he said without thinking. Rebecca had been very young when her mam died and Rob Middleton's second wife, Frances, had been presenting him with a new bairn almost every year it seemed. 'You've got four youngsters in the house now, haven't you?'

'Frank, the oldest's barely six, but they can all sleep in the one bed, except for wee Jessie who's still in her crib. They don't take up much room but they can make a terrible noise.'

He was still thinking about that when he left her at the gate. It was ever the same: women everywhere had the worst of it. Even Rob Middleton, a man of principle if ever there was one, always willing to give a neighbour a helping hand, thought it just the thing to lumber his young wife with one bairn after another. And there would be more bairns still to come. At least Rob had done things the decent way and wed Fanny, as he called her, not just used her the way those men had used mother.

God, where did that put him? What sort of family was this he belonged to with two half brothers and three fathers. Who was he anyway? What sort of passions had he inherited? When the Dominie had asked him, he'd boasted that he'd got his mother's brains and his mother's thoughts. But what about father? They said he'd got father's face and father's long, curved nose, an aquiline nose, he'd discovered. And his mother's wide mouth, somebody had said. But these were only two of his forebears. He'd read once that if you went twenty generations back in time you'd discover more than a million ancestors. And it doubled with every generation. He'd check on that some day. So who was he? Among those millions of ancestors were murderers and rapists, child killers, and thieves, folk like those Roman butchers he'd read about, far worse than this Kaiser Bill they were all going on about. When he was older he'd go north to Aberdeenshire and check up on those Gibbons and Grassics his mother had come from. But mother herself had been one of a family of twelve and look what had happened to her. At least father had married her. He couldn't hold that against him. But what did marriage mean at the end of the day?

So, who was he, and what was he? He was as bad as the rest of them. He'd been having strange urges of late and look how he'd behaved last night when Rebecca had kissed him back. He never called her Becky as the others did. He had more respect for her than that. But had he? What might he have done if they'd stayed out longer and the night had been warm? Those bothy billies and their coarse tales among the harvest stooks were no worse than he was. He'd had a dreadful time falling asleep last night and when he wakened that morning he'd felt awful. He was sick with himself, and sick with that smug, stupid crowd in Stonehive who never got down to the real problems of the world. He had to get away from all of them.

'It was a real daft thing to do, Leslie, and you'd never have got away with it.' Alex Gray, the Dominie, shook his head. 'It's all this talk of white feathers and patriotism's got into you, I suppose. I've heard of sixteen year olds cheating on their ages, but you've just turned sixteen and you're young looking for your age.'

The two of them were walking down the road to the Academy. Leslie had scarcely spoken a word since the Dominie had met him at Stonehive's station. He'd better pull himself together before he met those teachers and those sniggering tounies. What a fool he'd look. It had seemed a good idea at the time, rushing off to join the army. They were none too worried about your age, folk said.

'It wasn't like that,' he said at last. 'I just had to get away from the place. Joining the army seemed the only thing to do.'

'But you liked Stonehive, you said. They read out that essay of yours and you got into that big library of theirs. That's what you wanted, you said.'

This was going to be difficult. They'd be there in five minutes. How could he tell the Dominie what he really felt? That talk he'd had with John about mother had been hard to take. He could never mention that. And that business with Rebecca. Was Rob Middleton getting her digs in Stonehive just because of the weather? Was that really the reason? Yes, he was sure of that. Rebecca would never have said a word. But the whole thing was a mess. Strange how he'd missed her company that last week. The whole thing had been building up in him for some time now. He just couldn't fit in to the kind of teaching that went on at the Academy. But he'd better not say too much about that to the Dominie. Imagine having to swot up the dates of all those obnoxious Stewart kings and their stupid capers to prove you understood the history of your country. What about the ordinary folk who had to suffer for their extravagances; farmers and fisherfolk that had to work for all that wealth. No wonder he'd got poor marks for what he'd written, something father could never understand. And look at how they studied English, droning on about every comma and paragraph in Shakespeare and destroying some of the best poems in the language. A good teacher should get his class excited about those books, not bore them with useless exercises in grammar.

'I got fed up swotting up all those dates,' he said at last. It sounded pathetic. He knew that and kept his head down.

'Ah well,' the Dominie sighed. 'We've all had to swot up a few dates in our time. But I'll speak up for you to the rector again, and I'll try to persuade him to give you just one more chance. It's more difficult for young lads who travel in from the country. I told him that the last time you fell out with them and he said he understood.'

But Sammy Dreep, as they called the new rector, had little patience for this Smart Aleck from the country. They called him Sammy Dreep because of his perpetual snivel. A tall, rake of a man, Sammy was never in the best of health, but school bairns are cruel by nature and care little for things like that. Sammy, for his part, was for ever on the lookout for signs of rudeness, and this cool teuchter who made a practice of raising an eyebrow at times got right under his skin.

On fine weekends, Leslie would chuck Sammy's book under the dresser and head up the brae to his favourite spot, and it was there, in the shelter of the Big Stane, he read William Morris and other socialists he'd found. So there were others besides himself who'd seen the coarseness that went on! The cure, it seemed, was socialism. He read on and on about the thing, forgetting all about Sammy and his Shakespeare. He fair let himself go on those essays for Sammy after that!

'A revolutionist, are you, Mitchell?' Sammy asked him one day.

'A socialist, sir,' Leslie proclaimed, feeling proud.

'Ah, a pro-German then. Maybe you'd like to study what the Kaiser and his German philosophers would like to do to us all?'

'Surely you know the difference between a socialist and a pro-German,' Leslie began.

'Leave the room!' Sammy shouted, getting red in the face.

For once there was total silence in Sammy's classroom. Leslie collected his books and strolled slowly out the door. He was seething by the time he reached the foot of the Academy stairs. The ignorance of the man! How could anyone, never mind a Rector, think of the Kaiser as a socialist!

Father had little time for problems of that sort. When Sammy Dreep's letter reached him, he shoved his plate away.

'I canna eat,' he growled. 'How could you do it, lad? Sticking up for the Germans like that, and disgracing your folk. It'll be the speak of the Parish!'

Mam was at her wit's end. 'After all those years,' she sobbed. 'Your father working like a slave and you lying about there, reading and dreaming.'

Father said more than that to him. 'You'll not stay on here, living off your folk,' he shouted. 'You'll get yourself out of the place and get a fee like the rest of them.'

'Oh, go to hell,' Leslie muttered. He slammed the door and ran back up the brae.

SIXTEEN

Madge was real proud when the *Advertiser* printed a photo of the 64th Divisional (Highland) Cyclists Company on 24 August. There were over a hundred of them, all smartly trigged out, their genteel officers sitting with their legs crossed in the row in front. And there was her Jim standing with the rest, fine and handsome like, in the second row, fifth from the left.

You could hardly say the 64th were battle hardened. For the whole of

1916 and well through 1917 they never fired a shot in anger. But no unit in the army had trained as much, been drilled as much or manoeuvred or practised with their guns as much as the bikers of the gallant 64th. If ever they'd to storm a castle or capture a wee hoose, there would be none that would do it better. But that sort of Border Reiving you'd only find in the history books. Machine guns and barbit wire had made capers of that sort as auld-farrant as the cavalry.

It could never last of course, and it was near the end of their second summer, in early August, 1917, that the Colonel broke the good news.

'Lucky lads,' he said. 'Jerry is on the run and you're needed to chase him all the way back across the Rhine.'

The Americans would be coming in their thousands, but they thought it best if our lads finished the thing off first, so they'd all be transferred to the infantry. 'You'll get a grand welcome from all those fine French and Belgian mesdemoiselles,' he grinned.

It was cold, wet and windy when Jim turned up on Madge's doorstep. A 48 hour pass was maybe long enough, for it gave them little time to think and Jim got on his way to the Aberdeen barracks with the first bus next morning. But Bervie in the early morning is scarcely the most romantic place on earth. There was little left for the two of them to say. They'd said it all the night before up there in the parlour, with Father through the wall in his sad wee room.

'Not long now Madge,' said Jim. 'Jerry's on the run and we all want to get it over with. I'll send you a postcard the minute I arrive in dear old France.'

'Oh Jim,' Madge hugged him close. What a boy he was still. Dear old France, for heaven's sake!

Jim cuddled her for the last time and felt her cheeks, warm and wet. He climbed on to the Stonehive bus and both of them waved. The bus jolted off in a rush and coughed its way down the King Street. Jim leant out over the open side and held up his hand. Madge and Jim had a blurred look at each other as the heavy contraption shuddered its way passed the Auld Kirk.

The whole thing was unbearable and sad, Madge thought, as the bus veered left and out of sight down the Cowgate, past Jim's wee office at number three. It was such a wee office, and how proud he'd been of it. How long was it now, four or five years? He'd worked so hard at it, and what was this they were sending him off to do? Madge burst into tears and rushed inside. Father left her to her thoughts that morning and let himself out to his work.

That same autumn of 1917, young Leslie Mitchell took himself back down the track by Mondynes and boarded the train at Drumskite. He too was headed for Aberdeen. There had been smirks and nods when the news got out about Sammy's letter and he'd spent weeks of hell, rowing with his folks and dodging the neighbours. The best place, as ever, had been the Big Stane up there on the brae.

'Write off to those editors,' Dominie Gray had urged, handing him a list of addresses. 'You've got a big advantage being just sixteen. The newspaper billies are short-staffed now that all their reporters are being called up. Write a good letter in a clear hand, but don't breathe a word about socialism. They don't like that! I'll write you a good reference.'

That fair did the trick, and he accepted the best offer, a job with the *Journal* at Aberdeen at two pounds five shillings a week, a lot better than he'd have got by taking a fee.

He settled in at his lodgings with Mistress MacDonald at St Mary's Place and soon learned the ways of the newspaper world. It was an odd sort of world, but it got clearer by the day. He'd to change his style, he discovered, and learn all about composing sticks and copy, caps and quotes. He'd to master the art of journalese too, which was odd like and daft.

What an exciting place Aberdeen was. For the first time in his life he was independent and free, his own master, with two pounds five shillings a week plus expenses in his pocket. Free of all that Mearns glaur and the sneers he'd had to thole, he got himself a notebook and a fountain pen, bought a slouch hat to look like the rest of the reporters and strode off to the docks. An older man who'd just been called up showed him round the warehouses and offices, the tea-rooms and pubs and introduced him to folk that could be of help.

'Keep your wits about you lad,' said the old hack, pointing to a sharp eyed character at the bar. 'That's one will spin you a yarn for the price of a beer. Don't believe everything they tell you.'

The trick was to look older than his years, but he'd a sixteen year old's sharpness and energy and soon saw how things worked, listening politely to the harbourmaster's tales and swapping jokes with every bobby on the beat. The sub-editors mangled his prose, but he put up with that. He'd get out of this work in time, but for now this was the life! There was no shortage of tales down at the docks with all those U-Boats on the loose. Some day he would write about it in his own way, but for now, those editors got those tales the way they liked them. What a time he was going to have. There was a whole new world out there and it was his to explore.

For Jim, Aberdeen was a place for changing his kit, being inspected, shouted at, and marched around. There seemed to be an indecent haste about the whole thing, he thought, but then they'd all have to hurry if they were to catch up with those Jerries now they had them on the run.

The new squad mustered and paraded on the barrack square. The Colonel seemed fine pleased. This was no crowd of raw recruits the Gordons had got hold of this time. He'd never seen a body of men so well drilled and so well turned out. The Fourth Battalion had been terribly mauled on the drive for Poelcappelle. These replacements looked well capable for the job they'd be asked to handle. They drilled and marched as well as any regulars he'd ever seen.

The Colonel spoke a few cheering words to them under a black, louring sky. The rain had held off. If only they could make that train before the storm broke. He welcomed the lads to the regiment and gave them a speil about its history and its traditions. This was Aberdeen's regiment and now it was their turn to show the world what North East sodgers could do. He congratulated them on their parade ground precision. They were second to none, he said, and they knew it. That bucked them up no end.

So they marched out of the barracks, one more crowd of mother's sons, on down Union Street to the train waiting at the Joint Station. It was a special train, all brushed out, polished and cleaned, ready for the long haul Sooth. It looked as if the whole of Aberdeen had turned out to see them off. This was more men for Aberdeen's own regiment and they'd rounded up some pipers and drummers to make a good show. They'd a real professional look about them, Jim and the rest, for they'd practised and drilled long and hard and this was their chance. Their bikes had been of little use against the Germans, but for near two years they'd drilled and trained for this. This was the real thing.

There was something about this lot that was different. Man, it was a grand sight. You were real pleased it was your Gordons, going out to finish off the Huns. You cheered like mad when they swung into the Station Square.

'What crowd of kilties is that?' Leslie asked, pulling out his notebook and fountain pen.

'That's the replacements for the Fourth Gordons,' said a chield standing by. 'For the lads they lost at Poelcappelle.'

'Poor devils,' Leslie whispered, feeling sad of a sudden. 'They look so terribly neat and tidy. Their kit's so clean and fresh looking for the job they're having to do.'

SEVENTEEN

His lance-corporal's stripe lumbered Jim with a draft of men he'd to see across the Channel. Cruising in Norfolk had done little to ready him for the Channel and Jim was sick as a dog. The equinoctial gales, the Major said, but Jim had little interest in meteorology or his draft either by that time. It was as well he'd a good grip on his rifle and his kit when he landed in dear old France.

The first news Madge received was a note: 'Arrived safely in Dear Old France. Got rid of my draft. Will write soon. Love, Jim'. Madge shook her head. Dear Jim. He wrote as if he were away at one of his scout camps. Jim was never stirred up; a drunken tramp at the Modelly or a councillor havering on about the ratepayers' silver, it was all one to Jim. Now there he was, as douce as ever, in dear old France, as he had it.

It was November when Madge got Jim's note. Two weeks past she'd been at Hazelgrove, the Websters' Big Hoose out the Montrose Road. Was it really five years since she near grat about the Christmas dance? She'd blamed Jim for that. What nonsense! Jock Webster had been there then and the dance had been for an older crowd, Webster's cronies and their wives. David had told how he'd escaped from the thing.

It was a year since Old Jock had died, and Young Alice had asked them along. They called her Young Alice, but Madge found that odd. David's mother was in her forties now. The party though was for a younger crowd, David's friends mostly.

It was a cheery night with singing and dancing. Madge played the piano and some of the lads brought out their fiddles. They frolicked about at party games, charades and the like. Teen was there of course, and young Douglas Ogg, David's friend. Douglas was flirting about with Alice, which Madge found indecent, what with the difference in their ages and David's dad not long dead. Alice was old enough to be Douglas's mother after all. Alice Goodfellow was there and Maggie Elliot, the stationy's lass. Maggie was worried about her brother John. She'd joined the VAD and was going over to France, she hoped. Maggie was all for women sharing the dangers with the men.

Madge stayed on at the end with Teen, and David brought out his autograph book. Madge inked out a picture of a lass staring, sad like, at the moon through her curtained window. The night sky in the background was inked jet black. She flipped through David's book and read a light hearted bit of nonsense young Alice had penned: 'Mary Rose went to repose – but sister Clare put a tack on her chair'.

That summed up Alice nicely, Madge thought, frivolous and full of fun. Now she'd be able to have all the fun in the world. Teen whispered that Alice was contesting her man's will and David had persuaded the trustees to be generous and make her a better settlement. That was typical of David, but Madge remembered then what Jim had said about being business-like. How would his business, the Bervie Mills, fare in the long run?

Madge wrote Jim long sentimental letters and gave him the news. Young Laurie was still quite safe in the Royal Garrison Artillery in London, a sergeant now. Dear Bert was in Ireland trying to keep things in order there, but not over happy as usual about the whole business. Albert was a corporal and had written a letter from Egypt, of all places. His wife, Annie had moved back to Bervie from Johnner with her two boys, Robert and Alick. Poor Harris was back in France with his seige artillery. Madge couldn't bring herself to respond to Jim's description of dear old France. It sounded a terrible place with those awful trenches.

Jim hadn't yet got up to the awful trenches, but he'd met up with Ginger, a biking pal he'd known in Norwich. Ginger came from Dundee and had worked alongside Jim in the paymaster's office. The two of them had had a grand time of it sailing about on the Norfolk Broads. He met up too, with another, older man who'd worked for the Council in happier days. His first name was Cameron and he came from a farm somewhere in Buchan. It had a foreign sounding name Jim never quite got the hold of. Cameron was a big man, an inch or two over six feet. Ginger argued big men like Cameron should never be sent to the trenches at all. There were bits of the trenches, he'd heard, if you didn't bend down, a sniper would clip the top of your head off. But the army made no allowances for big lads like Cameron. Yet he'd survived, though that had been a miracle. He'd been through hell the last twelve months, and was one of the few that were left of the old Fourth Battalion.

The train journey from the Channel coast was a nightmare. They suffered crowded compartments and endless waits at junctions for trains that never appeared. They had restless nights in orra transit camps they could have done well without. They thanked God Jim's draft had been whipped off him. There were 45 in their group, mostly bikers that they knew, all smartly kitted out in their Gordon Highlander uniforms, with the 'HD' badge stitched on the shoulder to show they belonged to the 51st Highland Division. Jim had never seen so many sodgers. They swarmed over the platforms and into the streets. The Colonel had been right, he thought, Jerry would never stand up to this crowd. One more push and they'd have Jerry over the Rhine. He'd soon be on that train, back to Madge and his wee office in the Cowgate. Ginger had his doubts. 'It looks like an absolute shambles to me,' he said. 'The Germans could handle things a lot better than this.'

Shambles or not, the sergeant got his 45 wide-eyed replacements from one draughty train to the next, and then on to the lorries which landed them at a camp outside a toun which had seen better days. It had a daft sounding name, Lattre-St Quentin. Jim jotted it down along with the date. It was Wednesday, 14 November, 1917. They jumped off the trucks and passed through the camp gates, the home for a short time at least, of the Fourth Battalion, The Gordon Highlanders.

The Gordons had been expecting a longer break this time. In and out of the trenches they'd been, in one stramash after another. They'd had a terrible time of it at Poelcappelle. But Jerry had pulled back from the killing fields of the Somme to a line that was the pride of the German commander. They named it after him. The Hindenburg Line was a masterpiece with its deep concrete trenches, and its deep concrete dugouts, the deepest and cosiest dugouts they'd ever built. There was not just one line of it, but three, flanked, covered and surrounded by the toughest barbed wire on earth, not the barbed wire you'd find straggling round those parks back in the Howe, but thick, coarse jagged stuff you'd never hack through with the skimpy clippers they handed you. No, the daft days of the Somme were over, they said. They'd all settled down for the winter, Jerry as well as ourselves. So what was this tale these keen young lads had brought out with them, about one last push across the Rhine?

Cameron had a laugh at that. Jim and Ginger had dumped their gear and collapsed on to the beds next to his, fagged out and exhausted with all the humping and jostling they'd been through. This hut would suit them fine. They'd get a rest and a long lie at last, thank God.

Cameron, as well, had thought the battalion would be getting a break, and this Lattre-St Quentin place had looked fine enough at the start. But he'd a feel for things, had Cameron, and was scunnered with what he'd seen. The generals would be looking on the Fourth as a fresh battalion now with all these new lads still turning up. They'd been arriving since he'd got here, with their bright, eager looking faces. It was just a sodger's luck for Cameron and the lads that were left to be moving up the line again with this bright, keen looking bunch of boy scouts! Jim eyed the craggy-looking Aberdonian sitting there on the next bed. A settled sort of man, he looked, in his forties, maybe. He'd a typical Aberdeen look about him, Jim thought, the kind of face you'd see any Saturday night at the market off the Castlegate. He was a big rangy chield with a long, lantern-jawed face. His flappy ears stuck out sideways from his rough granite-like cheeks, and a wee brown mouser sprouted beneath his long Aberdeen nose. Once upon a time, Jim imagined, his eyes had shone with an Aberdeen sparkle, but they were dull now and tired looking. Jim was just dropping off, when Cameron stirred himself. Cameron glowered at the two of them, fair forfochtin they were, the two lads lying there. So they thought this was a rest camp they'd arrived at. He'd soon put them right on that score.

'You arrived a day late, lads,' he glinted, giving his mowser a twitch. 'The holiday was yestreen. The whole 51st got the day off to celebrate. It was November the thirteenth,' he added, by way of explanation.

'And what the hell has November the thirteenth got to do with it?' asked Ginger, opening his eyes. Ginger's language had got steadily worse, Jim noticed, once they had landed in Dieppe.

'The first anniversary of Beaumont-Hamel,' said Cameron, fair annoyed. 'As big a soss as any other, but the head billies made a bit of a caper of it. We'd the day to ourselves yestreen. The Brigade laid on a Sports Day, and we'd a slap up meal and a concert at the end. Oh you missed yourselves lads. It's back to hard graft the morn.'

They fell asleep after that, but that night they knew they'd be up early for manoeuvres the next day. Like Jim, Cameron had been an Auld Kirk man back home, but what comfort he'd had from that religion was hard to tell. There was no bitterness when he spoke, resignation more, just an acceptance maybe, of the whole bloody business.

'Na, na, Jim lad,' he said, when Jim asked him how it was. 'The less said about that bit soss, the better.' But he said it in a tired kind of way. There was little need to upset the young lads there beside him.

Next day was a Thursday and Cameron was proved right. They were rushed off to a place named Noyellette, a short run on the lorries. Then they'd a day of it, just as they'd had back there in Norfolk, and that seemed a bit odd, attacking and deploying in open country in artillery formations. What was it those men from the Front had said about that being more fit for Flodden than the Western Front? A young officer from Aberdeenshire was in charge of their platoon, a fine, strapping lad, as keen as you'd find. He'd been through the worst, said Cameron. He didn't look the kind would be training them for Flodden. Cameron could make little sense of the thing.

It was much the same again on Friday, but later in the day, they got some time to themselves. It made Cameron more wary than ever. They could watch the football game, they were told. Cameron nodded at that.

'We'll dander along and see how they get on, The battalion's got a grand team. It's the div. championships. Last week we beat a team from 255 Brigade in the second round. That was down at Acheux and we won 5–3.'

The three of them dandered across to the playing fields, pleased enough to get some time to themselves, though Jim felt he could have done with a laze in the hut. It was time he wrote another letter to Madge. The match was against the sixth battalion of the Black Watch, so there should be a bit of fun there. Right enough, some truck-loads of the Black Watch were rolling up singing Dundee songs and making odd cracks about the teuchters from the north.

It was a dry, cold day, and hundreds had turned up, jostling and enjoying a fair bit of fun when the teams ran on to the pitch. The three of them found a place on some high ground further back, and at first they'd a good laugh and gave a cheer or two when their team got the ball. But the lads from the Black Watch scored early on and then a sharp wind sprang up. Jim could see that Ginger was restless. Cameron too, was stamping his feet and glowering at the sky. When the Black Watch scored their fourth goal, Cameron had had enough. 'I'm off,' he said. 'There are better ways of passing a Friday than catching your death at a caper like this.'

The Black Watch team had just scored their fifth goal when they pushed their way through a crowd of their supporters, laughing and cheering at the edge of the crowd.

'Can they no teach you to play fitba' in Aiberdeen,' shouted a cocky wee sodger, egged on by some of his mates. A big lad beside him turned to Cameron with a wide smirk on his face, and in a voice straight from the mills of Lochee asked, 'Wha' shot the cheese then?'

Cameron turned round in the slow, teuchter way he had and, taking another draw on his woodbine while they all waited, nodded canny-like, then speired back in his droll Buchan drawl, 'Oh aye, and wha' was it snickit the barbit wire?'

'What the hell was that all about?' asked Ginger.

'Oh just a wee game they play with the Gordons,' Cameron grinned. 'The tale is that one of our staff sergeants opened fire on a big cheese he saw lying at the side of the road. Thought it was a Jerry.'

'And what about the barbed wire?' asked Jim, determined to get at all of the facts.

'Oh Jerry was short o' barbit wire one nicht,' said Cameron, 'so he crawled across and snickit the lot frae the Black Watch. At least, that's the way we heard it.'

Ginger threw a look at Cameron; a weird bunch those lads from the north.

But that was the end of the holiday. That night they'd a busy time of it. The battalion's transport set off at half past ten with all the heavy gear. Next day, Saturday the seventeenth, the Fourth Gordons left their cosy huts at Lattre-St Quentin and headed for the Front. At four in the afternoon they boarded a train at Beaumetz bound for Bapaume.

A quietness came on them as they tramped through the rubble of the place they'd called Bapaume. The whole toun was in ruins. They tramped on, going south all the while, to a camp at a place near Beaulencourt, and they stayed there the night. The days that followed were marching days, mostly in the dark. They were close to the Front now, and the odd thump of a shell a deal closer and harder to bear. It was true then, what you'd heard. With Jerry dug in safe and pleased like in those concrete dugouts, there was little chance of anything starting up till the winter frosts had passed.

On Sunday night, the eighteenth, the battalion tramped in the dark late and arrived at their next camp at eleven. They'd named the camp Littlewood. Maybe the French name had been overmuch for them to handle. The huts were near invisible from the road, being so smothered in camouflage nets, and the whole crowd of them needed little encouragement to throw themselves on to the beds. It had been a long, bothersome sort of day, so they slept well on through the Monday. There was little rush to get them up, for that was to be the last real sleep they'd have until the whole bloody business was over. They spent the whole of that Monday inside, listening to the regular crump of the shells. Most of them were far off, but every now and then, there would be a whistling roar and a crash like a clap of thunder would rattle the windows and make some of them loup. Jim and Ginger got a bit excited at times. Were they really going to chase Jerry back over the Rhine? Cameron tried to dampen things down. They looked so keen; he owed it to them to keep things steady. Excited capers had ever only one kind of ending, he'd seen it often enough when he'd first come out.

Ginger tried to explain that it would be different this time. Jerry was ready to crack at last and they were off now to give him his last final shove. Cameron nodded quietly. So that was the way of it. He'd heard that tale before, but he held his peace. Yet, things did look different, Jim and Ginger were convinced of that; all that practising they'd had, out in open country, the kind of manoeuvres they'd practised – daft-like said the older men – back there in Norfolk. Cameron admitted this was new but it made little sense. He set off to speir at some of his cronies if the top brass had gone clean skite. Cameron knew one or two officer lads from his own corner of the world that had spent the last year with him, in and out of the trenches.

Back he came with a new look in his eyes, the first real sparkle Jim had seen since he'd met him. 'We are going to capture Cambrai,' he whispered. 'We've got four hundred new tanks and they're going to chairge the barbit wire. We'll just walk in behind and step over the Hindenboorg.'

The Hindenburg line? With tanks? Could it be true? It was only daft generals sent men to the wire and the machine guns at this time of the year.

Jerry's Hindenburg was wide and deep, three lines of it, and he'd settled down for the winter which had made you wonder what the Colonel had been raving on about when he'd said all he needed was one last big shove. Well, here was the answer – tanks!

'Have we ever used tanks?' Ginger asked. He'd heard the rumours, but thought the things unlikely, something out of H G Wells, he'd thought.

'I've never seen any,' said Cameron. 'They used two or three on the Somme, but they made a real hash of things and they stuck in the mud. They tell me this lot are different. They've got hundreds of them. But maybe we'd better wait and see,' he added, gloomy again.

They hadn't that long to wait. The rumours were wild, but soon most had a fair notion of what was on the go. Later that day, they were handed out their battle stores. They were in earnest.

'Here we go, lads,' said Cameron when they loaded him up. But there was time enough yet and they made the most of that rest. It was three o'clock on the Tuesday morning when they all tramped out in the dark, weighed down with all the kit and ammunition they were ever likely to need.

It was a weird, uncanny business when the mist closed in on them. Things were different now. They'd been threatened, a bit uncouthlike, with shooting if they as much as lit a fag or spoke above a whisper. The road was staked out with posts and tapes. A military policeman would loom up out of the mirky swirl with a shaded lantern at times and there was the feel that other men were on the move besides themselves. It was ghost like, and even Jim, who aye laughed at such tales, began to wonder if there could be any truth in the supernatural. There was a cough here and a stumble there. The mist deadened the din, but times they heard it, a deep trudging noise it was, as though hundreds of boots were thumping away over there in the fog.

But it helped. Their battalion, a thousand men maybe, had company. There were other battalions beside them, the whole brigade would be there. Jim kept himself going, rehearsing the statistics he'd studied back in Norwich. It made sense to know the facts, and army facts were little different from facts about ratepayers and councils. Four battalions made a brigade, he knew. Theirs was 154 Brigade, so there would be three other battalions there beside themselves. Ginger had gone up ahead the last time they'd stopped, but Cameron and Jim were taking it nice and steady like. One of them would give a whispered grunt at times. They'd to stick close and keep near to the tape. The mist made things worse, but it had pleased the Colonel. Jerry wasn't that far up in front. There was little gunfire, just an odd machine gun rattled away, far off in the fog.

They were a part of the 51st Division, of course, and that was three brigades. Jim made a rapid calculation. 'Twelve battalions, over 12,000 men,' he whispered to Cameron.

'Aye, and the rest,' whispered Cameron. 'You've all the support companies a division has. But we're not attacking Jerry with one div, Jim lad. You're now a member of General Byng's Third Army, and God knows how many divisions that's got.'

Jim was quiet at that. How many divisions made up an army was something he'd never checked up on when he'd thumbed through the manual back in Norwich. The mist lifted at times and, even in the dark, they saw this land had been stripped clean. The road they were on had been re-laid and the shell holes filled in. The trees still standing were stunted and bare. Those mounds of stones had been homes once, with mothers and bairns, and they passed the ruins in silence, just one more place turned into rubble. So on they went, trudging and resting, resting and trudging. It was a quarter to five the next morning when they reached it, a couthy wee toun they'd once called Metz. Now it was a sea of tents, looming up there in the greyness, the sappers and the pioneers had put up earlier that night. They were still struggling with the camouflage nets as they moved in.

'Changed days,' grunted Cameron. 'They'll be putting up beds for us next.'

Ginger worked his way through a mob of men. He was grinning. 'They're giving us cooked food. There are field kitchens just across the road.'

'You're joking,' said Cameron, who'd never seen kitchens that near the Front. Maybe things had changed since Harris had first come out. Jim wondered about that. But Ginger wasn't joking. They were to eat early, for this was the day of the attack. There were shaded lanterns stuck on poles, but not a peep of light escaped the tent. They shuffled and guttered in the gloom, making a din like the shooch of the sea, before it was their turn to feed. Now that was a feed. They could see it in the brighter lights of the tented canteen. There were lashings of hot tea and bread and butter, but what really perked them up were the huge platefuls of thick stew.

'That's the best burgoo I've seen since I joined the army,' said Cameron. It was a mixture of well cooked beef mixed with vegetables.

'None of your French horse meat here lads,' he murmured, 'that's good Aberdeen beef. The best.'

The whole crowd munched on in contented silence. More than one company in here, reckoned Jim, at his sums again. This burgoo stuff would go down well with his scouts next time they were camped at Arbuthnott. There was no hurry to the meal. The CO of the 51st must be a deal better at his job than others he'd heard about. No sense in dishing up good meat then spoiling it with a bit of panic. Before they moved out, the Colonel came in and spoke, low and friendly like, but crisp and clear, to tell them the tale. They were to stick there in the place they'd called Metz till the order came to move on. Then half the brigade, themselves and the 7th Argyll and Sutherland Highlanders, would set off quietly to a place up the line, another heap of ruins, by the name of Trescault and that would be their starting point. The attack would start at 6.20 a.m. Their job was to move down the brae when they got the order, and occupy their own Front Line. By that time Jerry would be on the run, for at 6.20 a.m. the tanks would have crashed through the Hindenburg wire and the two other brigades of the 51st, up there in front, would have crossed over behind them. Their job was to follow up and take over the trenches they'd left behind. He paused at that. This was not going to be another Somme, he said quietly. The Third Army was going in on a six mile front from Arras to St Quentin with a battering ram of four hundred tanks. They had 72 with their own division and they were to catch Jerry sudden like. There would be no long artillery warning, the guns would start when the tanks started, something that had never been tried before. The important thing now was to keep total silence – and no smoking.

'Good luck, lads,' said the Colonel. 'God be with you.'

Jim scribbled the date down on the back of an old envelope. Back in Bervie he'd a habit of writing things on old envelopes. November, 20th, 1917, he wrote.

It was after six by the time they got all their gear and mustered in the dark. Jim remembered his English class in Dollar. What was it Henry the Fifth had said before the battle of Agincourt? 'And gentlemen in England, now a-bed Shall think themselves accursed they were not here And hold their manhoods cheap whiles any speaks That fought with us upon Saint Crispin's day'.

Jim laughed quietly to himself. He was becoming more of a romantic every day he thought. If dear Madge could hear him now. But nothing

99

could stop this great army with all its tanks. He drew the line though at crying out as Shakespeare had it: 'God for Harry! England and Saint George!'

The English were here too though, in great strength along with the 51st. Cameron had found that out. Over on their right, in the next sector, were the East Surreys, the Buffs, the West Kents, the Queens and many others. It was an all-British show this time. Near four hundred tanks! It wouldn't be Agincourt they'd talk about in the years to come, but the turning point of the War, the time the Fourth Gordons and the rest of them smashed the Hindenburg Line at the battle for Cambrai!

On they trudged. Fanciful notions flit through a man's head at times like that. Jim thought of that time Madge sat beside him on David's Rock. That was another world now, a world when the sun shone out on Bervie's Bay and the blue of the North Sea. Here the road was churned and pitted, the chalk of it glinting at times as the mist lifted and the first glimmer of a new day broke through. On and on they trundled, every man with his own dreams, his own notion of things and his place in it all.

They were jolted out of their dreaming. The column had halted and were settling down behind some ruins. They waited there in the lee of some bricks. It was near twenty past six and daylight was filtering in. Jim could just make out the shape of a man at about 50 yards. It was cold and dank and he started to shiver. Odd bursts of gunfire broke the quiet for a time, sporadic, normal, somebody mumbled, for a quiet night. After a year of suicidal attacks, neither the enemy nor themselves expected an attack at this time of the year. They'd all dug themselves in and settled down until the spring!

An officer close by started to whisper the seconds away. 'Four, three, two, one, zero.' He was dead on time. All hell broke loose. The guns were behind them, one thousand, or was it two thousand the Colonel had said, the biggest and most concentrated artillery barrage in history. Jerry must be getting the shock of his life, deep bunkers or no deep bunkers. The black sky was streaked with stabbing shafts of light. It was like a roll of gigantic drums, but it was more than that, and it was on both sides of them, for six miles, they'd said. Up above, the shells howled like fiends out of Hell. The pain of the noise drilled through them and they covered their ears and swallowed.

Then it happened. The tension snapped and men everywhere burst into a babble of chatter and shouting. The whole battalion spoke and nobody listened. There was no need for quietness now. They had a few minutes of that before the order came and up they got. It was then they saw the tanks looming high out of the fog. They were like huge lumbering toads, their camouflage gone and their engines roaring, smoke belching from the exhausts and swirling with the mist. There were huge mounds of stores too, strung along by the roadside, still hidden under their netting. The sappers and the pioneers had been busy right up to the edge. And there were horses, hundreds of horses standing in the wood over to the left. The cavalry were there. Jim and Cameron exchanged a look. Cavalry?

The shell barrage stopped as suddenly as it had started. The tanks were going in and they could hear the rattle of machine guns and the thump of the German artillery on the open land out there in front. The Fourth Battalion was resting now. The first huge tank attack in history had started. It would be their turn next!

EIGHTEEN

It was daylight now, and they could peer over the ground which sloped away down there in front. It was chalky and churned, and there, clear in the brighter air, were the snake-like marks of the two Front Lines and the places where the wire had been dragged away like so many strips of old curtains. The tanks had done there work. Some had dropped wooden bundles on to the wider trenches and rumbled over. One or two had stuck, but away beyond, they could see other tanks, rovers the Colonel had called them, climbing the slopes out in front. They'd burst through the front line of the Hindenburg. Swarms of German prisoners were at the foot of the slope, down there below. Their hands were in the air.

By ten o'clock, the Argylls and the Gordons had taken over the old Front Line. Up in front a battle was raging, the trouble coming from the top of a long sloping ridge ahead. Guns were firing from a line of trees on the summit and giving the tanks a hard time of it.

Cameron lifted himself up to have a better look. 'That's a devil of a thing,' he said, 'I wouldn't like to be with the lads facing that bit of wood.'

'That's Flesquières,' said a voice behind him. It was the young lieutenant again, he'd been with Cameron on the last stramash. 'There's a small château behind those trees we'll have to get hold of.'

Cameron nodded at that bit of helpful news, but gave the lieutenant a grin. They'd been through some hard times together.

'Here we go again, Cameron,' the lieutenant muttered in a strong Aberdeen tongue. Then he turned about and rumbled along the trench.

'That's Douglas Leith,' said Cameron, 'an Auld Kirk man like yoursel. His father's minister at Meldrum. A university man, of course. A great athlete back in Aberdeen; a long distance runner.'

Jim looked at the retreating lieutenant. He'd always had a friendly word for them, and he certainly knew his job. He'd have to have a crack with that young Aberdonian when he'd a chance. But this was not the time. The rattle of guns could be heard the rest of that day and they could see some more of the tanks had been knocked out, some were still burning. Ginger counted five in all. Injured men staggered or were carried back over the trench, but with them came crowds of prisoners. The word was the attack had gone well on the left and on the right but this Flesquières place was holding things up.

They huddled down for the night and Cameron introduced them to the daft ways of life in the trenches.

'No lashings of hot burgoo tonight then,' said Ginger.

'No lad,' said Cameron, 'but this chalk-like ground's a deal better than the mud and slime we had on the Somme.'

Jim counted his blessings for that and gave up a bit prayer. He made no great display of his religion, but the habit was with him still, and he seldom forgot a quiet prayer at the day's end. Maybe there was no mud and no gunfire just then, but sleeping rough in this weather could bring on double pneumonia or worse. He was put on guard and on out-post duty for a while, then down he got into the dug-out, cluttered and evil smelling, but at least it was warm, and soon he was fast asleep.

Sometime before six they were roused, and by half-past six that morning, 21 November – Jim wrote it down – the Fourth Gordons moved up out of the trench, and crossed the no-man's-land between the old front lines. The barbed wire had been cleared and the 7th Argylls moved forward with them, over on their left. The 9th Royal Scots, the third battalion in the brigade were following right behind. They crossed the empty front trench of the Hindenburg Line and marched on as far as the railway embankment below Flesquières and its château. The battalion stuck there for an hour and then they got the news, Jerry had slipped away from the château in the dark. The tanks had stormed ahead on either side of him, and he'd seen he was being surrounded.

Cameron said that casualties had been light, but they looked bad enough. Burnt out tanks stood around at strange angles and sad looking bundles had been covered over. Batches of weary but relieved looking prisoners passed them on their way back down the line. There was a noise of gunfire, but it was far off in the direction of Cambrai. It was still only half past eight in the morning when the battalion received its orders to move forward with the 7th Argyll and Sutherland Highlanders over on their left. It was their turn to move to the battle zone.

Trudging on over open country in broad daylight was a strange thing. A Jerry plane, its big black crosses sharp and clear, dived down on them with its guns blazing and they dived for cover. Nobody was hit. All four companies of the battalion moved forward at a steady pace. Strange to think this had been enemy land yesterday at sunrise, but the debris of battle left little doubt about that. This was a different kind of march, not the eerie, uncanny tramping of night time, nor the usual kind of march they'd often made, with marching songs and uncouth choruses to keep their spirits up. This march had a mark of belligerence about it. The men were quiet, every man had things of his own to think about.

Round a bend, they came on what seemed a whole army, straddled along the road and over the fields on either side. Most were flat out on the ground. Tents had been pushed up in places, and machine gunners stood guard, their guns pointed skywards.

'That's some of the brigade from Flekeer,' grunted Cameron. 'We're going out in front of them now.'

'Steady the Black Watch. Let the Gordons past,' yelled a sergeant ahead of them, and a crowd of men moved off the road. Jim felt a tingle of pride at that as they swung along through the resting men. Heads were higher now, and strange, there was none of the usual banter as they passed. The thing was too grim for that, and the men of the Black Watch looked shattered. There were Gordons, too, in the crowds they passed.

'Fifth or Seventh Gordons in that brigade,' growled Cameron, who'd seen a well-kent face in the distance.

The whole battalion spread out as they moved in on Cantaing village. Behind them were the 9th Royal Scots and the 4th Seaforths, the other battalions of the Brigade. The Argylls had been diverted to the village of

Anneux.

Holding a line in front of Cantaing were two battalions, the 5th Seaforths and the 8th Argylles. The battalion halted and a reconnaissance was made before they crossed over. It was the turn of the Fourth Gordons to mount an attack.

At 10.30 a.m., C and D companies edged forward slowly, with A and B companies close behind. They'd gone some distance when a fierce burst of rifle and machine gun fire signalled they'd gone close enough. Some mortar shells were falling harmlessly short in front. A double belt of barbed wire about fifteen yards deep stopped any thought the Colonel might have had of asking them to rush the place. The machine gun positions were well protected and Jerry would have deep dugouts as well to secure his defenders, for this was part of the third line of the Hindenburg. The one thing the battalion needed now was missing, for the main tank force had by-passed Cantaing and rumbled on to their main objectives, Fontaine and Bourlon Wood. Once these had been taken, the way was open to take Cambrai itself – so they'd planned it.

There was nothing for it but to lie low. Any move was met with a massive hail of machine-gun and mortar fire, so they waited. It was about twelve noon when they saw them, six tanks lumbering up from the direction of Premy Chapel. There was a moment's pause, then all the months of open country warfare they'd rehearsed back there in Norfolk was put into operation. The tanks charged the wire, firing as they went, and then in they went, the Fourth Gordons. The first rush was easy with Jerries being passed back, their hands in the air. After that it was text book stuff, from house to house.

Jim's heart was pounding when his turn came. Up he got and rushed with the rest. There was little time to think, he was back in Norfolk again and this was the drill, cover and charge, cover and charge. They leapfrogged each other in groups, bullets whining past. Men were hit, but Jim's life and the lives of most of his platoon seemed charmed. When he covered for others he'd little notion of shooting at anybody. It was rapid fire to keep their heads down. Then it was his turn to charge. The dead and the dying littered the street, but the months of practice focussed his thoughts on the next part of the action.

Excitement and noise and the sight of surrendering Germans kept him going through the heat of it all, and most of the village was soon in the hands of the battalion, the tanks rumbling off to deal with the fighting further on. One company was held for a while at the south western end of the village. The enemy had a firm hold of some trenches and a sunken road there, so a couple of heavy guns were brought in to dislodge them. But still they held on. At last a tank on its way to Fontaine was diverted and it was soon all over. By three o'clock, just three hours after the first assault, the whole of Cantaing was under the control of the Fourth Gordons. B and D companies went into the trenches to the North and North East, A and C companies linked up with men of the 29th Division who'd been moving up on their right flank. They'd done it! The new Fourth Battalion had won its first engagement, and captured its first wee village, just as the old regular army sergeants had trained them to do.

The reaction set in then. Bodies of men they'd known and men they hadn't known were everywhere. The screams of men from both sides still rang in their ears. Jim suddenly pushed a handkerchief to his mouth. He took a deep breath and saw the faces of the men beside him. In time they'd harden maybe, but now they, too, looked white and tight lipped. He wiped the sweat from his face. Cameron, at the far end of the trench, edged his way along to join him. It was quiet now although a battle was raging over to the west and north where the Argylls and the Seaforths had headed.

'All right Jim lad,' said Cameron, a man of few words, and he pressed a hand on Jim's elbow. 'We just wait here till the relief comes. They'll be cleaning up the place behind.'

Cleaning up, Jim realised, was Cameron's way of explaining how the wounded would be moved. The dead would wait a bit longer. Slowly his pulse settled down and his touch of sickness passed. It was Cameron now who chatted quietly and brought things back to a steady state. They were joined further along the defensive trench by men of the cavalry they'd passed on the way up, a squadron of the Queens Bays and a squadron of the 9th Cavalry Brigade.

'Without their horses, thank God,' said Cameron.

Then it was really over. The 9th Royal Scots from their own Brigade arrived and took over their trench. Back down from the Cantaing trenches they went. Ginger joined the two of them with a relieved look on his freckled face. All three of them had made it.

'Thank God we'd the tanks,' said Ginger.

'Aye lad,' said Cameron, his eyes a bit moist, 'if only we'd had them a year back.'

But there were jobs still to be done. A quick roll call was made and the prisoners handed out. They'd taken over 300 prisoners, and Jim got six into his care. They seemed decent young lads, now he'd time to look at them. No different to look at than any of his own crowd, and none of them looked anything like the cartoons of Huns he'd been looking at for the last three years. He passed a fag on to one of them who was trying out some polite words in English. It struck Jim as they all headed off, back down the line, he was taking more care of his prisoners than he'd done with the draft of Gordons he'd been lumbered with to cross the Channel.

The men of the Fourth Battalion that night were elated. They were dead beat of course, and shocked at the bloodiness of it all, but they'd really done it! Their leap-frog attacks, practised so often they'd become a bit of a game at times, had actually won the day!

'With the help of the tanks,' Cameron reminded them again.

The new Fourth Battalion could stand alongside the rest of the 51st. The whole of the 51st basked in the glory. Back home the news had spread that General Byng and his Third Army had won a famous victory at last. The Hindenburg Line had been breached on a six mile front and penetrated to a depth of six miles, yes, six whole miles. The thing was unheard of, six miles in one day! No wonder they rang out the church bells in London when the news got through. 'Byng's Boys' as the newspaper billies called them had shown the world what our lads could do!

'The old Colonel was right after all,' said Jim a few days later. It was the 26 November and he had quite recovered. After a few false alarms, when they'd to stop and man the defences, the battalion had been pulled back to their rest camp at Buire. The entire 51st were resting in the area around the toun of Baizieux which was close by.

'This is the turning point of the whole war,' Jim declared, 'We'll be crossing the Rhine any day now, Cameron, you'll see.'

But Cameron was not a man to be taken in by all the back slapping that had been going on, and he looked as dour as ever. He shook his head. 'I doubt it Jim lad,' he said. 'We'll all be seeing a bit more of that Flekeer place before the damned thing is over and done with.'

NINETEEN

Cameron was right, of course. The 51st Highland Division had been relieved by the Guards and were settling in at their rest camps near Baizieux, out of the battle lands at last. That flat, dreich bit of Northern France was little better than the land between Bapaume and Flesquières, but you could make out a street with a shop or a café maybe, sometimes a kirk even, standing straight above the dirt. As Cameron pointed out though, 'You'd get mair conveevial capers on a wet Monday in Cairnbulg than you'd find in those blasted villes.'

The weather was foul, splatters of rain or swirling fog could send you scuttling back to your hut. For all that, there was scarce a man but was not in better fettle that day. It was 30 November, St Andrew's Day, and the CO had promised a grand meal and a wild night of it by way of celebration. They needed cheering up and St Andrew's Day made a fine excuse for that. The supplies were in and the kitchens were bubbling away with a meal which would shame a highland wedding. They'd have *beaucoup* French *bière* and plenty of lemonade for the odd characters; Good Templars like Jim and the other thrawn Scots, who never drank what was good for them.

'Thank God for Uncle Harper,' Cameron nodded, 'if the generals Doon Sooth had half his gumption, the war would have ended years ago.'

The commanding officer of the 51st, General Harper, took a personal interest in his men. As often as not, he was up at the Front blethering away about things back home, with officers or privates, it made little odds to Uncle Harper.

Jim and Cameron were huddled by a red hot stove, enjoying what Scots like best when they're contented and in a big hearted mood. They were educating a Sassenach into the capers folk got up to north of the border. Mike, a young Englishman from Norwich, had asked them why Saint Andrew was so special when, as he saw it, most Scots were presbyterians and had little time for saints and ill-got Catholic relics like that. So they were hard at it, and enjoying themselves fine. A great night was in store,

107

and Cameron knew for a fact that loads of Aberdeen beef had arrived the day before.

Cameron and Jim never quite convinced Mike with a tale that made much sense. They were just coming to the convincing part, when the whole battalion was flung into the wildest carfuffle. The lazy peace of the day was ended, first by a bugle note far out at the edge of their dreich encampment. Men cocked their lugs at that, moved their buttocks, gave a bit stretch but did little else. Then the whistles started up, an odd peep to begin with, then fast they came, a whole damned chorus of whistles and shouts and a banging of doors.

'Damn them to Hell,' Cameron growled. Officers and NCOs were charging through the place, barking out their orders, buttoning up their coats. The sappy grins were disappearing fast. Out they tumbled. Cameron refused to budge, but he joined them in the end, shivering and forming up in the November gloom, in platoons and in companies. There was a bit of a muddle, of course, but things got sorted out. They'd to move, quick and fast, at the double and back again for more orders, in full marching kit. After all that bloody carry on, all those tanks, all that stramash and all the celebrations – Jerry had broken through!

The Cambrai Victory that turned into a debacle would be turned over in the months and years to come. The generals blamed their commanders, the politicians blamed the generals, and the men at the Front, as you'd expect, blamed the lads at the back. Tempers were roused in parliament. Lloyd George got mad at Haig, his Chief of Staff. The thing was, they'd punched a fine sized hole through the Hindenburg, but they needed another half million men to flood through and fan out on the other side. But they'd lost all those sodgers on the Somme the year before. The Jerries now had men in plenty, arriving by the train load, at Cambrai station, they were, fine pleased to get clear of the coarse times they'd had on the Russian Front. When 'Byng's Boys' had run out of steam, there were thousands of Jerries, willing and able, to pour into the place and give them all hell.

Cameron and Jim and Ginger and the rest had little time to worry about high strategy. It was enough that their St Andrew's meal was near ready and here they were on the road again, back to the old Front Line. Whoever did eat that St Andrew's Day meal has never yet been sorted out, but not scrap of it reached the men of the Fourth Battalion.

By five o'clock that evening they'd to be on board that train and heading for Bapaume, back to the place they'd started from less than two weeks before. By next day, 1 December, two battalions were back in the old front line, and by 2 December, two whole brigades of the 51st were further on still, in the spacious trenches and dugouts of the deserted Hindenburg. They'd to hold the line firm for the 56th Division, falling back before the swarms of Jerries. Over to their right, Jerry had broken right through and gone beyond the place he'd run from the day the tanks had gone in.

Back home the arguments started and there were red faces at the ringing of the victory bells. 'Where's your Byng's Boys now?' smirked the rest of the Jocks and the Tommies. The newspaper billies kept quiet about that. Up front though, Uncle Harper started straightening the line. He pulled some of his sodgers back from the Hindenburg to cover his flanks, but he was determined on one thing: they were to hang on to the Flesquières ridge and the bit of the Hindenburg that had held them up at the start.

So there they were, Jim and Ginger, Cameron and his cheery lieutenant, Douglas Leith from Meldrum. They were all back there with the rest of the Fourth Battalion, high up on Flesquières hill. The trouble was, that damned ridge Cameron had brooded over, was now sticking out, well in front of all the rest, glowering down on the German lines. Those Jerries from the Russian Front, had proved Cameron right, but a lot sooner than he'd imagined. They were all seeing a lot more of the damned place than they'd bargained for.

In the solid safety of Aberdeen's granite grey streets, the Russian collapse caused a stir of a different sort.

'They're setting up an Aberdeen Soviet tonight,' said George. 'We'd better get down there real early.'

George MacDonald, the landlady's son, was a sixteen year old reporter like Leslie. He was from a rival newspaper, but Leslie and George got on fine. The more folk you knew in the newspaper business the better. The two of them prowled the shipyards and the docks among all the odd looking ships, zig-zagged and daft looking in their war-time camouflage. Leslie would hunt down the weirdest chields from places like Russia and Poland and they'd spin him their tales.

Aberdeen was fitting in fine with Leslie's plans. Along Union Terrace he'd stare, fair impressed, at that grand statue of William Wallace clutching his muckle sword, his left hand pointing to His Majesty's Theatre just over the road. He was more impressed still by those stirring Wallace words carved round the plinth. Best of all though, were the socialist billies who climbed up there and ranted on about the war.

But this was news of a different sort. This was real action at last. 'We'll get down there at the start,' he nodded to George.

Leslie's eyes were shining. This was what he'd been reading about in all those revolutionary books and pamphlets. He'd a fair collection now, picked up from those scruffy wee shops huddled behind the hospital on Woolmanhill.

What a night they had of it. The cleck at the meeting was all about Karl Marx and Lenin, and grand folk like that. It was fell late before they finished and stormed up the Market Street brae, their slouch hats bent against a burst of sleet. The two of them could speak of little else. Leslie found it hard enough sleeping most nights, turning over all the excitements of the day. He would have little chance of sleeping this night. These were great times they were living in, the two of them. They chattered on about capitalism and the working classes, about life itself, freedom, oppression and revolution. They scarce noticed the burst of wet snow that was soaking their legs, and it was only at the last that they saw the two young prostitutes blocking the pavement.

'No, no,' said Leslie, amazed at the interruption. 'We've got work to do.'

That sounded a bit daft-like, in the glare of the night lights at the top of the Market Street brae. The wet granite blocks of Union Street looked bleak and threatening. At that time of night the toun was deserted but for the two hopeful prostitutes and a shivering bobby making his way to the Castlegate. Leslie noticed they were painted and powdered for the work they'd got in mind. He smelt a whiff of gin as he crossed the street behind a late night tram, clanging its way to the depot. Douce Aberdonians would all be tucked up in bed by now.

'Bastards. Awa' hame to your mithers,' one of the quines shouted. She slunk back into safety of the shop doorway.

The chief reporter had some coarser words than that when Leslie pushed his way into the *Journal* office with his copy for the day.

'And what about that Soviet crowd then,' the chief reporter growled. He'd just tossed some stuff into the wastepaper bin. It was a piece Leslie had taken some time over. A crewman had spun him the yarn for a few pints of beer in the harbour tavern.

'Oh, that!' Leslie was taken aback, and a bit confused. 'I can't write about that,' he stuttered, getting red and wondering how to tell it. 'You see, I've become a member. In fact they've gone and elected me on to the Aberdeen Soviet Council. They've sworn me to secrecy.'

TWENTY

Madge got the oddest collection of Christmas cards that year. In they poured with their messages of goodwill to all men, decorated with their regimental badges and their pictures of rifles and bayonets. Madge showed them to Father and he shook his head. Jim's Christmas card to Madge was the best of the bunch, and she kept it all her days. It was such a bonny Christmas card. On front it had a shield and crossed swords, with 1917 and 'Scotland For Ever' written underneath. On the back was a kilted sodger silhouetted against the sunset, his hand resting on the bayonet of an upturned rifle. Inside was some bonny art-work in pastel shades of red and green. On the left, framed in a strip of regimental tartans, a shield at each corner, was a pretty scene of kilted sodgers advancing with their bayonets towards a castle on a ridge at sunset.

'Flekeer, without a doubt,' Cameron had grinned when Jim had bought it. There were wee white puffs in the sky with a red dot in each, looking for all the world like the lights on a Christmas tree. On the right, was another bonny Christmas scene in different shades of pale green. Five trig artillery tents were spaced out with their guns sending out wee white puffs, their seasonal greeting to the tinted horizon. Underneath in Christmas lettering were the words, '1917 Greetings'. Jim had inscribed in neat black ink, 'From Jim, with fondest love and best wishes'.

In dear old France, Jim lay planning his concerts and his Games, his Burns Supper, his kirk picnics and socials, his scout camps and his football clubs for the year after next. On Christmas Day, the place was carpeted a damnable white. The snow showed them up to the pilots of the Gothas who came and straffed the Jocks just for the hell of it.

The Fourth Gordons had the good luck to be out of the trenches on Christmas Day. They had a special dinner that night, so Cameron and the rest got their *beaucoup* French *bière* at last, glasses brimming over with the stuff. They made up for the St Andrew's Day caper with legs and wings of chickens and turkeys. They pulled crackers and ate nuts, hoping all the time the fish net across their party hut would fool those pilots. Inside there were coloured streamers and candles. Dozens of Christmas-like biscuit tins were opened and handed round for greedy sodger hands to grab.

The Christmas Day meal was a deal better than they'd have had at Christmastime back in Buchan or the Mearns. An English caper, but none the worse for that. They'd soup before the chicken and turkey. Then came the plum pudding, carried in with a wee blue flame on top. Pipers played and a brass band struck up Colonel Bogie. The wilder lads hooched away at eightsome reels and foursome reels and the highland scottische and Rory o' More. They capered about with waltzes and foxtrots and sang songs in between times or listened to recitations and yarns. The battalion CO wished them well and said they'd be having their next Christmas dinner in dear old Blighty, wherever that might be. After singing Auld Lang Syne and God Save the King, the words sounding much the same with the French *bière* inside them, they stottered over the snow, back to their camouflaged huts.

The New Year capers were different though. A crowd of the Fourth Gordons had a treat, as they called it, in the Scottish Churches tent. Jim had a crack with Lieutenant Douglas Leith, the cheery lad from Meldrum. They blethered on for a while, about the war and the kirk, but could make little sense of the thing.

Leslie Mitchell had more urgent affairs in hand. He'd made his peace with the head reporter. Glowering through his glass partition in his corner of the reporters' room, the old devil speired if Leslie needed to take Sundays off.

'No, no,' Leslie was adamant on that. 'Sundays, weekdays, they're all one to me.'

The chief reporter nodded. He had plenty of stuff on those reds in the dockyard. There was no shortage of tales about their marches and demonstrations, and their scuffles with the bobbies. Besides, what you never heard, you could always make up. The *Journal* was losing its staff at a troublesome rate, off to the war or off Sooth for jobs with more silver. This eager sixteen year old, with his keen eyes and endless energy, was just what he needed to chase up all the gossip.

Being well versed in teuchter ways, Leslie was soon put in charge of agricultural matters. He fair enjoyed himself, making train trips to cattle shows, fairs and marts in places like Perth and New Deer, Ellon and Kittybrewster. He was sent out to get the gory details of any accidents or fires, and he soon learned the ways of big stomached bailies and how they handled those perky prostitutes or white faced keelies wheeled in before them.

'Soliciting in broad daylight, sir,' the bobby would smirk. If she'd done it in the dark, you felt, the bobby himself might have had a go.

Leslie's notions on bosses, bailies and bobbies got firmer as the winter passed and, away down in dockland, beyond Market Street and Guild Street, he worked away with the other chields in the Soviet. He could fair take a trick when he spoke about the workers and their rights, and how they should make a stand. There would be a hush once he started. When he got on though, about the things they were making, ammunition and gas shells and things of that sort, they'd shuffle their feet. Some chield would then shout out. 'What the hell has that to do with it? It's work, isn't it?' Leslie got fed up with the workers as well after sallies of that sort.

He was seventeen in February but that caused little stir. The commotion at that time was about Julian the Tank, named after that grand general Julian Byng whose lads had got them ringing the victory bells after the Cambrai caper. Julian the Tank paid visits to Dundee and Aberdeen on its fund raising tour. Leslie regaled Rebecca with the details when she met him later on.

Becky was up in Aberdeen to sit her entrance exam for the Civil Service, so Leslie planted his new homburg hat firmly on his head and, with his press pass in his hand, took her along to the theatre.

'Julian the tank fairly drew the crowds,' he laughed. 'They say they made over a million pounds selling their fifteen and sixpenny certificates and five pound defence bonds. They're raising money to buy hundreds of Julian tanks to finish things off. The photographers had a grand time of it in Dundee and Aberdeen. I doubt though, it will take more than all those Americans and even a thousand Julians to beat the Germans. There seems to be millions of them.'

Leslie was on his best behaviour now, but pleased and proud to be showing Rebecca the sights of the city, flashing his press pass everywhere they went. That long kiss that had stirred him so much was still at the back of his mind and could trouble him at nights, but this was not the time. He'd to make amends to Rob Middleton's lass for his daft behaviour in the snow. Becky was impressed, but much more concerned about the exam she'd just sat and the last train she'd still to catch to the station at Drumskite.

Becky's visit had stirred him more than he'd admit though, and, in between dashing from one assignment to the next, he started chatting to a most attractive lass who worked in the *Journal's* front office. He got fair carried away for a while and filled his notebook with sentimental verse, the kind that would have pleased Madge no end.

> And so I'll sing a song of Marguerite,
> She who is lovely, smiling-eyed and sweet

But Marguerite was more interested in a handsome sub-editor of a paper Doon Sooth. So she gave Leslie the bonniest of smiles and turned him down with thanks when he asked if he could take her to see Bernard Shaw's 'Pygmalion' at the theatre. Leslie swore at that, but consoled himself: he'd better things to do. Mrs MacDonald, his landlady, laughed when she heard. She put a table in his room, and he was soon hard at it, scribbling like mad. He had some notions now for the plot of his very first novel.

All this time the Gordons were digging for dear life. The winter frosts had brought the fighting to a stop. Uncle Harper had had a good look at Jerry's deep trenches and dugouts and thought his lads deserved nothing less, so he'd set them to building his own Harper Line. Uncle's trenches became the speak of the Western Front and commanders from all over began asking to get a look at them.

By that March of 1918 they'd built more than 60 new dugouts, enough to hold every man at the Front. General Julian Byng himself, paid them a visit and was fair impressed, but one of his brass hats thought the whole front was far too quiet and cosy like. They should 'get on with the war', he said, so they fired off a few rounds which entertained the Jerries and everybody else in the place, and sent him back to his cosy base camp fine pleased with himself.

Uncle's Quartermaster, Colonel Weston, got a free hand and soon had huts and tents all over the place, covered over with coloured fish nets. There were kitchens and canteens with stores for vegetables, fresh fish, eggs and drinks. There was even a soda water factory, and rest camps, a picture palace and a theatre for the 51st. Hot baths were built for the officers and men. Cameron could scarce believe it when they got a change of clothes after every wash. At Achiet le Petit, the 51st had its own theatre, and their Entertainments Officer, Captain Stanley, did a great job with a bunch of sodgers he named 'The Balmorals'. He wrote the words and music of a comic opera for them called 'Turnip Tops' and that kept the Division entertained on the coldest nights.

So the worst of the winter passed. On 5 March the Fourth Gordons moved in. It was their turn to hold the ridge up there at Flesquières, its château and all. They'd moved up to the ridge in broad daylight, three full companies of them, with Jim and Ginger, Cameron and the rest, in A Company, over on the far right. B Company took over the centre, and C had control of the left. D Company was close behind them all, and the battalion headquarters was close by in Demicourt. It had been a bright, clear day and nothing had stirred. The Gordons had moved in and the 4th Seaforths had left. It was uncanny and weird, and Cameron was ill at ease. They had a rare sight now of the country as far as Bourlon Wood and Cantaing village they'd fought so hard to capture back in November. It was all back in German hands again, but it would be Jerry now who'd have to charge up the hill against the machine guns and the barbed wire.

Jerry had numbers on his side. Eleven British and French Divisions with the 2nd Gordons among them had been sent off to help the Italians after their losses, so the brigades had been cut from four battalions to three battalions each. In the big shift round, the 5th Gordons had been moved to the right of Flesquières, which came under General Gough's Fifth Army command. That took over from Cameron and Jim's Company down the brae on the right hand side of Flesquières.

This bothered Cameron a lot. 'It's a bad position, Jim lad,' he said, one night when they were taking it easy in their dugout up on Flesquières. 'There's a lot going on over there and Jerry's not that daft. He'll be up to some mad ploy one of those days.'

'They say he's got some extra men from the Russian front, now they're out of the war,' said Ginger, a bit fed up with it all.

'It's this Flekeer place that scunners me.' Cameron had never been convinced they should have hung on to Flesquières, sticking out as it did in front of the rest of the line. 'We're the last battalion on this side. Down the brae there, on the right, it's a different command. If Jerry discovers that, that's where he'll hit us, in between our two armies.'

The young lieutenant dropped by to see how things were. 'Just four days of it lads, and you'll be back down below. Uncle's all for keeping us on the move. No time to get bored.' He went off with a cheery grin. He seemed to like the thing fine.

'That lad takes over many chances,' said Cameron as he left. 'He's forever on the move, scouting about there in front. Intelligence work, they call it. He got the Military Cross at the New Year, and not before time.'

Jim read his last letter from Madge just one more time. For a while, he was off in another world, a world of lush green fields, wooded dens and broom covered hills. It was a world where the trees were never stark and stunted. They'd be in bud soon, and the wee farms would be full of life, the only smoke would be the smoky wisps drifting straight up in the friendly air. He shut his eyes. The lads were there casting their lines in the trout filled Bervie, unbothered that the fish were holding back. He could see the sweetie shops and the school bairns, the mills he'd thought were a trial. Now they'd a better look to them, the mill quines laughing and joking. And there was his busy wee office – and Madge with her smiling, happy eyes. Jim read again the news of the place, the good news and the bad. Bad news came more often now, but she kept him up to date, all about the Games Committee and the cash they'd made for the sodgers, and all about the Gourdon Dominie's lads with their Indian Clubs – and how one lad had dropped a club.

J H's face had been a picture and they'd laughed, but clapped them just the same, loud and long. Jim read the postscript. Young cousin Alec in Montrose had got his commission. That was good. He was another Uncle Harper in the making. His young days in South Africa had fitted him out for that. Madge's uncles and their families had come home to Montrose when the troubles got bad.

'You're dreaming, Jim lad.' Cameron grinned across at him. 'It's our turn out in the fog next, so drink up your cocoa. There's nothing happening tonight yet, nor is there going to be. In four days time we'll be back down the Line, laughing our heads off at the Wooden Tops. Their new play hoose is starting up at Lebukeer.'

Jim laughed. They'd seen Captain Stanley's 'Wooden Tops' back in Achiet le Petit. The Captain's comic opera had been running since the New Year and had done over a hundred shows. The word was they sang the same songs and cracked the same jokes since the day they'd started, but that was hardly fair. The Captain had done his best to keep the show up to date with digs at the top brass as well as the Germans. 'Q' as Cameron called the Quartermaster, had been building the new camouflaged theatre for the Division at Lebucquières to be much closer to the front. That first show was something they could all look forward to.

'I think you fancy Gertie yourself,' Ginger grinned at Cameron, and they had a quiet laugh at that. Captain Stanley dressed himself up as Gertie, the Dame, and gave a great performance to the whistles of the men.

When the attack came, A Company were manning the new line between Morchies and Beaumetz, C and D Companies were up there on the ridge, with D Company in between. They'd spent the five days out of the trenches building up their new camp at Lebucquières, a short distance behind. The new theatre for The Balmorals was now complete and ready to start.

They were out on night patrol, very early on 21 March when it happened. The stroll in the mist as far as the barbed wire, was cold, wet and boring, and the three of them were just heading back to the trench when the guns opened up. It was half past four in the morning. Jim was sure about that. He liked to get his facts right, but he was shaken by the suddenness of it. Later on, he wrote it down on the back of an envelope – 21st March, 1918.

The bombardment back in November was said to have been the biggest gun barrage in history, but this was more massive than that. In November they'd all been waiting for it. An officer beside Jim had actually counted the seconds. But this thunder clapping bedlam from the enemy hit their ears like a blow in the face. They stumbled, then flung themselves flat on the hard, scarred earth. Every gun in the Fatherland had opened up, and they lay there, hands clapped to their lugs. It took a while to sort things out, to sort out the eternal screech up above, and solid thump of explosions nearer by. It was Ginger first that prodded them and shouted close up. 'They're not shelling us,' he yelled. They thought about that. It was true. They lifted themselves on their hands, breathed in deeply, then ran like mad.

That was a black day for the Fifty First – 21 March, 1918. The thing was done with ruthless German precision. The first salvo hit the 51st's HQ at Fremicourt and a plane downed their observation balloon. Every battalion and brigade HQ was hit and all the key positions behind the battalion were blasted. Bapaume, Albert and St Pol in the rear were battered by long range guns, and Jerry's Big Bertha let fly at Paris, far off in the rear. To let them know they were on their way. In the first fifteen minutes all communication lines were broken. This was Jerry's big breakthrough. The French had had their troubles, the Americans hadn't yet arrived and the British line was weak. A thick mist covered the whole land till about noon, and up in Flesquières they sat and waited. Any message sent up was by runner, up that long dreary slope. By the time it got there it was out of date. Later on, they would discover Jerry had flung nineteen divisions against Byng's fourteen. But over on the right of Flesquières, the situation was worse.

A massive 43 divisions were being flung against the twelve in Gough's army. German casualties were immense.

The artillery barrage was being directed by Colonel Bruchmüller. He'd made a name for himself on the Russian Front. The Germans nicknamed him 'Durchbruch Müller' (Breakthrough Müller). The Fourth Gordons up on Flesquières knew nothing of all this. They knew they'd be surrounded and cut off if they sat on up there. But no order came. When it did come, it was 1.30 in the morning. They'd to pull back to the trenches north of Hermies. They'd to get down out of Flesquières as fast as they could.

The rest of the 51st got battered from the start. The lads in A Company of the Fourth Gordons knew that the Fifth Gordons on their right had been overrun and the Sixth Gordons on their left were having a terrible time of it. Jerry had left the Flesquières ridge alone. He was probing for gaps on either side. By the sound of things he'd found them, just as Cameron had forecast.

Then A Company got it. Müller's shells started sceaming down on their trench near Beaumetz.

'Come on lads,' said Cameron. 'We're off to Lebukeer. Captain Stanley's having a German show this time!'

They scrambled and struggled down the communication trench, knocking into each other. Shells screamed and slammed into the chalky land on every side. Stones and rubble crashed down over them and they were flung into the dirt. Winded by one dive, Jim felt Cameron pull him up and grip his arm.

'Right Jim, over here. The dugout's just there in front.' The last men of the section stumbled past and Cameron waved them on. Jim staggered up. He'd knocked his knee in that last fall.

'Run Cameron,' he shouted and hirpled on behind.

'Down here, Jim,' Cameron shouted, looking back. A shell whammed into the ground. The place was jammed with men, pushing on into the shelter below. Jim scrambled down some steps. If only they'd move faster. The light from a lantern blinked from far, deep inside, and he made his way towards it. Somebody loomed up from the shadows and held out his hand. 'Here, Jim,' he yelled, 'sit down here. You're all right now.' The man gave Jim his seat and sat down next him, near to the entrance.

Jim eased himself along the wooden plank, but there was no room to go further. The men were slumped there and exhausted. Cameron sat opposite. Jim saw the man beside him who'd given him his seat had scarce enough room. He inched his way along. 'If Jerry keeps this up, we'll never get out,' said Cameron. The crash the shell made drowned the last of his words and it all went blank.

The place was thick with burning, choking dust, acrid smoke filled his lungs. Jim was lying on his side. He put out his left hand to lift himself. A pain stabbed up his arm and he yelled. They were yelling and screaming in the dark of the place, choking and retching in the dirt.

A gust of air was clearing the smoke. A figure from far inside was picking his way towards him, a lantern in his hand. Jim looked up at Cameron. Was it Cameron? He was still sitting there, his back against the wall, but part of his head was slashed. The side nearest the entrance was a mass of blood and torn flesh. His other cheek, a day's stubble of growth on it, looked calm and untroubled. Jim coughed and was sick. Cameron was dead. The man who'd helped him down was dead. Bodies were everywhere. There was little else to see in the glimmer of the lamp. Jim's head swam and he was sick again.

The air was clearing now and it was quieter. Someone was groaning, but the screaming had stopped. Jim looked down at his arm and saw the blood. He staunched that as well as he could, but the pain made him dizzy. They were shouting now and pushing from inside the dugout to get past.

'If you can move, get up and get out,' said a voice of authority. The two men beside him would never get out. Jim pushed himself up with his good hand and moved on with the others. The shelling had moved further on and he climbed up the steps to where the air was fresh. He fell in behind a line of staggering men. It was darker now, but he could see the way ahead. After that, they trudged on. For ever, it seemed. But at last, they turned a corner and entered another trench. The pain in his arm was unbearable and his head was in a whirl. It was hard to think straight.

Jim came to in a first aid tent, his arm and his hand had been dressed, and a label was tied to his tunic. He'd never felt so tired.

'If you can make it, follow that crowd,' said the orderly, 'they're off to the sick bay at Lebucquières. You'll have to hurry.'

Jim had little chance to write anything on his envelope. The words that crossed his lips drew strange looks from the Red Cross men at the Front and the nursing quines later on.

'Moshy Tite and Mossy White,' Jim muttered at times, and 'Hallelujah Lyon.' 'Toddler Ben,' he'd shout, and 'Barber John the Spanish Don.' Folk shook their heads, but then they'd never known happier times on Craig David's rock, discussing that happy breed of independents, the Bervie Worthies.

Jim was one of the lucky ones. He was got away before the bigger breakthrough. Bancourt and Bapaume itself were overrun and soon the whole army was back where it had started, to the Somme killing fields of 1916, and further back still, near to Paris before the murderous tide was stopped. In the mix up of the retreat, the Fifth Gordons had few survivors and the Sixth were cut to pieces. Brigades found themselves attached to different Divisions and Byng's Army alone suffered 10,000 dead. Among them were Cameron and Lieutenant Douglas Meldrum Watson Leith, MC, of the Fourth Battalion, Gordon Highlanders. Jim and Ginger were just two of the Battalion's four hundred casualties and were soon out of it all.

But just for a time. Men were patched up and pushed back to the Front if they could breath and stand up straight. There they joined the fresh drafts of new recruits, hurried over the Channel. Battalions soldiered on, it was the men in them who changed. So Jim went back when they'd picked out most of the shrapnel.

It was September when the telegram came. Madge was in the kitchen with Albert who'd just come back from Egypt. There was a knock at the door and she knew then, and looked at Ab.

'I'll get it Madge,' he said in the quiet way Albert had. But Father got there first and Madge stood at the kitchen door and heard. She listened to the rustle of the paper and the quick breath of Father. There was a quietness then, and Madge felt cold and faint. What a lonely, dreary world it was.

Father whispered and she heard his sad voice, shaky but clear.

'Don't tell Madge just yet, Ab,' he said, and he stifled a sob.

TWENTY-ONE

Jerry never reached Paris. It was a bit like Cambrai. Far worse. There were bodies everywhere, choking the roads and the ditches, cluttering the parks. By Armistice Day the Jocks were scunnered and too wearied to cheer.

The Fourth Gordons got to Cambrai, for what it was worth. The CO did his best and laid on a show of The Balmorals for them. Five Military Medals were handed out, out of the hat, some said. But the Battalion Diary tells it straight: '11th November, 1918. The men made no effort to rejoice. Such a day is difficult to realise. All parades cancelled. The day is regarded as a holiday.'

On 13 November, the Fourth Gordons celebrated the second anniversary of Beaumont Hamel with sports and a special dinner and tea for all ranks. It was Cameron, the cheery Douglas Leith and the rest that missed the celebrations that time. They were absent too at the grand meal that was laid on for St Andrew's Day. But the new lads of the Fourth Gordons were given a rare treat: 'Miniature Scottish National Flags were issued to all ranks, to be worn above the badge of the Balmoral.'

Madge tried to go flag waving with the rest. When Father told her it was Cousin Alec had been killed, she burst into tears. Father held her close, a thing he'd never done. How could she explain? It was Cousin Alec who'd brightened up their days with his gowf, his South African twang and his bright open ways. And she'd been glad it wasn't Jim! That last printed card Cousin Alec had posted from the trenches was to haunt her for years.

The line he'd left in was the one that hurt: 'Have not heard from you for a long time', it said. The words, 'short time', he'd scratched out.

The Paper Billies called it Spanish Flu, a pandemic, they said. The whole world caught it which proved it was a judgement on all of them, but that was daft. The science billies called it a virus and got out their microscopes, but damned the thing could they find. There were more dead from the flu than had been killed on the Somme and in the Kaiser's last fling combined, said the papers, but they'd say anything to cause a stir and put the fear of death in you. For yourself, you knew that folk had lost the heart to fight, the Jerries, the viruses, or even the lairds themselves. Folk had had enough, and maybe that was as near as you'd ever get to it.

Madge knew little of all this. Alec's death at the last, and the way she'd heard of it, had been over much for her to bear. Father could see she was ill and the Provost Doctor confirmed it on the spot. 'Madge has got a bad attack of the Spanish Flu,' he said, with a wearisome nod. The Provost Doctor had got himself a car by this time and had been out every night of the week with this trouble that had come to plague them.

You'd to hand it to the Bailie though, the coarse tink that he was. The jobs on his books and the whole damned business could go to hell, he said. Pappa Gibb could rage on about his drawing room ceiling, the Bailie had other work in hand.

Jock Low, the joiner, was soon making coffins full time. He had Mary Strachan and Jess stitching away to trig them out with soft padded linings. Well, Jock Low's coffins might be the best in the Howe, said the Bailie, but he'd get no orders from him! The Bailie summoned his womenfolk, and a hardy and determined lot they were. Still grieving at the loss of their Alec, they powered in with china hot water bottles, bread poultices, jugs of beef tea and remedies the Provost Doctor had never even heard of.

Madge rambled on in her delirium. The aunts exchanged looks and shook their heads when she came out with a lot of nonsense about barbit wire and gowfing niblicks, Alec and Jim and Barber John. When she started on about Moshy Tite and Hallelujah Lyon, they padded away at her brow and slipped some sugared toddy through her bonny red lips. It was touch and go for a time, but Madge pulled through in the end. The Bailie and those aunts would settle for nothing else, and maybe the Provost Doctor had a hand in things as well. Once the crisis had past, Madge got on to her feet. Father had a business to run and Jim was coming back!

The flu had set the whole country back and the Royal Toun was no different from the rest. J H Johnstone, the Gourdon Dominie and Games Secretary, pro tem, told of its progress with his canny like pen:

> Bervie, 6 November, 1918. A meeting of the Bervie Highland Games Committee was held in the Town Hall this evening at 8 p.m., Bailie Clarke presiding... owing to influenza, little had been done in obtaining artistes for the New Year Concert. – J H Johnstone, Secretary pro tem.
> Bervie, 13 November, 1918. ...Provost Boath presiding. (The Bailie had other matters in hand)... as influenza is still very prevalent little was done in the way of preparing for the concert. – J H Johnstone, Secretary pro tem.
> Bervie, 27 November, 1918... (no one presiding). On which night the Committee should have met, but owing to influenza and other causes, no business was done... J H Johnstone, Secretary pro tem.

A hardy man was the Dominie, J H Johnstone, Secretary pro tem, and very methodical in his reporting. By 4 December, he was able to get things on the move, with the Bailie presiding and seven others in attendance. The flu had passed its peak and thoughts were turning to some kind of celebration. The Bailie said he'd draft out a poster and an afternoon tea-dance would be held in the Burgh Hall from one o'clock to five. Maybe the hellish culture of the Germans had been stopped in its tracks, but the ways of the English were fairly taking a trick!

Madge got back to things slowly at first. Father brought in a buxom woman, a Mistress Melon from Stonehive, to look after the place and Madge was bundled out into the fresh air as soon as the weather improved. She took herself down the Kirkburn to the beach. The place was quiet, just the odd carter trundling his load of flax up from the station. Old Saxie Cameron, Ab's father-in-law, gave her a cheery wave as he rested his heavy horse between the Free Kirk and the old kirkyard before tackling the last stretch to the King Street. The mills were working away still, though the Auld Mill in the Haughs now lay in ruins and the plans for Jock Webster's new mill over the bridge had been laid aside for good.

'You're looking fine, Madge lass,' Saxie shouted. 'Get yourself a breath of good Bervie sea air and you'll be as right as rain.'

Madge gave him a wave, and Saxie gave the horse a smack on the buttocks. Roy, his douce, brown mongrel dog, trotted along at his heels.

Madge got as far as the beach. A shunting engine was working away in the sidings behind her, shunting coal for Cowie and Nicol, the two coal merchants in the place. The winter months were raw and cold, and near every house in the place, even down in David Street where they'd little enough silver, had a coal fire blazing at nights. Some along the Terrace had coal fires in their bedrooms forby, as she'd had those last awful weeks, but that was an extravagance they could ill afford. Some, like Pappa Gibb at Bridge End, had a coal fire in every room.

The forenoon sun glinting sharp and clear. The salmon fishers' cobbles on the beach had been laid up for the winter and the bonny white-washed bothy on the rocks O'er the Water, was padlocked and secure till the days of spring. There were few folk about, just old Andy, another Bervie Worthy, walking his dog along by the engine shed, taking the road to Gourdon round the headland there past the canons. The canons were relics of earlier guns where the Volunteers had exercised, antique reminders of olden times when the French had been the enemy. The boys would soon be back, Madge mused, glad to be rid of their guns and all that nonsense.

A Gourdon fishing boat was crossing the bay, heading for the harbour round the corner. Seas were like folk, Madge thought, unpredictable. Was it just three years since she and Teen, Jim and David had sailed out there on Jock Webster's boat, the Alice Webster? Old Jock was dead now and David would have the lot once the Trustees gave him full control. Folk said that David was determined to bring a deal more work to the place. But Teen would be taking no part in all that! Teen and David had fallen out when she'd seen him off at the station. David had told her of the fine times he was having in the new RAF down at Crystal Palace. 'There are lots of bonny lassies down there,' David laughed. Teen had said he was welcome to his English quines and that had been that.

Other men had been changed by what they'd seen in France. Some had come back looking fine at first, then, without a word or a nod, they'd up and left the place, their wives and their bairns fair dumfoonered, as the teuchters would have it, thrown on to the Parish silver without a word of explanation. And there were those that would never come back. Father had counted over seventy from the wee parish itself, including John Elliot, the Stationy's lad, and the Laird of Hallgreen himself, that had launched Gourdon's new lifeboat just a year or two before. Then there were all those sturdy lads she'd watched at the Games, pulling at the tug o' war and racing their hearts out for a five shilling prize. There were others too, from Arbuthnott and Kinneff, Garvock and those Mearns parks beyond the hill. What a miracle it was: Jim and the four boys had been spared.

Madge flung a last pebble into the sea and stepped back across the shingle. Father would be home soon. She'd better give Mistress Melon a hand with the meal. Would he still be the same dear Jim, she wondered, the same lad that stepped on to Davidson's bus, that morning, so proud at last to be joining the Gordon's? She looked up at David's Rock. What happy times they'd had up there.

But there was little help to be got from that bit of rock, however bonny it might look in the winter sun. Her Jim, she knew, would still be the same factual, kindly Jim with the same smiling, lonely eyes. The generals, the Jerries and even the French would never have changed her Jim. She was sure of that. Madge passed the Free Kirk and looked up at the square tower on the kirk of the parish, Jim's kirk, at the top of the brae. She sent a prayer up then. It was aye best to be sure!

TWENTY-TWO

'You mean it's a brothel?' Leslie put down his teacup and stared at the older man across the table. He'd had plenty of shocks since he'd come down to Glasgow and joined the staff of the *Scottish Farmer*. The sheer size of Glasgow had overwhelmed him. Aberdeen had been big and exciting with the commotion in its markets and docks, and all those garrulous seamen and farmers, but Glasgow was immense, more than five times the size of the Granite Toun, they said. You could handle a place like Aberdeen, stuck between those tram stops on the Dee and the Don, Hazelhead and the Sea Beach. Here in Glasgow, the trams disappeared into tenement jungles that stretched far down the Clyde, endlessly. Shipyards and railway yards spilled out peeked, white faced men in their droves. And the bairns were everywhere, swarming in and out of the close mouths, clattering up and down tenement stairs, moving in gangs from one court to the next. Aberdeen might produce a wheen of prostitutes down by the docks; in Glasgow they sidled out of every close.

It was the closeness of the squalor and the affluence, barely a street apart at times, upset him the most. And the rage that burst out when things went all to hell. Now here was this jovial colleague telling him that the place where he lodged in was a brothel. And he'd been living there for weeks!

'You never guessed?' Harry was entertained. Harry had been with the *Scottish Farmer* for as long as anyone could remember; he was part of the fittings. The day the young reporter had turned up with his heavy case, Harry had taken a friendly interest in him and pointed out the road to those digs in Hill Street. His room on the top floor was large and spacious, not as homely as Ma MacDonald's in Aberdeen maybe, but clean and reasonably priced. Very reasonably priced. It was a big house set high on the hill, so he had a clear view far across the city, beyond the ships and building yards of the Clyde. When the night air was sharp there were fantastic red sunsets he could brood on and that cheered him up. The landlady was a buxom, friendly soul and she'd been most impressed when he said he was a journalist. The last gentleman had been that, she'd nodded respectfully. He'd kept his place tidy and paid on the dot. She didn't look like the Madame of a brothel. Every morning she dished up a fine appetizing and substantial breakfast of bacon and eggs – bawdy house bacon and eggs, it seemed – to build up his strength!

'I just thought I'd struck it lucky,' Leslie frowned. 'She looks after me very well. I have noticed different men coming and going, at times. I pass them on the stairs. Young business men, I thought, though some are older, and some are on the scruffy side. But they are a breezy lot, and smartly dressed for the most part, all very friendly. They nod and grin when we meet. I took that to be a Glasgow trait. You Glasgow folk are more outgoing than we are up north. Some give me a wink as if there's some secret we shared. I have wondered about that at times.' Leslie stopped and looked at the character in front of him. 'I thought the rest of the building was let out as flats?'

'Oh aye, but they'll all pay their dues to Madame,' Harry chuckled. 'There are just the two of you there as legitimate lodgers. It gives the place an air of respectability. But you must have met some of those tarts on the stairs. They have strict instructions to leave the residents alone.'

'There are one or two mezzo-blondes I've a nodding acquaintance with.' Leslie shook his head. 'You must think me a real country bumpkin.'

The place was never quite the same after that. He took a greater interest in those mezzo-blondes and had short, polite conversations with them which they seemed to enjoy. It must have made a change from the usual chatter they'd to suffer. They were just ordinary lassies, he decided, forced to earn a living in the only way they knew. Socialism would soon put a stop to all that!

There was no getting away from sex. A cold shower was best, he'd read, but that only cooled you for a time. Now sex was all round him, through the walls, on either side, women's bodies were for sale. Every sound in the place, every creak and groan, conjured up an image of sex. His imagination began to run riot. He'd go mad if he just lay there and listened.

He got a book on the physiology of sex from the library and read on late into the night. He laid it down at last and put out the light. He stood at the window and stared out across the speckled blackness of Glasgow. Down by the river a furnace flared. A blue light flashed when a trolley hit the wire and a late tram whooped over the junction. Those exciting notions and sexual urges were bothering him again. Night time always had that effect, but it was far worse now and occuring more often. He was no different from the rest of them.

That book set him thinking. Sex and lust were at the root of all their troubles. Man was worse than the animals. Animals only copulated in their season, but man seemed to have this perpetual longing, in season and out, to fertilize the female of his kind. Unlike the animals, men looked on sex for thrills. Not content to treat it as just another bodily function, they dramatised it and complicated it for sheer gratification. If they remembered in time, they'd take precautions and there would be no fertilisation of the women that they used.

That hadn't happened with mother. Those brutes had taken what they could from mother and left her to cope on her own. Even the animals did better than that. No wonder mother was grim. All the romance and self-esteem had been driven out of her. And that was the mess he'd been born into! At least father had married mother beforehand, in spite of the two bairns at her heels. What did marriage mean, though, at the end of the day, but that mother could wear a wedding ring and behave like a licensed bed-woman in the sight of God! The Kirk approved of that sort of behaviour. The Kirk had built up a whole mythology to keep folk in their places. The Kirk's notions about right and wrong, marriage and morals were founded on sex. It had a virgin birth at the heart of its theology, as though a natural kind of birth was in some way indecent!

Next day he decided he'd better go back and see those pseudo revolutionaries he'd got caught up with. They were the reason for his coming down to Glasgow in the first place. It was to have been the start of a great new adventure, a new dawn for people like himself, a new start for the world. He'd never forget that great day they'd released John Maclean from his prison cell in Peterhead. What a stir that had created in Aberdeen! What a cheering and a shouting there had been, not just from rebels like himself, but from all sorts of folk. They'd been scunnered by what they'd seen in the war. The time had come to make a new start and let all of them share in what they'd won with their struggles. They'd paid dearly enough for it. More than five thousand had lost their lives from Aberdeen and round about. They all deserved a fair deal, not just those traders and profiteers who'd done so well for themselves. Aberdeen had gone wild for Maclean, he remembered. There had been a presentation dinner and speeches galore, but the Dominie had been less impressed when he'd gone on to him about it.

'You want to get involved with all those Red Clydesiders?' Alex Gray had asked. 'The Russians appointed Maclean as their Scottish Consul, you know, and that did him little good. It was never recognised, of course.'

'The government have Maclean on their conscience, all the same. They granted him a free pardon when they saw the kind of support that he had. He refused to accept it. It was adding insult to injury, he said. When Maclean got down to Glasgow the whole city went mad. The crowds were enormous. They say that half of Clydeside was up at Buchanan Street when he stepped off the train.'

'You really are determined to go down there and join them?' The Dominie was clearly upset. He shook his head. 'You'd be better to stay on in Aberdeen and make a reputation for yourself as a journalist before you get tangled up in politics.'

Well, he'd ignored the Dominie's advice and he'd come down to join them. Where exactly had it got him? The job had gone well enough. He'd worked hard at it and McNeillage, the editor, had been well pleased. He'd soon caught on to their own brand of journalese and their droll Glasgow jokes, writing screeds for them on all the gossip from the cattle shows and marts. He'd dug up some real life stories on the effects the new machines and tractors were having on those hard worked bothy billies and small tenant farmers.

'You're the best of my staff,' McNeillage grunted, which was high praise from a dour man like McNeillage.

He'd to lead a kind of double life through it all. The revolution in

Glasgow, some actually called it that, had got off to a bad start and when he'd got down there he found the workers had been squashed. They'd had the army out with machine guns and tanks in George Square. Bloody Friday, folk called it. Willie Gallacher got three months for his part in it all and Manny Shinwell got five. It had been an odd sort of revolution. A huge crowd had turned up to hear some speeches. They'd been in a holiday mood and fair enjoying things, but when the bobbies tried to clear a passage for the trams to get through – an impossible job as the Square was packed solid at the time – things had got fair out of hand.

So he made his way back to the ill-assorted bunch of revolutionaries he'd landed amongst. Editing their news sheets and writing up their minutes had taken a lot of his time, but they'd scunnered him in the end with all their arguments. They'd as many notions as they had members. The intellectuals among them, those sacked teachers and unfrocked priests with all their grand theories, had little in common with those rough lads from the yards. His credentials as a member of the Aberdeen Soviet had counted for a lot and they had made him their secretary, but he'd had other things in mind when the better days arrived, reporting on every show and mart from Perth to the Borders. And then at weekends, there had been the 'other matters', as he explained to the Prof.

The Prof shared the secretary work with him in the scruffy little shed they called their centre. The Prof was a white-haired Russian exile who'd got out of Russia when the Bolsheviks had taken over. He'd supported Kerensky in the summer of 1917, but the bloodshed in October had been too much for him. He was a gentle soul, and as out of place as Leslie in that odd crowd of rebels. The committee were forever short of silver and the two of them had the job of settling the bills.

The Prof was relieved when he turned up that night. 'You've much work to deal with these days?' He spoke wearily, more depressed than usual.

'And other matters,' Leslie answered, flushing a little.

'Ah! Other matters.' The Prof brightened at that. He was a romantic at heart, happier with his beloved Russian literature than the bloody carnage of strikes, riots and baton charges. His private hero was Prince Kropotkin, a writer of encouraging books on self-help and anarchy, easier to stomach than the mayhem he'd witnessed in Glasgow's George Square. Socialism to the Prof was a paradise of grain harvests and flowers peopled by happy, contented peasants and craftsmen. 'A lady friend,' he said, raising his eyebrows. 'How nice.'

It was then that he told the Prof a little about Rita, and how Scotland's spring sunshine and Rita had been an overheady mixture for him in the last few weeks. She was not really called Rita. That would for ever be a treasured secret, but the Prof deserved some explanation. The Prof and he needed each other's shoulder to lean upon. The Prof was a lonely exile, never quite in tune with Glasgow's mores and conventions. The two of them had a lot in common, forever supporting each other against the rapacious demands of the other revolutionaries.

'Thank God,' said the Prof when Leslie waxed lyrical for a moment on the sweetness and fairy-like innocence of this incredible Rita who'd seduced him away from the daft capers of the group.

'Praise be to God,' he nodded, 'there are still young men like you with dreams and visions of the future. All this talk about strikes and barricades makes the class struggle such a physical thing. But you should take more care of your money. We all take money from you. You will have need of it yet.'

Leslie had given the group some more money for their London delegation. He'd done it in a burst of generosity, fed up with all their bickering on tactics and the grotty schemes they kept dreaming up. 'I felt guilty, I suppose, missing those meetings and leaving you all the work to do.'

'But where does it come from, all this money? A young reporter like yourself cannot earn so much that you can hand all this to the group.'

That was the trouble. He'd resisted the thing for a while, but the Prof had once said that those capitalists had so much money to spare they wasted it on motor cars and grand houses out Kelvinside way. They should have shared some of it with the workers who'd made it for them in the first place. In the end he'd fiddled just a little bit on his expenses to help redress the balance.

Those weekends with Rita purged the cynicism from his soul. Sex was a brutal, lustful agony before the advent of Rita. It was all around him, in his family, out there in the streets, through the walls, above and below him in his lodgings, and at work there in the office, especially in the office from his fellow hacks with their innuendoes and their smutty jokes. A mention of a word like knickers sent them into paroxysms of hysteria. Yet he'd found Rita in the office, in an island of peace and calm. Rita, he discovered, had a steadying effect on all who came near her. In Rita's presence, the grubbiest scribbler would soften his voice and clean up his act.

His discovery of Rita was a moment of wonder. When he walked into her room he was caught by the fairy loveliness of the girl. Her fingers were dancing on the typewriter keys. She looked up and her eyes sparkled. They laughed together. 'Yes?' was all she said. He gulped and took it from there. Looking back on it later, he found difficulty with the detail. What exactly did she wear? Something crisp, yet soft. A pretty white blouse? He could never be sure. He always remembered the thin gold chain at her neck that dropped down to some locket, intriguingly, privately hidden from his sight. He never forgot that. It had stirred him, sharply. Rita radiated pure happiness that changed all of his thoughts.

It took a little time, but the sun shone and it was Spring. The laughter in Rita's eyes and the sweetness of her lips swept away all thoughts of the Soviets and daft notions like that. She was English, and a year or so older. That first time he held her she was so warm and child-like. He kissed her lips and for a moment she resisted. Her lips opened then and, unbelievably, their tongues touched and she kissed him in return. Flushed and breathless she drew her lips aside. He felt the beat of her heart, the warmth of her cheeks against his. He was lost to her then and Glasgow basked in the glow.

Of a sudden Glasgow was a different sort of place, with parks and theatres and folk who were friendly and warm. Tenements that had been squalid and seedy bubbled with humour and fun. The irrepressible confidence of the Glaswegian rubbed off on him and he picked up the infectious song of their speak, but the sweetness of Rita's pure English tongue kept that well in check. She was keen on Scottish culture, she said, and so, of course, was he. They explored Kelvingrove and its Galleries, the libraries and museums. They looked at plaster casts of the ancients. They held hands, naturally and untroubled, and together they looked at the naked Aphrodite. He wondered then why the world had got it so wrong. Sex for the young was clean and pure and always had been. It maybe didn't sell newspapers or magazines any more, only tales of perversion and the un-natural did that and filled the novels of the day. Had the world forgotten about romance and the joy of the young in being free and untramelled and unbothered? Surely the ideal age for mating was sixteen, he felt, hugging Rita close and regretting the years that he'd lost. At night he lay awake in his top storey room, brooding on life and what he had done. Life was passing him by. He was into his nineteenth year already and he hadn't even started to live!

'Scotland's such a beautiful country,' Rita sighed, in the musical English that made his bones want to melt. What a clumsy oaf he was, still unrid of those guttural Mearns grunts he'd inherited and tried to eradicate. Rita was etherial, too good for the world. They'd taken the train down to Balloch and were sitting on Loch Lomond's bonny banks that those folk in the Howe never tired singing about, though damned the one of them had the faintest notion of where they might be.

'Those hard-pressed workers in the yards should be out here on a day such as this,' Leslie murmured, slipping his hand under the warm silk on her shoulder.

'Those Moscow agitators are the cause of all their troubles.' Rita told him. 'They're lucky to be living in a place such as Glasgow.'

Lying there with Rita cradled in his arms, listening to the chirruping sounds of Spring and breathing in the scent of her hair, Leslie had no wish to argue. Rita enjoyed her morning read of the *Daily Express* and who could blame her for that. Rita's blouse opened slightly as she turned and she snuggled up close.

'McNeillage wants to see you,' Harry said to him next day.

He stayed a while in the washroom to gather his thoughts. He splashed some water on his face. Looking at himself in the glass, he appeared reasonably calm, but his pulse was racing. Better go in and get it over with, though. He hadn't taken a great deal. It was a slip of the pen, he would say, just a few pounds of the petty cash.

McNeillage sat at his desk, tight lipped. There was no mercy to be found in that quarter. The highlander's God was a vengeful God. He remembered a line the Reverend Dunn once read. 'Vengeance is Mine; I will repay, saith the Lord.'

'Sit down.'

Leslie sat down. He felt sick.

'It's simple theft,' he heard McNeillage say. 'From checking your expenses' account, I find you have forged bills for more than £60.'

Leslie drew in a deep breath. Had he taken as much as that?

'You may smoke if you like.'

'Thank you.' He lit a cigarette and inhaled deeply.

'What did ye do it for? Laddie, you're the best of my staff, you've no look of a thief, you've ruined a brilliant career. What did ye want with this

£60?'

Sixty pounds? Had it added up to all that? The delegates' fares, the printers' bills, bail for the 'victim' who had promptly vanished to Ireland, financing the group chairman in a threatened libel action – God, even the group chairman!

'I can't tell you – sir.' He found himself on his feet, listening to his sentence.

'Don't come back to the office, but don't attempt to leave Glasgow. I've got your address in Hill Street. When I've seen the directors I'll let you know what action they intend to take.'

The word had got around. He blundered through the front office. Rita was standing there, a sorrowful look on her face. There were tears in her eyes.

He struggled slowly up Hill Street and climbed the familiar stairs. His neighbour, the smartest of the mezzo-blondes, was locking her door. She returned his greeting with a warm, neighbourly smile.

It was a hot, sultry night. He'd opened the window wide and still he could scarcely breathe. He'd never sleep now. What a fool he'd been, and what had he achieved? They'd made a fool of him. Socialists or communists, bugger the lot of them! And sweet, elfin innocent Rita, how could she ever understand. He could never tell her the real reason. That would only make things worse. He rolled about in the sweat of his bed, and thought of Rita, on and on, he thought about Rita, her misty blue eyes, the sweetness of her lips, the hidden wonder of her breasts.

That warm and friendly mezzo-blonde is by herself now, all alone and only next door. I could knock gently on her door, he thought, and he struggled with that notion till it near drove him daft. He jumped up at last and strode across to the open window. Out there they were all at it. He stretched his hands high above his head and spoke out in a voice he'd never heard, strained and wearied. 'I'm not an animal,' he said. 'Damn the lot of you.' He reached out then for that bottle he'd once bought for a fever, and went slowly back to bed. The red print on the label said 'Laudenum'. He unscrewed the stopper and drank up the lot.

The stopping train back to Drumskite seemed to be moving faster than usual. It was time he needed, to think the whole thing through. He hadn't been thinking clearly when he'd swallowed that stuff. Sleep and some peace, that's what he'd near screamed for, but they'd been rougher than was necessary, when they'd pumped him out and trundled him back to the ward. They'd given him a day or two to come round and sent him on his way. McNeillage had looked in. They'd be taking no action, he said, 'for the sake of your father.'

He'd found an empty compartment. I haven't changed all that much, he thought. Once a loner always a loner. But he had changed, whatever they'd think back there in Arbuthnott. That was the most hellish part of it, crawling back there, facing all those smirks and sneers – and father's rage. But he wouldn't stay long. He just needed some time, time to clear his head and start out again. He'd got most of it out of his system now and he'd learned a lot, a helluva lot. There was nothing wrong with socialism or those other notions he'd read so much about. It was human nature and human greed that had fouled it all up. He'd lacked experience in the ways of the world, but he knew a lot more now. You'd to discover those drives in yourself before you could make sense of it all. He'd had his fill of daft politics, and women too, for a while.

Sweet Rita! Why had he called her Rita when he'd spoken of her to the Prof? It was a Freudian slip, of course. He'd fantasized often for Marguerite – Margaret Miller – the lass he'd written some verse for back there in Aberdeen. The Rita of his dreams had rejected him and that had hurt his ego. 'And so I'll sing a song of Marguerite,' he'd written.

That had been a short infatuation, of course. Dreams and fantasies in the night are made of such things.

Rita, too, was an infatuation. It hurt him to have to admit to that. Sweet Rita; it never would have worked. They were poles apart in their thinking. Sex, clean, honest romantic sex had drawn them to each other. Rita had helped him discover himself, and maybe he too had helped Rita. They'd both enjoyed their times together. Rita was bound to find someone closer to her way of thinking. She'd soon get over that petty thief who'd let her down.

But why had he boasted like that to the Prof? It was sheer vanity, of course, and the Prof, for all his intelligence had wanted to hear him say it. How had he put it? 'Yes, I did get to know the uttermost secrets of her body and soul,' he had bragged. It had seemed the kind of language that would most appeal to the Prof. He led a lonely life and needed some sort of titillation to compensate for the shattering of his dreams. All lies of course; he'd never have done *that* to Rita!

God, they were at Laurencekirk already. They'd be at Fordoun and Drumskite before he knew it. There was a danger of bumping into some of those coarse bothy billies and the rest. News travelled fast, and he could do without those knowing winks and nods. But he needed to be back in the peace of those hills, to lie down by the Big Stane. He drew strength and inspiration from that ancient place. There were good friends up here too, well, one or two maybe, like Rob Middleton and Alex Gray, the Dominie. And there were those bairns he'd spent his schooldays with, maybe one or two of them, like Nick Taggart, say. They'd got on fine after that bloody fight they'd had. They'd all be a lot older now. He was fantasizing again, the freudian part of himself, some would call it, though he'd little patience for most of Freud's nonsense. Chris Queen, how had she turned out? He wondered about Chris. She was the beauty of the class. She'd caught him looking at her, before he'd understood her attraction. She'd annoyed him with the daft books that she read, romance and sillyness, he'd thought at the time. Well, Chris and those quines had been maturing far faster than he and the rest of the lads in the class. It was Rebecca that had surprised him the most, however. She too, had been maturing faster. Chris had been the pretty one and intelligent too. They'd shared the glory in that essay competition. So what was it about Rebecca? Rebecca had more of a gypsy look to her, deep and dark and thoughtful, and her skin was a gypsy olive and smooth. Her hair was so black. When the sun shone sharp on Rebecca's black hair it was the deepest of black, it brought out the blueness of black that twinkled and shone. There was a hidden depth to Rebecca. He'd ignored her for so long. They'd trudged those miles together and he'd paid her no heed.

Of a sudden they were at Drumskite and he was fantasizing still. Thank God he was the only passenger to get off at the wee platform that night. He'd that coarse road to climb and a heavy case to drag. It was the last train of the day and it was early summer. Scudding clouds were darkening the track but there was light enough to pick his way up the brae he'd walked so often in the dark. It was the rickety bridge at Mondynes that put father's rage and mother's scowls from his head. The bridge brought it all back, the night of the storm and the snow, the night he'd put her frozen hand in his pocket and they'd laughed and sung all the way up that hill. That was the night they'd clung close at the gate and she'd kissed him back; for an age, they had kissed. He was being naive again, but he was only eighteen, he told himself, and the urge in him was strong. Anyway, it was summer, a time for holidays and fun. Was there a chance, he wondered, Becky might be back home?

TWENTY-THREE

'That's a fair pickle you've landed yourself into this time.' Rob Middleton came straight to it, stapping some Bogie Roll into his pipe. 'What plans have you got now?'

Leslie was relieved. There had been no talking about the thing to Father, or to Mother either. 'You'll get yourself a fee,' Father had said and that had put an end to it.

'I'll walk the streets first,' was the only daft answer he'd been able to dream up. But he'd have to leave, there was no escaping that. Rob Middleton and Fanny had moved over the hill to a bigger place at Nether Craighill, for there seemed no end to the bairns. Fanny sat in the corner with the youngest on her lap, shaking her head at the capers he'd had. Rob nodded the while as he burst out with the lot, about his job and the Bolshies, as Rob insisted in calling them, and how he'd kept them all on the trot. This was the first chance he'd had to get it all off his chest.

'Man, you've worked hard enough for all of them. One job would have done.' Rob was fair entranced by the tale of Bloody Friday. He'd read about the Red Clydesiders in the *Advertiser,* but Leslie gave it a different slant. He laughed loud and long when he heard about the brothel. The tears streamed down his cheeks and he looked as if he'd choke. Rebecca stood at the door, an odd look on her face.

'Losh man,' said Rob, 'so that's how they do things by the Clyde. I doubt the Reverend Dunn would have a sermon or two if they started capers like that at the Big Hoose.'

Rebecca stirred herself at that and rattled about with the tea cups. Her dad got carried away when visitors were in, and Leslie brought out the worst in him. Things quietened then and Rob reminisced on the antics of some characters they knew. Becky's scones were a treat and Leslie got some of his old confidence back. He was able to look her in the eye at last, but he said not a word about that lass he'd called Rita.

'There's nothing else for it,' he said at last. 'I never thought I'd hear myself say it, but I'll have to join up. The fighting's ended after all and I've no chance of a job. A year or two in the peace-time army will give me a chance to do some serious writing. They feed you and clothe you and they say there's plenty of free time now there's no war to fight.'

Rob nodded. 'Aye. You've no liking for farm work, lad, and there's little else to be got hereabouts.'

'I thought I'd give the Royal Toun a try first. They say the Inspector's back from the war and he's been told to get jobs for folk so they can save more of their precious parish silver.'

'That's a thought, lad.' Rob's eyes lit up. 'The Inspector's strong on the kirk though. The tale is he takes after his faither, an auld bit man from Banff. Shaking and done he was, before the young lad was born, aye preaching on about the olden days. This hardly fits in with our way of thinking, but you're fell keen yourself on the olden days, Becky tells me, so maybe he's the man for you.' Becky threw her dad a wild look, but Rob rambled on. 'He's full of new notions, they say, aye lecturing on this and writing on that. Maybe he's worth a try. They say if there's a job in the place, he'll ferret the thing out for you, the speerity Jim Geddes.'

Rebecca was setting out for the shop when he left so he walked alongside her as far as the main road. They walked in silence for a while. She'd got herself a steady job in a government office and would be going back again at the weekend. Rebecca always managed to keep her head in difficult times and press on with her life. What a mess he kept making of things. He was slipping back into his thoughts again, pondering and cogitating.

She knew him well, the way his mind worked. There was little point in making sympathetic noises, that would only make him worse. Better to be outright and realistic about the future. 'You could end up in India or some exciting place like that,' she said with a laugh. 'Be sure and send me a postcard if you do. One of the Taj Mahal would be nice.'

Leslie clasped her hand and looked into her eyes, they were deep, gypsy eyes, just as he'd remembered them. Her lips were soft and moist and she still had that sultry olive smoothness on her cheeks. They'd filled out a little since he'd seen her last. This lass by his side was developing into a young woman. The quiet little school lass had disappeared for ever.

'Oh I'll do that, if that's how it works out, but I'll give the Royal Toun a try first.' His pulse was racing and he squeezed her hand. They turned together and looked at each other, remembering.

'Promise me you'll write though,' he said. 'You're the only one, you know, who might.'

She put her arm round his neck and drew him towards her. He kissed her more gently, more confidently, more enjoyably than he'd done that first time. That time, he'd acted on instinct and roused the two of them in the darkness of the storm. This time they kissed in broad daylight.

The world out there was cold and unfeeling. A strange notion took hold of him. He wanted to be wanted. Then a strong urge came upon him and they both understood. For a moment nothing was said.

'I promise, I will write you,' Becky said, and they left it at that.

TWENTY-FOUR

'There's a Mr Mitchell would like a word.' Duncan poked his cheeky head round the door of the back office. Duncan Low, a bright, ginger-haired lad with chubby cheeks and a sprinkle of freckles, had quickly caught on to the ways of the Bervie office. Jim had persuaded the Bailie to let him take on the young lad. It would cost them only a few bob a week and the Council were screaming out for a balance sheet. The Bailie and a lass had kept things on the move during the war years, but the Council had stood by long enough. Those wastrels, they said, were a drain on the Toun's rates. What had become, they needed to know, of all their hard earned silver?

Short time working in the mills and changes in the countryside with bigger farms and the new machines were making the country a better place for fewer and fewer folk. Only in the Bervie office was there work in plenty. The front office was forever crowded with jobless mill quines and ex-servicemen, all dropping in for a crack. Duncan handled them fine, bright and cheery like. He knew every soul in the place and there was none that could spin him a tale.

'Mr Geddes has somebody with him just now,' Duncan would say, giving a mysterious look to the back office, and they'd nod at that. They'd

138

look back later, they'd scowl, and rush out to the summer glare, a bit conspicuous like, and over near to Pappa Gibb's house close by, next to the brig.

The wee office at number three the Cowgate was hardly the place if you'd secrets to hide. Jim and Duncan could do little to stop folks' troubles being public entertainments. The counter, with a flap at the far end to let you pass through, split the room in two and there was little enough room for you to squeeze past the legs of folk sitting on the long form with their backs to the wall.

Leslie was embarrassed when Duncan gave him the nod. He thanked them as folk drew in their legs and he made his way to the end where Duncan held up the flap. There was little to cheer a man on that grim wall, Leslie noticed. There were threats about unpaid rates or bills from the Bervie Gas Company, and there were huge posters listing the penalties you'd suffer if you went poaching for the odd rabbit or for one of their precious salmon. The only choice of a steady job, it seemed, was in the army or the navy, unless you took up the offer of some acres of land in Canada or Australia. The Inspector had a box of bonny leaflets with pictures of kangaroos on them he was tempted to pick up.

Leslie edged his way to the back office and closed the door behind him. The place was more cramped than out front. The Inspector was seated at his desk, fitted in between a filing cabinet and a huge iron safe. He was scribbling down some figures he was checking from a ready reckoner. Amongst the papers on the desk was a typing machine and a solid looking black telephone, its head stuck up through all the clutter. The telephone rang just then. The Inspector lifted the earpiece from its cradle and grabbed the phone in his right hand. 'Geddes, Bervie,' he said, nodding to Leslie to take a seat.

The phone conversation was about the hire of a dancing board, returned from the Arbuthnott sports. It was needed elsewhere. While the transport arrangements were being worked out, with odd asides about the fitness of the characters involved, Leslie gathered his thoughts. Wherever he looked, there were papers and ledgers, cases and sports gear, all presumably collected by this speerity man, as Rob Middleton had described him. The window ledge, the filing cabinet, the safe and the desk were piled with the stuff. Heavy equipment lay scattered on the floor. Leslie noticed a tea urn and a pile of coloured flags with bits of earth still sticking to their wooden posts. A partly opened parcel of football strips and a brand new set of bowls lay in the corner. Over on the window sill were some hymn books and a box of tiny paper flags – a flag day on Saturday, by the look of it. A scout hat and a lanyard hung from a peg behind the door. Sundry photographs had been pinned on the wall and, near to the telephone, scraps of paper with pencilled notes on them had been fixed to the woodwork by drawing pins. Leslie was fascinated but nonplussed. Where would this energetic but overburdened man, however speerity, find the time to solve his daft problems?

'My apologies, Mr Mitchell,' said Jim at last, pushing the earpiece back in its cradle. 'Busier than usual today, but things sort themselves out.' Jim smiled and sat back in his chair. He was quite a tall man, Five foot ten or more, and looked fit and sunburned. Leslie saw that he observed him in a penetrating, but kindly way. He'd sharp grey eyes and he wore a grey, slightly crumpled suit, complete with weskit and the obligatory gold chain looping grandly to the watch in either pocket. His grey tie was loosely knotted round a white, celluloid collar. His hair was jet black and neatly combed.

The last occasion Jim had seen young Mitchell had been at those boisterous Games they'd run, far back, before the war. What an age ago that was, and what changes there had been. Mitchell had been a schoolboy then, fair entertained at the Arbuthnott team pulling the Dundee bobbies over the mark. He was a young man now, but Jim recognised the likeness, that intelligent look and those clear, hazel eyes that summed you up shrewdly. He was about five foot six or so, and neatly dressed. His well pressed suit showed slight signs of wear if you looked closely enough. His soft brown hair was neatly combed, but it was that steady, thoughtful gaze he remembered from that time at the Games. You could see he was under some kind of stress by the tightness of his lips. He needed to unburden himself. Jim offered him a fag.

Leslie relaxed and responded to Jim's easy style. This Mr Geddes was not what he'd expected from an inspector, the guardian of the parish silver. He was a big improvement on that coarse editor who'd ranted away at him back there in Glasgow.

'I had a spot of bother when I lost my last job.' Leslie looked at Jim closely. The whole of the Howe would have heard about his troubles by this time, and no doubt this easy going Inspector had heard about them too, and a lot more besides. The Inspector, he'd heard, was forever hobnobbing with the Reverend Dunn and the Dominie.

'I heard they'd decided not to prosecute,' said Jim. 'That's a help for a start. There's little chance, you think, of getting back into the newspaper business. Could you make a fresh start south of the border, do you think?'

'I've thought about that, but it's time I need. Father's getting wild about things. I've got to get out of the house right away.'

Jim nodded. He'd heard how it was. The rest of the parish would be watching, a bit maliciously, to see what happened next. A nasty business. 'The situation here's getting worse by the day,' Jim said softly. 'The place is full of ex-servicemen, all looking for work. Any sort of work,' he added.

'There was plenty of work when the war was on,' Leslie started. They blethered away then about the politics of it all. Jim disagreed amiably with young Mitchell's notions, and he reacted differently from Rob when Leslie described the happenings of Bloody Friday.

'Most folk have had enough to put up with during the war years,' he said. 'They just want to get on quietly with their lives.'

Duncan pushed his head round the door. There was a pile of work building up in the front office. A bairn was crying and a young mother looked as though she was about to collapse.

'The army seems the only answer.' Leslie stood up. 'I've been giving it some thought. Things might improve in a year or two. By that time I might have worked something out.'

Jim shook his hand and wished him well. 'I'd some good times in the army,' he said, thinking back to those times he'd spent with Ginger and the rest, sailing that summer on the quiet reaches of the Norfolk Broads.

Leslie pushed his way out past the crowd in the front office. There was standing room only now. Something was far wrong with a system that found work for folk only when there was a war to fight. This Mr Geddes was a strange character. He acted more like a priest at the confessional instead of the stern guardian of the parish silver. There was little doubt though, this speerity Inspector was a man of the establishment. Nobody would trap him into one of those socialist cliques that had messed up his own career. One day this Mr Geddes would find himself a comfy wife who'd look after some local charity. She'd probably spend her spare time giving slide talks to the women's guild on her last holiday in the Alps!

There was little chance that year of Jim, or the boys either, getting wed, Madge and the rest of the quines soon discovered that. There was so much to catch up on and 1919 was going to be an exciting year, so Jim got to work on the peace celebrations, his Kirk picnics, his concerts and his dances. Committees were springing up for ploys Madge and the rest had never heard of.

One affair was in the social club down the Kirkburn. Some had started calling it the toffs' club which showed how things were shaping up. Jim planned a night for the ex-servicemen, an idea he'd had since he'd seen them knock back the French *bière* at that Christmas affair behind the Front. Jim still stuck to his ginger ale, but he got quite carried away along with the rest of them when they harmonised quietly, singing the soldiers' dirge for The Old Battalion:

> If you want to find the old battalion,
> I know where they are,
> I know where they are.
> If you want to find a battalion,
> I know where they are.
> They're hanging on the old barbed wire.
> I've seen 'em, I've seen 'em,
> Hanging on the old barbed wire.
> I've seen 'em,
> Hanging on the old barbed wire.

But they'd to put all that behind them. Jim had to look out for those folk who'd been hit the hardest and draw up a balance sheet for the Council. There were hard-pressed souls shivering out there in the country who'd slipped through the net, and a fair crowd in the Royal Toun had been caught by the short-time working in the mills. The Council were stunned when Jim said it was more silver he needed, not less, so they let him run a flower day for the ex-servicemen – an odd sort of thing for men who'd just won a war!

To be fair, the lads Doon Sooth had rewarded their heroes well. Field Marshall Haig and Admiral Beattie each got an earldom and a tax-free present of £100,000 for the hard times they now faced. Sir Julian Byng whose tanks near took Cambrai, though he'd ill-prepared for what to do next, was made a viscount with £30,000 to help him keep up with the times. And the Bervie lads were well remembered. The lowest private among them got a clear £20 to himself. He got another pound forby, it was pointed out, if he handed in his greatcoat at the railway station. A mill quine would work for twenty weeks and never see as much, they'd tell you at the Star.

The best news of all had come through on the 6 May. The Provost read it out to the Council himself. The lads in the War Office had decided to reward the Royal Toun for the loss of her 70 lads and all the work folk had put in, fund raising and the rest. Provided they paid the carriage, said the Provost, they would receive a free gift of one German machine gun (damaged), one German ammunition box, and one German machine gun ammunition belt.

In August the Council were awarded other trophies – a captured German gun and a 150mm howitzer. They got a share too, of more trophies still that had been handed in at Stonehive.

There were some ill-fitted agitators who said guns did little for the unemployed, like the tinks up at Nairn who dumped one of their German guns in the river and another two in the harbour. There might have been one or two tinks in the Royal Toun of the same mind, but that was soon hushed up. You'd little wish to embarrass a famous Royal Toun.

The Royal Toun never got back to those great days before the war. The old mill had gone and Pappa Gibb's new mill was shut for months on end. David did his best, keeping his three mills on short-time. Only Dave Burness with his Pitcarry Mill and Willie Peter's Selbie Works in Gourdon kept up a steady pace. With the Russian flax gone, the price of flax was astronomical. Some wondered if another fire might come to the rescue, but that was just coarse talk. There was no justification for it.

A fire did break out though, at Ed Gibb's Johnshaven mill. It did a thousand pounds worth of damage to some Russian tow and other odds and ends that were lying about. But the big fire, when it did come, was during armistice time in November at Pappa Gibb's New Mill down in the Haughs. It happened in broad daylight during working hours when an overheated bearing set things off. The talk was that the Montrose fire brigade had been held up at St Cyrus when some well meaning souls gave each of the firemen a drink. Like most Bervie tales, there was not a word of truth in that. The Montrose brigade would have been of little use in any case. Montrose, as folk know well enough, is over thirteen miles to the Sooth.

The year 1919 ended then, with another hundred workers on the dole. When young David Webster spoke to Pappa Gibb about doing something for the Royal Toun, Pappa's answer was short and to the point. 'The grass can grow on the streets of Bervie, David, for all I care,' he said.

TWENTY-FIVE

The winds howled through the Mearns in the twenties as coarse and as wild as ever. There were winds too, of a different sort, ripping away at the notions folk had held in those far off days before the war. They brought the quines the vote and that made little odds, but there was a freshness in the air and young folk everywhere perked up and fair enjoyed the smell of it.

The weddings came first, a whole spate of weddings. Jim wed his Madge in the Queen's Hotel at Montrose. The teetotal Bailie raised his glass as if to the manner born: 'I drink your health in clear cold water,' he said, but that raised a few titters, for most knew the Bailie had been slipping of late, throwing back the odd dram down there at the Crown. Bert wed his Janet, the nice teacher from Gourdon, and Harris got his Bella, the lass from Stonehive who'd kept things bright and cheery up by at Hazelgrove.

Hazelgrove provided the spiciest of tales. Young David was back from his English quines, as Teen had it, to put new life into the Bervie mills. David wasted no time in being hitched to the only lass of a wealthy Jute Merchant in Carnoustie. It was the wedding of the year, they said, with a grand reception at the Bruce Hotel. The best man was Johnny Burness, back from Borneo with his sun tan to have a look at the Burness side of the mills.

Stella David was a bonny lass and a cut above the Bervie quines, well suited to handle the running of Bervie's Big Hoose, so she and David set out to enjoy themselves and put the Royal Toun back on the map. It was only natural then, folk nodded, that Young Alice, as they still called her, should look around for a lad of her own. Alice had broken Old Jock's will and David had been glad enough at the time when she'd got her £50,000. She was his mam, after all, and that would keep her in some style. Besides, the silver was still there, and he'd got the three mills, Kinghornie Farm and half of Bervie forby.

It was the lad Alice chose that caused all the stir. Even Jim had to smile. 'That's romance for you now, Madge,' he laughed, 'as good as any you'll find in those novels you read.'

'But Douglas Ogg!' Madge gasped. 'David's school chum! Alice is old enough to be his mother. Whatever will David think of that?'

Whatever David thought made very little odds. He'd enough ploys of his own to see to and the new times to enjoy. Alice and her Douglas bought themselves the Heugh House in Stonehive, close enough to the Royal Toun, but not over near. A fitting place, you would say, for a grand lass like Alice, with big hooses nearby and lawyers by the score.

There was no Big Hoose for Jim and his Madge, though. A parish inspector can do better than most, but a place like Heugh House was far beyond Jim's reach. He settled for a snug, terraced house with an attic up top and a plot of land at the back. It was down in the Kirkburn, half way to the beach, next door to Elliot, the Stationy.

Jim looked out from his new terraced house, past the crossroads to the station and the sea beyond, lying quiet and still there in the clear morning air. The road across and to the left was the narrow, crowded David Street, shadowed by those jostling buildings the spinners had lived in and swarmed in for a century or more. To his right and just out of sight, was the Castle Terrace, a quiet, genteel sort of street, sheltered by the Castle Park trees, its houses set back a bit and better spaced with their trim gardens in front, well fenced from the street.

'They call the Kirkburn the Great Divide, Madge,' he smiled, 'separating the haves from the have-nots. I suppose that means we are now living in a kind of no-man's-land. I don't see any barbed wire there though.'

Madge looked puzzled. Jim's jokes were rare and not aye understood.

So things looked bright for the twenties. The bad days were behind you and the good times had arrived. The quines in their skimpy frocks and the lads in their flannel bags thumbed their noses at the sour notions of the Council and the Kirk. Even Madge and Jim bought a grand oak gramophone with doors on the front and stood it in the back parlour. You cranked up the handle, opened the doors and out blared 'Happy Days are Here Again' or 'Me and Jane in a Plane', thin and scrawny like, not deep and full blooded as Bert and the Bervie orchestra would have it, but it stirred you just the same – on week days that is, for Madge and Jim kept the lid and the doors of their new contraption tightly shut on a Sunday.

The new tunes and dances fair caught on and folk were set to enjoy things whatever the cost. There were some that looked back and spoke of the golden days, but even they got caught up in the times they were in. For the young and those that thought they were young, the jazz time had arrived and they danced the Charleston at Kinneff and in the Bervie Burgh Hall. Willie Lyon's picture palace and the newspaper billies with their news and their magazines said things would never be the same again. The times were modern. American slang was okay, though the speak of the Mearns, or Buchan, of Shetland or the Borders stayed much the same as ever. A trickle of American words slipped in and were added to the Scot's speak. You could all speak toity English when you had to, but you did it with a smirk and felt you were saying damn all when you did.

The more flirty quines put on powder and paint and bought long cigarette holders. It was good for a laugh. The newspaper billies called them flappers, but they had other names for them in the Howe. When the sun shone and the Mearns got its ten days of sun they called a heatwave, they got into the sea by the salmon bothy in a way that was scandalous. Bervie had no prissy shelters like Montrose, where there were Clydesdales to haul the wheeled bathing huts up and down with the tide so the quines could slip on to the sands, quick and decent like. In Bervie the quines squealed as they stripped behind the cobles and the salmon nets at the beach or 'O'er the Water'.

They went on charabanc trips to Drumtochty Glen and splashed through the fords. High up the Cairn o' Mount, they tumbled out and unloaded their picnics and their portable gramophones. The thin notes of 'The Japanese Sandman' or 'I'll Say She Does' drifted over the Howe and they felt like Jane in her Plane, high up in the clouds, away above the rest. Back in Bervie they'd scandalise the Toun by ending up in the Crown Hotel, sipping the latest cocktail Andra McLeod had dreamt up in the back kitchen he called his saloon bar.

David and Stella were no different. David had his mills to run through the ups and downs of trade, but that was little excuse for not enjoying the time that was theirs. He got himself a movie camera and flew over Bervie taking shots of the place. He'd then run a picture show of the Royal Toun from the air, and that fair caused a stir. David had his Air Force connections, but you could all get up in the air if you'd a few bob to spare when the Flying Circus came to Stonehive.

Jim Peter ran his buses and even Andra McLeod at the Crown ran a bus down the back roads of Kinneff. Andra had been a horse hirer once and he took on the Crown Hotel that his wife's folk had run, but he still had a flair for moving folk around. Up in Laurencekirk, Craigie and Mitchell built motors, as good as any you'd get Doon Sooth.

It was a time for experiment, and Jimmy Moir, who'd a flair for all things electrical, built a box wireless for Jim and Madge with valves and earphones, and batteries you could charge up at the garage. Through the earphones you could hear a wife shout out, 'hullo twins', clear as you like, if you fiddled the knob through the squeaks and the howls. There was magic in the air!

David thrilled the Toun when he and Stella got their third car. Few folk in Bervie had any car at all. Apart from the laird, the mill lairds, the doctor and Jim Peter who ran a taxi, there was barely a soul had the silver or the need to own a motor car. There were buses galore and still three trains a day came into the place, so what would a body need a motor car for? David and Stella's three cars brought a bit of a bustle to the roads and more trade to the garage where Jim Peter had a crowd of mechanics to handle his buses and the two or three lorries that had come in about. The Websters' cars would never all be on the go at the same time of course, for there was 'his car' and 'her car' and 'their car', as they would have it. Folk were fine pleased to see that David's car, a three litre Sunbeam, was the snappiest and sportiest of the three.

David got himself on to the Council and become a junior bailie and convener of the Gas Works. He got a big new gas tank and Bervie set itself against the electric company from moving in and upsetting things now the Toun owned its own gas company. They'd electricity of their own in the mills, in the picture palace and in the garage, and they could run a line to Hazelgrove and places like that, if there was a need for it. The Toun had new gas lamps too, and some had gadgets for turning them on without matches that were as handy as electric switches any day. Other touns could go in for electricity, but the Royal Toun had its own supply of gas.

That was only part of the tale, though. Jobs were harder to get now, and that gave a better shape to the tales you heard about those golden days before the war. Jim and Duncan struggled with the dole queues. Jim would get Peter's taxi to haul its way up past the dykes at Arbuthnott to check on the hardest cases on his roll. He'd come on the odd cheerless croft where bairns with not a bite to eat, would lie huddled in their quilts. Jim would load up with pies and bridies, but he'd fill the car as well with any bairns that were there. It made little sense for a seat to go spare if a bairn could have a hurl!

Young lads could do little else but join the army, even lads that had been through all the soss in France, so bad had things become. Leslie was not the only lad from the Howe to join up, but it hurt him more than most. He'd sworn they'd never conscript him to do all their killing. He'd been seventeen on armistice day, but principles are hard things to live by. That summer of 1919, when he'd made a last try for a job in the Royal Toun with that soft spoken man in the wee back office, he'd found he'd little choice.

There was no sense in railing against the army, he knew. The Royal Army Service Corps was no worse than any other, and he got his food and his shelter. There was time too, to sort out his thinking. He got on with his reading of Darwin and Huxley and those odd tales by H G Wells, but it was the morals and the speak of the barrack room that upset him the most.

Private Leslie Mitchell stretched out on the string bed and tried to make sense of the world. The rough army blanket would have been of some comfort back home on the Reisk, but out here in the desert it had him tearing and scratching at the bites on his back and the sores on his feet. He closed his eyes and tried to shut out the coarse guffaws from the other end of the hut.

You could never shut out that barrack room stench. What was it about army life that turned men into beasts, destroyed their self respect, and reduced their speak to a string of obscenities? Leslie discussed that at length with old Harvey who sat there, sucking his pipe, unbothered by it all. The worst of the brutes left old Harvey alone. Even the sadistic Sergeant Coster left Harvey to his thoughts.

'We'd a pride in fighting the Kaiser's war,' said Harvey, 'for all its bloody madness. Thank God that's over and done with, but sodgering in peace time is a job for the riff-raff.'

That scarcely helped, but he was developing a sense of humour. Seeing the comic side of things helped keep him sane. Army life had broadened his thinking, and he began to scribble tales about the Egyptians and their different ways to while away the time. Things looked sharper in the lands of the Arabs. He saw things he'd never have seen if he hadn't joined up.

He laughed at the sleekit look on the Sphinx and he ate peanuts on top of Cheops, the largest of the pyramids. Sitting there, he marvelled at the conceit of the human race. There must have been a time, he thought, after man had lost his animal swagger and the ape-like thumping of his chest, that he'd really been free. The evidence was all around him, five thousand years of it or more. They must have been mad, those Pharaohs, preserving their stinking bodies to keep them going on for ever. What an attraction it must have been, to think you could eat and drink and fertilise the wombs of your squaws through all eternity! All they'd got out of it, though, were those ugly pyramids of stone, surely the most boring and futile monuments ever to have been built.

He was forced to laugh at the madness of it all, when two natives settled down beside him and started scratching like mad. One was selling small bottles of lemonade and the other had a stack of obscene photographs. Was that the verdict of posterity on religions everywhere, he wondered. He dug out a wee coin and bought a bottle of their lemonade.

He made the most of his travels. He visited Hebron and Jerusalem, Cairo and Bethlehem. Bethlehem! It was Christmas Eve and he went along with the rest of his squad. What a shambles it turned out to be. There were crowds of different faiths, or were they all of the same faith crowding in to the place. What would Christ himself have thought of it all? And who was Christ, he puzzled, some sort of Judean Bernard Shaw, shocking the world to get his message across? He'd shocked them by blessing the poor and cursing the rich and powerful, yet he claimed more power than they could ever have.

He'd shocked them even more when he declared that prostitutes were their equals. How had Christ accepted that tale of his mother being a virgin? Had He wondered at that, wondered if he'd been fathered by a Greek or Roman legionary? Mother's first bairns, George and John, must have wondered at times, back there on the Reisk. It was an eternal problem all folk had to face, the true identity of father!

He rode a camel in the desert and looked up at an Arab sky, sharp and clear, with stars twice as big as any he'd seen on that rough road to Mondynes. The coarseness back in the Howe was nothing like this, with all the squalor and stench in the touns and their neglect of the dying. What a welter it was of beauty and filth, a loving and a hating all kirned in together. That Christmas Eve in Bethlehem had brought it all back, the way men treated their women. The clearest picture he had of that Christmas

Eve, was of the drunks in his squad, tightly hanging on to those brown, apathetic prostitutes outside the Church of the Nativity, groping and retching till the call came for them to hurry down and celebrate the midnight mass.

He lay there on the deck, sailing homewards at last, dreaming as ever of the broom clad braes and Arbuthnott's den in June. That burst of heat aye caught folk by surprise. He thought for a time of Rita, sweet delightful Rita, but that was over and in the past. He mused then on the wee school at the roadside, with the holidays near, and all those places he'd hated and loved, the snotty nosed bairns with their black, Pictish looks and their sniggers in the playground at strange tales they thought coarse. He dreamt of the quines, so slight and pale were some, how long would they last? Some were more rosy and plump, a life of toil and pain still to come. Some quines he dreamt on more, like the bonny Chris, sitting just across the aisle. So fine and swack she'd been, with her soft silken hair. Her smile was so warm. He'd been a bit sharp on Chris, he could see that now. He'd scarce been ready for quines at that early stage, and Chris had little time for his dry books and all his talk of flints and those stones on the braes. She'd laugh if he spoke of the den and its coarse like beasts. She'd laughed too when he'd spoken of the kirk the Norman knights had left behind. He'd been younger then with notions of his own, with little time for the romantic tales in those magazines Chris kept in her bag. But she was a sweet lass Chris, and that had been her way of it.

Rebecca was different. Strange how long it had taken him. He'd never thought of Rebecca in that way, trailing those roads together, first to the school, then on that other road to the station near Mondynes. That kiss in the storm had stirred him at first. He'd scarce given sex a thought until that kiss from Rebecca, so caught up had he been with those flints on the brae and those socialist books he'd discovered. But sex had brought its own agonies to plague him. The disgrace and the shame mother had suffered because of sex stirred a deep anger inside him. His own mother, humiliated like that, and men walking away from it all, boasting and proud of the wild times they'd had.

He agonised then on those bothy billies and their coarse talk, the overworked blondes and the grinning clowns on the stairs. It was even worse in the army with those squalid trips that were planned. Afterwards came the bragging! Women were fair game. They were the victims, there was a general acceptance about that.

How ever could he write about the world as it was then? Was there no place for loving and caring any more? He'd never sell books if he wrote about love. The world wanted to be titillated. Anything about sex that was clean and natural and honest would be censored. Sex and the human body were now classified as filth, to be enjoyed in a lecherous kind of way, out of sight but never out of mind. There must be a place somewhere between the Kailyard and the obscene.

Rebecca had written as she'd promised. He knew she would, and he'd poured out his thoughts to her. He'd overdone it, of course, with all his philosophising. When she'd had enough of his ravings she'd held back for a time, but writing like that had helped keep him on track, and he'd got mad at her when she failed to write. She was in London now, and had started writing again. London had horrors of its own, she'd said, and she'd been glad of his news.

After that, those long desert nights had been harder to bear and he'd told her so. He needed her more than ever now, he'd said. By the time he'd served his four years in the army, he'd be set up as a writer and the two of them would wed. That's what he'd planned and that's what he'd written.

He raised himself up and walked across to the rail. The air was heavy and nobody stirred. The troopship was shaping a course through the Straits. He caught a whiff of the burnt smell of Africa floating over in the stillness of the afternoon. In front, the huge Rock loomed, dwarfing everything below it. In an hour or two they'd leave Gibraltar far behind. They'd swing north then for the breezier seas of Biscay. A week from now he'd be back as a civilian; a penniless, jobless civilian. He'd been scribbling away like mad in the last four years, but there had been much better things he wanted to say. There were reams of the stuff stirring about in his head, books galore just waiting for his pen. That was the trouble, of course, he'd still to make a start. He'd have a job explaining that to Rebecca when he met up with her again in London!

TWENTY-SIX

Rebecca was wary of him at first. He'd booked into the YMCA and rushed round to see her in the morning, first thing. He felt awkward from the start. Had those years in the army changed him that much? Or had Rebecca changed.

'Clerical Officers are ten a penny in London.'

Rebecca looked at him. It was Saturday afternoon, and they were sitting, self-consciously, in Lyon's Tea Room, a pot of tea and some cream cakes on the table. Leslie had just congratulated her, for the second time, on landing a steady pensionable job in the metropolis. He'd really forgotten how it was, to sit and chat quietly to a lass. It was early spring, but London was warm and Rebecca was relaxed and cool in a blue cotton dress. He thought of Rita and those hot spring afternoons on the Campsies. Rebecca disturbed him more and he was tongue-tied. His talk had been clumsy. Those letters he'd written, saying they would wed. Suddenly he felt such a fool.

'We could go dancing, if you like,' he said.

Rebecca smiled. London had given her a new assurance. It unnerved him a little after years with those swaddies and their uncouth, loutish ways.

'This isn't Arbuthnott, Leslie,' she said. Her Mearns burr was still there, but she'd picked up a gentle English twang that sounded sweet to his ears. 'The ballrooms here are rather chic and overpowering. We're having a dance of our own though. It's the Civil Service Clerical Association's last dance of the season. You could come along to that and meet some of my friends.'

He wore his Royal Army Service Corps uniform as he was entitled to, being still on demob leave, but Rebecca's friends were a sophisticated bunch. They looked a bit askance at being introduced to a simple private, he thought, and that got him off to a bad start. What a tight little clique they were. Their talk was all about the office, their tea breaks and a dreadful Mr Brown who seemed to wield enormous power, something of an office tyrant, who dominated all their waking hours.

'He treats us like workers,' said a superior young quine, waving a long cigarette holder across the table. 'You'd think we were shop girls or waitresses, the way he speaks.'

Leslie took Rebecca onto the floor after that. 'That's a snobbish bunch of dames you're caught up with in the Civil Service,' he whispered. He was recovering some of his old confidence, and dancing close like this brought on that urge he'd felt that last time. That was when he'd kissed her on the long road from the Reisk, the time he'd spoken of joining up.

'They're a good crowd really,' said Rebecca, annoyed at the way he'd snubbed them. He hadn't even tried to be sociable. 'We've had some good fun over the winter months. None of us is that keen on the Association. It does precious little for us. The men get all the perks, and it's men who are on the committee. We only joined because of the dances.'

'The Association is your trade union,' Leslie began, 'you should bring up your grievances at their meetings.'

'Better not let them hear you calling their association a trade union. I should think they're all loyal true blue tories. They'd never go near an association meeting. Besides, the men would soon shout them down.'

Leslie gave up after that. Politics had got him into trouble the last time he was in civvy street, and it was too early to start all that again.

'What are your plans, now you've left the army?' asked the precocious dame with the cigarette holder.

'I've applied for a job as a salesman,' he said, thinking that would shut her up. What business was it of hers anyway?

They greeted that remark with silence. The evening never got going after that. They went on the floor again to escape the daft chatter, but everything went wrong. He couldn't get the hang of the syncopation and the strange rhythms of the new jazz. 'Forced and artificial,' he muttered watching a plump matron skirling away and swinging her hands in the air.

'People are throwing off their inhibitions and the old stuffy ways,' Rebecca explained, exasperated at his behaviour. He was making an exhibition of himself, not letting his hair down and joining in the fun.

This was not how he'd planned it, and he was annoyed with himself. The fault was his, of course. The sudden change from the army to this new world of the twenties was all too much to take in at once and he hadn't the patience to handle it. He was frustrated too. There was so much he'd like to do but first he'd to earn a living. He just had to get out into the fresh air, away from all this forced hilarity. Rebecca was upset, but then so was he. He needed to get away for a bit to clear his head.

She let him walk her back to her digs in silence. He was back to his old dour ways again, it seemed, so she left him to his worries. He'd have to work this one out for himself.

'I'm sorry I messed things up for you,' he said at last when they arrived on her doorstep. 'I've got out of the habit of this kind of thing. I'll get myself a decent job first. That'll put me in a better mood. Sorry I've been such an idiot.'

She softened to him then and made to say something bright, but he put his hand on her sleeve and kissed her briefly on the cheek. It was then she should have spoken, but the moment had passed and she watched him in silence as he walked quickly down the street.

The months that followed were his own private hell. The salesman's job, tramping the streets and knocking on doors, got him nothing but abuse and precious little silver. He tried writing but none of it would sell. Writing was a long term occupation and it was now he needed the cash. He moved from one dreary accommodation to the next but, by the end of summer, his savings and his demob pay finally ran out. For the third time in his life he was penniless and jobless. There was no question of heading for that Mondynes road on this occasion, and by the middle of August things were desperate. Before the end of the month, he made up his mind, braced himself, and walked straight down to the recruiting office. The Royal Air Force, he decided, had a better look to it than the army. A short spell there might give him just the time he needed to get on with that book. Life in the RAF could be no worse than what he'd already been through. It would provide him with his basic needs, and, just as important, he'd be able to look the world in the face again. He was still only 22, but for the second time in his life, and against all his convictions, he signed away his independence and swore a solemn oath to the King.

An aircraftsman's life could be just as coarse, he discovered, but it had its compensations and the army had taught him a trick or two. As soon as he'd completed his training at Uxbridge, he organised himself an office job, clerking at RAF Kenley, which was handily placed near London with all its libraries and museums.

He put in a power of work after that, doing two jobs as in his Glasgow days, but this time it was different. He did his Air Force job well and headed for promotion. His real work, as he saw it, was in the library, for ever reading and notetaking. On through Christmas and the New Year and into 1924 he went, catching up on the world, its history and anthropology. For recreation he caught up on those authors who'd made it, to see how it was done.

In the end, though, he had to get back to her. That warm, dark haired lass with the smooth olive skin and those deep, thoughtful eyes was never far from his thoughts. He sent her a telegram. 'Please meet me, Rebecca, outside the British Museum,' he said. He said a lot more. The telegram cost him a fortune, but he had a steady job in London himself now, and money in his pocket. In his RAF uniform, he felt he looked smart. He'd be more positive and more in charge of the situation this time when he met her.

Becky turned up smiling and pleased. He was thinking of her as Becky again, the name they used for her at school. Rebecca had too much of an Old Testament ring to it. Rhea might be better, he thought. Rhea suggested the mystery of ancient Greece, more appropriate to this dark-eyed lass with the smooth olive skin. But that could wait. At least she was smiling and she really looked pleased.

'I've missed you Leslie,' she said, and she came up close. He put his arms on her shoulders and kissed her on the lips. She kissed him back, gently at first, her mouth opening to his, slowly in a long smouldering kiss, right there in the open, out there in the street.

TWENTY-SEVEN

'That's Gourdon over there.'

Becky roused him from his slumbers and he raised himself on one elbow. He was on another ship now, an Aberdeen ship, with Becky in his arms. He eyed the sky, innocent and cloudless, and scanned the lush, green stretch of Scottish coastline. What a beauty was there of sky, land and sea. The sun sparkled on the white harbour beacons and the straight lines of Gourdon's fisher homes. Wheeling gulls trailed a small boat heading for the harbour entrance, and towering behind rose the Knox Hill hiding those Garvock lands and the distant touns of Laurencekirk and Fordoun, deep in the heart of the Howe.

'A picture postcard of a place on a day like this,' he whispered in her ear and pulled her close. 'Imagine those coarse fishers we used to steer clear of coming from a fantastic place like that!'

'You're prejudiced, Leslie,' Becky ruffled his hair. 'Our own bothy billies in Arbuthnott were every bit as bad.'

He breathed in deeply the salt tang of the air. This sail up from London was the best thing he'd ever done. Becky had been thrilled when he'd rushed her down the Thames to catch this boat to the north. What a difference a year could make. He was a leading aircraftman now with a little more cash in his pocket and he'd made a start on his writing.

That had been a good year. He'd planned his free time to fit in those hours at the library and those times Becky had free. Now it was a hot, sunny day in June 1925, which was turning out a rough year for many, but for the two of them, sunning themselves now on this slow boat to the north, it was shaping up as the best year they'd ever seen.

'Meeting your folks still bothers you?' Becky asked, snuggling a little closer.

He caught a whiff of that French perfume he'd bought her. It was a heady mixture. They'd searched out a quiet alcove on the deck, cut off from the other home-going Scots, lying all over the place, sprawled out and soaking up the unaccustomed sun. He was in his shirt sleeves and Becky in the flimsiest of summer wear was warm and soft against his breast. What a grand place a ship was for finding some peace and quiet.

'The Royal Toun's asleep too, by the look of it.' Becky smiled. 'It's fairly quietened down since those wild times they had away before the war. Dad said in his last letter that most of the mills are working short time now. Some have closed down all together.'

Leslie looked out over the blue stretch of sea to the white pebbles of Bervie's beach. At the centre, the grey road of the Kirkburn climbed straight on and up to the square tower of the Auld Kirk, its four turrets silhouetted against the sky, more blue than ever he'd seen it, the mill lums stark on either side.

'There's certainly no smoke from those mills stacks,' he said, 'but I suppose Jim Geddes and the Auld Kirk itself are still working on.'

'That's another picture postcard for you. The Knox Hill and Craig David make a pretty frame for the place. It's strange to think that Arbuthnott and our folk and all the world we used to know are tucked in over there behind that big lump of Rock.'

'The hills and the parks and the beaches are fine. It's folk who cause all the trouble, folk and the two things that drive them, greed and sex; especially sex.' ·

'Oh, you and your sex. You're forever going on about it.' She turned and he saw the tight shape of her breast. He kissed her gently behind the ear and moved his hand over the flimsy stuff of her dress till he held her in his hand. The steady throb of the engines and the summer sun worked on them for a time. They were passing Tod Head and its lighthouse when she eased slightly away and put her hand on top of his. Her softness was past bearing. He kissed her again, more deeply than before.

'Sex is beautiful and natural,' he spoke at last. 'It's the way it's regarded makes it sordid and sad. Look at us last night, the way that old dragon of a stewardess separated the women from the men, at least among those of us of the second class. I daresay they had other arrangements for the crowd upstairs.'

Becky laughed. 'She was making sure there would be no shenanigans as long as she was in charge of the deck.'

'But have you ever seen such a crowd of middle aged respectability? I'd say all of those matrons are respectably wed to those weary men they've dragged along. Not one of them is under 40. They'll have slept with their men and borne all their bairns for the past twenty years.

'But appearances are everything, dear boy.'

'That's what I mean. It's the dreadful difference between appearance and reality. It's dishonest and hypocritical. Look how they were all dressed when we pushed past them on deck.'

That was true, Becky thought to herself, those broadwaisted and well-corseted women must be sweating terribly under the layers of wool and heavy coarse tweed they had on, all in the cause of respectability. Their pasty-faced menfolk with their droopy mousers were no better in their thick drab clothing, their weskits cumbered with all those watch chains and medallions.

'Besides, it would take a contortionist to have any sex on those three-tiered bunks they gave us.'

'I still think she was doing her best to keep up the appearances.'

'Appearances are everything though. You know I'll get no great welcome from my folks tonight, not just because I've let them down, as they say, but because I've been traipsing around with you like this. "It's indecent," they'll say, we're not respectably merrit.'

'I'll vouch for you Les.' She gave him a cuddle.

'But it's all right, you see, if a bothy billy takes a young woman in the dark. It's being found out that's the sin. To traipse around, as we're doing, is immoral, no matter that they know you, no matter how we behave.'

'That prize you won in the short story competition will have pleased them surely?'

'"Siva Plays the Game." That was just a tale from my Egyptian days, a bit of nostalgia. It gave me a good boost, but I doubt if it's impressed my folk or the neighbours. *Cassell's Weekly* might be more prestigious than the *People's Journal,* but I doubt if anybody in Arbuthnott's ever heard of it. That time I won the medal for my essay before the war, you'd have thought I'd done something indecent. They said I should have been out there in the parks giving a hand with the hay.'

It was a scorcher of a day when they stepped ashore at Aberdeen. Fish market porters were stripped to the waist and folk were in holiday mood as they crowded the upper decks of the Tory trams. They had avoided the crush and the guff of the breakfast on board and had taken the chance to wash while the others took their fill. So they entered into the holiday spirit of the place as they strode along the quayside. The Aberdonians were as chirpy and friendly as always and they exchanged greetings with most folk that they passed.

'Aberdeen's at its liveliest on a hot summer's day,' Becky smiled. 'The trams will be packed with crowds off to the beach, the Duthie Park and Hazelhead. Dad used to take us on the tram to the beach in the summer. Travelling on the tram was the best part of the holiday.'

'Let's go into the Station Hotel and spoil ourselves with a good Scottish breakfast. We've got plenty of time before the train leaves.'

They were travelling light, just one small case each with a few changes of summer wear and a bundle of papers: the manuscript of his novel he'd started reading to Becky on board ship the previous night. They left their cases at the station, crossed over to the hotel and settled down to their feast. They thanked God the porridge had salt in it for a change and lashings of cream. That was followed by a giant pot of tea with their bacon and eggs. By the time they'd scoffed a good Aberdeen helping of scones and brown girdle-cakes, they were ready to face the Mearns. Becky's dad had arranged to meet them at Drumlithie station with his pony and trap so they'd time to spare till the departure of the local train. It stopped at near every cowshed on the way, the Aberdonians said, before it dandered its steady way through the lush farmlands of the Howe.

They found an empty compartment in the near empty train. After that blissful cruise and their leisurely breakfast, it made a perfect start to the holiday, to lie back on the well padded seat and feel the wee engine puff its way along the picturesque coast of the Mearns. The high cliff-top run from Cove to Stonehive was a joy to be savoured, never hurried or rushed. Leslie took off his Air Force jacket. He'd smartened himself for this important homecoming, but the warm sunlight streaming through the carriage window soon had him slackening his tie. 'This is what I call living,' Becky murmured, feeling the warmth of his arms. 'I could stay like this for ever.'

'If only we could. It's time that's the enemy. The notion haunts me wherever I am, that time's racing us on. Time never stands still, whatever we do.' They turned together then. That sex drive within him had never been so strong as it was now in the cushioned warmth of the railway carriage, the hot sun on the glass rousing them both. Far below, the wide stretch of the North Sea glinted up, blue and speckled in the summer heat. A lone fishing boat idled close to the shore, gulls hanging back at her stern. The wee engine stopped at times, panting softly by the deserted platforms at Portlethen and Newtonhill, Muchalls and Stonehive, but not a soul came near.

At Stonehive, Becky straightened her dress and he looked into her eyes. He spoke slowly then, choosing his words, watching her reactions. 'I've spoken a lot of rubbish in the past, about marriage and the way folk exploit it. Real marriage is about loving and sharing. It's about treating each other as equals. It's got nothing to do with the Kirk and Marriage Lines as they call them hereabouts, but you know I'd never let you down. You're adorable.' He kissed her gently. 'I need a short, fond name for you of my own. Becky's fine, but they called you that at home and at school. Rebecca's too formal. I've thought about Rhea, it's got a touch of Greek mystery to it that fits your dark, mysterious eyes, and it's nice and short. You spell it R-H-E-A. Can I call you that?'

Becky cupped his face in her hands. 'I'd have an awful job spelling that out to people. Why not just call me Ray. I'd like that. That would be your name for me, now there's the two of us. Others can call me what they wish.'

'Ray it is then,' he smiled. 'Ray and Les sound a matching pair.' He smiled that quiet, gentle smile of his that made her weak and silly. He'd been smiling more often of late, the worried look disappearing fast.

The train started up just then and they sealed their promise, steaming out of Stonehive. How often they'd journeyed on this little bit of track. They knew every twist of the line, every click of the rails. They knew when they'd come out of the cutting to the open lands of the Howe and at that they drew back together, and laughed, a shared knowledge that this place was theirs. They looked out then and saw the corn, green in the shadows still, but as the Howe opened out, they saw the early heat had brought it on, and there before them it stretched, to the foothills on either side, far into the distance, past Fordoun and through the Mearns to Strathmore and beyond, a carpet of corn sunturned to pure gold.

Leslie pulled at the thick leather strap. He gently lowered the heavy carriage window and they breathed in the tangy smell of hay, newly cut. The familiar noises of the hearst came through, sharp and clear. Ray put her arm round his waist, and they stood and listened as the clank of the mower and the cries of the peewits brought the memories flooding back. Sturdy, sark-sleeved men, their breeks well gripped by their galluses, were tossing the hay with long handled forks. They did it slowly and steadily with a rhythm that pleased. Beyond stood the Grampians. He held her close, content at last, feeling the warmth of her dress and the incredible softness of her arms.

Round another bend, and there was Drumlithie station. 'Drumskite's steeple's safe enough today,' he laughed. 'No need to haul her indoors on a day such as this.'

Becky's dad was waiting there quietly with his pony and trap. 'There's another picture for you,' she whispered. 'Communicating with nature those two.'

Rob Middleton was puffing slowly on his pipe, his sark wide open, near stripped to the waist. Suddenly he eyed them both and a wide grin creased his weather wrinkled face. There would be a warm and happy welcome for both of them from Rob and Fanny. That had never been in doubt. The problem for him lay up there at Bloomfield. He'd still to make his peace with father, and explain his affair with Becky, as she knew her, to his dear, overburdened Mam.

TWENTY-EIGHT

'So we're husband and wife, Ray. Does it give you a strange turn?'

She put her arm round his neck and kissed behind his ear. He kissed her on the lips. 'I want to kiss you all over,' he said and he did, undressing her the while. They slept on through the long afternoon till daylight had gone.

It had been a hectic, tiring, glorious day. The fifteenth of August, 1925, as unsettled a time as any in that unchancy year, but they'd hurried along to the Registry Office in Fulham and signed the big book. The bit of paper he'd collected was lying on the chair where he'd dropped it.

He woke to find her asleep in his arms. There was a strangeness in that moment, awakening like this with her close nakedness beside him. He'd never thought of it till now, but she looked so young and trusting there, feeling safe in his care. The euphoria settled into a pleasurable content-ment. This was his life now, there are two of us, he thought. Better not move just yet though, she needed her sleep.

Those two weeks in the Mearns? Rob and Fanny had done their best, ever bright and cheery with it all, but overburdened with bairns, they were forever on the move. From Hareden they'd gone to Nether Craighill, then the Gobbs, and still they were moving on. Times were hard for all of them, but they'd kept that well hid. Not a man to girn, Rob still had them laugh-ing at all his tales. He'd got them a pair of shepherd's crooks that first morning and they'd tramped the whole parish. With their sleeves rolled up, they'd headed for the sun, rising over Barras way, and they'd crossed the Moor at Auchendreich. He'd guided Ray to those cairns and standing stones by the Leys of Barras and Gallowhill, and he'd touched, one more time, the Big Stane of his youth.

'I have a feel for those early folk,' he'd murmured, the rough cold of the Stane sending a thrill through his hands. They'd snuggled down behind the Stane after that and the Picts and all their capers were very soon forgotten.

It was Rob McCombie at Pitcarles who told them how it was, with the cutting down of the trees, and the wee crofters being driven out by the machines and those lads that had made their silver in the boom years of the war. Rob's place at Pitcarles was fell handy, tucked in behind the wee school and the village shop, but for all his fine parks, Rob had hit on hard times along with the rest. He had harvested and stacked a grand crop of spuds that nobody could buy.

'We dumped the whole crop,' he told them, 'in that wee pond by the Kirkton.' Beside those ghosts and those gryphons, Les had been tempted to say, but he asked instead about the bothy lads and their jobs.

'They've gone to the Royal Toun,' said Rob, 'but they'll find little work down there.'

Wherever they went the tale was the same, folk were leaving the place and faring no better. Young Madge McCombie, Rob's lass, told of being the only quine left in the Dominie's class when she'd left it a year past. The Dominie nodded when they asked. 'We'll carry on for a long time yet though. Meg Archibald's class is as big as ever. Times may be bad, but they still keep having bairns.'

That was true, it seemed. Bad as things were, folk were still getting wed. Down at Millplough, Ray's cousin Archie was planning to wed Molly Cushnie, the lass who'd started school in that terrible year John Queen had died. That made them feel their years. They were both of them 24 now, a terrible age! Was it that that had spurred them on?

He smiled at the thought. Ray stirred gently beside him; her thighs were so soft. More likely it was that time at Dunnottar that persuaded them both. What a glorious, sun burning day that had been, the high point of their holiday. They'd cleared off for the day and taken the early train to Stonehive. They'd walked the Bervie Braes to Dunnottar and scrambled down to that sheltered bay, so haunted by the past and so private, hidden by the rock rising sheer to the castle walls. Ray's head had been spinning when she'd looked back.

'Don't look up,' he'd called. 'Remember what happened to those Covenanters.'

They'd lain there, near naked, on a patch of sand they'd found among the pebbles, eating fruit and dreaming their dreams. The hot sun worked on the two of them in their deep sided cove. For a time they worried about the Covenanters and those coarse times of the past. He'd been fair carried away by it all.

'It makes me mad when I look at those dungeons,' he said. 'They were our ancestors, all those mothers of ours. My mother's mother and her mother, back to the Covenanters and back to the Picts and the Romans, and further back still. I think of all those poor damned women who've been abused and been given all the dirty jobs to do. Women have been raped and jeered at down the ages and flung into dungeons just like those. What sort of blood have we inherited? The bitterness must be in all of us still.'

Ray lay thinking about that. 'And all the time the gentry were up above them dining and dancing. But those gentry were our ancestors too. Those millions of ancestors you speak about included all sorts. Those mothers of ours were among the gentry, but even they were robbed of their fun and their independence, crippled in crinolines and the dreadful rules made by you men. It's time we women of the world really got organised and asserted ourselves.'

Ray's thinking matched his own at times, though she usually lost patience with his wilder notions. Those arguments of his had been getting through to her it seemed. He grinned at her fervour, she was getting quite passionate about it all. He had a strong urge for her then. She sensed that and jumped up.

'Let's go for a swim,' she pleaded.

'We've no bathing things.'

Ray was exasperated. 'Leslie it's hot. After all you've said about the joys of living thousands of years ago, before a naked body became something to snigger over, you worry about bathing things.'

The heat was overpowering and she just had to jump in. 'Come on. You think of nothing but sex. I just want to be cool. No-one will see us. My dress will soon dry out afterwards.'

With that she ran quickly to the edge and started leaping from one rock to the next. She looked so lithe in her skimpy dress and, without pausing to turn, she stepped on to a high ledge and slipped gracefully into the water. It had happened in a flash and he'd been spellbound at the sight. She was swimming now and heading rhythmically and leisurely towards a high rock far out in the bay.

He laughed and stripped quickly right down to his underpants. With an urgency that surprised him, he traced her steps to the ledge. The shock of the plunge took his breath away, but he gulped down some sea air, and chased her out across the bay. His heart was pounding and he felt excited. She looked back at him and increased her pace. The race was on and he caught up with her just as she pulled herself on to the rock.

They lay on the rock, panting and laughing. There was some sand and soft grass in a hollow, an ideal spot out of sight from the shore.

'Our own private island,' he said, 'we're cut off from the world.'

They lay side by side, their bodies heaving and drying in the sun. The sounds of the sea and the gulls lulled them to a drowsiness and time stood still.

When he opened his eyes she was looking down at him, eyes thoughtful and deep, naked-looking in her wet shrunken dress. He reached up and pulled her down. They clung close after that, sea sounds and bird cries mingled with their breathing. He wondered at his heart beats, before realising they were hers.

'You're day-dreaming again.'

He flushed slightly, startled by her voice.

'I've been watching you for ages. Tell me about it.' She was so relaxed now, and happy, yes happy.

'It was that day at Dunnottar. Time never really stands still. I suppose others have lain in that grass hideaway in the past, and others will come again. The time and the place and folk like ourselves, how to match all three. What a lottery life is.'

'I think that's when you decided we'd sign the big book.'

'That's telepathy for you.'

'A pity about your folks. Your father never did make his peace with you, and your mam was never happy at the way we were traipsing around together.'

'We said a few polite words to each other before I left. I suppose I could hardly have expected more. But let's talk about us. We really are married you know, and we're in bed together. Tell me how it feels.'

There was no answer to that. His nakedness was stirring her too, and they'd all the time in the world, just the two of them, there on their own.

It took them a day or two to come back to earth. On the day they were wed though, he'd bought himself a typewriter. 'Not very romantic,' he'd said, a bit embarrassed. But he knew he'd little choice. He had to earn for the two of them now that Ray had lost her job. Women were of no use to the Civil Service, it seemed, if they dared to take a man. That was another example of those modern, civilised times.

He'd to get on with that book, but what a winter it was turning out to be. His airman's pay could never keep the two of them in London in a style that was decent.

'We've been moving from one damned awful lodgings to the next, each one worse than the last.' Ray sounded miserable. She wasn't one to complain and he looked at her with concern. They'd discussed it often enough, each time they'd moved to a shabbier place in a poorer part of the city. It had always seemed worth it at the time. It gave them just that little extra money to spend on themselves. He'd been working really hard on his book too, typing late into the night. Next day he'd be off to his Air Force office, dodging the traffic on his bike. He'd got home that night and found her upstairs in bed. She'd been under the weather, she said, but there must be more to it than that.

'I'm pregnant, Leslie.' She looked apologetic, wondering. This would hold him back, she knew. He needed all his time for his book.

'Ray, that's wonderful news.' His eyes shone and he rushed over and hugged her close. 'What an idiot I've been, so wrapped up in that book of mine. I should have noticed.'

'I had an odd turn today. Things will get better soon. Away down and make me a cup of tea.'

Leslie ran downstairs, singing as he went. Easy for him to sing, she thought. Then she felt sorry for that thought. She'd be singing herself once the bairn was born.

'This bairn of ours is just what we need.' Leslie was back with the tea things, grinning all over. He held her flushed face in his hands and smiled into her eyes. 'I've been over tense of late, working on that dratted book. I'm going to ease up now and spoil you for a bit.'

As winter wore on and Christmas drew near, Ray took to her bed on most afternoons. He'd park his bike and rush upstairs to find her still there. She felt so bad about that. She was holding him back. Those sturdy wives back in the Howe took things in their stride, helping with the hairst right up to the last, and here she was lying about like an invalid. But what a place to be bringing Leslie's child to the world, down here among the winter fogs, choked in by buildings and strangers in the teeming London sprawl. If only she could get back up there by the Bervie flow. She lay and dreamt of Arbuthnott's braes in the late days of Spring when the trees were in bloom. The corn would be growing and the peesies calling. The air would be fresh and clean and the sun would be burning the whirling mists in the den, round the old kirk and the manse.

Ray's fever got steadily worse. In February, she had convulsions.

'Mrs Mitchell's suffering from eclampsia,' the doctor said. 'It's a toxic condition which sometimes develops in the later stages of pregnancy. We'd better get her into hospital.'

Time dragged its heels after that. The hours stretched into days and Leslie paced the corridors and waiting rooms of Purley Cottage Hospital. The ward sister and the night nurse seemed unbelievably cheerful.

'There's no change yet,' they'd say. 'Blood poisoning like this is not a pleasant thing to see. You'd be better to go back home to bed.'

'I want to see my wife.'

'All right, if you must. But she's sedated. They're to operate in the morning,' Matron told him.

He tramped the streets that night, convinced that he'd lost her. After the operation they let him in. When she opened her eyes, sick and weak with all the agony she'd been through, he was close by her side.

'You're fine, Ray,' he said, 'the worst of it's all past.'

She managed a weak smile and looked straight into his eyes. She knew then, for certain. 'What happened to our baby?' she whispered.

'The baby's gone Ray, but you're doing fine. Get your strength up now and we'll get you safely back home.' Leslie put his cheek to hers and they held each other close. She caught the wetness of his tears, the first she'd ever felt. She shut her eyes and her own tears held back. After all he'd been through, she'd presented him with this.

That night he wrote her a love letter, something he'd have jeered at in the past. Love letters were for the Victorians or the Scottish Kailyard scribblers. Today's writers were hard hitting realists who wrote about sex, about fornication and adultery. He was to be one of their number!

'Oh, I love you,' he wrote. 'I saw the tears in your eyes.'

He added some verse:

> Now that we've made our sacrifice of mirth
> In agony, we'll seek respite from pain
> In quiet places of the mourning earth,
> In the sea's song, in fall of autumn rain.

'I'm a worry to you,' she said when she got home. 'I've been a drag on your work.'

For all their memories of the land and the speak they had known, the two of them had another tongue now. He'd never given much thought to writing in Scots. His verse and his tales were in English and he worked at them real hard.

'We'll go down to Devon, Ray.' His eyes lit up. 'Spring comes early down there. What you really need is a spell of good Bervie sea air, but they'll be having sea-piners up there about now, so we'll go down to Devon. I'll organise some leave and we'll do nothing but laze and breathe in the West Country air.'

He drew her into his arms and whispered, 'We need some time to be together again.'

There were few folk about and the weather was mild. He took a book of verse with him and recited some Shelley and Rossetti and some lines by Rupert Brooke. There was not a word by Rabbie Burns though, and Scot's dirt like that. On 13 February they celebrated his twenty-fifth birthday and he wrote some more verse in English.

She still needed a strong dose of Bervie sea breezes to get her on the mend, so in March she was back in the Royal Toun filling her lungs with the stuff.

'I'm in my ain countrie again,' she wrote to Dorothy Tweed, one of the friends she'd made since travelling south. '...enjoying the lovely air. My husband has given me leave until the end of June. Isn't he a dear to let me have such a long holiday. He expects to be transferred to Uxbridge sometime in June, and then he intends coming north for a fortnight at the end of which time we will journey south together.'

The Royal Toun set her on her feet. It really was a more douce place, she confirmed, than that wild place she'd been scared of, in those far away times. Pappa Gibb's mills had all gone, but David Webster's three mills and Burness's mill at Pitcarry were still throbbing on. Bert Clarke's piano playing kept things cheery at Lyon's Picture Palace for those who'd trouble with the captions, and of course, there were all those Arbuthnott chields and quines like the Queens and the Bannermans who'd moved into the place.

Things picked up after that. Leslie had got a better place out on Angel Road in Harrow and the two of them then spent the last two weeks exploring the Royal Toun and their old haunts through the Howe.

Back Doon Sooth again, and he was writing like mad.

'It's sex that bothers me, Ray,' he burst out at last. Ray was towelling herself, glad to be free of the steam in their small, overheated bathroom. She'd drowsed away over long in the bath, willing his typewriter to stop.

'I wouldn't have thought sex was your problem.' Ray laughed and dropped the towel, putting her arms round his neck. She was her dear, sweet self again and the night was late. 'Let's talk about it in bed and see if that helps.'

'We both needed that,' he whispered later. 'But it's putting sex into print that makes a book a best seller. Galsworthy and Bennet, for all their acclaim by the literati, have no appeal for the masses. It's titillation the world wants nowadays.'

'You're not going to write muck, Leslie?'

'It's muck that sells. Yet the world's sick too, of novels that simply catalogue a succession of matings. The world thinks it's grown up, more mature. It wants a writer to project himself. It wants a writer's honest beliefs, his hopes and hates, and how he sees the world. It's a serious and frivolous world we've landed ourselves into.

'Sounds a perverse kind of world to me.' Ray was drowsy now and at peace, but Leslie's overactive brain was more alert than ever after their lovemaking. She cuddled up close. Would he never let up?

'It's a human characteristic, worrying about the universe and knitting our brows about eternity. But we like the odd distraction. A bit of lewdness and lingerie appeals to all of us. We need to laugh and relax at times with an occasional snigger at the daftness of the thing. What a fuss the world makes about the simple process of procreation.'

'You're too cynical, Leslie. You make it sound so mechanical.'

'The war's made us all cynical. Sentimental tales of love are old hat. The world's looking for some purpose in its novels, but it needs a bit of titillation to make them easier to digest. I'm afraid I'm a damned poor novelist when I shy away from a little muck in my books. I'm too much in love with my heroine to subject her to an honest to goodness seduction.'

'You're making me jealous now. Who's this sexy heroine you've fallen in love with?'

'Who do you think? I've got to write about what I know and what I feel strongly about. Our days in the Mearns and down here in London, that boat trip to Aberdeen and my days in the desert are the stuff of my life. My job in the RAF too, makes me what I am. Most of all, my darling Ray, there's you,' he whispered. 'I keep seeing you in this heroine I've conjured up. I'd need to go through some shattering experience before putting her seduction into print, a crashed pilot in flames, maybe. Something of that sort.'

'Why don't you then?' Ray kissed him on the mouth and stopped his blethers for a while.

'We'll both sleep now,' he murmured at last. 'And I'll shut up, I promise. I know I can make my tales exciting. There's a tale about Spartacus and his revolt against the Romans. There's exploration and discovery crying out for a fresh interpretation. I could write some good Wellsian yarns on time travel and I'm determined to re-write the history of Scotland, telling it truthfully for a change. But I've still this problem about sex. To write a best seller and make money, these days, you need purple patches and lots of sex, with a few ingenious prostitutions and seductions thrown in. If I could do that with conviction, my book would be made. In three years time I'll be out of the Air Force. Just think of that! In 1929 I'll be out once again in the cold, indifferent world. For good this time. My best seller has to be in the shops before the 1930s are with us.'

'The thirties will be our great times.' Ray squeezed his hand. He needed all her support from now on, and he'd get it. He mustn't lose heart. 'Forget all those rejection slips. Publishers need lots of prodding when it's someone they've never heard of. I'll handle that side for you and write to some of the critics. I know you can do it. Write those seductions if you must. Don't worry about them. Folk will maybe buy your books for the seductions and that way you'll get your message across. Let's aim for 1930. I think there's a touch of magic about that year; 1930 will be your *Annus Mirabilis.'*

Where had she heard that odd phrase for the first time? It had stuck with her all those years. It had something to do with those Queen girls, Chris or Jane, away back in those near forgotten Arbuthnott years. It had a fine ring to it, though. Their *Annus Mirabilis* would come to the two of them in 1930, she was sure now of that. They both fell asleep then, his arm resting on hers, exhausted but content. What a pleasant notion it was, just four years from now – 1930, their wonderful year!

TWENTY-NINE

The twenties were disappearing fast along with all the silver. They called it the Great Depression. Back in the Howe it made little odds, you'd no silver to lose. Your wages had been cut or your dole maybe stopped. So roll on the thirties, you said, things can only get better.

Ray and Leslie were having a hard time like the rest. They'd rooms in Hammersmith now, still spartan and drear, but his first book, *Hanno: or the future of exploration,* had been published and Leslie was writing short stories for the Cornhill Magazine. By September he was out of the Air Force and writing full time. 1930, that great year they'd both talked about, lay just around the corner!

In the Mearns, it was the Royal Toun that suffered most. The year had started well enough, but folk saw that those wild capers of the twenties could never last. For David, there had been some good years and some bad. He'd only to keep Alf Forbes at the bank in good fettle, he thought, and things would work out in the end. A great lad Alf Forbes. Alf had a fine singing voice and his duets with Annie Neilson aye found a place in Jim's concerts. When Annie and Alf got harmonising with 'The Crookit Bawbee' on New Year's Day, there was scarce a dry eye in the place. There would be no trouble there, David thought. Alf Forbes, the banker, would see him through, but he could have done with that £50,000 mother had got when she'd broken dad's will. The money was still there, of course, and she'd set some aside. The lawyers had seen to all that.

Alice, and young Douglas, his chum that mam had wed, were living in grand style now in a place called The Grange, down at Ealing in London. A bit out of the way maybe, but better placed than the Heugh House at Stonehive for theatres and the like. It was a fine place to stop by in if he and Stella ever headed Sooth.

Early in the year though, Alice fell ill and two days before Burns Night, in that year of disasters, Alice lay dead. They buried Young Alice, as some still called her, in that lonely glen beyond Edzell in the Oggs' family plot. So that was Young Alice, a bright and happy lass from the Bellfield at Kinneff. In her time she'd been mistress and a grand hostess at her Big Hoose, Hazelgrove, and she'd sailed out round the bay in her trig wee boat, 'The Alice Webster'. Being wed to old Jock with his three Bervie mills, his farm o'er the water and half of Bervie forby, she'd been a queen among the gentry in those days before the war.

But the tale soon slipped out: no will could be found and, though David searched high and low, he could find not a trace. Young Douglas had scooped the lot! David pressed hard but the law Doon Sooth was clear on that. Scots lawyers and the like could whistle in the wind, they'd no jurisdiction down there. Alice's silver had left Bervie for good and David made a quick change of tack. He'd looked on Alice's silver as real cash in the bank.

David's fling in the twenties had cost him a lot. Folk were never quite clear when things started to crack, but they wondered in the Spring when the tennis crowd met up the Glebe Close, and there was no sign of Stella. David and Stella between them had run the tennis club in grand style, and Stella was aye very keen.

The thing could scarcely stop there. There was not a soul in the Toun but had a tale for you, and folk laughed at the lengths some would go with their speak. You got the best tales from the Crown where Andra McLeod had a good eye to trade. In the raw days of Spring folk would slip in there for some heat. Most would head straight for the Crown bar, but some, more genteel, or more sleekit you could say, would slip through to the kitchen for a news, about trade it would be, or on politics maybe. By politics they'd mean the Council and how it spent all your silver.

Andra aye had a fire going in that kitchen of his and, if the wind was in the east, there was no better place to be. A man would hand over his shop to the care of some lass and spend an hour in that kitchen putting the Council to right. He might have a dram or two to keep out the chill and get back in fine fettle with a shine on his neb and a pan drop on his tongue.

Millar the chemist from over the road would make up the day's mixtures and powders and then don his muffler and hat. He'd leave a lass in full charge of the mysterious drawers with their latin labels and the big blue and green jars stuck high in the window. As often as not, he'd get into one of Andra's big armchairs by the kitchen fire just as the Bailie settled down, real comfy like, in the chair straight across. There was aye need for a crack on how the last Council meeting had gone, for things had fair got out of hand since the Bailie had left. It was some years now since the Bailie had fallen out with the rest of the Council over the cuts they'd made to the wages of the scaffy and the rest, but the thing still needed going over.

'The rates can aye stand another penny,' the Bailie growled, 'but a man has a wife and bairns to feed. The labourer is worthy of his hire.'

He'd quote scripture, would the Bailie, to ram home his point. Andra would agree with him there and fill his glass to the brim.

David came in on them once, to get in out of the rain. He'd a cheery word for the two politicians. David was a Bailie himself now and had full charge of the Toun's gas.

'I'll hand you this David,' said the Bailie, 'you've done a grand job at the Gassy. We'll have no dipping of the lights now with that new tank you've had built.'

'Aye, and it should give us a good cut in the rates,' said old Millar, 'with all those profits you'll make.'

'In time, in time,' David laughed, and winked at Andra's lass, Ella, who'd just come ben. 'We'll have to consolidate first. There's a bit of profit just now, but we've some costs to be met.'

'Oh I'll warrant you that,' growled the Bailie, 'exig-en-cies turn up.' He spoke out exigencies, slow and steady like and never a syllable was missed. It was now three in the afternoon and the word was that Millar and the Bailie had been at it since eleven. He could fair handle his drink could the Bailie. Having come at it late with being teetotal so long, he took his drink canny and steady like, in an intelligent sort of way.

'Have a dram with me David,' the Bailie said, hoping for a crack.

'That's good of you Bailie, some other time,' David laughed, 'but I promised the girls I'd try out George's new cocktail he's gone and prepared.'

'Cocktails!' howled the Bailie. 'American abominations. Whisky was good enough for Burns and it's good enough for us. A drop of the Auld Kirk will keep out the cold. That's more than your American cocktails will ever do.'

'You should try one Bailie,' George Ranson declared in his deep baritone of a voice. George had arrived with four cocktail glasses on a tray. George was the strong, handsome lad of Bervie. He'd a deep commanding voice that made folk sit up, and he carried himself well. He carried not an ounce of spare weight and his clean, good looks, his tall spare frame, drew glances from all the lassies when he was down there on the football pitch. He was Bervie's goalkeeper, and on Saturdays when the team was at home, George in his yellow goalkeeper's jersey was an inspiration to the rest of the team as much as was Tommy Beedie, their captain, out there in front. George's dad was another thrawn Bailie. Bervie seemed filled with Bailies, but there was only one, of course, they still called The Bailie.

'This new cocktail is the best thing to have hit the Royal Toun since the new Craigview Mill opened her doors,' George assured them with a grin.

The Bailie and old Millar gave a bit of a snort at that and turned back to their whisky and their notions on the Council.

George and David left the older men to their fireside politics and sat down with the two quines at the table. Red haired Ella McLeod and the bonny Jane Queen had brought with them a breath of summer sun into that back kitchen of the Crown. In their short skirts and their frilly satin blouses, which were all the fashion, they'd drawn dour looks from the two politicians by the fire, but George and David thought they looked fine. George aye had an eye for a pretty lass.

'Here's a toast to the new Crown Cocktail,' said George, lifting his glass, and they all laughed at that and sipped from the fancy green glasses with the red cherries on top.

The girls had never tasted a cocktail before, or anything stronger than apple cider, but George had persuaded them to try his new cocktail, because it was special.

'It's sweet and it stings,' said Jane just then and she gave David the warmest and sweetest of smiles.

When David first fell for Jane has never been told, it's aye been one of the best kept secrets at the Linty. His Craigview and his Springy mills might be the biggest and the best, but David aye had a feel for the wee Linty mill, down under the brig. The world was less rushed down there at the Linty, and the water from Fordoun and Arbuthnott Den still flowed on, and splashed round the big wheel as it had in the past. It might flood or go dry but, year in and year out, the sluice at the lade would keep things in check.

Young Jane was sixteen when she started down the Linty Brae, a bit odd, you might think, 1923 being a bad time for trade, and Jim's dole queues getting longer by the day. David had aye a cheery word for her mam, Jane Ann, when he passed her terraced house at the end of the street, and they'd pass on the news in the way that folk do.

'This one's looking for a job,' said Jane Ann one day, and she nodded to the young Jane, helping there with the weeds. It was a little enough patch of garden they had, but it had neat rows of bonny flowers once the sea piners had gone. It was Queen's Corner, after all, a kind of landmark in the place.

David looked then at the young lass. My hadn't she grown! She'd be a real beauty yet!

'There's aye work for lassies willing to work,' said David in a flash.

He'd to sort out that promise fast when he got down the Linty brae. Mary Smith, a slick reeler at the Linty, was found a job up the brae, with the reelers at Craigview. That suited her fine, and young Jane got Mary's reel which was now going spare.

When young Jane Queen first turned up at the Linty, she was fine pleased with the place. She'd heard tales of the on-goings at some of the mills, but the tales were pub tales and little more than that. Whatever went on at weekends or at nights, she could only but guess, but during the day, the Linty gaffers kept a tight grip on all the quines and their work.

There was a fine feel about the Linty. So long had it stood there, and seen folk come and go. You thought the mill itself had a mind and a speak of its own, with the 'thump, thump, thump' of its wheel, steady and sure.

Some said Madge Gibb's ghost was hanging about still, keeping a watch on them all. If she did, she was doing a damned good job, looking out for her quines. Jane stumbled her way down the Linty Brae with the rest. In black winter mornings there was barely a flicker from the mill house close by. They'd the feel of the cart track and the sound of the flow to help them. Near to the roof tops, they'd turn sharp to the left. The thing was to grope for the crossing, clear enough in the daytime and wide enough for Sy Stewart's station cart to cross, but there were no side rails to the brig. The mill race was quick there and, more than once, Jane near stumbled in. Was that where Madge Gibb had slipped those many years back?

There were some quines there from Johnner, getting more silver than Ed Gibb would provide. They were bonny quines too, the Johnner quines, but they were odd, fisher stock with a strange kind of speak and an odd sort of dress. They were chirpy though, and well able to take a care of themselves, which was just as well when the rammy began. How it started, you could but guess, but a Johnner or a Bervie quine would give a bit laugh, then the shouting would start. Once, it got clean out of hand and, when the foreman turned round, the Johnner quines were flinging mill bobbins and fair set with their nieves. The foreman soon silenced the lot of them though, with words even the Johnner lot had never heard. They lost some silver for that bit stramash, but it fair cleared up the air and got rid of all their spleen. They were shamed then and laughed at all the soss, and the quines from Johnner and Bervie got on fine and stuck up for each other after that. They were all Linty quines together, and that counted a lot.

David enjoyed his trips down the Linty Mill brae. He'd aye get a cheery smile when he went in through the door. They said the work got on better when the boss was down by.

For all the Linty's couthy ways though, none would refuse a chance to move up the brae. The new Craigview was more spacious, and the machines were brand new. It was just down from the Square, so you'd no long hill to climb, when your day's work was done and your back ached with the strain of it all. There was little surprise then, when young Jane got her chance.

From low down there in the Linty, Jane found herself high up in Craigview's garret, where the reelers all worked. It was fresher up there, fans sucked out the stour and you breathed in Bervie's clean salty air. Jane brought some brightness with her too, and she soon settled in. She was a dab hand as a reeler, whipping the spun yarn from the bobbins and on to her reel, making neat hanks, for the bundler to stack. The bundles were all ready then for Saxie Cameron and his carters to wheel off to the station.

David had to keep an eye on all of his mills, of course, not just the wee Linty. So it was but right that the reelers' garret in Craigview should become a part of his tour. It was Paul Gray, the foreman, noticed that some hanks were in a helluva mess.

'What in God's name is that?' David burst out.

'Oh that was Jane Queen,' said a young lad nearby, though he'd no notion at all how the thing had come about.

'I'll have a word with her,' said David, and put on his grim look.

David met up with Jane round the end of the frame, and gave her a scolding the whole garret could hear. The while he was grinning, Jane kept her face straight.

Maybe it was the short working weeks that helped on that romance, but Andra's back kitchen had a hand in it as well. Andra's lass, Ella, was a college lass at Atholl Crescent, and great friends with Jane. Ella would help her dad out at the Crown, and Jane would drop by, just to see how things were. George Ranson would judge his time then, 'to come in out of the rain.'

'These two girls were born under a lucky star, David,' said George in the strong speaking way that he had. Like most folk in Bervie, George never said 'quine', which some thought was a teuchter way of speak.

'They were born in Bervie's great year, 1907, when your Craigview Mill opened its doors.'

'Both of you?' cried David, hearing the spaewive's tale for the very first time. 'We'll all need to drink to that!'

'Craigview's Silver Jubilee is in three years time,' said George, a sharp man with his calculations, and aye looking for some excuse for a celebration. George was forever taking charge of the fancy dress parades Jim

175

would organise, togging himself up in some smart military uniform, an old Bervie Volunteer's helmet maybe, then leading the crowd out of the Square and on round the Toun.

When Stella heard of those goings on at the Crown she made up her mind. Things had been going not so well, and she'd heard most of the gossip. So the Royal Toun woke up one day to find Stella had gone. Like Alice before her she'd set off for Stonehive. She knew they'd grand lawyers in Stonehive, the very best in the Mearns.

By the tail end of 1929 then, David had a deal of problems to solve. He resigned from the Council along with Willie Lyon, the Provost, when coarse things were said about the way his Gas Works was run. They had a good laugh in Stonehive when they heard that bit tale.

'You'll be selling the Provost's chain then?' they laughed, fair tickled at it all.

But that wee storm had barely begun when it was spelled out in the papers, for the whole world to see: 'A decree of divorce was granted in an undefended action by Stella David or Webster, Hamewith, Stonehaven, against David Webster, flax spinner, Hazelgrove, Bervie, Kincardineshire.'

Madge shook her head when Jim showed her that piece of news. The twenties that had started so well were now ending like this. The divorce, she heard later, would cost David a lot: £12,000 or more. What would this do for David's mills and the Toun itself, she wondered.

By Hogmanay though, things had started to stir. Johnnie Burness stepped in as the new Provost, and David took a good look at things and made up his mind. The thirties seemed the time to be making a fresh start. All you needed was a good dose of Scottish smeddum.

There was no shortness of smeddum in the Royal Toun that Hogmanay, and Herbert Stephen, the Beadle, gave the Auld Kirk bell an extra heave to bring in that special New Year.

The 1930s had arrived!

THIRTY

Jane laughed as Bailie Couper caught her eye. He'd just walked into the morning room. Hazelgrove was at its best, the bright spring sunshine streaming in through the large windows behind her. It was mid-May and Jane was sitting there, needle in hand, smiling up at him with a happy shine in her eyes. The trees and the wide sweep of those immaculate lawns outside completed the scene.

'A picture she looked,' Bailie Couper said later, 'with masses of cut lillies all round about her.'

'You know my wife, Jane,' said David, with a grin. Always a lad for a laugh was David. The Bailie near tripped just then. It was the first that he'd heard. To give the bailie his due, he took it in his stride. Bervie was changing her bailies and her provosts at a steady rate those days, with all the rowing that was going on about their gas works and their water supplies. Bailie Couper had survived the last Council barney, and his quiet, mannerly style had cooled things down for a time. The Bailie needed all his tact now, and he handled it well. He shook Jane by the hand and turned then to congratulate David, which showed quick thinking, you could say. Bailie Couper's head was in a whirl. The bonny lass from Queen's Corner, he was thinking, settled here in Hazelgrove! She looked just right for the place though, but whatever next? What a speak there would be when news of this reached the Toun!

'I'll leave you two to your business,' said young Jane, with that bonny smile that she had, 'I've a few things to get and the day's turning out fine.'

Twenty-two year old Jane looked no different that day as she strolled into the Toun. They'd got back late the night before, and there was so much she'd have to do. She was aye neatly trigged out was Jane, even off to Craigview or the Linty, she'd make the heads turn and draw approving looks from the dourest spaewife in the place.

Today was a weekday though, and she had on her Sunday best. She'd a song in her heart as she strode down Montrose Road to Number One, Queen's Corner as they had it. The sun pierced through the high trees of the Castle Park on the right. Through some gaps in the trees she could see the spring lambs frisking, tumbling and prancing with the sheer thrill of it all. The whole world was so pleased with itself. It was one of those Bervie spring morns makes you glad to be alive. The greenness and freshness of the place made up for all the rain and all the storms that had passed. The wet of the night was rising from the slated roof of the old Savings Bank on her left, an odd wee place where Maisie Deans checked your silver and Tommy Johnston, the Factor, hovered at her back. Maisie had won that other consolation prize along with Chris when Leslie'd got his medal in those far off days before the war. What a time ago it seemed now. And what a distance they'd all come.

The world was a much better place, Jane thought, smiling. The only traffic on the deserted, steaming road was Willie and his sheltie, his cart piled high with vegetables and last year's spuds. Willie gave her a droll kind of look but raised a cheery hand as she passed. Not a man to gossip, was Willie, but he'd be keeping his lugs cocked from here on. What in God's name was Jane Queen doing out here at this time of the day? All dressed for a holiday too, by the look of it. What an odd sort of thing.

She'd carry on just as normal, Jane told herself. Surely the word would be out. She spied old Lizzy Watson come out from the Terrace. Lizzy was heading for Townhead and she crossed in front of her as Jane turned into Mam's gate.

'Taking a day off Jane?' Lizzy asked, looking fair puzzled at it all. 'It's no a Bervie holiday today?' she added, making to stop for a news.

'A fine day for a holiday,' Jane laughed and gave her a cheery smile as she passed through the gate. So the word was still not out. That was odd. News usually travelled fairly quickly in the Royal Toun. Maybe Lizzy had been away and missed all the speak. She did scuttle down to Montrose at times for days on end. That would be it. The word would be all over the Toun by now, she was sure. Davie Annand had run the four of them to Aberdeen, and Ella's folk would have let the news slip.

She and Ella McLeod had had a laugh at that, when they made all their plans. All that talk of the spaewives, they'd whispered. Both of us born on, what was that thing George had called it? Bervie's *Annus Mirabilis,* the year Craigview had been built. George Ranson was an awful man for high falutin' phrases when he got going. *Annus Mirabilis,* for goodness sake – Bervie's glorious year! Well, maybe there had been something in it after all. They'd set out for Aberdeen, Davie Annand with the four of them, she to wed David, Craigview's laird, with her sister Mary and Ella to be their witnesses. What fun it had been doing it like that, Davie Annand, the chauffeur, driving them north and doing things that way, with no fuss and no nonsense. David had fixed it by special licence, with no ministers and no crowds to glower at what they did.

A fine holiday? Jane smiled at the thought. A fairy tale come true, it had been. David certainly did things in style. After the short ceremony, Davie Annand had driven off with them from Aberdeen, the two of them in the back of that daimler, what luxury and space. With a chauffeur to take care of things, she and David could spend all their time with each other. Only David would have brought his own chauffeur. He and Davie Annand had planned out every inch of the route, and she and David had lain back there in those luxurious seats without a care in the world. Those beautiful runs round the lakes, along Borrowdale and Derwent Water. Then that sumptious hotel in Keswick!

She'd worn a neat grey costume and her new shoes for that trip. Oh, those shoes, and her aching feet! Davie was the ideal chauffeur, he'd a remedy for everything.

'What you need, is some sheepie's wool, Jane,' he'd grinned and louped over the fence. They'd thought that a bit daft at first, but my, what a difference! The doctor might have other notions for blistered toes, but the sheepie wool Davie collected from the fence, had been a balm to her then. After David had tucked those tufts of softness round her toes, she was walking on air.

The Aberdeen Tivoli was a grand place, in its way, but sitting there with David in the dress circle of that London theatre, she'd felt on top of the world. Davie had run them to the coast after that, and the trip to France had been the holiday of a lifetime. They'd a cabin to themselves on the crossing to Dieppe; there was so much to tell her Mam. There was that time David had gone down to the bar. He'd shaken his head when he came back and let himself in.

'You've to lock your door when you're Doon Sooth, Jane,' he'd explained. 'Folk are more trusting in the Royal Toun.' They'd laughed at that, but it was true, she supposed, pushing open Mam's unlocked door. It never occurs to folk in Bervie to padlock themselves in.

The news would be out by now though, and Lizzy would read all about it in the paper. Well, maybe not it all. They'd never hear that. But her Mam was different. There was so much she could tell her Mam, she'd be just dying to hear.

The Royal Toun had to be content with the short note in the papers that day, they digested every word of it, and some read it twice, 'to mack sicker,' they'd say.

'On the 14th of May, 1930, at 35a Union Street, Aberdeen, by declaration, David Webster (33), Jute Spinner (divorced), Hazelgrove, Inverbervie, wed Jane Ann Davidson Queen (spinster) (22), 1 Montrose Road, Inverbervie, in the presence of Ella Diack McLeod, Crown Hotel, Inverbervie and Mary Burnett Queen, 1 Montrose Road, Inverbervie.

Well, the Royal Toun took that bit of news as it did every other. Barely six months since David's divorce and he was wed to Jane Queen! It was the speak of the place for days, until the next bit stishie came along. Some of the young quines felt their noses put out of joint and some tried to stir up tales to get rid of their spleen, but most took it with a bit of a laugh. They had other things to worry about, and young David was a fine lad for all his silver. Jane Queen deserved all the luck she could get. They were a popular crowd the Queens.

So the thirties began in great style. Old Jess, the spaewife that began that tale far back, was real pleased with herself. If she'd read the tea leaves again, she might have looked a few years on and seen David and Jane make another trip to the Granite Toun, to witness the same ploy with Ella McLeod and George Ranson. But it's rare for spaewives to get things right twice on the trot, and besides, Jess was a bit dottled by now, and was as likely to spill all her tea leaves if she carried on with her capers.

You'd have found omens enough, if you'd bothered to look, that first year of the thirties. There was that grand hairst for a start, down in the Haughs and up the water side by Arbuthnott way. The stooks had all been set out in bonny straight rows, and there were the usual capers when they'd thought the job done. The quines and the orra loons were all in fine fettle. They'd have fared a lot better if they'd hauled in the stooks, for fine days in the Mearns are chancy things at best. There's aye a black cloud or two hanging about in the Sooth. This time the clouds were real, all black and bursting to go. They hit the Howe hard and kept at it for days. Arbuthnott Den had seen nothing like it since the days of the gryphons. The banks burst near to Fordoun and closed Arbuthnott's main road. From Allardice to the sea the red mud of the Howe churned down in a torrent and filled the whole of the haugh floor, from Pitcarry Mill on one side to Newbigging's braes on the other.

'I've heard tell of the Red Sea,' said Scaffy Duncan, looking down on the huge red-brown loch, 'but this is ridiculous.'

Only the ruins of old Jim Gibb's mills could be seen, their two silent stacks sticking up from the flood. The haughs were swept clean, fences and gates and uprooted trees were all swirling down to the old bridge. They churned about there awhile, then got sucked through the big arch, on towards the Linty. There were sand bags round the Linty and the torrent was lapping at the brim. The worst damage though, was to the hairst. There they were, the bonny, neat-tied stooks of grain they'd slaved at for so long, bobbing and bouncing their way down to the Bervie mouth and on out to sea beyond the gravel bar. That was a sign that said things were afoot – the red mud of the Howe stretching for a full mile or more into Bervie's bonny bay.

Folk looked on the bright side. There was a lot going on. When Madge first heard of Jane and David she gave a gasp at first, but then looked on it fine, as she did at most of the antics folk got up to. She'd go up to Mackenzie's and get them a card. She did that for all the weddings, even for the tinkers Jim fixed up to wed down there at the beach. Weddings were aye happy, romantic things for Madge, and Jess McKenzie, at the paper shop, did a fair trade in the coloured cards she was for ever buying there. She'd spend ages in McKenzie's shop, swithering. It was important that the words were just right.

The dole queues were now so bad that the lads Doon Sooth forked out some silver to build five new brigs between the Dee and Montrose. The biggest of the lot was to be a substantial eight arched concrete brig for the Royal Toun itself. The old one-arched brig that delighted the old Bailie, was a fine brig to look at and would last a thousand years. It was as strong as on the day it was built for the new mail coaches back in 1799, but there was scarce passing room now for the buses Jim Peter was putting on the road. The only problem, Jim could see, was that their grand new road would cut slap through the middle of his own wee office at number three the Cowgate.

Well Jim took that fact like every other, and posted up some bonny blueprints of the new brig in his office. The sound of the pile drivers banged away for months on end, but the time came and Jim moved on to a bigger office back up the King Street. It was across the road from the Bailie's place of business, handled now by Bert and Harris. The Bailie contented himself these days by doing art work and shop signs, in between his drinking sprees with Millar, the chemist, in the back kitchen of the Crown.

When Pappa Jim Gibb had lost the last of his mills, he moved out of the Big Hoose at Bridge End and became the new laird of Hallgreen, the old laird having been left out in Flanders with the rest of his regiment. The old puffer captain was well suited to be laird since he'd no mills left to glower down upon. When he died, he left Wilhelmina and her crowd of bairns an estate of near £62,000, a tidy sum for a man that had lost all his mills and been hit by the depression. Jim Gibb had known when to get out, folk had said.

But David took a different tack. Before he wed Jane, he had switched the mills from flax to jute, for the price of flax was astronomical. Alf Forbes at the bank was real pleased at that. Alf was in good voice, and Hazelgrove was a bright and canty place once more. Jane had settled in, and folk were reminded of the times when old Jock had brought Scott Skinner in and he'd stirred them up with his Hazelgrove Jig and his Bervie Quadrille. They had grand nights at the piano. David had a good ear for music and he could fair rattle out the latest tunes from the films like 'Love is the sweetest thing', and 'The Sun has got his Hat on'. Alf Forbes still liked it best though when they let him have a turn at his 'Crookit Bawbee'.

Things were on the mend, you could say, that fine summer of 1932. But the gods had started some ploys of their own, that year, that would turn the whole thing on its head. Before the big disaster hit the Toun, some folk were fair fashed at tales leaking through the Howe. It was Jane's sister Chris who was bothered the most. She'd been taking things quiet-like in Hazelgrove's front room at the weekend with Jane tending the bairn. Chris had come up from the beach where the waves had drawn a bit of a crowd, wondering if the salmon bothy would catch it this time, but the tide had receded with only an odd swish of spray washing the bothy roof. Folk were aye keen for excitement when the tides were running high.

Chris had come up the Terrace, kicking the leaves as she went. The high Castle Park trees had long shed their leaves, but there were heaps still lying about in their autumn yellows and reds. For the last half hour she'd been finishing a book she'd picked up in Montrose a week back. She was aye delving into books was Chris.

She looked up at Jane at last. 'It's true what I told you,' she said, nodding her bonny head. 'It's real folk Leslie Mitchell's put into his book, and there's little disguising it's Arbuthnott he's writing about.' She flung the book aside on the sofa. 'How could he write such stuff? About his own father and his mother too, that have wrocht all their days and got little thanks for their pains. He's even put a map at the front to show that his folk's place at Bloomfield is the real Blawearie.'

It was the speak of the place that back end of 1932. *Sunset Song* was hailed by all the scribblers and clever chields that fancied the doric but never dared put it in print. Clean living lads that would have blushed at such speak, now started on about coo sharn and dung as though they'd invented the stuff. The clever lads found the Mearns speak had a richness and a raciness they'd never have guessed. Young Mitchell had fair opened the doors and shown folk how it was. You had to laugh when you read that bit he had about his Chris quine, baring her legs like that to tread her blankets in the tub. Then he had her looking at herself in the moonlight, and her Ewan lad kissing her breast. Then he told how Chris's mam hit back at her man, old Guthrie, when he'd gone skite at seeing Chris trampling the blankets with her skirt off.

'Ah, well, it wouldn't be the first time you've seen a naked lass yourself; and if your neighbours haven't they must have fathered their own bairns with their breeks on,' she'd said.

Was there need to put stuff like that in a book, you wondered? Folk kept stuff of that sort for the Sally on a Saturday night. Some of the sharper lads looked then for what was behind all the muck and, right enough, when you read the stuff, you'd to hand it to him about the hellish chauving in the parks that could drive a man mad. Those bloody parks. You'd dream on them yourself if you went to foreign parts, or were laid low for a while.

He was right too, about his two Chrises. You felt that yourself at times, when you blethered on in English, fair chuffed with the swank of it all. Then you'd come back to the real world and the real words that got right down to the guts of things.

They liked the book fine in New York and in other foreign parts. It was a new Scottish renaissance, they said, a Scottish writer at last! In the Mearns and in Aberdeen some had other things to say. In Edinburgh, where they print books in Scots they were fair kittled up with it all, but his Mam, that hard tried woman away up there on the Reisk, was anything but pleased.

'Laddie, what did you want to write all that muck for? It's the speak of the place. Your father's fair affronted and I'm ashamed of you,' she said.

In Aberdeen, they banned the book in the library. A few years back they'd have put this Gibbon man to the torch, but now they threatened him with the Mearns presbytery, which was a bit daft and fushionless, when you came to think about it. Down in the Howe itself, a chield would shout out, 'The bugger's maligned me and named me a thief, the ill-fitted tink!' An odd poverty toff in Stonehive was a bit put out by it all, but most thought it a good laugh. Down Bervie way and in Gourdon they gave never a damn!

Chris was fair beside herself when she opened up to Jane. 'These are real folk he's describing. They've their own lives to live. They've worked hard all their days and he makes fools of them like this.'

Jane tried to calm Chris down. 'You said yourself, he could write a good essay. Remember that time both of you put Arbuthnott on the map with your tales? He got keen on those heavy books long before you did. Remember how he laughed at those romances you read? He's just writing literature after all. Shakespeare and the Bible are full of dirty bits that no-one seems to mind.'

'Oh, I don't mind that,' said Chris. 'He can write all that romantic stuff in any way he likes. I quite enjoyed it. I never thought he had it in him. Leslie was never much interested in lassies at school. What I think is mean, is the way he picks on real people, our people.'

'You don't think his Chris Guthrie, you were telling me about, is you by any chance,' Jane laughed.

'Oh no. Leslie's Chris Guthrie's nothing like me. Becky Middleton was the only quine Leslie ever opened up to in those Arbuthnott days. He could do little else with the two of them struggling up and down that wild road on the Reisk.'

'But it's your name he's used, in the same way as he's done with old Pooty and the rest. You did say he was always glintin' at you in the class and making coarse comments on those magazines you read.'

'Oh, I dare say he'd got me as well as Becky and a kirn of other quines in his mind when he dreamt up his Chris Guthrie for his tale. There's a good bit of Becky in that lass. Mind you, I have a feel for the way his Chris Guthrie thinks. Leslie Mitchell must have a good notion of the way a woman thinks and that comes as a bit of a surprise. He's made a good job of his Chris Guthrie. I've gone through those trials of hers many a time, the way she feels about men, and how she has to pretend to be English, and – well, everything,' Chris added slowly. 'He's possibly used my name. He does that, uses all the names and the places he remembers. He moves a farm or a house around, but you can easily see who or what he's talking about. At least he's given his Chris a good Bervie surname – one with a bit of history to it, and I suppose he meant that. Old Gut Three the Bervie folk are for ever going on about, makes his Chris something more than a country lass – gives her a deeper and a wider significance I suppose.'

Chris was a bit of a poet herself, and had a good notion of the different levels writers could get on to. She'd a notion too that some day, she might land herself a job working with all those books she liked to delve into.

'Well, I can't sit here blethering like this,' said Jane, laughing at the way Chris's thinking had gone. 'David will be home quite soon. I just hope he's got on all right with Alf Forbes at the bank. He seems to have something on his mind just now.' She lifted wee John out of his pram and gave Chris a look.

'I can take a hint,' Chris laughed. 'But I think I'll write a letter to our old friend, Leslie Mitchell. I needn't be unpleasant. I'll write him a nice letter and congratulate him on his latest book. I'm not bothered about ourselves, but I'll point out that he might have found another way of writing his masterpiece. He'd little need to miscall those hard pressed Arbuthnott folk we all grew up with. They'd to struggle long and sore for every penny they earned. We only remember the happy times we had then, but it was coarse for the older bodies, the way things were. He does show up a few good characters, like his Chae Strachan and his Long Rob of the Mill, and I can guess fine who they are, but farming folk were nowhere like as coarse as he makes them out to be. It was pretty tough for that crowd before the war. I'll write to him tonight,' she added. She could be real determined, when she liked, the bonny Chris.

Chris patted Jane on the shoulder and threw a kiss to baby John as she made for the door, but Jane had a far away look in her eye just then. Something was troubling David just now. What in God's name was going on?

THIRTY-ONE

Leslie Mitchell read Chris Queen's letter and grinned. He could see her yet with that teasing smile, sitting over the aisle in the crowded Arbuthnott school room. Her slate pencil set his teeth on edge when she scratched the sums down from off the blackboard. She'd written a nice letter though, not as fulsome nor as coarse as most he had got.

They were piled on the table before him, threatening letters and scholarly ones, jumbled in a heap. He'd never manage to answer half of them. He'd answer this one though, for old times sake.

He gave a wry smile as he singled out some of the more critical among them. *Sunset Song* had fair caused a stir, far more than his English books had done. It was a strange world. *Three Go Back,* that experiment in time travel, had been well enough received, but had sparked off no sensation like this. Those short stories, *Persian Dawns, Egyptian Nights,* were surely better than *Sunset Song?* There was no accounting for taste.

It had been a grand notion doing *Sunset Song* that way. He'd brother John to thank for that. That trek round Arbuthnott's parks had fairly opened his eyes to the changes. John had suggested he could write a good tale there. 'A saga of the Mearns in the style of Hardy's Wessex', one critic had called it. Maybe 1932 would be his big year after all. Some had called it a new era in Scottish writing! They were a fickle lot.

The 'Golden Age' myth had fitted in well enough, though some thought it far fetched. At least he'd got them arguing about it, and some had seen there was more to what he'd written than just the coarse on-goings in one small part of the Mearns. 'The universal out of the particular', somebody had said. Most had a good word though, for the way he'd tackled that linguistic nightmare. That was something you could never dodge if you tried to write from the inside about how it is to be Scottish.

Leslie looked awhile at the letters, ripped from their envelopes and spread out before him. He should really sort them out. He'd worked himself overhard, he knew, but Ray had put up with it well. She'd little Rhea to see to now, and she still managed to cope with all those folk he brought into the place, but he should never have let them stay so late. He got carried away with things once they started their discussions. Ray deserved better from him after all those years in London suffering those bloody landlords and their filthy little rooms.

Thank God things were looking better at last. There was a funny side to it all. The two of them were no different from all those middle class white collar workers living round about them, with their detached villas, their trees and their shrubs. Welwyn Garden City was one of the plusher parts, the heart, you could say, of post-war suburbia. Well, there was nothing wrong with that. No worker should ever accept what was second best, and Ray deserved the best. It would have to be paid for, of course.

It was a relief to be back into the mind of his Scottish Cousin again. Having two personalities made things a lot easier. Leslie Mitchell was fine for all his English books, his writings on exploration and history, and all the work he'd done for his 'Spartacus'. Ray had helped him a lot there, doing all that research. You really needed to change your personality and take on a new identity to write as a genuine Scotsman. Mother's family names were just right for that. After all, we were all born with the two identities our parents passed on to us. Maybe Lewis Grassic Gibbon would have a lot more luck than Leslie Mitchell ever had.

The second tale of this trilogy was a bit of a problem. The theme for *Cloud Howe* was clear enough, but he needed a piece of real drama to sharpen up the plot.

'I was never at home in the Royal Toun,' he said to Ray, who had come in just then, 'not the way I was in Arbuthnott, or in Aberdeen or Glasgow even.'

'It's Bervie you're writing about next?' Ray sounded surprised.

'Well I'm calling it Segget,' Leslie laughed, 'after the wee farm toun that gave me birth. I want to show how it is in Scotland, so I've to see the thing whole. It's the land grips me most, the wonder and the smell of it, and how it torments and destroys the men bondaged to it. I'd Arbuthnott's Kinraddie for that.' He stretched his weary arms above his head and reached for her hand. 'I've a feel too, for what I found in the Granite Toun and in the slums of Glasgow, so there should no problem with the third tale. But I've never lived in a Scottish burgh, and I've no feel for what really goes on in such a place.'

'But Bervie's such a douce wee place, with two of its mills burned down and the rest on short-time. The dole queues have knocked all the spirit out of the place. They're certainly a much quieter lot than they used to be. Remember those wild capers round the dancing board we used to watch before the war? And the daft rhyme we used to chant:

> Oh, Bervie it's a dirty hole,
> A kirk without a steeple,
> A midden-heap at ilka door
> And damned uncivil people.

'Oh Bervie's square tower's as good as any steeple,' Leslie laughed, 'and the Scaffy aye did his best with those middens in the David Street. But the same disasters have hit the wee burghs as have hit the touns and the countryside. It's little wonder they've all lost heart.'

'But Bervie?'

'It's the place I know best. I think of it still with its smoking stacks and the hundreds of spinners pouring out from the mills. It was full of odd characters and shopkeepers who'd grab your last penny.'

'The only characters now seem to be that odd lot on the Council,' Ray laughed. 'In that last letter I got, Molly talks about the coarse heckling there was at the election with the candidates going on about their gas works and their water supplies.'

'You've a better feel for Bervie than I ever had, Ray. The Bervie air brought the colour back to your cheeks that last time. I've always felt a bit of an outsider there myself.'

'All of us in Arbuthnott were outsiders. Remember how it was when we went down to the Games, how those coarse mill workers laughed at us and called us country teuchters?'

'It never bothered me,' said Leslie. 'We got the last laugh that time we knocked out their tug o' war team.'

'The Gourdon fishers were even coarser, but I always found that a great comfort. The fishers and the mill men were so busy having a go at each other, they'd leave us country bumpkins alone.'

Ray could stand back from things now, after her years in London. Leslie squeezed her hand. 'But you can see the problem. The letters I like best are not all from the literati, but from exiles like ourselves. My scribblings about Kinraddie brought back odd memories to some of them.'

Leslie picked up a note from the pile. 'Here's one who tells me how I took him back from his foggy London to the days of his youth, how it was, he says, "with the sweetness of the broom in the air, and the long grasses bending under the fresh North Sea breezes". Over there,' Leslie pointed, 'another lad says I took him back to happier days, and the tales he'd listened to many times at his ain fireside about gryphons and other monsters down Arbuthnott's Den. I could write from the heart about Arbuthnott's parks and their peesies, and I might even stir an odd Clydesider or Aberdonian with my *Grey Granite,* but I have little feel for life in a wee burgh toun.'

Leslie reached for a note he'd set to one side. 'This is an invitation from one of my new admirers. She's invited me to stay the night with her next time I go north.' His eyes twinkled as he passed her the letter.

Ray read the letter slowly. 'It looks like an older body, judging by the writing,' she laughed. 'You'll be safe enough there. She seems quite taken with your tale of life in the Mearns. She devoured it, she says.'

'It took her back to her early days when she lived in Montrose. Her father was a plumber there, but she knows the Mearns well. She says her man came from a farm up Auchinblae way, so she's well versed in the speak of the Mearns.'

'The invitation's in the postcript. Written by her daughter, it looks like.' Ray lifted her eyebrows.

'Helen Cruickshank? She's a civil servant. I should know of her, I suppose. Says she's the secretary of the Scottish branch of PEN. That stands for Poets, Playwrights, Editors, Essayists, Novelists. It was set up by Chris Grieve in Montrose a year or so back. She must have taken on the secretary's job.'

'Well she's never heard of you, Leslie. She's not quite sure if you're male or female.' Ray ruffled his hair.

'I'd have thought Lewis Grassic Gibbon sounded masculine enough. But it's a friendly note. She says she'd invite a crowd of writers to meet me, if I let her know in good time. They're all agog apparently, to meet this new writer who's caused all the stir.'

'Fame at last,' Ray smiled. 'I think you should write her. You've to go up to Arbuthnott soon, and it would make a break to your journey. Meeting those folk could be useful. I've got enough to keep me busy down here.'

'I'll maybe do that, and take her up on her offer. I must send a note, as well, to Chris Queen. She's written a friendly wee note, though she's bothered by some of the names I've mentioned. Did you see much of Chris when you were up in Bervie?'

'We had a bit of a gossip about the old days. We never hit it off too well in those days, but then the Queens moved over to Mains of Kair when their dad died, so we saw little of each other after school. They seem to be doing a lot better now though. It was Jane that married that millowner you felt annoyed about.'

'David Webster?' Leslie looked surprised. 'Well, I wish her all the luck. It was the system annoyed me. Some folk get the best of it all. But the Queens had as rough a time as any of them. She deserves a change of fortune.'

'You'd better go carefully, if you're writing about the Royal Toun, Leslie. I doubt if the folk there will take things as lightly as the country chields seem to have done.'

'Oh, I'll watch my step,' Leslie laughed, 'I'll camouflage things a bit better. But you see the problem. I can strike a chord when I write about the folk and the land that I know about. Life in a burgh toun is quite different. The plot's no problem, with my Chris Guthrie into the place as the minister's wife. She can look askance at all their notions in the same way as she did in Kinraddie. The Royal Toun's got more than enough history for any tale you could write, with yarns about their Kaims and their Sheriff's Pot. Then there are the mills and all those tinks they brought into the place to work them. They say they still swarm away like lice down in David Street upsetting all the gentry. I can make good use of all that. Did you hear if David Webster is still swanking around in his big motor car. Is he still telling folk how he'll put some order into things?'

'The last I heard was that he and Alec Queen had crashed his big Sunbeam into a wall, somewhere near the Crawton. He got off with nothing worse than a sore wrist. You'd better be careful and not write your tale too close to life.'

'I'll take care,' Leslie smiled. 'I've moved my workers over to the west of the toun and I've placed my Segget on the other side of the Howe, somewhere near Fordoun and Laurencekirk. I've brought my spinners up from Bervie too, so that separates Bervie from Segget.'

'I still think Bervie's on the small side, for what you have in mind.'

'It's symbolic,' Leslie explained. 'Segget stands for all the smaller touns, the Hawicks and the Huntlys, the Forfars and the Kilmarnocks, with their mills and their train stations, their thrawn councils and their proud burgh schools.'

'I suppose that's where most of those independent characters came from, that built up the Empire, with their railways and their bridges, their kirks and their mission stations.'

'Aye, and provided the cannon fodder too, I'm afraid, but the wee burgh touns can scarce be ignored. Bervie's the one burgh toun I can write about. Before the war remember, it was growing at a great rate, and it had all the stir and animal spirits you could ask for. It was the only place in the Mearns with mills in any number, and it had enough local worthies in it to fill a book. Does George Shand, the baker, still preach his own brand of the gospel out there in the streets, I wonder?'

'Yes, but those Brethren or Meeting Folk, whatever you call them, have given up their wee chapel behind David Street. They used to call it the Kail Kirky.'

'Kail Kirky?'

'Yes, you got a plate of kail broth if you turned up at their meetings. A welcome feast for most folk on cold Bervie mornings. But that's one lot that have come up in the world. They've moved into a much plusher place up in the King Street which they share with the Freemasons. I hear they've fallen out with the old Bailie, on some obscure point of principle.'

'Oh they're great lads for principle, the Bervie worthies,' Leslie laughed.

'Maybe it's the Bailie's drinking, as much as the principle, that caused that little stishie.'

'The soft spoken Mr Geddes is still running the parish, I suppose?'

'That and everything else in Bervie and in the parishes round about. He supervises and teaches in the Sunday school, looks after the football league and even coaches young lads in double entry book keeping, Molly says. Some call him the School Master.'

'He never mastered a job for me, I'm afraid. He was very much an establishment man our Mr Geddes, for all his gentle ways.'

'The whole place is a lot more gentle now than the smoky, rowdy place it used to be. Remember that day we strolled down the King Street to Miss Davidson's Garden Café? The place was deserted. With the mills idle at the time, it was a mystery where folk had all got to.'

'No union leaders then, stirring things up?' Leslie suggested hopefully.

'Fred Mason's the only union leader Molly ever spoke of, and he seems a quiet, decent-like man. He runs the Unemployed Workers' Union which says something for the way things are. He and your Mr Geddes have got hold of a hut up the Glebe Close. The unemployed go there to play cards and dominoes. They say you can cut the air with a knife. There's no short-age of fags in the Royal Toun, whatever else they're short of.'

'Oh, Woodbines are cheap enough,' Leslie nodded. 'The Segget I have in mind is the wild Bervie we knew before the war. I've placed it in the present with all the troubles of the Depression. What I need now is for something drastic to happen to give a bit of bite to the thing.'

'There's little chance of that. From what Molly says, life in Bervie is set to jog along quietly now, douce and steady-like for evermore. But I'd better leave you to your correspondence. I've got work to do.'

Dear Ray, he'd never have done it without her. He needed her more than ever now. Leslie turned to the letters lying in front of him. Some of the literati were a bit upset at his misuse of the English language. He could ignore that, but he must type a quick note to this Helen Cruickshank. Yes, he'd love to stay overnight with her and her mother. He would be travel-ling north soon, and he'd very much appreciate an introduction to the members of her Edinburgh PEN group.

Chris Queen had taken care to show her disapproval in a friendly kind of way. She deserved a friendly answer. He picked up another sheet of his headed notepaper. He'd write this one by hand. He grinned to himself, headed notepaper? That should impress the bonny Chris. '28 Edgar's Court, Welwyn Garden City', it said, and his telephone number: 658.

'Dear Chris Queen,' he wrote. 'I'm just off for a few days holiday, so I hope you'll forgive a scrappy note... Glad you liked Sunset Song... 'Pooty', like all the other characters in 'Kinraddie' is, of course, quite imaginary; it's a common nickname. Thanks for all the kind wishes, and I hope you'll accept mine, very sincerely sent, in return. Yours sincerely, L Grassic Gibbon.'

Chris read Leslie's reply with a touch of exasperation. 'Well, I suppose he would say that, wouldn't he?' she said to Jane.

'Fancy addressing you as Dear Chris Queen. Dear Chris would have been more appropriate. He does know you after all.'

'And signing himself L Grassic Gibbon,' Chris looked puzzled. 'Leslie would have done fine. I suppose he's become a bit of a Jekyll and Hyde. When he's writing like that, he must feel he really is Lewis Grassic Gibbon.'

But Jane had other things beside Leslie Mitchell to trouble her just then.

David had had another long talk with Alf Forbes that day, and he'd come back looking fair upset with himself. It looked as though his last meeting with Bervie's singing banker hadn't gone at all the way David had planned it.

THIRTY-TWO

It was Harris who first gave Madge the news. Madge would look out for his cheeky grin and his kenspeckle figure striding up the Kirkburn real early each day. They would crack a joke about the latest stir in the Toun and Harris would swing on his way. Coming back at night, Harris would peer round the kitchen door before striding on down to his Bella and his dahlias as Madge was setting the table. Jim would aye be held up over some ploy or another, so there was little need to rush.

Madge and Harris between them had all the tales before the newspaper billies got wind of them. If the gales were at their worst, Harris would put a worried look on his face and say, 'The Sapey Wood craws are coming down the Toll Road to shelter under the brig. It's so windy they're having to walk it.'

Madge would look suitably impressed. She'd heard all his tales before. She'd 'put them all in a book', she once laughed.

It was St Andrew's Day when Harris had the news. Bad luck seemed to strike on St Andrew's Day. Jim had never quite forgiven Old Fritz for spoiling his St Andrew's Day meal back in 1917. Harris had no cheery grin this time when he looked round the kitchen door. Madge could see something big was amiss.

'David Webster is ruined,' said Harris. 'He hasn't a penny to his name and half of Bervie is mortgaged to the hilt.'

'But that's impossible,' said Madge, 'things have been going so well since David switched to jute. Jim said David and Alf Forbes were getting on fine just now. And David's never looked cheerier,' she added, as if that settled the thing.

'Those Stonehive lawyers have settled Bervie's hash for good this time,' said Harris, and he shook his head, for a disaster like this would hit them all. Trade was bad enough, but this would rip the heart from the Royal Toun. More than one wee business could be forced to close its doors and sell up. 'It's the gospel truth, Madge. We'll all have to tighten our belts a bit more now. You'll read all about it in the *Leader* in the morn.'

Before the morn though, rumours were sweeping the Toun. Most put the blame on Alf Forbes. He'd have been far better employed fixing ways to keep the mills on the go than wasting time rehearsing his Crookit Bawbee and daft songs like that. A banker should stick to his trade and look after his clients. But some said no, Alf had done his best and got David his new loan. David had been set to carry on when the inspectors turned up. They'd been suspicious of the large amount of stock in his books. The stock had been there for some time, so it could hardly be jute, for that was new to most of Bervie's mills.

An odd like tale began to take shape in Madge's kitchen that night. If Jim's committees ran the Royal Toun, it was Madge's kitchen that settled things in the end. As Harris explained once, you'd find half of Bervie inside Madge's kitchen most nights of the week.

Albert's Annie had it first, 'straight from the horse's mouth,' she said, and Bert had some wind of it from Jim Peter at the garage. If Albert had heard it at the tailoring, sitting there with his legs crossed on that board all day, with a stream of folk looking in with their tales, it could be taken as gospel. Ab and Jim Cameron and the rest of the tailors aye checked their facts, they'd have heard all the ways of it by the time they had lowsed that night. It was the same up at the cobblers where Ed and Arthur Strachan hammered in nails at a steady rate, cracking jokes and giving as good as they got with whoever chanced by. If one half of Bervie was out of a job, there was no shortage of places they could drop in at 'to get out of the cold' or to 'pass on a bit news'.

Frank Williamson, the blacksmith, was all right for heat, but the infernal racket he made clanging his hammer, the smell of horses' hooves and the sparks flying about the place gave you little chance for a crack, if you could get a word in edgewise, that is, when he'd stopped his blethering about Garvock. But then his mouth would be full of nails, or there would be over many school lads standing inside the smiddy door which was right next to the school. There aye seemed to be a playtime on the go when you went near the school. Jimmy Edward the saddler now, he aye had a welcome, and you'd little need for a haircut if there was a spare seat at the barber's.

The best place for news that was official, was in Jim's back office, the Bervie Office, they called it. He'd a lot more space now that he'd moved and there was aye a big fire at the back, where you could warm your hands and peer at his photos pinned up on the wall, the secretary lass rattling away at her typing machine over in the corner. Most had aye a good excuse to be there what with all the committees there were, and Jim would catch odd bits of gossip dashing back and fore between customers at the front and the phone through at the back.

But Jim had little time for long, drawn out tales, and he'd miss out what he thought was of little worth. So, in the kitchen that night it was left to Maggie Burness to set out the thing as it was. Maggie's days were spent checking the books at the wee Pitcarry Mill over by the Bervie stream. Dave Burness, Maggie's brother, had kept a tight grip on the Pitcarry along with that other mill, the Invercarron, he'd taken over at Stonehive some seven years back. He'd kept them both on the go through all the ups and downs of trade, so Maggie's tales were given more respect than most.

'David took Alf Forbes down to the sheds,' explained Maggie, 'and he showed him his stock. The shed was stacked high with bales of jute, as high as the roof and near bursting the door. You could never squeeze past. Alf was real pleased at that, so he gave David his loan.'

'So what went amiss?' Madge asked, trying to get Maggie to the point.

'Ah well,' said Maggie, warming to her tale, 'the bank inspector was suspicious. He came down a week later to see for himself. The sliding doors were pulled back again and, sure enough, it was just as Alf had said, jute bales stacked high to the rafters. But the inspector lad took a dander round the back and keeked in at it from there. That's what finished the mills for good. The shed was bare, just a thin curtain of bales had been stacked at the far end. His exact words were,' said Maggie giving a wave of her hand, for Maggie liked telling a good tale, 'this place is as toom as your hat!'

Well, that fair set the tongues going again, but there was no denying it next day when Jess McKenzie sold all her *Mearns Leader* by nine o'clock. The paper billies in Stonehive had fair licked their lips when they'd heard and they'd printed the lot. They listed all the profits and losses since old Jock had gone, how Kinghornie had been sold and for how much and why. They told of Alice's £50,000 and Stella's big cheque. It came out then, all about the stock in the sheds and what had been claimed. David had expected to get £20,000 from Alice and when that failed to arrive he'd reduced the figure for his stock by near the same amount.

'When you realised you could no longer carry on,' the lawyer lad had chipped in.

So that was the ruination of the Royal Toun – not a word in the *Leader* though about the inspector and his keek in at the back door, and the tale about the place being 'as toom as your hat!'

Some laughed at that tale, and most said there was not a grain of truth in it. 'It has the smell of Stonehive about it, that bit tale,' said Andra McLeod at the Crown. 'It's the kind of joke the Stonehive lawyers tell when they've put by a dram of two.' But the tale of the Toom Shed was never forgot.

Dave Burness still had his mill at Pitcarry, of course, and Willie Peter down in Gourdon was doing away fine, but that court case fair knocked the guts out of the Royal Toun. When the mill doors clanged shut that last time it would be forever, they said. This was no short time closing as they'd seen in the past. This time it was for ever. With trade the way it was, there would be none willing to take the mills on. It was the end of a Lang Sang, for the huge Springy with its Klondike, and it was the end too, for Jock's grand new mill at Craigview. They closed the doors for ever at the couthy wee Linty that had chattered away down the years beneath the Auld Bervie Brig. These were the last of the quines who would dream their dreams to the steady thump of Jock's old water wheel.

The whole Toun suffered then, not just the spinners and reelers, or the firemen and the preparers. There were drivers and carters, office folk and managers all joining the queue at Jim's office on the Monday for their few shillings off the dole. Houses and shops were now held by the bank, as were Jim and Madge's terraced house and the ones alongside. The houses still standing in David Street, most in the High Street, the Square and God knows where else were all caught up in the sorry mess.

'Will this make any difference to us?' Madge asked.

'No difference to us Madge,' said Jim. 'We'll just pass our rent to the bank, but there will be trouble for some. David never pressed too hard for his rents. The bank will take a harder line, and what with the Means Test doing its worst, things are going to be bad. Some of the traders might have to close down.'

David had lost most. Some said he'd not been left a penny, but most took little pleasure in that. The strange thing was, David faced up to things best. He'd never dreamt things would go the way they had. He'd aye done his best and the bank could surely have given him another year to pull things round with the jute making a profit. But now it had happened, he just gave a bit laugh and tackled things head on. He had a cheery way with him and, in no time at all, he'd a job in the book trade and was doing away fine. Madge and Jim got themselves a grand new set of encyclopedias, on the empire no less, with fine pictures of New Zealand and Canada and other healthy British places like that.

'That's what a St Andrews education does for you,' said Jim, 'but I think there's a bit of the old Jock in David there still.'

David and Jane got out of Hazelgrove, and held on to what they could. They found a wee place at the top of Farquhar Street, and then a terraced place half way up the hill road at Bervie's Townhead, with a skelp of garden out in front. David and Jane moved in and looked as happy as the day they were wed. They polished all Jock's cups and trophies and set them on the sideboard. David had a lot more time now for his painting and his piano playing, and more time as well to enjoy those big collections he had of moths and butterflies, and the things he liked doing best.

'They're very much in love,' said Madge, and she nearly added, 'and they will live happily ever after.' Madge still hung on to her romantic notions of the world, though she was finding it a bit harder now with every day that passed.

David's mills stopped dead at the news of the court case in November, and the dole queues stretched longer as the winter closed in. Jim worked harder than ever, but still managed his bible class for young Rob Middleton and the rest in that little back room in the Kirkburn. Rob's parents were another hard pressed pair that had moved into the Royal Toun to find work in Bervie's mills. Their bairns were all scrubbed clean and turned out neat and tidy like, their clothes well darned and patched. They all crowded together in a couple of wee rooms in that square off David Street, where George Shand's preachers still did their stuff on Saturday nights, but it was Jim's bible stories that pulled them in on other coarse nights. Jim's bible tales got Rob and the rest a wheen of certificates when they sat their Sunday School exams for the Kirk lads in Edinburgh. Harris said it was Madge's lemonade and biscuits that brought about that improvement to their education. Harris was never far off the mark, apart from Willie Lyon's cinema and those slide shows in the Free Kirk, there was damn else for bairns to do that wild and hungry winter.

It was a bare six months after the Royal Toun's disaster, when the

Arbuthnott chield brought out his next Grassic Gibbon book. He named it *Cloud Howe*. David's mills had given him his disaster. Some said said the Segget place was nothing like the Royal Toun and they were right enough there. Forby he'd placed it over by Fordoun on the Aberdeen railway line, though if you'd found a mill toun in that part of the Howe, you'd have been certified clean skite. What the Gibbon lad had done, of course, was to parcel up a wheen of tales and moved things around to put folk off as he'd done with his Kinraddie. There were characters in plenty you could spot fine from the Royal Toun, and as many again that he'd simply made up.

Chris was far less hassled when she read *Cloud Howe* than she'd been about Kinraddie. 'The Bervie Worthies are well able to take care of themselves,' she declared. 'He's caricatured folk he knows much less about than he did up there in Arbuthnott.'

'I wish he wouldn't keep calling all the men spinners,' Jane complained. 'Every spinner that I've ever seen in the place is a lass. Men would never work for the wages they pay the spinners. Besides, men are too ham fisted. A man would never be any use as a reeler or a spinner.'

'Oh, that's just the way folk from the country look on the mill workers,' said Chris. 'There are a good few in Bervie much the same. They've precious little idea of what goes on inside the mills. They never talk about the mills in the school. To most folk, the mill workers are all spinners.'

'But there's little doubt he had the Royal Toun in mind,' said Jane, who was more than halfway through the thing. 'We were the only Queens Leslie Mitchell ever knew. Which one of us is Else, do you think?'

'Else Queen? Oh, your guess is as good as mine, Jane,' Chris laughed. 'You'd better read the thing through, then let me know.'

'David just laughed when I told him the tale about the Bervie mills. He said he was far too busy to worry about fairy tales of that sort.'

'I think that's how most folk here will look on it,' said Chris. 'But he writes some scurrilous things about the shopkeepers. There's a bit of truth in some of it, but most of the shoppies I know are just doing as best they can to make a living for themselves. They're aye willing to give a helping hand with any ploy Jim Geddes dreams up for the place.'

'There was little need for Leslie to get a cheap laugh out of Jim's wife though. There's no one more willing than Madge to give folk a helping hand, yet all he can drag up is that she's keen on the Guild and its lantern lectures, and that she sucks pandrops in the church. There's scarce a body I know but doesn't suck pandrops in our kirk!'

'He's not really writing about the folk in the place,' Chris explained. 'He's doing what he did in *Sunset Song,* picking out things he's seen or heard and using them for the sake of his plot. Sometimes he makes use of more than one person to build up a character, as he does with his Mr Geddes and his Robert Colquohoun. Ella Macleod says her dad thinks he's picking on him with his blethering Will Melvin, just because her dad ran a transport business along with the hotel at one time. Will Melvin's nothing like Andra MacLeod and was never intended to be.'

'Well old Andra does go on a bit, when he's a tale to tell,' laughed Jane. 'Just as does Frank down at the smiddy, when he gets those nails out of his mouth.'

'I think all that stuff is by the way,' said Chris. 'He's more concerned with getting over those notions of his, the clouds, as he sees them, of fascism and nationalism sweeping over the Howe. And he shows how we womenfolk are treated, in this world that's run by men. I must hand it to him there. The place and its worthies are just a frame for what he has to say. It's much easier for a writer than just thinking up happenings and characters from the top of his head.' Chris was fair tricked with notions of that sort, and had been reading some biographies of late.

'Maybe so,' said Jane, none too happy that her dear David should have been caricatured just because he'd driven a big car and come back to the place with a St Andrews accent. 'But he doesn't tell of those folk as they really are. That's maybe just as well, for they can ignore it if they're not bothered by it all.' Chris could see that Jane was not bothered herself.

In Madge's kitchen though, Maggie Burness was less keen to let this Arbuthnott teuchter off so lightly.

'The bobby is real upset by the things he said about him,' said Maggie, 'and I don't know if George Shand sees himself as the bible-thumping grocer. George is nothing like that coarse Macdougall Brown. What about yourself Jim? He says a few coarse things about you and Madge.' Maggie's eyes were shining with indignation.

Jim waved his hands in that quietly dismissive way that he had. 'No, no Maggie,' he protested. 'Leslie Mitchell's not writing the history of Bervie. The Dominie, Andrew McAllan, was telling me he's read it and he thinks it's a fine piece of literature. It's a bit strong in its language for us to take into the library, and it's a bit over the head of most folk. The Dominie says *Cloud Howe* will be studied in the university one day. There's a lot of philosophy in the book, he says.'

Jim had never read the book himself and was never likely to. He was far too busy with his committees and his work in the Bervie office to read books of that sort. The only books Jim read were books on local history. He'd become a bit of an authority on the history of the Royal Toun, forever writing stuff for the newspapers or for the speeches he'd to give on Bervie's Charters, Bervie's Meal Mob, her brig, her mills and, of course, tales of their own King David who'd been washed ashore and had given the name of Gut Three to the chield who'd fed him. The one thing that had put Jim out slightly, was the point the Dominie, Andrew McAllan, had made about young Mitchell shaping Bervie's history to suit his plot.

'Andrew McAllan says Mitchell has moved the Kaim of Mathers from the coast up to the place beyond the Auld Wood where Mathers and Arbuthnott boiled the Sheriff. That distorts the true history of the place.' Jim was more concerned about sacrilege of that sort than any nonsense written about Bervie worthies, real or imaginary. To Jim's way of thinking, facts of that sort were not to be tampered with.

Maggie slapped her hands on her knee with some glee. 'Oh, so you admit it Jim. He really is writing about the Royal Toun,' she laughed. 'But how could you do otherwise, when he tells the tale of how David went bankrupt and left half the place mortgaged to the hilt, right down to the last detail, where the mill inspector turns and says, "This place is as toom as your hat!"'

Jim smiled a little at that. Whatever the truth of that bit tale, it was all now in the past and of no consequence to the real history of the Toun.

Madge, all this time, was sitting in the corner by the fire looking over tense and troubled. Albert's Annie had moved over beside her earlier. The cheerful, romantic Madge had not been herself of late. Something was happening to the lass, and Annie was determined to have a word with Jim about it. If only the rest of that noisy crowd would see something was amiss and take themselves off. The wind was starting to rattle the kitchen window, and Annie had little doubt the storm would get a good deal worse. She was scarcely looking forward to that trek up the Kirkburn, but she'd have to do something soon. Madge looked as if she might collapse at any minute.

THIRTY-THREE

Madge's turn that night owed little to *Cloud Howe* or the closing of the mills. The thing had been building for longer than that, and at times the room swam as it did that time of the flu. It was no virus that brought the vertigo this time, just an empty despair at how things had gone. She'd watched Father slide and give in to the drink. He'd fallen out with the Council when they'd cut the men's pay, and he'd fallen out with his Kirk and with those folk at the meeting hall. She felt for Father, but as with everything he did, he went too far. Her embarrassment with Jim and the bairns was more than she could handle, and she'd rush the bairns upstairs when his language got really bad.

That Land Fit For Heroes had been lost early on. There was little justice in any of it, and poor Jim bore the brunt every time. Means Testing, they called it, folk thrown on to relatives who'd little to spare for themselves.

Annie was giving her a wee hug and holding a glass to her lips. The room had spun just a trace, but she was all right now. Jim was seeing the last of them to the door.

'You had a turn, Madge,' Annie said. 'Too many folk here tonight and the kitchen's far too warm.' Madge burst into tears.

'Madge must rest awhile,' said Dr Mulligan next day. 'She's been pushing herself too hard.'

Jim got Peggy Proctor, a slip of a lass from Gourdon, who scampered about the place and put everything to right. Jim blamed himself for what had gone wrong, for ever out at his meetings and seeing to other folks' problems. But the Bailie too, had a lot to answer for.

The Bailie changed tack overnight. He went full tilt at everything he did. He could drink Millar, the chemist, under the table any day of the week, but all that now stopped. He did nothing by halves. He was teetotal again, and not a drop passed his lips. He smoked a bit more, and flung back at his work, graining his doors and tickling away at his fancy shop signs. He was forever prowling and growling about the shop again, checking up on the work. Harris wished him back in the Crown for an odd dram with old

201

Millar. It would get him out from under their feet!

There was none that could point to any committees Jim had given up, but he spent more time with his Madge. As the days grew brighter, the two of them would dander down by the waterside again and Jim would entertain her with tales of the latest antics of the Council. This was the way it used to be, Madge thought, in those days before the war, Jim confiding his secrets and holding her close. Things were on the turn. The deep boom of the Springy's horn had sounded the other day. Willie Peter that ran the Gourdon Mill had taken the Springy over, and folk were drifting back to work. There was word too, that Willie would be taking over Craigview as well. The high pitched horn of old Jock's last mill would be sounding out soon. It would be like old times again. Jim looked down at the stepping stones and laughed as they watched a young lad clutching at his lass when she slipped on the big shiny boulder.

'Remember that first time I held your hand on those stepping stones?' he said. It had been a long time since Jim had talked of their courting days.

'I wonder if Postie Mollison's doing the right thing raising money for a new footbridge,' Madge said. 'Those cruives are so much a part of the place.'

'Thereby hangs a tale,' Jim laughed and then explained the early happenings of what was to become another Bervie saga. Postie Mollison was another of Bervie's long line of thrawn Bailies, but folk still called him Postie Mollison, for that's what he'd been before he retired. He was a quiet, gentle spoken, spare sort of man, with a white goatee beard and sharp, bright blue eyes. Postie was fair set on building a new concrete footbridge on the sight of the old Bervie cruives. He was too old himself now to negotiate those slippery stanes. He'd had the place surveyed and the contractors had named a price, but the thing had been held up, as ever, by the Council's lawyer chield up in Stonehive.

'Better get permission from Doon Sooth,' said the lawyer chield.

'But Bervie owns the rights of the whole damned water,' Postie Mollison was outraged. 'It says so in our charters.'

'Did Postie Mollison ask for permission then?' Madge asked.

'Oh yes,' Jim grinned. 'I persuaded him and we drafted a note for our lawyer to write out. It was just a formality, I said to Postie, to keep them all happy.'

'How can you be sure of that?' Madge gave Jim a look. 'You know how these lawyers are, and you know how they are with our notions down there in London.' Madge was less amenable to the antics of the lads Doon Sooth than she'd been in the past.

'Oh, if a Bervie Bailie gets stuck into a fight about our Charters, he'll wear them down in the end. Postie's every bit as thrawn as the rest of them. It seems to go with the job.' Jim's eyes twinkled at that bit of repartee.

Postie Mollison did wear them down in the end, but his battle with the Mercantile Marine Department kept the Toun entertained for months on end. The arguments were all about whether the brig was to be above or below the High Water Mark. It seemed the admiralty controlled all the waters round the coast, and that included the tidal waters of the wee Bervie stream.

'Maybe they want us to build a drawbridge, so they can send a gunboat up past the Linty Shotts,' suggested George Ranson with a dead pan face. A droll lad George, when he liked.

In the end, Mollison's Briggy, as it's been named ever since, was opened in the spring and in the summer of 1934; the spring, because that's when it was ready, and in the summer because the douce Bervie stream, true to its reputation, rose up that year at this latest affront to its independence.

The floods on the Bervie that wild April of 1934 were worse than any that had gone before. The spaewives had little doubt that something was amiss. This was an omen you'd ignore at your peril. The floods which hit Arbuthnott and Bervie, Kinraddie and Segget if you like, were more destructive than that deluge four years back, and came in wilder waves than the ones which had threatened the boiler house door of Jock's Linty Mill back in 1898.

The red deluge powered its way under the Auld Bervie Brig, looking to smash to hell the brand new brig in reinforced concrete they'd near completed. It swept up all the builders' gear, two engines and a screening plant, and flung them far out into Bervie Bay. That was the last anyone saw of them. The big new brig stood the strain, but Postie Mollison's wee briggy had little chance in the storm, and one of its concrete supports was thrown flat on its side. The torrent burst through the shingle bar at Bervie beach, the first time ever, the Worthies said, and demolished Jock's old boat house that had stood firm for years. Folk in the Linty House were rescued in time, but Jock's old Linty Mill, now derelict and silent, was finally swamped and ruined. The Royal Toun itself, high standing as it was above the Bervie stream's tantrums, had no escape from it either. Water poured down from Townhead and folk in King Street, thinking they were well clear of it all, found holes being gouged out in the street and their shops under two feet of water before they could stir. The flood then swung round at the top of the Kirkburn and piled straight down to the sea, turning the bay to a dark gloomy brown.

This was Cloud Howe with a vengeance, the black nimbus clouds had dropped their heavy load of water, fair and square, the Kaiser's gunners would have cheered. There was a canny cunning to that storm in the targets that it struck. Madge's kitchen and her back parlour were soon piled high with boulders and red mud. Jim's Michelin illustrated *Guides to the Battlefields* were sodden, the pages glued and stuck fast. If that's where your plans are hatched, it seemed to say, we'll soon put a stop to all that!

In Arbuthnott things were as bad if not worse. The brigs at Whitfield and Mondynes – yes, Mondynes! – were smashed down and carried off through the Haughs. Arbuthnott's low lands were flooded and her main roads shut off.

'If it's not one damned thing it's another,' said Scaffy Duncan. 'We've no sooner sorted out the gods from Doon Sooth, but we've to take on those gods up abune!'

There was little need, you would have thought, for the Scaffy, who was also the Toun Crier, to be sent round, for the soss was there for all of you to see. But no, Jim summoned the Scaffy, or the Toun's Officer if you like, for he had a top hat and a red coat he'd put on for ceremonials. The Scaffy'd to shake his bell and shout it into the wind that the water was bad. The rules were clear about that, and folk had to be warned. You'd have been clean skite though, if you'd touched the stuff. The Toun's water was a sharp bright colour of red when it splashed out from the taps.

So that was 1934, a year of floods in the Howe. As clear a sign as you could get, there was worse still to come!

THIRTY-FOUR

'Before a Gourdon quine speaks the truth the Bervie burn will run backwards through the Howe.'

Helen Cruickshank's mam slapped her side and laughed. 'That fair tickled the both of us when we read it. I just had to write and find out more about this new writer from the Mearns. We maybe live in Auld Reekie now, but our hearts are still up there in the Howe. Helen could fill a book with odd tales from Angus and the Mearns.'

He got a lively welcome at Dinnieduff, the semi-detached villa on the slopes of Corstorphine Hill where Helen Cruickshank handled her work with Scotland's literati. She'd a busy time of it, walking her dog, tending her garden and keeping an eye on her effervescent mam. She put in a seven hour stretch at her Department of Health office in Princes Street, and managed her secretarial work for the PEN Club forby. That night she'd crowded twelve of them, poets, writers and the rest, into the wee front room to meet Scotland's newest author.

'Eighty years young and getting younger every day,' Ma laughed when Helen introduced her. She fair spoke her mind, did Ma, and she soon got their Scottish night going with her renderings of The Laird of Cockpen and Kate Dalrymple.

He'd been pushing himself over hard of late and this was just what he needed, a chance to stand back and take a broader view with those like minded folk up here in the north. Ray had urged him to get away and take his turn of Bervie's sea breezes. He'd been working flat out, and she needed time on her own with baby Rhea. His late nights at his typewriters were disturbing their sleep.

Well, the sea breezes had been fine, but Father still found it hard to forget, and Mother too was as overworked and as upset as before. Here at Dinnieduff, he found a boisterous outspoken lot, full of something they called Scotland's literary renaissance and daft notions like that.

'We were an irreverent lot ourselves at Montrose Academy when I was a lass,' said Helen's mam. 'We made up parodies of the psalms about the places and folk that we knew. Mind you, some of those psalms just ask to be mocked. It's the way they're translated, I suppose.'

'You're not going to deave Leslie with those awful psalms of yours, Mam,' Helen screwed up her face.

'Just the one tonight lass, since we're on about Bervie and Gourdon. You know that awful psalm number 137?' She looked at him and he gave a half nod.

'I'm not all that up in my psalms,' he grinned.

'It goes something like this,' said Ma, 'a terrible bit of verse.' She crooned away quietly with a mischievous look on her face:

> By Babel's stream we sat and wept
> When Sion we thought on
> In mids't thereof we hanged our harps
> The willow trees upon.

'Our own version, we composed Under the Dome, was so much better. I'll sing it to you more slowly.' Ma had a good church voice when she was in the mood, and she gave it all she'd got.

> By Bervie's stream we sat and wept
> When Gourdon we thought on
> On partan's cleeks we hung our breeks
> The water to drip from.

'That was fine, Mam,' Helen burst in. 'Now we'll turn to loftier themes. This is a literary discussion we're having, not a Montrose Academy Old Girls' Reunion.'

'I must remember that piece,' Leslie grinned, 'and work it into my next novel. It's on the coastal touns of the Mearns.'

'We'd a notion you were a woman when we first read *Sunset Song,*' Helen explained. 'Your characterisation of Chris Guthrie was a master-piece. I said you'd too much of an empathy with the woman's point of view for a man to understand.'

'It's the injustice of the modern world bothers me most,' Leslie said, 'and the biggest injustice of all is the way men treat the other half of the human race.'

That fair got them all arguing and it lasted well into the night. He fell into the soundest sleep he'd had for years after Helen left him in the wee room they called the Prophet's Chamber, the bedroom they reserved for honoured guests like himself.

Ray was right, after all, he thought to himself later, one of those 1930s years would be his *Annus Mirabilis.*

But which one? 1932 had seen his big breakthrough with *Sunset Song.* It had caused such a stir with the literati, including those friends he'd made in Corstorphine. He'd had another half dozen of his books published by then, and some he'd thought were a damned sight better, but it was *Sunset Song* had stopped folk in their tracks.

The next two years, were the busiest of the lot. He kept up his visits to Dinnieduff whenever he travelled north and Helen met Ray the next time she was on her travels Doon Sooth. Helen and Ray hit it off at once, two women civil servants together sharing views on Britain's chauvinistic Civil Service.

'Your man wants us women to run around naked and pick out a new man for ourselves each year,' Helen laughed.

'You've been reading his *Three Go Back,*' Ray looked embarrassed. 'He believes Elliot Smith's notion of a Golden Age in the past, when we were all a lot more natural about each other, is far better than all the pretence and double standards we've got so used to in the civilised world.'

'It's as good a myth as any other for explaining the way the world's gone.' Leslie wasn't going to let them laugh off this piece of serious thinking. 'If we could do a bit of time travelling, we might appreciate better, the terrible mess of the present time.'

'Oh, I agree with the thinking behind it all,' said Helen. 'You've chosen a woman again for your principal character. I don't take to Clair Stranlay as I did to Chris Guthrie, but you've a surer touch with your women characters than you have with some of your men. I still think your Chris Guthrie's Ewan acts well out of character.'

Helen never pulled her punches, but Leslie gave as good as he got. 'I've seen men behave like animals,' he argued, 'brutalised by those atrocities on the Western Front.'

That started the two of them off again about human nature, the Diffusionist Theory and much else besides. Ray was happy to leave the two of them to battle it out. When Leslie was waving his hands like that, she knew he was fine pleased with himself.

They were hectic years. He had two typewriters on the go now, and by the end of 1933 another three books were published, including *Cloud Howe* and *Spartacus.* In November he wrote to Helen 'I've got a publishing list as long as my arm for next year. My only hope for a rest is the revolution, and that still seems an infernal long way off.'

The year 1934 had the look of an *Annus Mirabilis* about it. *Grey Granite* came out in September, but before that he got out four more books and a string of short stories and articles. Hugh MacDiarmid joined him in the production of 'Scottish Scene'. The two of them described it as 'The Intelligent Man's Guide to Albyn'. Helen enjoyed that touch, they had dedicated it to her 'with affection and appreciation', and had a good laugh when Helen showed how contradictory he and MacDiarmid had been in their descriptions of the Scots. 'But then that's how the Scots are themselves,' Helen beamed.

As Christmas neared, it looked as though 1935 would be even better. The newspaper billies were stirring up the notion that 1935 would see a new age of prosperity, and there would be a great ballyhoo to celebrate the Silver Jubilee of King George and Queen Mary. Whatever you thought of that as a cause for a jamboree, at least it gave a brighter look to things than all that talk you'd had about the Depression.

Nineteen thirty-four had been Leslie's best year yet, Ray knew. If he took more care of himself, they'd have a grand time of it in the year that lay in front.

Nineteen thirty-five had a grand look too for Jim and Madge. The flood damage in April had been cleared up. They'd lost a few of their things when the waters burst through their front door, but Madge's kitchen and her parlour had been refurbished when the insurance lads paid their dues. Mollison's briggy had been repaired along with the brigs at Whitfield and Mondynes. All that nonsense about premonitions and omens was nothing more than the haverings of those daft spaewives and their like.

There had been changes as well, up there in Arbuthnott. When Jack, the new laird, and his wife, Dorothy, had stormed in straight from their ranching years in Canada, they'd set to with a vengeance to clear up the shambles. That had been back in 1920, and now in the thirties the whole estate had a bright and healthy look to it. The Big Hoose and its gardens had been restored, and the Home Farm was back in good working order.

The ranching laird, the 14th Viscount Arbuthnott and Baron of Inverbervie, soon had Jim's scouts organising jamborees and scout camps in his parks. By 1934 a younger generation had taken over and the scout camps on Arbuthnott estate beside a pool of the Bervie stream had become an annual event. The Bannermans who'd run Arbuthnott shop before the war now had their shops in the Royal Toun and in Gourdon. Young Peter Bannerman could scarcely believe the thing.

'The place is nothing like you described it when Grandfather camped in those woods before the war. Our tents were pitched on a well trimmed park by the Bervie. We went swimming every day, and in the evenings we'd singsongs by the campfire. The laird could fair spin a yarn. He'd sit down with us by the campfire and tell some great tales about his early days in Canada. It was Bonzer, Mam,' Pete said. Willie Lyon's Picture Palace had a lot to do with the new words now mixing in with the Mearns Speak.

In the Royal Toun, Willie Peter had put new machines into Craigview, and every spinner, reeler and preparer in the place was back at work again. The new machines worked a treat with folk being trained as shifters to change the bobbins. This left the spinners free to speed the work on. The corner had been turned, folk said, and the silver was rolling in.

'What a shame it was,' said Madge, 'the bank could surely have given David just one extra year.'

By the end of 1934 the deep blasts of the Springy and the high pitched horn of Craigview sounded first thing each morn and kept folk on the go for the rest of the day. It was good to see the dole queues shrink. That Means Test had been so unfair, a hard thing to thole.

There were celebrations to plan for the Jubilee Year, and Jim was back at the things he liked doing best. The big new brig would be opened and he'd have to plan for that, sometime in August, they thought. Lord Arbuthnott would be there to cut the cord and folk would be crowding into the Toun from all over the Mearns. It would be as it was in the good old days when folk crowded in for those great days of the Games. The Council planned to fill a bronze tube with some mementos and silver 1935 coins which they'd drop inside one of the big concrete piers. That was real history in the making. Jim was pleased. They'd be Jubilee coins for the Silver Jubilee Bridge, for so it would be named.

Then there was the Silver Jubilee itself. Jim had plans for that with parades and parties and dances. He'd have to order flags and bunting in good time for the occasion. This was a royal toun, after all, and things would have to be just right for the Royal Jubilee.

They had another grand time of it that hogmanay night. Herbert Stephen near rang the New Year bell clean out of the belfry. It was Jubilee year at last. It would be a year none would forget!

THIRTY-FIVE

The dice were loaded against Leslie that New Year's Day, but he didn't think so. He thought he was on the mend at last. He'd been wrong not to listen to those doctors, and he'd been out of sorts and argumentative on that last trip to Dinnieduff, but he'd seen to it when he got back. That nagging pain had eased, and he was definitely on the mend. He'd explained himself later:

'Dear Helen,' he scrawled, 'this must remain the merest scrawl as I am prostrate in bed (gastritis) for a fortnight on diet, forbidden cigarettes and loathing humanity. Wish I could come up in early Spring, but I am too busy...'

Nineteen thirty-five was here at last and he'd that other problem on his mind. Of a sudden the publishers were keen and he'd promised them so much. Ray herself was busier than she'd ever been now she had the two bairns to see to. He smiled at the thought. They were developing into a neat middle class family group with their wee lass and baby boy in this suburban garden city! He'd better keep a tight grip on things if he wanted to put his grand theories into practice. Women always did get the worst of the bargain however hard you tried, but he had done all he could to help Ray with the chores. She'd helped him with that mountain of research they'd done for his book on Spartacus. He'd certainly never have done any of it without her, but he should be helping her more. Maybe he had taken on too much.

There was all the correspondence too, and those folk who came to visit. He'd never turn them away. Tossing ideas around till the wee sma' hours was the very stuff of life. The eternal puzzle and mystery of it all. You just couldn't crawl through life with your eyes shut and not question the thing.

It was the first weekend in February and they were having a grand time of it again. He really was on the mend at last and Willa Muir was quizzing him about his last book on time travel.

'I don't believe your *Gay Hunter* has no serious intent, as you claim, Leslie. It certainly glories in the sun and wind and rain and those dreams by smoking camp-fires, and I enjoyed it for that. I think you've a more serious notion behind it and you were just a shade embarrassed when you wrote the dedication. I liked the points you made too, about those terrible fascists.'

'I made a mention of glimpsed immortality in the dedication,' Leslie grinned, 'but what do any of us mean by immortality? Do we mean the immortality of the human race or are we thinking of the life force in Nature? Can we somehow share in that immortality? Organised religion has distorted the message, if there ever was a message.'

'I was glad to see you built your tale around a woman again. Gay Hunter on her trip to the future is much improved on your Clair Stranlay in the prehistoric past. It's a pity you'd to destroy the world with those atomic explosions first. Will we need to go through all that, do you think, before women are seen as equal to men, and can be carefree and uninhibited?'

Dear Willa, another Scottish quine who'd suffered because of her sex. Vice-principal of a London teachers' training college, no less, but she'd to give all that up the moment she dared to wed!

'I meant that to be taken with a pinch of salt, Willa, light hearted reading,' he laughed, 'but you never know. It didn't worry you that I had all those folk romping around stark naked then?' Leslie was enjoying himself.

'Weren't you just showing us the unhealthy attitude we all had to sex? I'm at one with you there. You'd a Nurse Geddes as Gay's mentor, I noticed. Wasn't it a Dominie Geddes your Robert Colquhoun looked to for help in *Cloud Howe*? Any connection?'

'Just a Freudian slip on my part.' Leslie's eyes twinkled.

'I still think your Chris Guthrie is your most rounded female character. I like the way she sees beyond the politics of her young Ewen. She's fascinated by what lies behind it all and sees the need for there being constant change in the universe. A developing universe makes some sort of sense. I would say those clouds that sweep the Mearns and bother your Chris have as much to do with time and place as do your novels on time travel.'

'Maybe we're all being too analytical about things,' Leslie laughed. 'I used to feel that way when those dreary teachers went nit-picking over Shakespeare up there in Stonehive.'

'We've had a grand night of it again tonight Ray,' Willa whispered as she took her leave. 'Thanks again for all your hospitality. I hope we haven't over excited that man of yours. He's pushing himself too hard you know. What he needs is a good long holiday, back up north where the air is clean.' Ray nodded at that. If only he would.

It was only a few days later that the news filtered back through the Howe. Leslie Mitchell was dead. He had died on 7 February after an emergency operation on a gastric ulcer. It was one week before his thirty-fourth birthday.

Madge had taken the soft brush to smooth the nap of black silk on Jim's bonny lum hat she'd fetched from its box in the wardrobe. She'd smoothed the fine crown with her long tapered fingers, a piano player's fingers, Jim called them, and pondered on the things Grassic Gibbon's Chris Guthrie had said about her Segget. Segget was, she remembered, 'halted here in these Segget years, waiting for the sound of unhasting feet, waiting for a Something Unnamed...'

Madge loved the smooth feel of the soft silk on Jim's lum hat. Why was it mostly at times like these she'd to lift it from its box?

Jim wore his lum hat, black jacket and striped trousers for formal occasions. He'd come this time, not just as Inspector of Arbuthnott Parish, a post he held with the inspectorates of Kinneff and Bervie, but because there was a strong sense of occasion about this gathering. He'd glanced at, but never read, Leslie Mitchell's books that he'd seen Madge read. He'd recollections too, of the few times he'd met and talked to that quiet, deep thinking man with the bright, intelligent eyes. It was a good many years since they'd met in his first wee office in Bervie's Cowgate.

Jim attended most funerals when he could, as he attended most happenings in the parish. Funerals like weddings, council meetings, kirk socials and Remembrance Sundays were events of significance. At times like these you took stock of the folk that were there and the folk that were not. He'd a great sense of local history, had Jim, the only history, he thought, that really mattered, the moving on of the lives of the folk that you knew and the places you knew.

Jim stood still at the graveside. It was a bright afternoon, 23 February, when they brought Leslie's casket to the corner grave of Arbuthnott's auld kirkyard. There was a sharp bite in the air and Jim buttoned up his coat. It was here the young Leslie had browsed on his own, wondering at those stones and the folk gone before.

There was a troublesome note about this burial. As with the cremation at Golder's Green, no prayers would be said in the hallowed kirkyard. In London, Ivor Brown had said some words about Leslie's writing and his compassion. Even in the Cambrai mud with men shattered and deserted, they'd sent up a prayer at times. There would be no kirk prayers here though, just the silent prayers, sent up by the ones that cared, better prayers maybe, not troubled by the rote words of the minister.

James Mitchell, the lad's dad was there. The square set of his beard hid any sign on that strong weathered face. A much misunderstood man, Jim thought, eyeing the defiant face, held high now and taking on the world. James Mitchell had that dour Scottish look, the incarnation you might have said of old John Knox himself.

Leslie's mam was near to tears. She'd expected no crowd like this. How could those strangers even guess at the agony of her man and herself. It was her own family names, Lilias and Grassic and Gibbon, he'd used for those uncouth books he'd written. George and John had been born to her before she'd wed her James. This was James's only son they were burying and he was taking it badly. She despaired for her man just then.

Jim knew most of them, but some were strangers, writers and journalists by the cut of their clothes. They stood out from the crowd of farmers and locals gathered there in the Den. The crowds had come down from both sides of the kirk, on those roads that looped from the Bervie road and the crossroads to the Reisk up there behind. Some had crossed the wee brig down there in front, over the Bervie stream, sparkling and clear in the sharp afternoon sun. Up past the ruined mill they'd come, their dark bonnets and clothes at odds with the sheets of white snowdrops on the banks at either side. Most of them had halted out there on the road, on the far side of the wall, just beyond the open grave.

Ray carried the small casket slowly to the grave's edge. The crowd stood still, heads bowed and bare to the chill of the slight breeze that had sprung up, a bit unsure of this way of doing things. Ray bent forward and let the casket drop. It had a short distance to fall. She spoke some words Jim barely could hear.

'A great man is dead,' she said, and stopped a moment, to catch her breath. 'The body is dead but the spirit will remain and be an inspiration

213

to the people of Scotland now and for many centuries to come.' An arm stretched out and drew her gently back. Jim sent up his own silent prayer.

'How was it,' Madge asked later.
'Folk here are of two minds,' said Jim. 'He's little understood.'
'I little understood myself, some of the things that he said, but I had a strong feel for the way that he said them. He'd a great love of the land and the folk that worked it, but he'd a bitterness too, at the lives they had to lead.'
'There were writers up there and I listened to their talk. It was the primitive goodness in folk he believed in, so they said, but he'd little time for the kirk.'
'I sometimes think there's a shape to everything, almost as though it had all been worked out in advance.' Madge looked worried. 'When you look back, it sometimes seems that way. It all fits to a pattern.'
'We've all to work out our own salvation,' said Jim giving Madge a tight hug. 'Leslie Mitchell was maybe not so very different from ourselves. We're looking at the same thing from different angles, but we all believe in the power of Good over Evil, in the end that is. There's an awful lot of unfairness and injustice about in spite of what we all went through, and young Leslie Mitchell was just not willing to put up with any of it.'
'There was something he said about how nothing would endure, how we are all halted in these Segget years, waiting for something terrible to happen. What's going to happen, Jim, in the years that lie ahead of us? What will happen to the bairns and the place we are in? Nothing stands still, he said, and he's right enough there. Where will we all be in ten years time, or in the next five?'
Jim hugged Madge closer. She was back to her old worries. 'Everything is on the turn now, Madge. Things can only get better. The mills are busy again, there's a new brig and a Silver Jubilee to celebrate. The bright days of Spring are just round the corner.'
Madge looked doubtful at that. 'They're still talking about another war, you know. That man in Germany was telling thousands of his Nazis that he'd conquered democracy and he wanted to be hated by his enemies. I thought we'd ended all that when you came home from those terrible trenches. Those lads we lost then were just like young Rob Middleton and Peter Bannerman and the rest. Even the laird of Hallgreen, remember, was

lost that last time. I thought about that when I spoke to young Edwin Gibb
the other day. He'd come home on holiday, he said. He likes Bervie best,
and so do they all, however far they travel. But here we are again, nearly
twenty years on and other young lads are coming to that age. Are we all
sitting here in Bervie waiting for the sound of Unhasting Feet, waiting for
Something Unnamed? That's what Grassic Gibbon would have us believe.
That's what he said.'

'Madge, Madge,' Jim laughed. 'You've been over serious of late.
'Grassic Gibbon said a whole lot of things. I heard those writers discussing him. Grassic Gibbon thought that one day women and men would be
free and equal in everything they did and there would little need for folk to
marry any more. Can you imagine the Kirk agreeing to anything like that?'

That would be impossible, Madge could see. All the pleasure in life de-
pended on happy, healthy marriages. What would happen to the bairns if
they did away with weddings?

'Your Bervie's in real safe hands, Madge,' Jim smiled. 'There's as
much chance of young Peter Bannerman or Rob Middleton, or even young
Edwin Gibb going off to another war as, well, as there is of them doing
away with the Bervie Council and all those thrawn bailies that keep a good
grip on our affairs. I mean, thrawn bailies like your father, of course, or
that stubborn Bailie, Postie Mollison.'

Madge laughed. That was something that could never ever happen. How
could they possibly run the Toun and get things done the way they wanted
them done without their thrawn Bervie bailies! They were as likely to have
half the Toun living in sin, she thought. As for another war, surely no government would let things drift that far after all the ugliness and the killings
they'd suffered last time.

Helen Cruickshank walked along the waterside and thought about the
words Ray had spoken at the graveside. She'd been there with Nan
Shepherd and Eric Linklater from the PEN Club, but she was alone now,
and had time for her thoughts. It was this notion of time and place again,
Leslie's theme. His spirit had forever been reaching backwards and for-
wards down the years to that Golden Time where the body could free itself
from the clutter of taboos and fears that suffocated the world. She'd write
her poem for him in the Royal Toun that night.

The February gloom was settling in as Helen passed Mollison's Briggy, as good as new again, strong, straight and trim. It was almost a year since that douce wee burn, rippling quietly there, had risen up and smashed its pillar away. Leslie had told her about that and his wee brig at Mondynes. There had been the whole gamut of the year since then, from seedtime to harvest, and now they were back at the beginning again, with the unfurrowed fields before them. The poet was at work in Helen, the crowds and that kirkyard had cut very deeply. She'd write it tonight. It was all so clear and sharp.

On the Auld Bervie Brig she looked deep into the Howe. The burnt out mills and the old Games Park were empty and still. Leslie had talked of those days, of those Mearns crowds, their pipe bands and brass bands, their sturdy lads at the tug o' war and the big Gourdon Dominie, J H Johnstone, with his bristling moustache. Golden times are aye in the past and Leslie was no different from the rest of us, she thought. His hands were forever waving as he talked about his memories, those orra lads and those spinners, the fisher lads and the quines, dancing the night away with their hoochs and skirls through the long *Simmer Dim*.

That had been another time, in high summer. The place was the same but this was February and beyond the park she could see the unfurrowed fields. Away on the high slopes, beyond Pitcarry towards Auchendreich way, the burning whins were lightening the shadows. Out of sight lay Leslie's Kinraddie, and before her the Haughs, stretching as far as Castle Allardice and Guthrie's Dam that took its name from that strange tale of the past. Behind the castle and out of sight, round the bend of the Bervie flow, lay the kirkyard and the Den.

Helen stood there in that place and at that time, a poet's look in her eyes. She saw the burnt out mills and the blazing whins. Ashes from the mills, ashes from the whins, aye and ashes from the Den were mingling in the burn now and washing to the sea. They'd bring their own seeds with them to bring on other births. She'd write about that. Nothing endures, Leslie had argued, except the land itself. There was truth of a kind in that, but ideas lived on, and spirits lived on. Others before them had looked at that view. Helen started to dream. That Provost Alf had been no poet. Not a man for whins or notions, Alf, no doubt, saw the things he knew, his two grand mills. What else would he have seen? And those wild, excited crowds what would they have seen? What would they have looked at damned mills for on a day such as that? And that Captain Pappa Jim, they all spoke about, how would he have looked on those burnt out mills?

Given a bit of a nod, maybe?

The poem took its shape as she passed the Big Hoose at Bridge End, and carried on up the Cowgate, past the Market Square. It looked smaller than she had imagined it. But what a stillness there was in the place. This was nothing like the Royal Toun of Leslie's younger days. She stepped up her pace and got back to her hotel. They'd put a fire on in her room and she sat there a while, the day's events still paining her mind. 'Spring in the Mearns', she'd call it. She wrote all of it that night in her wee Bervie room. She read the poem aloud slowly, then read the last verse again... he'd worked so hard, poor Leslie, on those dreams he'd caught and held.

What was that remark Gay had made in that last book of his on time travel? '...events don't happen. They're waiting there in the future to be overtaken.'

Gay had been talking to that fascist, Houghton, she'd met. He'd seen a future of hardness and hierarchy, the scum put in their places again, and that had apalled her, tempted her to dabble in that 'Experiment with Time' her father had learned from the American researcher.

Helen was half dreaming now, another verse taking shape... It had been a stressful day. The hotel had gone quiet, and all around her, the Royal Toun was asleep. She kept thinking of Leslie, how he questioned it all, taking nothing on trust. There was nothing bleak and despairing about him though. He'd worked out something positive for himself, found his own epiphany, freedom from that odd notion of God most folk were cumbered with. A 'glimpsed immortality,' he'd said, forever looking beyond the present. He'd taken his Gay Hunter through the millennia, beyond the holocaust of the atom, and she'd found her freedom there.

Helen had no wish to go that far, but it would be worth while, as Houghton, the fascist, had said, to have just a glimpse of the future, to project herself into it 'for no more than a blink. Worth while trying half a night of sleeplessness to see that.' Helen's imagination ran away with her then. She too was halted 'in these Segget years waiting for the sound of Unhasting Feet, waiting for a Something Unnamed...' Another Great War was possible, but this was 1935 after all and there was an optimistic mood in the land. If only she could have a glimpse of it herself, no more than a blink, say twenty or thirty years ahead. What was lying out there in the years that lay ahead?

What was that trick Leslie had described? 'Dreams and a floating edge of mist. But you must not dream. You must just stay on the edge of sleep, concentrating... Twenty, thirty years on, that's all any of us would ask...'

'I could scarce believe it when I heard. Archie Middleton and Molly settled down in Pappa Gibb's Big Hoose at Bridge End!'

Ray's eyes twinkled as she handed her case to Cousin Archie. 'Those Bervie Spaewives had some of it right in the end then? Jane Queen had her turn at Hazelgrove and now the two of you have moved in here!'

'Come away in and stop your havering.' Archie grinned. He hadn't the least notion what she was blethering about. 'It was Molly fancied the view by the Bervie brig. We'd a long, hard time of it at Millplough but things picked up after the war and this place came on the market. You can see the Grampians from here and those Arbuthnott parks on the braes.'

Molly came out just then and laughed. 'They're all over there, Becky, Millplough and the kirk, the wee school and the shop, just tucked out of sight behind Castle Allardice and the braes. You get some grand sunsets at this time of the year. Just the place for us to live out our days.'

Ray had a strange turn just then. She was Becky again, back with her ain folk. 'That must be Madge McCombie's place down there in the Haughs,' she said, pointing. 'Madge described it to me that time she came down.'

'Madge Laing she's been, a long time now, Becky. She and Jim moved about at first when they left Pitcarles. They went to Craighill for a time, but they're fine and settled now over there in Bervie's Haughs. That's their place, beyond the burnt out mills. It's good growing land down there, black and rich, none of that red clay stuff you had up there on the Reisk.'

'Till the Bervie bursts its banks,' Archie laughed. 'but it's the Bervie burn makes it growthie.'

'Madge is a great lass on the roads with that car of hers,' said Molly. 'She's forever driving up and into the Royal Toun. But that was a fair trip she took us that last time, all that way down to Welwyn.'

'She likes driving,' said Becky, 'You're all welcome back as soon as you're ready. I've invited Chris Queen down, when she's free, and we can all crack on about the old days. I wonder why Chris never wed, she and Jane were the two most glamorous quines in the place.'

'Chris had charge of the NAAFI in Perth during the war and now she's fine pleased with herself looking after those library books up the Glebe Close. We've to call it Church Street now, Glebe Close has too coarse a sound for modern lugs! Chris is another Arbuthnott quine that enjoys that view. She says she has the best of both worlds nowadays. She can see most of *Cloud Howe* just by standing at her library door. Inside she's got books in plenty on all those clouds Leslie warned us about.'

'It's strange, how you've all ended up in the Royal Toun, the two of you settled here in Pappa Gibb's old place. Remember when Jane lived in Hazelgrove when David still had his mills? Leslie used that affair for his Segget tale.'

'Some were none too pleased at your Leslie for that, but it did little harm. David had a good laugh about it at the time. He and Jane were a lot happier, I often think, when they moved to their wee place up in Townhead. David had more time after that for his piano playing, his butterflies and the rest. He was fine pleased to get back with those airmen again. They made him an officer in the RAF when Hitler's war broke out.'

'I was telling Archie that tale the Bervie spaewives put about,' Becky smiled, 'but he looked as though he'd never heard of it.'

'Oh Archie's got little time for nonsense of that sort,' Molly laughed. 'Besides, that tale was a bit muddled in the end. I landed up at Mill of Arbuthnott and attended the school. Jane left Milltown that year her dad died.'

'We used to laugh at the Provost Doctor and his *Annus Mirabilis*. I never forgot that phrase.' Becky had a faraway look in her eyes.

'Things are looking brighter with you now though Becky?'

They had moved inside and Molly was rattling away with the coffee cups. So this was where Provost Alf and Captain Pappa Jim with his big crowd of bairns had hatched out their plans for their Bervie mills. Spacious enough for Provost Alf, but Pappa Jim had taken his brood with him to live out his days in that other castle on the sooth side of the Toun. Now wee Molly, as they'd called her at school, and Archie had settled in, looking for all the world as though they'd grown up in the place!

Becky started at Molly's voice. 'Brighter? Oh much brighter, but it was a long hard struggle at first. I got a good deal of help from those friends of Leslie who got me back into the office again. That's all in the past though, and we've got a land fit for heroes at last, no more worries about doctor's bills or how we'll fare when we're old. There's to be the best of treatment for all of us, not just the wealthy few. If we can be one nation in the war years, they say, we can be one nation in peacetime. All of us matter now. It's a pity it's taken two terrible wars to bring that about. And women, especially mothers, are to get a much happier life of it in our new Welfare State. Leslie would have been really happy about that.'

'You're managing to get his books reprinted?'

'*Scots Quair's* doing well. It was good to see those three tales under the one cover. They're allowed to read them in Aberdeen, would you believe it? They even study them at the University! Changed days! You never know, they might even make that film we've been talking about for so long.'

That evening they stood on the auld brig of Bervie as the sun was setting. It was high summer and a tumbling of cloud glowed and gleamed above the white walls of Castle Allardice. The sky darkened on Pitcarry hill and streaks of red were fading on the Reisk, above Mondynes and the Howe beyond.

'Archie and I come down at times,' said Molly, 'just to watch the sunset. Archie never says much, but he feels the mood that's there. The whole of our past is behind those braes, in Millplough and Hareden, Milltown and Pitcarles, Greenden and the rest.'

The sun had all but gone now, a splash of red on the white of the castle. 'That's Madge Laing down below, seeing to her chickens and the kye that she keeps. Her corn's coming on fine this year. She's got that park too, below the brig, between the lade and the Bervie burn. You'll see Madge and Jim take a dander whiles, when there's a redness in the sky.'

Beyond Madge's croft lay the dam of old Guthrie. Behind them they could hear the sea, splashing away there in the dark.

'It's the winter snows I remember,' Becky whispered, 'climbing that rough brae at Mondynes with Leslie clutching my hand. There was no sunshine then, but we were happy, the two of us, singing away in the snow and in the dark. You think little of it at the time, but Leslie thought a lot about sunsets when he got into his writing. The sun would aye be shining somewhere he used to say. He called it the best deliverance of all. I still remember how he ended that book. "The day that did not die there," he said, "but went east, on and on, over all the world till the morning came, the unending morning somewhere in the world."'

EPILOGUE – 'NEMESIS'

Peter Bannerman had joined the Royal Corps of Signals and we were both back home in the Royal Toun before our overseas postings. We had a last long blether – crossing Mollison's Briggy, where else, and on 'O'er the Watter' as far as the Salmon Bothy.

'How do you like it?' I asked.

'Boring,' said Pete, 'working in an office full of lassies. But I've joined the paratroopers,' he added.

'What in God's name made you do that?' I looked at him, fair amazed. Pete was always a canny, soft-spoken sort of lad. He'd worked away quietly in his dad's butcher shop in the King Street. He and Alastair Reid would trundle their bicycles up those Arbuthnott braes together, delivering orders to places like Pitcarles and Mains of Allardice. Alastair worked for Joe Glegg, another Bervie butcher, but that made little odds to the two of them. Pete had never been my idea of a swashbuckling hero diving down from the skies.

He thought for a while before he answered me. 'You've got to do something,' was all he said, and we talked on about better things. Pete was a bit upset at what had been going on over in France.

What Pete could never tell me was that his paratroopers belonged to the GHQ Liaison Regiment, popularly known as 'Phantom.' They were an exclusive kind of private army which included charismatic characters like David Niven, the actor, who was their CO, and John Hislop, the famous jockey.

The object of 'Phantom' was 'to obtain first hand information of the most forward fighting and relay it straight back to GHQ.' They were divided into small patrols of four or six, with an officer, a corporal, a wireless operator and, maybe, a dispatch rider or two. It was all a bit different from the capers Pete and I had got up to in the Scout Curlew Patrol when we camped beside Arbuthnott's woods. Pete had been chosen because he was a good wireless operator and, as all messages had to be transmitted in morse code, Pete's training in the Scouts had served him well.

Pete's Phantom group were finally based above a small village called Moussay in the Vosges Mountains. For over a month they harried the enemy and tied down an entire SS Division which was diverted from the front to destroy them. Of the 93 men who took part, 31 were killed, all but three of them after capture.

Pete was ambushed and fatally wounded on 29 September, 1944. Namesake and grandson of that other Peter Bannerman who'd run his cheery shop and blended his 'Howe o' the Mearns Whisky', young Pete was 23 years of age when Nemesis caught up with him.

Robert Middleton from David Street joined the 2nd Battalion of the Royal Highlanders (The Black Watch). On Christmas, 1939, Madge received a Black Watch Christmas Card with a map of Galilee, Samaria and Judea on it. There was a picture of a highland soldier holding the scales of justice, evenly balanced, with a Jew on one side and an Arab on the other. 'To my dearest friend,' Rob had written, 'with Best Wishes for Christmas and the New Year.'

Madge had taken up her letter writing again, where she'd left off twenty years earlier.

'I shall never forget you,' Rob wrote, 'for all the things you taught me… don't think that I am a Christian. No man in the army can be that exactly… It hurts me to say so, but your efforts, so well meant have been wasted. Not entirely, but the army does this to me… This may be my last letter, I do not know, but I look forward to your answering letter… my love to all and my regards to Jim. I am, as ever, your sincere friend, Rob.'

Rob was wounded at Tobruk in 1942 and he sent Madge a photograph of himself with a group of soldiers convalescing in the desert. On the back he'd written: 'With all the best to you from Rob. Taken in Egypt after the relief of Tobruk. In the rear rank, wearing cap, is Pipe-Major Roy, DCM – the Piper of Tobruk, February, 1942.'

It was to be another two years before Nemesis caught up with Rob, namesake of that other Rob Middleton, *Long Rob of the Mill.* 2756007 Private Robert Middleton, 15 Platoon, 2nd Battalion, The Black Watch, India Command, was killed in Burma in May, 1944. He too, was 23 years of age.

❦

Edwin Gilchrist Gibb of Hallgreen Castle, like his father, Captain Pappa Jim Gibb before him, went to sea. Edwin served as a radio operator in the Merchant Navy. He'd been born on 18 July, 1914, two weeks before the outbreak of the first Great War. Edwin was lost at sea in November, 1942. He was 28 when he died.

That 'Something Unnamed' was not long in coming to Leslie Mitchell's Segget.

Maybe Leslie's verdict on it all says as much about us in the late 1990s as it did back then about that cheery, thoughtless crowd in the Roaring 1920s:

FOR I WILL GIVE YOU THE MORNING STAR

In the sunset of an age and an epoch we may write that for epitaph of the men who were of it... They went quiet and brave from the lands they loved, though seldom of that love might they speak... lest we shame them, let us believe that the new oppressions and foolish greeds are no more than mists that pass. They died for a world that is past, these men, but they did not die for this that we seem to inherit...

Sunset Song, Lewis Grassic Gibbon

BIBLIOGRAPHY

Bing, Christie, *The Lairds of Arbuthnott* (Capability Publishing, Edzell, 1993)

Brewsher, Major F W, *The History of the 51st (Highland) Division 1914–1918* (Wm. Blackwood & Sons, Edinburgh and London, 1921)

Broom, John, *John Maclean* (Macdonald Publishers, Loanhead, 1973)

Campbell, Ian, *Lewis Grassic Gibbon* (Scottish Academic Press, Edinburgh, 1985)

Coppard, George, *With a Machine-Gun to Cambrai* (HMSO, London, 1969)

Coupar, Alexander K (ed.), 'Bervie Remembered', a collection of Bervie Verse, including 'The Bervie Worthies' by William Scott, 'The Bervie Volunteers' and 'The Bervie Lassies' both by William Gall (A K Couper, Bervie, 1985)

Cruickshank, Graeme (ed.) 'A Sense of Place: Studies in Scottish Local History', Article by Ian Campbell on 'Lewis Grassic Gibbon and the Mearns' (Scotland's Cultural Heritage Unit, Edinburgh University, 1988)

Cruickshank, Helen B, *Octobiography* (Standard Press, Montrose, 1976)

Falls, Cyril, *The Life of a Regiment. Vol. 4: The History of the Gordon Highlanders 1914–1919* (Aberdeen University Press, 1958)

Gifford, Douglas, *Neil Gunn and Lewis Grassic Gibbon* (Oliver & Boyd, Edinburgh, 1983)

Hislop, John, *Anything But A Soldier* (Michael Joseph, London, 1965)

Jervis, Andrew, *Memorials of Angus and the Mearns* (Vols. 1 and 2, David Douglas, Edinburgh, 1885)

Malcolm, William R, *A Blasphemer & Reformer: A Study of James Leslie Mitchell* (Aberdeen University Press, 1984)

Michelin Illustrated Guides to the Battlefields (1914–1918) (Michelin & Co., Clermont-Ferrand, 1919)

Middlebrook, Martin, *The Kaiser's Battle: 21 March 1918* (Allen Lane, London, 1978)

Mitchell, James Leslie (Lewis Grassic Gibbon) All works but especially *Sunset Song* (first published by Jarrolds of London, 1934). Also the semi-biographical *Stained Radiance* (Jarrolds, 1930; Polygon, 1993) and *The Thirteenth Disciple,* particularly Chapter 4 re the dismissal etc., (Jarrolds, 1931; Paul Harris, Edinburgh, 1981; B&W, Edinburgh, 1995) *The Speak of the Mearns,* Campbell, Ian (ed.), (Ramsay Head Press, Edinburgh, 1982; Polygon, Edinburgh, 1994)

Munro, Ian S, *Leslie Mitchell: Lewis Grassic Gibbon* (Oliver & Boyd, Edinburgh, 1966)

Smithers, A J, *Cambrai-The First Great Tank Battle 1917* (Leo Cooper, London, 1992)

Souter, Roy, *A Wild and Windy Coast* (Roy Souter, Gourdon, 1988)

Souter, Roy, *Call Out* (Roy Souter, Gourdon, 1992)

University of Aberdeen, *Book of Remembrance 1914–1918* (Aberdeen University)

War Diary 1/4 Gordon Highlanders 1917–1918 (Gordon Highlanders Museum, Aberdeen)

Whitfield, Peter, *Grassic Gibbon and his World* (Aberdeen Journals Ltd, 1994)

Whittington, Graeme W, 'The Regionalism of Lewis Grassic Gibbon', *Scottish Geographical Magazine* (September 1974)

Young, Douglas, *Beyond the Sunset* (Impulse Books, Aberdeen, 1973)

Much information was also gleaned from the Minutes of the Bervie Highland Games Committee, the Minutes of Bervie Town Council, past editions of the publications listed below and the diaries, writings, scrapbooks and autograph books of Bailie Robert Clarke, Jim and Madge Geddes, and Alice and David Webster.

The Courier
The Dundee Advertiser
The Evening Express
The Kincardineshire Observer
The Mearns Leader
The People's Journal
The St Andrews Citizen
The Scotsman
The Scots Magazine